THE HANDMAID'S SECRET

A Starstruck Novel

BRENDA HIATT

dolphin star
PRESS

THE HANDMAID'S SECRET

A Starstruck Novel

Copyright 2018 Brenda Hiatt
Cover art by Ravven Kitsune

Dolphin Star Press
ISBN: 978-1-940618-92-0

*+

DEDICATION

For everyone who's ever felt like they didn't fit in

*+

THE STARSTRUCK SERIES BY BRENDA HIATT
Starstruck
Starcrossed
Starbound
Starfall
Fractured Jewel: A Starstruck Novella
The Girl From Mars
The Handmaid's Secret

Contents

Equilibrium

Molly

"MOLLY, are you ready to try that new move we talked about yester-day?" Trina, our head cheerleader asks as we finish our pre-practice warmup on the track by the football field.

"Sure." I step between the two girls who act as my "bases" for most of the flyer routines. "I have it looking pretty good on the ground, anyway. Where's Amber?" She's usually my back spotter.

Trina looks around, frowning. "This is the second time this month she's been late. If she doesn't— Oh, here she comes."

Amber trots up, all smiles. "Sorry I'm late, but I come bearing gossip. Believe it or not, we're getting *another* new student tomorrow!"

All the girls start talking excitedly.

"Seriously?"

"That will make nine in one semester!"

Just three weeks ago we got eight new students all at once. That would have been a huge deal for a school as small as Jewel High even if they *weren't* all from Mars. Not that any of the other cheerleaders know that particular detail.

"Boy or girl?" Trina demands, cutting through the chatter.

"Boy." Amber waggles her eyebrows. "Sounds like *his* parents will be working out at NuAgra, too."

NuAgra is the new company on the outskirts of Jewel supposedly responsible for the recent influx of newcomers to town. Along with its stated purpose of conducting top-secret agricultural research, it's also supposed to become a sort of government headquarters for Martians on Earth.

"Hm. I wonder if he'll be as good looking as the other new guys?" Trina's eyes narrow speculatively.

I suspect he will, since *Echtrans* in general tend to be unusually attractive by Earth standards.

"Did you hear what year he'll be?" she asks then.

Amber nods. "A junior, I peeked at his paperwork. His name's Tristan. Tristan Roark."

"Ooh, yummy name," Donna declares, to general agreement.

"Tomorrow we'll see if he lives up to it," Trina says, but then she's all business again. "Okay, time to get serious, girls. It's barely two weeks till our first playoff game and Jewel's bound to go to State this year. We need to be in top form by then. Molly, you ready to fly?"

I am. We start our latest choreographed routine with its synchronized dance steps and kicks, then Donna and Tiffany, my base girls, hoist me up by both legs to their chin level. I wait a beat, lift one knee into my basic Liberty pose, wait three more beats, then transition into an Arabesque, extending my raised leg straight behind me as I lean forward slightly and spread my arms out to the sides.

I'm about to shift from that to the Needle, the new move, when Donna changes her grip slightly.

"Ooh," she exclaims, looking back at Amber. "You said this new guy's a junior. Did you hear what classes he'll be in?"

I wobble for a second, but then I feel pretty solid again. Tipping further forward, I point my back leg straight up until I'm doing a vertical split—the Needle. I hold that pose for a beat, just like I rehearsed in the gym, then take two beats to return to my prep position so I can do my pop-cradle dismount.

"I did!" Amber replies from behind me. "I even jotted his classes down, so I'd remember. Remind me after and I'll—"

"Quiet!" Trina yells. "Do the finish first."

My bases pop me up for the cradle dismount but Donna and Amber, both distracted, are out of position to catch me properly. I hear everyone screaming as I pitch backward and see the asphalt track hurtling toward my face.

In desperation, I tuck into a last-second reverse somersault and miraculously manage to land on my feet, well behind everyone else. I'm still marveling at my close call when I belatedly realize no *normal* Earth human could ever have pulled off that maneuver. It was purely my Martian reflexes that saved me from a cracked skull.

"Omigod Molly!" Amber shrieks. "I'm so sorry! How did you—?"

Trina shoulders her aside. "That was amazing, Molly! You should always dismount like that."

The others are still staring at me with expressions of shock mingled with relief. I force a laugh.

"Um, no thanks, Trina. That was *way* more up-close than I ever want to see the pavement again. I'm just glad I remembered that gymnastics move from when I used to compete back in Ireland. I only ever managed it twice before, and that was with nice thick mats under me."

Not true, of course. I never actually competed in gymnastics, though I took a few classes as a kid. But claiming that keeps the other cheerleaders from freaking out over my superhuman flip, which is all I care about. I'm just glad there were no other *Echtrans* around to see me do it, or I'd be in big trouble.

On that thought I glance up at the bleachers to see M there, staring right at me…and looking more than a little upset. Oops.

With a sheepish grin, I wave at her. To my relief, she smiles back as she returns my wave. I hope that means she's not *too* mad at me. Because in addition to being my best friend, M also happens to be our people's supreme leader, Sovereign Emileia.

From beside me, Trina makes a disgusted noise.

"Do you *have* to, Molly? It reflects badly on the whole squad when you insist on hanging around with a loser like Marsha Truitt. If you weren't such a good flyer, I'd be tempted— Never mind. Let's practice that routine again. And Amber, try to focus this time, okay? Injuries reflect badly, too."

I want to tell Trina—again—that M is the exact opposite of a loser, but I know it won't do any good. She's apparently been determined to hate M since they were both in elementary school. So I just shoot another quick smile M's way and get back into position.

At the end of practice, when the rest of the squad heads to the locker room, I sprint up into the bleachers to talk to M.

"Guess you saw that, huh?" I brace myself for a well-deserved scold, even though I can't remember her ever yelling at me before.

"Yes, I saw! What happened? I was scared to death you were going to break your neck."

"The girls were gossiping about this new guy instead of paying attention to my dismount. I *think* they all bought my excuse that it was something I learned in gymnastics, but it was dumb to panic and pull such a crazy stunt in front of everyone. Are you mad?"

She looks startled. "Mad that you didn't break your neck? Are you kidding me? Anyway, it sounds like you came up with a good cover story. You always do. I'm just relieved you're okay."

Her concern warms me. "Thanks, M. So, about this new guy who almost got me killed. Sounds like it'll be another *Echtran*—Tristan Roark?"

"Roark?" she repeats. "Connor has a son? I didn't even know he was married."

"Connor's last name is Roark?" I wince. Connor is easily my least favorite member of the *Echtran* Council, which meets at my house most weekends. "Did you know he was moving to Jewel?"

She lifts a shoulder. "Sure, eventually, because of the new government center at NuAgra, but not this soon. It's weird he didn't say anything about it last Saturday. I wonder what his son is like?"

"Snooty and arrogant, just like his dad," I predict.

M laughs. "Come on, you don't know that. Maybe he'll be nice, like the rest of the newcomers."

"None of them are Royals. You watch, this guy will look down on me for being a lowly Ag the way Connor always does. Like father, like son."

"Well, he'd better not do it in front of me or I'll— Oh, there's Rigel."

I turn and see Jewel's quarterback—M's boyfriend—jogging toward us.

"See you later, M. I'd better scurry if I want to catch my ride." With a smile for Rigel, I trot off to the locker room.

I doubt Amber will really leave without me after her screwup earlier, but I know M and Rigel like to have a few minutes together before taking their separate late buses. Even if playing chaperone *is* technically one of my duties.

It was a huge honor to be appointed M's official *Chomseireach*, or Handmaid, before we went to Mars last spring. While we were there I selected all her outfits, chaperoned her when necessary and kept presumptuous favor-seekers from getting too close. Sure, she had a Bodyguard, but I was always her last line of defense—and did a great job, according to M.

Since getting back to Earth, not so much. For obvious reasons, she doesn't want me tagging along whenever she and Rigel are together, and it's not practical for me to pick out what she'll wear to school every day. As for being a last line of defense—hah! I didn't even hear about last month's attempt on her life until the day after it happened, because I was at some stupid cheerleading party.

I need to seriously up my game...if M will let me.

.⁺.⁺

LIKE FATHER, *like son.* My words to M yesterday echo in my head when the new boy waltzes into Pre-Cal the next morning like he owns the place. His Adonis-like profile is remarkably like Connor's, his deep gold hair only a shade darker. In other words, outrageously handsome, same as his dad—and probably just as stuck up.

Sauntering up to the teacher, he hands her a slip from the office and turns to survey the classroom, his gaze lingering on M. Then, with a confident smile, he ambles over to the empty desk closest to her—which happens to be on my other side. Before sitting down he pauses, one proprietary hand on *my* desk, and inclines his head to M. Not a bow, which would be too obvious, but respectful.

"Hi, I'm Tristan," he says, looking right past me, "and you must be... Marsha?" It's like the people sitting around her, even those of us who are obviously *Echtran*, don't exist.

"Hello, Tristan." M's voice is a tiny shade cooler than normal. "Welcome to Jewel."

"Thank you. I very much look forward to getting to know you better." There's something distinctly suggestive in his low, smooth voice that puts me on high alert.

Rigel, on M's other side, leans over to see past M and me. "We'll look forward to that, too. We all will." His glance includes me and Liam, another *Echtran*, sitting just in front of me.

Tristan's dark brown eyes slide over us negligently, then refocus on M as if Rigel hadn't spoken.

"Maybe you and I can get together after school to, you know, talk."

By now every girl in the room is staring at him with blatant interest, though as over-the-top handsome as he is, I'm sure he's used to that. I get the distinct impression he's disappointed M isn't reacting the same way. He finally sits down when class starts but continues to direct intense, almost smoldering glances at M every time the teacher isn't looking. If M notices she doesn't let on, though Rigel occasionally glares back.

When the bell rings, Tristan quickly stands, then sidles forward in an attempt to wedge himself between M and Rigel as they move toward the door. Finally, a chance for me to do my job!

Stepping in close, I cut Tristan off just before he reaches them. "Hey, Tristan." I stick out my hand despite my reluctance to touch him. "I'm Molly."

He totally ignores my hand, still watching M. "O'Gara, right?" He sounds bored.

"That's right. Sean's sister. Have you met him yet?" My only goal is to keep him occupied until M and Rigel are out of the room where it will be easier to avoid him. Creeper.

"Not yet. Why? He's renounced his claim there, hasn't he?"

His smirk when referring to my brother makes me bristle. Because that was definitely a smirk.

"Yes, and for good reason. So there's no point you trying to stake one, if that's what you're planning."

Whether it's my words or the acid in my tone, he finally looks at me. "No point? What makes you think so?"

"The fact that I know a lot more about them both than you do. Trust me, you'd be wasting your time."

M and Rigel reach the door and a moment later they're gone. He isn't watching them now, though. Instead he looks down his perfect, aquiline nose at me, still with that slight curl to his lip. "Of course *you'd* think that. You're Sean's sister."

"That has nothing to do with it," I assure him. "I just happen to know—"

I break off, suddenly aware of several interested pairs of eyes, most belonging to girls. At least half a dozen of them have moved in close, obviously hoping to introduce themselves to Tristan before he leaves the room. With a tiny smirk of my own, I step back to let them converge.

"Have a nice day," I toss over my shoulder as I walk off to French class.

UNFORTUNATELY, Tristan shows up there, too. Rigel's not in this class, which Tristan takes advantage of by trying to chat M up before the bell. I'm ready to run interference again if necessary but she shuts him down just fine on her own.

"You're Connor's son, right?" she asks when he stops at her desk to suggest getting together that evening.

He frowns. "Um, yeah. Why?"

"You look a lot like him. And I get the impression you share his opinion of my relationship with Rigel. Am I right?"

Blinking, he flushes noticeably. Clearly, he didn't expect such a direct question—or that she'd see through him so easily. Idiot.

"Hey, I don't even know him," he responds after only a slight hesitation. "For all I know, he's a great guy. Really good at football, from what I hear. I'm just trying to be friendly. There's nothing wrong with that, is there?"

"That depends on your reasons." She turns a shoulder to him to face me. "I forget, Molly, which set of vocabulary words were we supposed to go over last night?"

WHEN TRISTAN TURNS up in Chemistry third period, I begin to suspect he signed up for every one of M's classes. At least Rigel's in this one, though the lab table he shares with Trina is on the opposite side of the room from M's and mine. He obviously took Tristan's measure as quickly as I did, judging by the way he watches him.

"Everyone welcome Tristan, who's with us for the first time today," the teacher—also an *Echtran*—announces after signing him in. "Since we're starting a new module tomorrow, I'd already planned to have you select new lab partners. With Tristan here our numbers are even, so nobody will need to triple up this time around."

He nods to two girls and a boy near the back who've been sharing a lab table since the start of the year. Both girls immediately look hopeful.

"Since Tristan's new, it would probably be best if someone very familiar with the material partners with him. Beyond that, I can either assign you alphabetically—" There's a collective groan. "—or let you choose your own partners, as you did at the start of the year. Try to pair up with someone new but don't waste too much time. You have ten minutes, after which I'll start assigning partners. Go."

With a hasty scraping of chairs, every single girl heads for Tristan.

Even though she was all the way across the room, Trina reaches him first, elbowing the others out of her way.

"Hi, Tristan." She gives him the brilliant smile that tends to make guys go nonverbal around her. "I'd *love* the chance to show you everything we've covered so far." *Among other things*, her tone implies.

Though he manages a bland smile in return, he barely glances at her before turning a charm-infused smile on M. "I was hoping maybe Marsha here might be my partner? I'll bet you're one of the best students in the class, aren't you?"

"Not really." She looks more amused than flattered. "Molly here is better at Chemistry than I am. Anyway, I have a different partner in mind." She looks past Tristan's shoulder at Rigel, shouldering his way through the gaggle of girls still vying for Tristan's attention.

"She's right," Rigel says, joining us. "I'm pretty sure Molly has the best grade in the class now. Right, Molly?"

Though I'd far rather leave him to Trina's tender mercies, I'm forced to nod. My grades *are* better than M's or Rigel's, though that's only because they've had way more important stuff to deal with this semester. Like saving the world.

"Er, yeah, I think so. I guess I can help you catch up, unless you'd rather—" I look pointedly at Trina. She isn't a great student, but those two definitely deserve each other.

Tristan doesn't even glance at her—or at me. He's still completely focused on M, like he's trying to use that "push" thing some Royals have. Rigel moves to M's side and faces him, a faint challenge in his eyes. There's a tense silence for a moment before Tristan finally turns to me.

"Sure, Molly, that would be great. Thanks." He sounds anything but grateful.

With a huff of disgust and a poisonous glare at M, Trina moves off. So, gradually, do the others, not wanting to risk being randomly assigned. Meanwhile, Rigel joins M at our old lab table and Tristan and I move to an empty one two rows back.

"You're her Handmaid, aren't you?" he mutters, sitting down next to me. "Maybe you can tell me what I'm doing wrong."

I stare at him incredulously. "You mean other than being an arrogant jerk? Even if you weren't being totally obvious about what you're trying to do, M is nearly impossible to fool and totally in love with Rigel. Give it up."

He looks startled for a second, then the smirk is back. "After only a couple of hours? Not a chance. But...I guess I can be more subtle."

"Yeah, good luck with that." I turn away with a snort and open my lab binder.

Tristan watches me while I flip pages looking for the next module on the schedule. When he finally speaks again, I can tell he's working hard to suppress his instinctive disdain for everyone but M.

"Look, Molly, I can see I got off on the wrong foot with you, too. I'm sorry. I probably shouldn't believe everything my father says, especially about—"

"No," I snap. "You shouldn't. He's convinced M is too young for her role and he's as opposed to her relationship with Rigel as my Mum is. Whatever your father has told you about her, or them as a couple, I guarantee he spun it in the worst possible direction."

Tristan directs a smile at me that would likely make most girls turn into a puddle of goo. Even irked with him as I am, I can't *completely* ignore its effect. Probably some special Royal ability of his, like Mum's lie-detecting talent.

"You're probably right." He looks me directly in the eyes, turning on the full power of what he no doubt intends to be an irresistible charm assault. "In that case, I should find out what our Sovereign is really like, don't you think? Surely there's no one better than you, Molly, to tell me that."

Instead of melting on the spot, as he clearly expects, I laugh in his face. "I'm sure whatever you're doing works on most girls, but you can't seriously think I'll *help* you steal M away from Rigel? Even if it were remotely possible."

He blinks, then frowns. "I didn't ask you to. But...don't you think I should have a more accurate picture of her than the one my father has painted?"

I still don't trust his motives an inch, but I guess it can't hurt to disabuse him of whatever misinformation his father has fed him. "Fine. What do you want to know?"

The chaos in the room is starting to die down now that most people are paired up so he lowers his voice. "Is it true she has a habit of putting this non-Royal boyfriend of hers ahead of her duties to our people?"

"No. Not at all. M's done more for our people, for everyone on this planet, than anyone, risking Rigel's life along with her own in the process."

"But she *has* shared classified information with him, hasn't she? Even after promising the Council she wouldn't?"

This is stickier ground, since there were extenuating circumstances that aren't public—not even *Echtran*-public—knowledge.

"Only when she had no choice." Which is true, though I don't elaborate. "And it turned out to be a good thing she did." Also true.

"If you say so." He doesn't look convinced but the room is quiet enough now we can't keep talking, especially about Martian stuff.

I'M RELIEVED Tristan isn't in my Creative Writing class next period…until M tells me at lunch that he was in her Comp/Lit class instead.

"Wow, stalker much?" I glance back. He's several people behind us in the cafeteria line, surrounded by flirting cheerleaders.

"You're getting that impression, too? Luckily I had not only Rigel, but Trina there. She did everything she could to keep him away from me."

We both laugh.

"Hey, if she can convince him to be her lab partner instead of mine in Chemistry, I sure won't argue."

M nods sympathetically. "Yeah, sorry about that. I kind of threw you under the bus there, didn't I?"

"No, it's fine. I hardly do anything to justify my, er, role lately but this falls smack under my job description."

"I guess it does," she agrees. "But it's not true you're not doing anything else. I depend on you way more than you think, even if it's not for all the, um, traditional reasons."

She's probably just saying that to make me feel better but I still appreciate it. M is always thoughtful that way, one reason she's such a great friend—and a *dabhal* good Sovereign, no matter what anyone says.

I groan aloud when I see Tristan heading toward our lunch table a few minutes later. He slows when he gets close, scanning for a seat. Rigel is sitting next to M, of course, and I'm on her other side, with Sean and Kira next to me. In fact, I'm pleased to see there are only two empty chairs at the whole table, none close to M.

"Move along, move along," I mutter under my breath.

But then M's friend Bri spots him and immediately motions him over.

"Hi, Tristan, remember me? My friend Deb here introduced us after your Pre-Cal class first period. Are you looking for a place to sit?" She nudges Deb, who nudges the boy next to her. They both scoot down, opening up a seat practically across from M. Gah!

But now Tristan seems to be on his best behavior. Hm, maybe my comments in Chemistry actually had an effect?

"Are you sure you don't mind me joining you?" he asks the group in general. Then, turning to Kira and Sean, "Hi, I don't think we've met yet. I'm Tristan."

He must know who they are, but they introduce themselves and welcome him to Jewel. I doubt Sean would be so friendly if he'd seen the way Tristan was coming on to M earlier. Or maybe he would. Since getting together with Kira, he finally seems completely over M, for which I'm truly grateful. I hated seeing him suffer. And things are massively less awkward these days when we all get together.

We can't talk about Martian stuff with so many non-*Echtrans* at the table, but luckily I'm not the only one with questions about Tristan. One is answered early on when Deb asks him if his family moved here because of NuAgra, like the other new kids.

"Yeah, my father was coming to Jewel for so many meetings, it made sense to relocate him."

Bri leans in next. "Where did you move from?"

"Denver. The suburbs, anyway. I mostly grew up there."

She and Deb proceed to pepper him with questions about how he likes Jewel so far, and how it compares to Denver.

"It's a lot flatter, that's for sure," he says, getting a general laugh.

"And a lot smaller," Deb says longingly. "I'd love to visit Denver someday. I hear the mountains are beautiful."

That topic takes up the rest of the lunch period and I'm grudgingly impressed by how easily Tristan carries it off, never giving even the slightest hint he's anything more than a normal, if outrageously hand-some, *Duchas*.

I'm not the least bit surprised when Tristan accompanies us to U.S. Government after lunch. Maybe it was his dad who signed him up for all of M's classes? I can't imagine the ladies in the front office denying Connor anything if he turned on the charm. Though he's never wasted it on me, it's probably even more potent than the taste I had of Tristan's.

Like Chemistry class, this one has a high concentration of *Echtrans* —me, M, Rigel, Sean, Kira, and Alan Dempsey, another newcomer. And now Tristan. At least the teacher is *Duchas*.

"Everyone, please welcome Tristan," she says, smiling at him a little more warmly than strictly necessary. I remember her doing the same to Alan his first day—another particularly handsome *Echtran*.

Alan catches me looking his direction and smiles. I smile back. Though Alan's an Ag like me, I don't know him very well yet. Maybe it's time to change that?

Since M isn't in my AP Psych class, I'm surprised to see Tristan there next period. I guess even Connor's charm couldn't get his son into a one-semester Econ class this late in the year?

He snags the desk next to mine and proceeds to pump me for more info about M every chance he gets, using the almost-sub-vocal whisper only other Martians can hear.

"That cheerleader, Trina, tells me Marsha and Rigel broke up more than once last year. What was up with that?"

"I wasn't here the first time, but M told me they faked it to throw off Faxon's assassins. The other time was fake, too, and only because of a deal she made with the Council to save Rigel's life—or didn't your dad tell you that part?" I whisper back without moving my lips, keeping my eyes on the teacher.

"He told me that deal was her idea."

I huff out an exasperated breath, drawing a glance from the boy on my other side.

"Of course it was her idea," I quietly reply after a moment. "It was to save Rigel's *life*. She knew it was the only way they'd agree to let him come back here."

"But—"

The teacher looks our way and he breaks off. I use the opportunity to turn half away from him and he seems to take the hint, saving whatever other questions he has for later. Hopefully *much* later.

————————————————————————

2

Malleability

————————————————————————

Tristan

When the bell rings at the end of sixth period, I'm tempted to leave without another word to Molly O'Gara, who's been more hindrance than help so far. I have to force myself to be polite when I say goodbye.

Not that she returns the favor.

"Guess I'll see you tomorrow," she says with her distinctive Irish lilt, stronger than the average Nuathan accent. "Unfortunately."

Her addendum nearly makes me snap back, but I restrain myself. It's too soon to alienate her completely, since she seems closer to the Sovereign than anyone. Except for Rigel Stuart—not that I believe in that *graell* bond mind-reading thing they supposedly have any more than my father does.

Thinking about Father makes the space between my shoulder blades itch. He's not going to be happy with how little I've accomplished today when I give him my update—which will be all too soon.

I head to the front office to sign myself out and find four other *Echtrans* already there, all recent immigrants from Mars. Like me, they're going out to NuAgra for our seventh period work-study program.

"Hey, Tristan," one of the Walsh twins—Liam, I think—greets me. "Our dad said you might be joining us today. Do you know yet what you'll be doing at NuAgra?"

"Whatever my father put down on the form," I reply since we're still

13

within earshot of the woman at the front desk. "Guess I'll find out when I get there."

I suppose the others are doing actual work out there, growing plants or building stuff or whatever their *fines* are suited for. Me, I'm just going out there to report to my father. Which I could do just as well at home, but he claims pretending to be like the other NuAgra kids is less likely to make the *Duchas* suspicious. Whatever.

Liam nods and turns back to the others and I realize my tone was probably off-putting. Again. I'll have to work on that if I want to fit in here. Not that I do, particularly, except as a way to ingratiate myself with the Sovereign.

The only girl in our group is Kira Morain, who I met at lunch. She's kind of famous, or was. I used to hear her name on the delayed-broadcast *caidpel* feeds from Nuath. Not that I follow the sport all that closely, having grown up on Earth.

Then a couple of nights ago I heard her name again, when my father went on a rant about her, calling her an Ag traitor. He said she was involved in a recent assassination attempt on the Sovereign, though the Sovereign and Sean O'Gara somehow convinced the Council not to press charges.

I couldn't believe it when Father told me Sean's actually dating Kira now, instead of the Sovereign. I mean, famous or not, she's still just an Ag. But they did seem awfully friendly with each other at lunch and in Government class after.

"Ride's here." Alan Dempsey leads the rest of us outside, where we pile into a silver van.

I wonder why Kira and Alan aren't together. Like Sean, they're both seniors, but Alan's in her same *fine*, nearly as tall as Sean, and nearly as good-looking as me. Okay, even in my head that sounds stuck-up, but I'm just being honest. Alan probably had *Duchas* girls swarming him when he first got here, too. That got old for me within a week of starting at my *Duchas* high school in Denver.

It takes more than ten minutes to get to NuAgra, which is even more in the middle of nowhere than the rest of this godforsaken town. The others talk about school and the projects they're working on at NuAgra but I barely listen. I'm too busy dreading the coming interview with my father.

The van drops us in front of an opaque glass door that we each have to palm open. Inside the huge entry area, a uniformed woman approaches me while the others head for their various workstations.

"You would be Tristan?"

"That's right."

"Your father is waiting for you in his office. Right-hand corridor, first room on the left. His name is on the door."

I turn on a little bit of the charm when I thank her, mostly to check that it still works on *Echtrans*. Molly O'Gara acted like she didn't even notice it. To my relief, this woman blushes and stammers a bit as she assures me it was her very great pleasure to help.

Reassured, I head for the hallway she indicated and tap on the door marked "Connor Roark, *Echtran* Council."

"Come," my father calls. I go inside, where he's seated behind an imposing desk of some dark wood.

"Hello, Father."

He waves me to the chair opposite him, about half the size of the throne-like one he's sitting in. "Well? Despite your reluctance to relocate to Jewel, you seem to have survived your first day of high school here. I assume you've met the Sovereign by now. Were you able to become acquainted with her?"

No, "How was your day?" like most parents might ask. Nope, not my father. He always gets right to business.

"Of course we met. I'm in most of her classes. You saw to that."

"And?"

I start to shrug, then stop myself because he hates that. "I introduced myself to her, though she already knew who I was. There wasn't much chance to talk in class, and during passing periods and at lunch she was always with friends."

"Friends. You mean Stuart, I suppose."

"Not just him, but yeah. I mean, yes, sir. She also seems tight with Molly O'Gara."

He nods. "Her *Chomseireach*. Not surprising, I suppose, though I'd have thought the Sovereign's treatment of Sean O'Gara would have created a rift with his adopted sister as well. May I assume from your response that you were unable to contrive any private conversation whatsoever with the Sovereign over the entire course of the day?"

The way he says it makes me feel like a failure—as he no doubt intends. "It was only my first day," I remind him.

"Begin as you mean to go on," he snaps, one of his favorite maxims. "Were you at least able to convey your interest in doing so?"

"Yes, sir. More than once I suggested getting together after school, but she never really answered because either Stuart or Molly interrupted."

He gazes at me appraisingly. "Perhaps your gift is not as strong as I had begun to believe."

Though he'll never admit it, I know it bothers him that I apparently inherited more of his Royal charming ability than he has himself.

"Or maybe she's immune because she's the Sovereign," I suggest. I don't mention that Molly, who's just an Ag, was similarly unaffected. Even when I turned it on full force in Chemistry class.

"Perhaps. In which case you will need to fall back on whatever other resources you might have. Befriend Stuart, if nothing else will serve. Learn where the weaknesses lie in their relationship so that you can exploit them. One way or another, that relationship needs to end. It has been the driving factor behind the Sovereign's most appalling lapses in judgment, starting well before her Installation."

"Molly O'Gara said—"

"Why should I care what some Ag girl told you? She has done enough damage, prejudicing her adopted family and the Sovereign in favor of her inferior *fine*. That no doubt made it far easier for the Ag traitor to impose upon them all."

I know better than to point out that if Kira were *really* guilty, Lili O'Gara would have known. Even Father has admitted her lie-detection ability is generally considered infallible by the *Echtran* Council.

"I didn't— That is, I'm not giving up, sir. But if the bond between the Sovereign and Stuart is as strong as those Scientists claimed, it may take a while. I, um, might have come on a little too strong today, tried to move too quickly. Especially if she really is immune. I'll do better tomorrow."

"See that you do. Should you persuade the Sovereign to meet with you after school, that will of course take precedence over coming here. You can report to me when I get home, instead."

"I understand."

"Good. Now, find someplace out of the way to wait until I'm ready to leave. The lecture hall at the end of the corridor should be empty this time of day. You can spend the time on *Duchas* homework, if you have any."

He doesn't actually say *you're dismissed* but it's implied. Picking up my backpack, I leave his office without another word, fully aware I've disappointed him.

Again.

I find the deserted lecture hall and sit at a table in the back where I can spread out my books. I'm about twenty minutes into my stupid-easy Pre-Cal homework when my cellphone vibrates in my pocket. It's my mother.

Before I can even say hello, she whispers, "You're not still with your father, are you?"

"No." I wouldn't have dared answer if I were, she should know that. "We only talked for a few minutes."

"Then tell me about your first day at Jewel High. Have you made any new friends yet?"

Other than being a high-ranking Royal, my mother is nothing at all like my father. For one thing, she likes to hear all the little details about my life that he can't be bothered with. I've never seen her use her Royal status to gain advantage over anyone else, unlike him. And she's really smart, smarter than Father, I'm positive.

"Not friends, exactly, not yet, but I met a lot of people. Nearly all the other *Echtrans*, I think. Plus a bunch of *Duchas*."

"You shouldn't use that tone of voice when you talk about them, Tristan. They can't help their descent. You're not your father."

As he makes clear constantly.

"I know, sorry."

I probably should work harder at showing compassion to people without our advantages, like she kept telling me to do when I started at my *Duchas* high school in Denver. Though only when Father wasn't around to overhear.

"I assume you met the Sovereign and her friends?" she asks. "Do they seem nice?"

Nice. A quality Father generally equates with "weak."

"Sure, I guess they're nice. So far, anyway. I sat at the Sovereign's table at lunch, and Father signed me up for most of her same classes. It's such a small school it'll be hard to avoid getting to know people."

"Fewer than five hundred students, your father said? It must seem very different from your last school, though of course much bigger than your previous one."

She means the one I attended through eighth grade in Fiarway, the *Echtran* compound a few miles outside of Denver.

"It's an okay size, I guess. I forgot you haven't seen it yet."

"I'm sure I will sometime soon."

I doubt that, actually. Mother almost never leaves the house. That was even true in Denver, where she mainly worked remotely from home at her research job. According to Father, she's one of the top political and cultural historians on Earth, and probably Mars, too. Before we moved, she worked for a university in Denver as well as one back in Nuath. Here, she plans to spend more time on the Nuathan cultural history she loves, though she's still doing some remote work for UC Denver.

"Father wasn't too happy with my report," I tell her before she can ask. "He seemed to think I'd be going steady with the Sovereign by the end of the day."

She sighs. "I've warned him his expectations are unrealistic but he seemed convinced it would be an easy matter for you to disengage her from her relationship with Rigel Stuart."

"Even though he read the same reports on their bond that we did. I don't think he trusts our Scientists much."

"No. He never has. Perhaps you should focus on simply becoming her friend. That alone should allow you to exert a positive influence on her future decisions."

I'm sure she's just saying that so I won't feel so pressured. She knows better than anyone how important it is that the Sovereign's Consort have the proper Royal lineage and training.

"I still plan to become a lot more than friends with her," I insist, "though it may take a little longer than Father would like. I have to. Remember what you told me about one of our earliest Sovereigns, Vevilana, who never paired at all?"

"Of course. The Scepter went to her nephew Eamon, who created all manner of problems because he was so ill-equipped to lead. His half-Royal Consort was even less prepared for the responsibility. Thankfully, their son Tiernan chose a well-educated, fully Royal Consort, and together they set Nuath on its proper course again."

"Exactly. That mixed-*fine* upstart, Rigel Stuart, has no training at all, so I'd obviously be a massively better Consort than he would."

Which is why I'm on board with Father's plan, though he seems mostly concerned with keeping the Sovereign bloodline pure—and the prestige that would go along with me being Consort.

"True," Mother agrees. "Though if the Sovereign can be persuaded to give Sean O'Gara another chance, that would serve the same purpose."

"If Sean O'Gara really cared about our people's future, he never would have stepped aside," I point out.

Of course, Sean isn't the only Royal who's fallen down on the job of creating a better future for the Martian race—supposedly the whole reason our *fine* exists. Even before Faxon decimated our numbers, way too many had perverted that purpose into consolidating as much power for themselves as possible. Like Father? I quickly push away the disloyal thought.

Sure, I know actually becoming Consort myself is a long shot. But totally apart from Father's insistence, knowing how much good I could do in that position makes me determined to give it my very best effort.

"I'm not giving up yet, don't worry," I assure my mother. "There's too much at stake."

3

Bond substitution

Molly

TRISTAN IS the main topic of conversation among the girls in Chorus seventh period, and again at cheer practice that afternoon.

"I was next to him in the lunch line earlier," Amber says when we're changing in the locker room. "His voice is nearly as dreamy as his looks."

"And those eyes!" sighs Donna. "They're like melted fudge. I could drown in them and die happy." She pantomimes sliding to the floor.

"Uh-uh, hands off, girls." Trina shuts her locker with a snap and smooths her low-cut, form-fitting t-shirt. "I'm claiming this one for my very own."

Immediately there's a chorus of protest.

"No fair!" Amber exclaims. "Last month you warned us all away from Alan Dempsey, remember?"

"That was before Tristan got here." Trina smirks and waggles her eyebrows. "Anyway Alan's not in any of my classes, since he's a senior, so I haven't had much chance to make an impact there. I've got Tristan in Chem and Lit, plus he'll be here another year, so I'll have more time to enjoy him."

She turns to me with a frown. "*You* weren't planning to move in on

20

him, were you, Molly? I saw how that loser Marsha pitched him your way in Chemistry, just to spite me, but you didn't look like you were that into him."

"Definitely not," I tell her without hesitation. "He's all yours, as far as I'm concerned."

Trina and Tristan would be a right perfect match, since both consider themselves a gift to the opposite sex. Unfortunately, I can't imagine someone so scornful of lower-*fine Echtrans* ever looking twice at a *Duchas* girl, no matter how pretty.

Despite everyone's continued mooning over Tristan-the-jerk, we manage to perfect our new routine during practice—this time without any near-injuries. M's not here today but I hope I'll get a chance to talk with her tonight. If we put our heads together, maybe we can come up with a strategy to make him back off once and for all.

.⁺⁺.

I'M JUST PUTTING AWAY the last of the dinner plates that evening when I hear a familiar argument out in the front hall. Closing the dish cabinet, I push the hidden ionic sterilizer button and march out of the kitchen to enter the fray on my brother's behalf.

"Why don't you take Molly with you?" My mother has her back to the front door, like she's trying to physically prevent Sean from leaving.

I step between them. "You're being ridiculous, Mum," I tell her. "Sean will be eighteen in just a couple of weeks. He doesn't exactly need a chaperone."

But our mum gets that stubborn look on her face that never bodes well for anyone. "You're friends with Kira too, aren't you? And her sister? As you're all from the same *fine*, I'm sure you have a lot in common. You should go along."

"Kira and I just want to go for a walk." Sean keeps his tone reasonable, though I can tell he's frustrated. "I thought you were okay with that now."

I can't imagine why he'd think that, when our mother keeps making it clear in a zillion different ways that she's *not* okay with my Royal brother dating a girl who's just an Ag, like me. But that's Mum's problem. If she can't see how much happier Sean is these days, it's only because she refuses to. I'm not about to let her spoil this for him, after all he went through this past year. And I can be pretty darned stubborn myself.

"Fine, Mum, I'll go along," I tell her with exaggerated exasperation.

Sean frowns at me. "We don't need—" he starts, but when I give him a tiny head shake he breaks off. "Fine. Come on, Molly."

The moment Sean and I are outside, I say, "Don't worry, I'm not really tagging along. I just said that so Mum would stop hassling you."

"Guess it's a good thing she didn't focus."

I grin. "I figured out a long time ago that if I don't make her suspicious, she usually doesn't bother. Anyway, I'll just pop over to M's and see if she can hang out."

His relief is obvious. "Thanks, Moll. I shouldn't let Mum get to me like that. If she'd just get to know Kira—"

"She'll come around…eventually. It's only because she wants what's best for you."

He snorts. "For me? Or for our family's status? She's all about appearances these days."

"That's not fair, Sean," I argue, even though he has a point. "You know she'd do anything, sacrifice anything, if she really believed it would benefit you. Or me."

I believe that last bit's true, too, even though I'm just an orphaned Ag they adopted. She and Dad have always treated me like a daughter, hardly ever mentioning my inferior *fine*.

Turning up the collar of my jacket against the chilly October breeze, I say goodbye to Sean at the corner. He continues on toward Diamond Street and Kira's apartment complex while I head down Garnet toward M's house. I'm halfway there when I see her walking toward me.

"Hey," she greets me. "I was just on my way to your place."

When she gets closer, I can tell she's upset about something. "What's wrong? Your aunt isn't giving you a hard time, is she? I though she was better since learning the truth about you."

"She is. She even lets Rigel come over twice a week, but this is an off day."

I turn back to walk with her. "You must miss him a lot on the off nights?" I try hard not to be jealous of what she and Rigel have together. Especially because they went through so much awful stuff to get to a point they could finally be a couple openly.

"I do, but that's not what has me annoyed right now. Nara called me just before I left the house—it's why I was coming to see you."

I'm puzzled now. "Nara, from the *Echtran* Council? She's the little one right? I thought she was your biggest fan."

"She is. That's why she alerted me about what Connor's up to. He hasn't just moved his family to Jewel, he's also taking steps to certify Tristan as next most qualified to be Royal Consort after Sean."

"Seriously?"

She nods. "And the other Royals on the Council will probably be *fine* with that, considering how much flack they still give me about Rigel."

"Mum won't be fine with it," I assure her. "She may not like you being with Rigel but she'll see this as a direct insult to Sean." We reach my street then and I hesitate. "Speaking of Sean, Mum thinks I went with him to see Kira. I don't know if I should go home yet."

M frowns. "Then she still has issues with them being alone together?"

"Crazy, isn't it? But since all these new *Echtrans* moved to Jewel last month, Mum cares more than ever about all those stupid Martian traditions—like the ones that say who can properly get chummy with who."

"She's not the only one," M grumps. "Did you read the most recent *Echtran Enquirer*? Gwendolyn Gannett never did publish any kind of retraction for her last nasty article about Rigel, and now she's written a piece claiming more than sixty percent of *Echtrans* think Rigel should step aside now that the Grentl are gone."

I did see that article, but I kind of hoped M wouldn't. "It's probably not true. She makes up statistics all the time," I tell her, like it's a well-known fact. She still looks worried.

"Come on," I say on sudden decision. "I'll just tell Mum I ran into you on the way—and that my *Chomseireach* duties take precedence over her stupid prejudice against inter-*fine* romances. We need to put our heads together and figure out the best way to handle this."

MUM'S clearly not happy that I'm back so soon, but she tries to hide it in front of M. I snag some pumpkin cookies and milk from the kitchen while my parents exchange pleasantries with her, then M and I head upstairs to my room.

Closing the door, I set the plate of cookies on my desk with a thump, still outraged over what she told me. "So Connor's real reason for moving to Jewel was so Tristan can mess things up for you and Rigel?

That whole story about him helping to set up the *Echtran* headquarters at NuAgra was just a cover?"

"Not completely. Connor really is involved in getting the new government center ready. But he could have done that without moving his family to Jewel and making Tristan change schools partway through the semester."

"*Making* him? Tristan seems totally on board with his dad's plan, so excuse me if I don't feel sorry for him. Especially since he's kind of a jerk."

That gets a smile from her. "Kind of? He reminds me so much of his father it's scary—and not just in looks. Tristan seems to have bought into that whole Royal privilege thing as much as Connor has. I'll bet they even used Royal "push" in the school office to get him into most of my classes."

"Did he manage to join the newspaper staff, too?"

M gives a little laugh and shakes her head. "No, thank goodness. I think he went to NuAgra with the others seventh period."

"Oh, right, that makes sense." I know Kira and Alan work in the same greenhouses as their parents, while Liam and Lucas are doing something engineering-related with their folks. I wonder what Tristan will do there, being Royal and son of a Council member. Take arrogance lessons from his dad? Not that he seems to need them.

M plucks a cookie from the plate. "I was hoping you could help me strategize ways to keep Tristan from goading Rigel into a fight at school and maybe getting him suspended. For all I know, Connor suggested Tristan do exactly that."

"Rigel knows better than to rise to his bait, doesn't he?"

"I warned him against it, but if Tristan goes too far—" She shakes her head. "Thanks again for agreeing to be his Chemistry partner, by the way. As obnoxious as he is, that was a real sacrifice."

I roll my eyes. "Sacrifice? This from the person who risked her life to save the world? Keeping jerks like Tristan away from you is part of my job—and he hasn't been downright awful to me yet. I think he's trying to stay on my good side, hoping I'll help him steal you away from Rigel. I told him flat out it's impossible but he still seems determined to try."

"What *is* it with these Royal boys?" M shakes her head, then shoots me an apologetic look. "Um, no offense to Sean."

"That was different." I instinctively come to my brother's defense. "He didn't even know about Rigel before we came to Jewel. And Uncle

Allister seemed sure you'd automatically fall for Sean the second you met."

It was a right shock for Sean—and for me, too—to discover M already had a boyfriend and wasn't the least bit interested in fulfilling her role as Sovereign. Especially the part involving her so-called destiny with Sean.

"I know. I was mostly kidding," she says.

But I know she's not, not completely. Sean *did* act like he already had a claim on her last year, and now Tristan's acting the exact same way.

"This must seem a little too familiar, yeah?"

She grimaces. "A little. I mean, Allister moved you guys here last year for the identical reason and… I just don't want to go through that again."

I don't blame her. Uncle Allister, my mum and most of the Council did everything they could to keep M and Rigel apart, supposedly for the good of our people. Last spring, they even erased Rigel's memory of M, then told her it was his idea. The two of them had it unbelievably rough for the better part of a year, right up until Rigel suddenly got his memory back last month.

"Don't worry, this won't be anything like that," I insist, trying to sound upbeat. "You're Sovereign now, fully Acclaimed and Installed. The Council can't *make* you do anything you don't want to. Plus you've got me now. I'll keep Tristan out of your way so you don't have to deal with his stupid entitled attitude."

"How, exactly?" To my relief, the worried crease between her brows disappears and her green eyes twinkle mischievously. "Are you going to seduce him yourself?"

I burst out laughing. "Oh, aye, like high-and-mighty Tristan would ever touch a dirt-grubbing Ag like me? Especially a defective one who kills plants instead of growing them—not that he'd know that part."

"Hey, don't you run down my best friend," she scolds, though she's laughing, too. "But that reminds me. Has Alan offered to work with you on any Ag stuff yet?"

"I haven't asked him to. It's…kind of an embarrassing thing to admit, especially to another Ag. It's bad enough Kira knows."

She nods sympathetically. "I can understand that. Sorry. I just think you and Alan would be really cute together."

Mum has hinted she wouldn't mind if I went out with Alan—and I'm not exactly opposed, handsome as he is. When he first got here, it was pretty obvious he had a thing for Kira. But now she's clearly with Sean, maybe Alan will be open to other options...?

"We would, wouldn't we?" I grin, Tristan momentarily forgotten. "Maybe that's who I should try seducing, yeah? Oh, Alan!" I put on a silly, falsetto voice. "Can you please help me grow this plant? Maybe if you put your hands on top of mine...no, tighter, tighter..."

M and I both dissolve into giggles.

"So, um..." she says after a moment, sobering slightly. "Would you be mad if I told you I might have hinted to Alan you've been wanting a chance to develop your Ag skills?"

Laughter abruptly forgotten, I stare at her. "You did not."

M bites her lip, her guilty expression answer enough. I groan.

"Now he'll think I'm a total loser who not only can't make grass grow, but puts her girlfriends up to asking boys out for her."

"No he won't!" she protests. "I did *not* tell him to ask you out. We were talking about how the new folks are fitting in so far, his research at NuAgra, that sort of thing, and I just casually dropped in a comment about you wanting to practice your Ag skills. Because you're always around Royals, so you never get to use them. But I thought I should warn you, in case he *does* ask you to work with plants together or something. I didn't want you to think I...well, what you just said. Because I swear I didn't. And you *did* say you thought he was cute..."

I regard her suspiciously for another long moment but she looks so contrite I can't be mad. "In that case...thanks. I think."

"And thanks for not being mad at me. I just...want you to be as happy as I am these days. Maybe Alan can be *your* happy ever after."

When she says that, for some weird reason Tristan's face pops into my head. Which is crazy, because the only reason *he'd* ever want to make me happy would be to get to M. Alan definitely has potential, though.

"Maybe," I say. "If he's finally over Kira. I noticed he was still trying to chat her up last week. But if he offers to help me with Ag stuff, I won't shoot him down."

"Like you did to poor Pete?"

I snort. "'Poor Pete' nothing! I told you what he was like at Homecoming...especially on the way home. He was an octopus, hands everywhere. Lucky I have *Echtran* reflexes. Besides, I could never have any kind of long-term relationship with a *Duchas*."

She quirks an eyebrow at me. "Wow, you sound almost as prejudiced as your mother."

"No, I meant even if I find a *Duchas* guy I really like, I'd have to keep so many secrets from him we could never be a proper couple. Sean told me that's why he never tried to get serious with Missy, even when he was desperate to move on after—"

"I know," she interrupts me before things get awkward. "I was teasing. Anyway, now you've got at least three eligible *Echtran* boys to choose from, right here in Jewel. Five, if you count Grady and Tristan."

"I don't, no."

Grady's just a sophomore and about as dweeby as it's possible for an *Echtran* boy to be. And Tristan obviously considers himself way out of my league—not that I *want* to be in his league.

"Liam and Lucas are both nice," I concede after a moment, "but all Liam wants to talk about is sports and Lucas is so shy I can hardly get him to talk at all."

"Maybe he acts nervous around you because he likes you?" M suggests with a wink.

I laugh. "I doubt that, but I suppose it wouldn't hurt to try again to draw him out—for his own sake, of course." I wonder if Mum would mind me dating a guy from one of the Science *fines*, or if it's only Royals she thinks should stick to their own kind?

"Worth a try," M says, grinning, but then she becomes more serious. "Molly, this is going to sound kind of weird, but I need a little, um, alone time with something of mine in your closet."

"Huh?"

Since our return from Mars, she's kept a few dresses from her Martian wardrobe in there, along with her Royal Scepter and a genetically locked box of other items she brought back from Nuath. The Grentl communication device was hidden there, too, until the Council moved it to Rigel's house during last month's crisis.

For a moment M looks conflicted, then she shrugs. "Okay. I'm really supposed to keep this secret, but...one of the things in there is an archive. Remember how frustrated I got when I couldn't find anything on Faxon's rise to power in the regular Nuathan archives when we were on our way to Mars?"

"Yeah, I do." I especially remember her pissing off a room full of Royals by asking a bunch of questions about it at a formal dinner while we were on the ship.

"Well, after we moved into the Royal Palace, I discovered a much better archive, only accessible to Sovereigns."

I stare at her. "And you never told any of us?"

"I couldn't. Right up front it warned me to keep it *super* secret—so I did. But now we're back here, and it lives in your closet…which means can't use it without you, at least, knowing it exists. And I really do need to use it."

I'm incredibly honored that she's telling me this—but also confused. "Why would an archive have to be so secret?"

"Because there's a whole lot of classified stuff in there along with detailed historical records. I guess if too many people knew about it, someone might try to hack it or steal it or something."

I guess that makes sense. "And you need to use it right now? Tonight? Is it to do with what we were just talking about, or something else?" I immediately realize I shouldn't be asking that. "Sorry, never mind. None of my business."

"No, it's okay. I mean, it *is* in your closet. I'd keep all my Martian things at home, except I don't trust Uncle Louie after that incident with my omni that got my aunt and me kidnapped."

"I don't mind your stuff being here," I assure her—truthfully. In fact, I appreciate discovering another job I can do as Handmaid, keeping such an important archive safe, and secret. "Seriously, you can do whatever you need to in there and I promise not to ask questions." *No matter how badly I want to.*

She smiles, clearly relieved. "Thanks, Molly. So, um, I'll just go in there now, if that's okay?"

"Sure, of course! I can even go downstairs if you'd rather not stay in the closet."

"No, that's okay, I don't think it'll take long. And it'll look odd if you go downstairs and I stay by myself in your room."

"Oh, right." I work hard to subdue my raging curiosity. "I, ah, I've got homework to do anyway. Maybe bring your milk and some cookies, in case it takes longer than you expect?"

She does. Then, with another apologetic smile, she shuts herself into my closet. I stare at the closed door for a long moment, dying to know what she needs to look up, and why—especially when I hear her *talking* in there. Her secret archive must respond to voice commands.

With a sigh, I sit down at my desk and open my French book, trying not to eavesdrop any more than I can help.

4

Activation energy

M

I STILL FEEL a little guilty as I pick up my Scepter and settle myself on a box of books in Molly's closet. I was really, really tempted to tell Molly the whole truth about the Scepter just now, but my ancestors have stressed repeatedly how important it is to safeguard knowledge of this incredibly valuable resource.

And to be honest, deep down I kind of like it being my own, personal secret. Only two other people anywhere know about it—Rigel and his grandfather Shim, my Regent back on Mars. And neither of them have actually seen it work.

Since coming back to Jewel, I've only managed to use the Scepter once, while Molly was in the shower. Ever since, I've been waiting for another chance to access it without her knowing. I'm supposed to regularly update my own entry in the Archive and a *whole* lot has happened since I was last able to do that.

After waiting more than a month for another opportunity to open the Royal Archive, I decided my only option was to tell Molly *part* of the truth about the Scepter.

Just not the most important part.

Placing my palm over the large pink stone near the top of the ornate staff, I whisper, *"Chartlann rochtana."*

The last time I used the Archive I warned the other Sovereigns that we'd all need to be quiet if I was going to keep the secret. Because their stored images, memories and personalities are capable of virtual intelligence, they're easily able to adapt to changing circumstances—like keeping the Scepter hidden in Molly's closet.

"Hello, my dear." A remarkably lifelike hologram of Sovereign Aerleas, my great-grandmother and the last Sovereign I consulted, appears before me. My grandfather, Leontine, is great for strategy and technical stuff, but Aerleas, I've learned, is the most gifted at interpersonal relationships and political maneuvering. Maybe she can help me now.

"Hello," I respond with a smile. "It's been a while since I was able to access the Archive, so I need to add a lot of stuff to my entry. I could also use some advice."

Her smile becomes motherly. Or, I guess, great-grandmotherly, though her image doesn't look older than forty or so. "Of course. Go ahead with your update, as that should make it easier for me to address whatever it is you need help with."

When I couldn't get to my Scepter for so long, I started worrying I'd forget stuff, so I made recordings on my omni and stored them on a Nuathan data chip. I pull that chip out of my pocket now and insert it into a slot hidden between two jewels midway down the staff. Then I quietly recount the most recent events aloud.

Once that's done, I feel a lot better. "Now maybe you can tell me how to deal with a few things—and people," I say to Aerleas.

Quickly, I tell her about how public sentiment is already turning against Rigel and me, after that brief outpouring of gratitude the week after we foiled the Grentl attack. "How can people supposedly so advanced have such short memories?"

She shakes her head sadly. "I fear it is partly a result of our technological advances, particularly in the areas of media and communication —something I attempted to mitigate somewhat during my reign."

"The Great Unplugging. Yes I read about it. But I thought after the people's initial resistance they agreed it was a good thing? That interacting face to face was better than spending their lives, um, online?"

Before her edict, people had actually started getting semi-permanent implants to keep them connected to the *grechain*, or Nuathan internet, 24/7.

"True, they did. But while our people spent less time than previously communicating with each other technologically, they continued to access most of their news and entertainment that way. Competition for audience attention gave rise to the polling that is still so popular in Nuath. Over time, our people have become overly dependent on those polls, allowing them to shape opinions that should instead be based on reasoned analysis."

I had firsthand experience with that myself. It was those stupid polling numbers that almost prevented me from getting Acclaimed Sovereign in time to keep the Grentl from destroying Nuath last spring.

"I know it's still like that back in Nuath, but I thought here, away from the constant polls and poll results, that would change."

"According to your recent Archive entries, a large percentage of the *Echtrans* on Earth only arrived a few months ago. Old habits can take quite a long time to change. As unused as they've been to forming their own opinions unassisted, I imagine many now rely on other sources to help formulate them."

Like the *Echtran Enquirer.* Ugh. "That makes sense," I reluctantly admit. "So what can I do about it?"

"I recommend co-opting those sources, to whatever extent is possible. Perhaps you can communicate your own messages via the media our people here already use and trust, rather than relying solely on the official channel used by the Council."

"Then…you think I should write articles for the *Echtran Enquirer* myself?"

She inclined her head. "That would seem the most obvious first step, yes."

"Thank you. I'll do that." It's a great idea. I even have some experience at that sort of thing, as a member of the school newspaper staff.

By now Molly must be wondering what's taking me so long, but I quickly tell Aerleas how the Royals, who have a majority on the *Echtran* Council, keep dragging their heels on implementing certain reforms of mine they've already agreed to.

As before, she listens without speaking, though her facial expressions perfectly reflect the emotions I'd expect her to feel if she were really alive and in this closet with me. Which, come to think of it, would be awfully uncomfortable, since her image is superimposed over Molly's shoe rack.

"I understand why you are concerned, Emileia. It appears that some Council members still have difficulty accepting that a girl your age might have either the wisdom or authority to suggest measures they did not think of themselves. I wonder if you should consider appointing a second Regent who might shoulder some of your responsibilities on Earth?"

"Sovereign Leontine suggested that too, but the only person I trust enough for that role is Mr. Stuart, Rigel's dad...or maybe Dr. Stuart, his mom. And even I can see the problem with having two Regents from the same, non-Royal family."

She frowns thoughtfully, which usually means she's searching the Archive. Then, "My apologies, dear. I do see that you already explained this to Leontine. I should have checked that log before offering the suggestion."

Not for the first time, I marvel at just how human these images seem, right down to making occasional human mistakes like that.

"As that solution does not seem viable at this time," she continues, "I recommend you enlist the aid of those Council members who do share your concerns. It may be necessary to dissemble somewhat in order to persuade one or more of the resistant members that an idea is theirs when it is, in fact, yours."

Kind of like what I did with that last MARSTAR release I sent out in the Council's name to give Rigel credit for helping to save the world. Except this time I'll probably have to be even sneakier about it. I thank Aerleas again for her help, then deactivate the Archive.

Standing up, I set the Scepter back in its corner behind Molly's old bathrobe, half-wishing I could tell her the *whole* truth. Still, I told her enough that I should be able to access the Archive a lot more often now. Which I will. After all, my combined ancestors are way smarter and more experienced than any Regent could ever be.

Fortified with at least the beginnings of a plan of action, I open the closet door.

5

Reduction potential

Molly

"I'M SORRY, MOLLY," M says when she finally emerges from my closet after almost half an hour. "I didn't think it would take so long. I'm supposed to add my own updates to that archive, too. For, um, posterity. And a whole lot has happened since the last time I used it, even more than I realized."

"It's fine. I was doing homework. And yeah, a lot *has* happened these past few weeks—you foiled an alien attack, then got kidnapped, then there was that assassination attempt a couple of weeks ago... What am I forgetting?"

She chuckles. "I think that's most of it. Like I said, it was a lot to add to the Scepter."

"The Scepter?"

I can immediately tell from M's "oops" expression she didn't mean to say that.

"I, um... Yeah. That's what the archive is stored in." Then after a pause, "I wish I could tell you more about it, Molly, really I do, but I'm not supposed to."

"No worries. If it's secret Sovereign stuff, it's secret Sovereign stuff. It's not like being your Handmaid comes with any kind of top security clearance. I remember last spring you weren't allowed to tell me or Sean about the Grentl until you had no choice. Um, nothing *that* scary is going on now, right?"

To my relief, she smiles. "No, nothing scary at all. And I'm not keeping any other secrets I can think of. I just can't give you all the details about the archive. Sorry."

"No, really, it's fine. I'm still here for you any time there's something *not* so secret you want to talk about."

"I know. You always have been, Molly, and it means more to me than I can tell you. You're way more than my Handmaid. You're the best friend anyone could have."

Her words and the look that accompanies them actually bring a lump to my throat. Sometimes I forget how few friends M had before I got to Jewel.

"Ditto!" I say it from my heart.

And then we're hugging each other, both of us crying just a little. After a lovely, emotional minute or two, M sits up and clears her throat, giving me a watery smile.

"I did just remember something else I was going to tell you about. It might not turn out to be important, though."

Maybe she just wants to distract me from the other secrets she's keeping, but I can't resist asking. "What?"

"Rigel told me last night that his dad has intercepted some communications from what he called 'rogue' *Echtran* settlements."

"Rogue settlements? What do you mean? Like...Faxon sympathizers?"

"Maybe? Even though Faxon's in prison, there are apparently still some Martians who believe all the stuff he spouted. About how our people are superior, so we have some kind of right to take over on Earth and lord it over the *Duchas*, maybe even enslave them."

I suck in a breath. This is scarier stuff than I was expecting. "But...I thought his followers were all rounded up after he was deposed and imprisoned. Weren't they?"

"Not if they didn't commit any actual crimes. Just holding an unpopular opinion isn't illegal, so there wasn't much the interim government could do about them."

I snort. "It sure wasn't like that under Faxon."

When my family still lived on Mars, my parents had to be careful to hide who they really were and what they believed in, or risk arrest. Or worse. When a Resistance meeting was raided, my older sister was taken prisoner and the rest of us had to run for our lives—to Earth.

The sympathetic look M gives me almost makes me wonder if she can read *my* mind the way she does Rigel's. But no, I usually have a pretty good idea what she's thinking, too, and I'm for certain no mind reader.

"We don't actually know yet who's in those rogue settlements," she continues, "but if there are other threats out there, we need to find out."

"Yeah, I'd say so! What kinds of threats do you think there might be?" I wasn't any help at all when M was kidnapped, or later when she was nearly assassinated. *This* time I plan to be ready to spring into action if necessary.

M pats my arm soothingly. "Don't worry, it's probably nothing. I mean, it only makes sense people with really unpopular views would leave Nuath when they could, especially if they were being ostracized by their neighbors. If any *did* commit crimes under Faxon, they'd worry that might come out if they stayed. On Earth, they probably figured they could get a fresh start—especially if they avoided any *Echtrans* who knew them back in Nuath. Maybe they just want to be left alone."

"Then you don't think they're banding together, maybe forming some kind of neo-Faxon movement here? You said 'rogue settlements.'"

"It's possible," M admits. "Mr. Stuart thinks the Council should keep tabs on them, though they insist there can't be enough of them to cause problems. The only reason we know about these settlements at all is from concerned family members sending inquiries to the immigration office, trying to track down relatives who disappeared after getting here. Mr. Stuart is hoping to find out more before the Council meeting on Saturday."

She frowns thoughtfully for a second. "Hm, I wonder if Kira saw or heard anything that might give us some clues about these groups. Some of those people might have been on her ship or in Dun Cloch with her. Maybe she'll have some idea of whether they're an actual threat or just technophobes or something. Do you think she and Sean will come back here tonight?"

"I doubt it. Mum is still being such a pain, they mostly just go for walks or meet in town. Whenever she's at the house, Mum makes it way too clear she doesn't approve."

M winces. "Doesn't she want Sean to be happy? Do you think it would help if I talked to her, pointed out how unfair she's being?"

I consider that for a moment, then shake my head. "Probably not. She'd smile and nod while you were talking. Then as soon as Sean gets home she'd go off on another rant about how he never would have lowered himself like this if you'd stuck to tradition."

"*Lowered* himself?" she repeats, clearly outraged. "Did she actually say that?"

I nod, trying not to let M see how much Mum's words hurt *my* feelings—but of course she can tell.

"Okay, now I really do want to talk to her. How can she—" She breaks off at my alarmed expression. "Never mind. Anyway, I should go. It's getting late. Just remember that people sometimes say things when they're upset they don't really mean. Stuff they'd never say if they thought it through."

"I know."

But Mum has said other things lately to make me more aware than ever that I'm not Royal—and that I'd better not forget it. I want to believe she only makes those references to my *fine* for my own good, but they also remind me how much I don't fit in. Not in my Royal family and not as an Ag, either—not unless I can somehow develop the traditional skills of my *fine*. I'll just have to work harder at that.

Maybe with Alan's help?

As I GET ready for bed later, I think over everything M told me tonight— especially about the secret archive in her Scepter.

On impulse, I go into my closet and flip on the little overhead light to stare at it. As usual, it's propped innocently in the back corner, next to the box of books that used to have the Grentl device on it.

It's gorgeous—ornate but not gaudy, despite the gems embedded along its length. The jewel colors all complement each other and, not-coincidentally, every single one of M's Royal outfits. I've always liked looking at it. Now that I know it's more than just a fancy staff, I look closer. I've never *noticed* any buttons or controls on it…

Even though I know I shouldn't, I lightly run my fingers along it from the big, translucent pink jewel at the top to the comfortable grip about halfway down the staff. There, just above the grip, I discover a tiny slit I never noticed before, hidden between two green gems. A slit just the right size for a Nuathan data chip.

Huh. That's probably how M added her report to the archive, since she wasn't in the closet long enough to dictate *everything* that's happened since we got back to Earth. I wonder how she looks stuff up? Maybe she just…asks?

"What is the population of Nuath?" I say aloud to the Scepter, uncomfortably aware that I'm crossing a line.

When nothing happens, I'm more relieved than disappointed, then swamped by guilt that I even tried. M *trusts* me. And here I am, betraying that trust by prying into her secrets. Shaken, I back away from the Scepter and exit the closet as quickly as I can.

THE NEXT MORNING, remembering my resolve to work harder at becoming a proper Ag, I make a point of catching Alan's eye when I pass him in the hallway before school. Even knowing M mentioned me to him, I'm a little surprised when he immediately stops.

"Hey, Molly, I'm glad I caught you. I was wondering if you were planning to go to the football game tonight?"

I have to struggle not to laugh. "I, ah, sort of have to, since I'm on the cheer squad."

His confusion is comical. So is the way he immediately tries to cover for it. "Oh, um, yeah, of course. I knew that."

Not. He's probably been too busy watching Kira and Sean in the stands to even notice me on the sidelines. There's no point embarrassing him further, though, if I want to be friends—and maybe get his help.

"I guess I'll see you there, then?" I give him an encouraging smile.

"Yeah, for sure. I was sort of hoping—oops, there's the bell. I'll, um, talk to you later, okay?" He hurries off, apparently still feeling foolish. Which is *not* my fault.

Before and after Pre-Cal, Tristan again talks to M every chance he gets. I'm pretty sure he's trying to use his charm thing on her but it's having no more effect than it did yesterday. Despite what he said about being more subtle, his attempts to flirt with her are still blatant enough that when we all get to French, I try to draw off his attention.

"So Tristan, have you had a chance to start catching up in any of your classes yet? I can point you in the right direction if you need help."

"No, I'm good. At least ten other girls have offered me their class notes already. Though if Marsha here wants to tutor me, I'd be fine with that." He slants a glance M's way but she just rolls her eyes.

I pull out a sheet of paper, jot down the school website address and hand it to him. "Here. Almost every class has everything you need online. So you don't have to pester anyone else."

He looks like he's about to tell me off but the bell rings first so he just shakes his head and turns away. Too bad. I was ready to zing him right back if he had.

I hope he's irritated enough to avoid talking to me in Chemistry, but no such luck. Instead he tries to convince me he'd be a way better match for M than Rigel is, claiming he's practically an expert on Martian traditions.

"You say they're great together," he whispers, "but it has to bother her at least a little that he's not Royal. I guess I can understand why they got together early on, since he was the first *Echtran* she'd ever met. But once word went out about her and more of us started coming to Jewel, someone really should have explained the whole *fine* thing to her, considering how important a proper Consort is for our people."

Keeping my voice super low, I reply, "Someone did—me. I told her all about *fines* myself, just a week or so after we moved here. I explained why our people pair within their same *fine* and why she and Rigel weren't a good idea. My Uncle Allister also lectured her constantly about her duty to our people and Sean did everything he possibly could to convince her she should be with him instead of Rigel. None of it mattered because it was too late. She and Rigel were already bonded."

"Bonds can be broken. Just like in Chemistry." He thumps our textbook for emphasis. "For the good of our people, that one *needs* to be. One way or another." His intensity is unnerving.

"You're wrong. Without that bond, M would probably be dead right now. Maybe we all would. Their bond has done more good for our people than you can possibly—"

The teacher gives me a frowning glance and I break off, suddenly remembering he's an *Echtran*, too, and can probably hear our whispering. After watching us for a second, he continues with his explanation of the labs we'll be doing next week.

At lunch Trina waylays Tristan long enough for me to make sure the only empty seat at our table is well away from M. Once he sits down, Bri and Deb do the rest, monopolizing him until the bell rings. It's almost fun to watch Tristan struggling to be diplomatic as he parries their flirting. He clearly realizes it could hurt his case with M to alienate her best friends, even the *Duchas* ones.

On the way to Government class, Bri and Deb continue talking to him, apparently trying to learn every tiny detail about his life. Again he does a surprisingly good job of answering their questions without giving away anything that might make them suspicious.

"Yeah, I went to private school through eighth grade," I hear him tell Deb. "It was even smaller than Jewel's middle school, only fifty students or so. After that I attended a public high school more than three times the size of this one. Took a little getting used to."

I'll bet. That "private school" must have been in Fiarway, the *Echtran* compound near Denver.

When we get to class, the teacher has us get with our partners to finish up the project we've been doing on the electoral process. Tristan doesn't have a partner so Bri and Deb immediately invite him to join their team. To their disappointment, the teacher instead has him sit up front with her to review what we've covered so far. That effectively keeps him from hassling M and Rigel while they work together, though I notice he still stares at them a lot.

In Psych class, he takes the desk next to me again, ready to continue the conversation we started in Chemistry.

"What did you mean earlier, about that bond thing supposedly saving M's life?" he asks in a sub-whisper the second he sits down. "You said yesterday that she made some deal with the Council to save Rigel's, but when did he ever save hers?"

"The *first* time was when Faxon's people came after her last year. You must have heard about it, with your dad on the Council and all. We did, and we were living in Ireland then."

He frowns. "I heard it was Regent Shim and some of his people who fought off those attackers."

"Only for the final showdown. Before that, they tried to kill M in a car wreck—and would have succeeded if not for Rigel and their bond. And even in that big battle in the cornfield—it was the one right behind this school, by the way—it was M and Rigel together, using their bond, that brought down Faxon's Ossian Sphere. My dad says it almost certainly would have killed M and most of the rest of our side if they hadn't."

"Used their bond how?"

"That electrical thing they can do. It was mentioned in the report our Scientists put out, though they played it down some so it wouldn't scare people. Your dad was right there the last time they tested it, though. *He* knows what they can do together. Why don't you ask him?"

Tristan is still frowning but I see doubt creeping in.

"Yeah. Maybe I will."

He continues to look thoughtful through the rest of class but doesn't ask me any more questions. I'd like to think I've finally said enough to discourage him but I doubt it. Still, with any luck I won't see him again before Monday. Thank goodness.

$$\rule{6cm}{0.4pt}$$

6

Blocking effect

$$\rule{6cm}{0.4pt}$$

Tristan

I MAKE sure to get to tonight's football game early. Every time I've tried to talk to the Sovereign at school, either Stuart or Molly O'Gara has blocked me. Tonight they won't be able to, with Stuart out on the field playing and Molly doing cheers on the sidelines. I need to make the most of this chance to finally have a one-on-one conversation with her.

Scanning the dinky little set of bleachers, I spot the Sovereign near the fifty-yard line. There are no other *Echtrans* around her, at least not yet. Just those same two *Duchas* girls who flirted with me all through lunch today. Now, though, I can actually snag a spot next to the Sovereign. Perfect. Wearing my most charming smile, I head her way.

"Hey, mind if I sit here?"

Just like at lunch, her two girlfriends fall all over themselves to make me welcome, simpering and flirting for all they're worth. The Sovereign, not so much—but she doesn't object to me joining them. I sit on her other side.

"Did you go to many football games in Denver?" the darker haired girl, Bri, leans over to ask before I can even try talking to the Sovereign.

"Yeah, I was on my school's team, actually. Quarterback, just like Stuart. It sucked that I had to leave before the end of the season."

Both *Duchas* girls exclaim about how unfair that was, but I'm watching the Sovereign. She doesn't say anything, but she does look sympathetic. I consider that a hopeful sign.

"Do any of you do sports?" I ask, in an effort to get her talking.

"Not me, I'm a total klutz," the little blonde one says, "but Bri played soccer in middle school and M does Taekwondo."

Which I knew, though I pretend otherwise. "Taekwondo, huh? Wow, that's really cool. How long have you been doing that?"

Her green eyes reveal a trace of suspicion but she answers readily enough. "I started a year and a half ago, but missed almost six months over the spring and summer."

"Oh? Why was that?"

Again, I know perfectly well—and this time her expression makes it clear she's aware of that. But because the new *Duchas* student I'm pretending to be wouldn't, she answers anyway.

"I went to Ireland to study abroad, then I was in an accident there that kept me from coming home until August." The cover story my father told me they'd used to explain her absence while she was in Nuath getting Acclaimed Sovereign.

"Wow, sorry about the accident. Looks like you're okay now, though, huh? How often do you do Taekwondo now you're back? What belt level are you?" Anything to keep the conversation going.

Unfortunately, the suspicion doesn't leave her eyes. "Twice a week, usually. I'm just a blue belt, though I'll be testing for recommended-red later this month."

I keep asking her questions, first about Taekwondo, then about her classes and Jewel in general. I'm careful to call her "M" now, since I finally realized at lunch today that none of her actual friends call her Marsha. Even though the other girls butt in every chance they get, she's still talking to me a lot more than she has at school so far.

As much as I can without being obviously rude to her friends, I keep my focus on the Sovereign, working my charm thing for all it's worth. But just like in school, she acts like it has no effect on her whatsoever. In fact, her gaze keeps straying to the field, where the players are warming up. Watching Stuart, no doubt. I need to try harder.

I get her to answer a couple of questions about her favorite things to do in Jewel, but when the game starts, her full attention shifts to the action on the field. So does Bri's, though Deb, the little blonde, keeps smiling over at me. Since I can't ask the Sovereign the kinds of questions

I *really* want to anyway, with her friends there listening, I start watching the game too.

About a minute into the first quarter it's obvious the only decent player on the Jewel team is Rigel Stuart. I was the standout on my team, too—not that that's saying much compared to a bunch of *Duchas*.

A few plays later, I have to grudgingly admit that Stuart's at least as good a quarterback as I am. Maybe better. Because of that bond he and the Sovereign supposedly have? I'm sure Molly would say so.

The Jewel team scores, Stuart running the ball into the end zone. As they set up for the extra point, I turn back to the Sovereign.

"So, do you have any hobbies other than Taekwondo?" Not that she *should* have time for any hobbies at all, what with school and her official duties.

"You're still into astronomy, aren't you, M?" her friend Bri says before she can answer.

She nods. "I'm still hoping to talk my aunt and uncle into getting me a decent telescope. Maybe for Christmas."

The idea of the Sovereign needing to ask her *Duchas* guardians for anything—especially something as basic as a telescope—boggles me. Don't they know the truth about her? I could swear Father said they were told recently.

"What kind of telescope do you want?" Maybe if Stuart can't buy it for her, I will. Doesn't matter how expensive it is, I know Father will be fine with anything that might make her feel obligated to me.

"Well, my dream telescope would be a ten-inch computerized go-to refractor," she says, "but I'd be happy with just an eight-inch reflector. The little one I have now can barely resolve mid-sized craters on the moon."

Before I can ask for more details, the crowd erupts in cheers as our team makes the extra point—and the Sovereign's attention turns back to the field.

I continue to use every time out to talk with her—or try to. Unfortunately, she starts deflecting more and more of my questions to her *Duchas* friends, even when I direct them specifically to her. By halftime I'm getting desperate to make some real headway with her. I don't know when I'll have another opportunity as good as this one.

"So M, what can I get you from the concession stand?" Turning on the charm, I lean over to direct my very best smile into her face. "Popcorn? A drink?"

"Nothing, thanks," she replies coolly as her friends get up. "But if you're going, Bri, get me a coke, okay?" She hands the girl a dollar.

As a brushoff, it couldn't be more obvious. Or embarrassing.

"Hey, I would have—" I start to protest but she cuts me off.

"I know you would. Just…don't, okay?"

I sit there for a second, not sure what to say to such a direct rebuff, then shrug and follow Bri down the bleachers while I consider my best way to regroup. I'm maybe halfway to the concession stand when I get waylaid by Sean O'Gara.

He doesn't mince words either. "Man, you don't give up, do you?"

He's so tall, I have to look up to face him—which irritates me. "What, the way you did? I've never been much of a quitter."

His lip twists in a sneer. "Better a quitter than a nuisance. Because that's all you are to her, you know."

"Did she tell you that?"

"She didn't have to. Listen, I know M a lot better than you ever will and you're deluding yourself if you think you'll ever get anywhere with her. Won't happen. You'll just end up looking like a chump if you keep trying."

"I guess you'd know, huh?"

I expect that to piss him off but he surprises me with a grin. "Better than anybody. But hey, you want to keep making a fool of yourself, be my guest."

"I'd rather be considered a fool than turn my back on my obligations and settle for an Ag, like you did."

The grin disappears. "Watch it. Kira's got more going for her than you'll ever have. I'm sure you were raised to believe Royals are superior to everyone else, just like I was, but I happen to know firsthand just how fallible they can be. Even more than the other *fines* are, because most Royals are so cocky. Didn't your daddy tell you what Allister Adair and Lach Lennox tried to do to M? *Fine* has nothing to do with character. Obviously." He looks down his nose at me, his meaning clear.

"The Royal *fine* originated from our smartest, most talented people. They've had leadership qualities bred into them for centuries," I remind him through clenched teeth. "Sure, your Kira was a great *caidpel* player, but let's face it, Ags are basically farmers. Not even close to being on the same level we are."

"Maybe you should get to know a few. They might surprise you."

For some stupid reason, I glance at the sidelines, where Molly's been doing cheers, though she's not there now. Unfortunately, Sean notices.

"I didn't mean my sister—not that she'd be interested in *you* anyway. She's seen the way you've been panting after M since you got here. We all have. Trust me, I was doing you a favor by trying to give you a heads up. You want to ignore it, that's on you."

With a parting smirk, he turns and walks off. I wait a minute, then continue down to the concession stand, fuming. Jerk. Just because *he* wasn't able to convince the Sovereign her responsibility to our people includes a proper pairing doesn't mean *I* won't.

Because I will. I have to. The future of our people, both here and on Mars, depends on that.

7

Asymmetric induction

Molly

"COME ON, Molly, head in the game," Trina scolds me when I get out of synch again, my third time in the first half. "Watch me for the cues if you have to."

"Sorry." I pay closer attention during our next cheer routine but it isn't easy. Up in the stands, Tristan is sitting way too close to M and it's beyond frustrating I can't do anything about it. Some *Chomseireach* I am. Bri and Deb are doing their best to keep his attention on them, but I can see from here it isn't working.

When the whistle blows for halftime, I toss my pompoms on the bench in relief and head for the stands.

Only to find Alan blocking my path.

"Hey, Molly, you're looking really good out there."

Like this morning, it's all I can do not to laugh since I've been messing up left and right. "Um, thanks. Great game so far, huh?"

He glances at the scoreboard, which shows Jewel ahead 21-6. "Yeah, Rigel's doing an awesome job. So anyway, I was wondering—"

"Um, can we talk later?" I interrupt him, glancing up at the stands again to see Tristan leaning toward M, a wheedling expression on his face. Jerk. "I, er, don't get a very long break and I need to hit the loo."

"Oh. Of course. Sure. Maybe after the game, then?"

Oops. I promised M—and myself—I wouldn't shoot Alan down if he acted interested, and it must sound like I'm doing just that.

"After the game will be great. Thanks!" I put some extra enthusiasm into my voice and give him my best smile. Then I hurry away to intercept Tristan, who's now heading down the stands. Before he reaches the bottom, though, Sean cuts him off. With all the crowd noise, I can't hear anything they say from here, but it's obvious Tristan isn't happy about it.

Good.

Sean warning him off M should be more effective than anything I can do anyway. He outranks Tristan and I totally don't—and if anyone *were* going to take Rigel's place, Sean obviously has first dibs. Not that I expect that will ever happen, especially now he's with Kira. Even if public acceptance of M and Rigel as a couple *has* declined from where it was last month.

Sean finishes talking and moves away and Tristan continues toward the concession stand, scowling. Figuring a little reinforcement from me can't hurt, I head the same way.

"So, did Sean convince you to sit somewhere else for the second half?" I ask as I pass him. "If not, I'd like to suggest it myself."

The look he turns on me is totally devoid of his usual charm. "When I want your advice I'll ask for it, okay? Meanwhile, how about you stay out of my way?"

"Fine, as long as you stay out of M's. Otherwise, expect to find me in your way at every turn."

"Why? What's it to *you*, anyway?"

Yeah, Sean definitely warned him off. I give Tristan an exaggeratedly patient look.

"I'm her *Chomseireach*, in case you forgot. It's my job to keep irritating creeps away from her, as much as it's her Bodyguard's job to deal with any physical threats."

He snorts derisively. "Oh, right. Yet another way she flouted tradition, appointing an Ag to a post that should have gone to a Royal."

"All the more reason for me to take my responsibilities seriously," I snap, ignoring the sting from his words. I'm not likely to forget what a huge honor my position is when Mum reminds me of it regularly.

"Whatever. But you can't be with her 24/7 any more than Stuart can. While he's showing off on the field and you're dancing around on the sidelines, I can get to know her better. At some point she'll wake up to what she's missing."

That gets a laugh from me. "What, one more arrogant jerk telling her what to do? She's had plenty of those along the way and doesn't miss them a bit, believe me. But hey, it's your time to waste."

Shaking my head at such willful self-delusion, I continue on to the restroom, mostly in case Alan is watching.

JEWEL WINS, of course, 33-13. M did get Bri and Deb to sit between her and Tristan for the second half, not that they probably needed any convincing. That makes me feel a little less lame for not being up there myself.

At the final whistle our fans rush the field. Tristan follows M down, trying to stay close, though the crowd makes it hard. I head toward them in case he catches up with her—but then I see Alan coming my way from another direction. Oops.

Torn, I flash a smile Alan's way while anxiously watching M's and Tristan's progress. Not until M reaches Rigel, with Tristan still well behind her, do I turn to give Alan my full attention.

"Hi," I say brightly, determined to make up for being short with him earlier. "Sorry I rushed off before."

"No problem. You have a little time now?"

"Sure. What's up?" Out of the corner of my eye, I see Tristan stop, frown, then shrug before turning toward the parking lot. Excellent.

Alan clears his throat and shoves a hand through his white-blond hair, clearly embarrassed—which somehow makes him even cuter. "I, ah, just recently found out that even though you grew up with the O'Garas, you were actually born an Ag?"

"That's right. They adopted me when I was a baby, after my real parents were killed." I thought everyone knew that by now.

"Killed. Do you mean—"

"By Faxon's *bullochts*, yeah. At least, that's what I was told, though no one seemed to know why."

Alan shook his head. "Not sure they always needed a reason. It was really smart of the O'Garas to pass themselves off as Ags when they decided to stay. I thought they really were until word started to leak out about the Resistance right before they left Nuath. I grew up in Holly-doon," he adds by way of explanation.

"Oh, not far from Glenamuir at all." A wave of nostalgia sweeps over me, making Alan suddenly seem like a little piece of home.

"Yeah, next village over. Your brother and I even played *chas*— er, basketball together a few times when we were kids."

I don't think anyone is likely to hear us over the crowd noise, but he's right, there's no point being stupid about it. "I remember him mentioning that, your first day at Jewel. Do you miss it as much as I do? Home, I mean, not playing ball."

"Yeah. I'm kind of surprised you do, though, considering…everything." His blue eyes are sympathetic.

"Most of my time there was fine. It was only right at the end things got scary. Don't get me wrong, I do like it here. I've made lots of friends, my family's great and M is awesome, of course."

"Must be a lot of responsibility, having such an important position, huh?" The respect in his eyes is flattering. "One reason I was surprised to hear you weren't Royal. It's so cool they were willing to appoint an Ag."

So different from Tristan's condescending attitude! "Yeah, it is cool. As for the responsibility, I don't really have so much now. When we were back…home last summer, in the Palace and all, I did, but I really enjoyed it. The best part is M herself, though. She's about the best friend anyone could have."

Now the respect becomes tinged with awe. "You're really friends then? Not just—?"

"We really are," I assure him. That's one thing I *don't* have doubts about. Behind Alan, I see Sean and Kira coming our way. "Oops, I'm going to have to go in a minute, I'm getting a ride from my brother. But, um, do you think you could do me a favor sometime?"

"A favor?" He looks confused.

I nod. "I don't know if anyone's mentioned it to you, but I'm not… super great with the Ag skills and obviously no one in my family is any help. I've got some plants that aren't doing too well and I wondered—"

"Oh. Sure! I was, um, actually going to ask if you wanted to get together sometime to talk trade secrets, that sort of thing. I'd be happy to take a look at your plants, too. Will tomorrow work?"

"Tomorrow would be grand. Say around noon? Do you know where we live?"

He grins. He really is awfully cute. "My folks do. I'll see you at noon tomorrow, then."

Sean and Kira reach us then. I probably imagine the slight longing in Alan's glance at Kira because he's perfectly nice to Sean—and gives me another big smile before walking away.

"That looked promising," Kira teases as we head toward the parking lot. "Making plans?"

"Yeah, he's going to come by tomorrow to help me with my, er problem."

Kira nods sympathetically. Last month she also tried to help me awaken my latent Ag skills, using some rose bushes at her apartment complex. With zero success, unfortunately, though I was seriously impressed when I saw what *she* could do.

"I'm sure it's just a matter of practice."

I hope she's right, though I'm not especially confident. Still, it's a decent excuse to hang out with Alan and *maybe* he'll have better luck putting me in touch with my dormant plant affinity. Even if not, it surely can't hurt to get to know him better. And who knows? Maybe it'll turn into something more.

M will be pleased to hear her hints worked.

.⁺✦

"What time is Alan coming over?" Sean asks as we're finishing breakfast the next morning.

Mum instantly perks up. "Alan? Alan Dempsey, do you mean?" She turns to me, curiosity sparkling in her bright blue eyes. "You've invited him here?"

Shooting an irritated glance at Sean, I nod. "We talked a little after the game last night and he, er, offered to stop by to take a look at my poor plants, maybe show me how to take better care of them."

"Well, isn't that nice!" Mum exclaims delightedly. "It's lovely you're making friends with other *Echtrans* your age. I've worried a bit you only socialize with those *Duchas* cheerleaders. And the Sovereign, who's far too busy to spend all her precious free time with you."

"I don't think M minds. But yeah, I'm getting to know the new students a bit better."

Mum and Dad have both cautioned me against depending too much on M as a friend or being too informal with her, though they should know M better than that by now. Despite the difference in our stations, she *hates* when I say or do anything that emphasizes her rank, like bowing or calling her "Excellency." Though I still have to in front of other Royals, like the Council, because Mum insists.

"Pleased as I am that an Agricultural boy is showing interest, you're not to be alone in your room with him," Mum says then, with a glance at Sean. She's strict about that rule with him and Kira. "Perhaps you should take your plants out to the front porch? It's a lovely day, after all."

"Oh, good idea. He said he'd swing by around noon, so I have plenty of time to do that."

"I'll be sure to have a few sandwiches and some biscuits ready for you, then."

The relieved smile she and Dad exchange tells me they've also noticed how I don't really fit in anywhere. Maybe that'll change if things work out with Alan?

AT FIVE MINUTES TO twelve I'm setting the last of my pathetic house-plants on the front porch when Alan drives up. I take his punctuality as a good sign.

"Hey, sorry I'm a little early," he says, coming up the front walk. "I wasn't sure how long it would take to get here. Figured I'd just sit in the car until noon but since you're outside…"

"Yeah, that would be a little weird." I laugh. "It's such a pretty day, it made sense to bring my plants out to the porch. I'm sure they can use some fresh air anyway." No way will I mention what Mum said about him coming up to my room.

He surveys the five potted plants, down from the six I left with Heather while we were in Nuath—and that she returned in better shape than I left them. Unfortunately, I managed to kill one after getting them back.

"Good idea," he agrees, concern creasing his brow. "Looks like they're not so happy with wherever you've been keeping them."

"Yeah, maybe they need more sun. Or less. Or something. I'm hoping you'll give me tips. But first come in and meet my parents."

He follows me inside, where Mum and Dad hurry forward, all smiles.

"Hello, Alan." Dad extends a hand. "I've spoken with your parents a few times at NuAgra and they say you're settling in well?"

"Yes, sir, everyone has been great." Alan's marked deference toward my dad startles me. "They wanted me to thank you again, both of you —" he gives Mum a tiny bow— "for all the help you've given us here, and for everything else you've done for our people."

"And we appreciate you taking the time to work with Molly and her plants," Dad replies. "Since moving to Jewel last year, she's been around very few *Echtrans*, I'm afraid. We're pleased she's finally making more friends."

Blimey, does he have to make me sound so pathetic?

"Well, um, we'll go mess with the plants now, I guess," I say before Mum can reinforce what a complete loser I am.

She gives Alan a complacent smile. "Yes, do. I'll bring some snacks out shortly."

We retreat back to the porch and my sorry collection of plants.

"So, any ideas?" I gesture at their drooping leaves. "I've tried every-thing. I read everything I can about gardening, but…"

He cocks an eyebrow. "*Duchas* gardening? They try, and some appar-ently aren't bad at it, but we Ags can go way beyond what they put in books. I guess you haven't been around that many Ags, though?"

"Not since we left Glenamuir, no. Even in Bailerealta, most of the kids my age were from the Science and Mining *fines*. And my parents and Sean know even less than I do."

"That's too bad. There are several basic tricks your real Ag parents would have taught you. Like this." He picks up my poor peace lily, whose leaves are browning at the edges even though I water it faithfully. "Watch."

Like Kira did when we worked with the rose bushes outside her apartment, Alan runs a finger up each stem, starting from the bottom. It's like magic the way each leaf is standing up straighter by the time he reaches the top. I can swear they look a little greener, too.

"Wow," I breathe. "I've never— That is—"

"Try it," he urges, pushing the pot toward me. "Do a different leaf."

I mimic Alan's motion along the stems exactly, remembering what Kira told me about trying to sense the life inside the plant and encourage it. Unfortunately, I don't sense a thing, any more than I ever have when I've tried this. Nor does my leaf look the least bit different afterward.

"Huh." He frowns at the plant. "I, uh, guess it takes practice. Remember, I've been doing this since I was a little tyke."

Glumly, I nod. "That's what Kira said."

He gives a tiny twitch and I wish I hadn't mentioned her. "And my mum and M and pretty much everyone else," I add quickly. "Let me try again."

I pick a different leaf and do the finger-stroking thing again, concentrating as hard as I can. Nothing.

"Okay, well, let's try this philodendron, instead. You're sure you watered—?" He tests the soil with a finger. "Um, yeah. Guess so. Here, we'll do it together."

Alan and I both reach for the nearest sad leaf at once and our hands brush. The tingle I feel startles me—though it shouldn't, since it's the first time we've ever touched. I felt a similar *taghal ardus* when Liam tapped me on the shoulder his first week at Jewel, and even from sophomore Grady when I shook his hand at a party. Pretty typical between Martian teens at first touch. I tell myself this *taghal ardus* was stronger than either of those, which only makes sense given we're both Ags.

Then, remembering how I joked with M about *exactly* this scenario only two days ago, I have to suppress a sudden urge to laugh.

"Here, you draw your finger up that side of the leaf while I do this side," Alan says after a tiny pause. I guess he noticed that tingle, too. "You should be able to feel the plant's life force moving up the stem as we go."

Forcing myself to focus on the plant, I mirror his motion with my own and sure enough, the leaf straightens noticeably as we progress upward. Though I want to believe I'm helping, I'm pretty sure it's all Alan.

"There. You felt that, right?"

"Um…yeah." I'm too embarrassed to deny it. "That was really cool. Thanks."

"Now try it on your own."

Predictably, my touch unaided by his has no discernible effect. He shoots a slightly confused glance at me, then looks back at the plant. "I, um, think that helped some. Try again with the same leaf."

I do. Still nothing, though again he pretends he can see a slight difference— which is nice of him, even if it makes me feel lamer than ever. I'm about to apologize for wasting his time when Mum opens the front door.

"I thought you both might like a spot of lunch," she says cheerily, setting a tray with sandwiches, cookies and big glasses of milk on the table by the porch swing. "How is the practice going?"

"Thank you so much, Mrs. O'Gara." Alan surveys the heaped plates. "I, ah, think Molly is starting to get the hang of it."

"Well, that's just grand!" Mum exclaims, beaming at us both, then at the peace lily. "Oh, my. Yes, that plant looks a great deal better than I've ever seen it. Lovely, just lovely."

With another big smile, she goes back inside.

"Thanks, but you didn't have to do that," I say with a little grimace.

"Do what? You said you felt it that last time. I think you really are making progress. Do you want to try again before we eat?"

I shake my head and pick up a sandwich, feeling guilty now for lying to him. "I'll concentrate better after some lunch."

While we eat, he asks about my life in Glenamuir and what it was like to leave.

"Was your first view of Earth as amazing as mine? Even though I'd read so much about it, I still didn't expect it to be so…blue."

"Same here. And I was really blown away by my first glimpse of the ocean. It's so big! There was nothing in Nuath to compare it to, at all."

His smile is a little wistful. "I haven't had a chance to see an ocean yet, except from space. I'd like to."

"Oh, right, landing in Dun Cloch I guess you wouldn't have. Bailere-alta is on the west coast of Ireland so we went several times while we lived there. I'm sure you'll get to visit someday."

He nods, taking another bite of sandwich. "Was it weird going back to Nuath after being gone more than two years?"

"A little. I mean, I never saw much of Nuath outside of Glenamuir before we had to leave. Then our trip to the spaceport was at night, so I couldn't see much then, either."

"Leaving must have been scary, huh?"

"If it hadn't been for my sister Elana being taken, I probably would have found it more exciting than scary. I wasn't quite thirteen at the time, so I didn't completely understand what was going on until later. Mum and Dad hardly ever talked politics around Sean and me."

"That makes sense," he says. "You were so young, they probably didn't want to risk you accidentally repeating anything at school that could link them to the Resistance. When did you realize what amazing heroes your parents are?"

The reverence in his expression seems to include me, too—which is silly, since I've never done anything particularly heroic.

"Um, to me they're just Mum and Dad," I tell him. "They never made a big deal about it, so it feels odd when people get all tongue-tied around them. Or around M—though I did that, too, first time I met her." I laugh at the memory of my first day at Jewel High, when I felt so overwhelmed by everything that now seems normal.

Alan shakes his head, the admiration in his sky-blue eyes unmistakable. "The way you talk about the Sovereign, like she's just any other girlfriend… I don't think I could ever do that."

"We *are* friends. Really good friends. Of course, she wasn't Sovereign yet when I met her. Faxon was still in power back on Mars."

"Oh yeah, right. Still…" His expression grows warmer for a moment, then he looks away like he's embarrassed. "Looks like we pretty much polished off all the food. Ready to tackle your anthurium?"

"Er, sure." It's kind of sweet how he's embarrassed around me. I usually feel like such a nobody compared to M and my family.

We spend another hour with my plants. They all improve enormously, thanks to Alan, but I don't seem to.

"Hey, this was just the first day," he says when I voice my discouragement. "You haven't spent your whole life doing this stuff like I have. We can give it another go sometime."

"Okay, if you think it'll do any good."

He shrugs. "Even if it doesn't, this was fun. So…are you busy Monday night? We wouldn't have to work on your Ag skills again if you'd rather not."

Huh. Alan Dempsey, the cutest senior at Jewel High, is actually asking me out. Mum will be over the moon. "No, I'm not busy Monday. But yeah, let's do something different." This session was humiliating enough.

"We could go to Dream Cream after dinner," he suggests. "Or maybe the Lighthouse Cafe?"

Other than a couple of bars, which we're both too young to get into anyway, there aren't many other options in tiny downtown Jewel.

"Either sounds great."

When he drives off a couple of minutes later, I decide I really am looking forward to going out with him Monday evening. Alan *is* very handsome. And nice. Plus, it'll make my parents happy. Considering everything they've done for me over the years, I'm especially glad about that part.

8

Coordination complex

M

Taekwondo class Saturday is fun, especially when Master Parker lets Kira and me spar against each other. That's the only time neither of us has to hold back, like we have to do when we're paired with *Duchas* students.

I catch her eye as we're pulling off our arm and shin guards after class, and as soon as she finishes taking off her body pad she comes over to me.

"Something up?"

"Sort of. I was wondering if you might have time to talk once we get out of here?"

She hides it well but I can sense her sudden nervousness. "Nothing to worry about," I quickly assure her. "I just need to ask you some stuff about…before you got here, that's all."

She relaxes—or at least her emotions do. "Of course. Whatever you need."

Since finally accepting me as Sovereign, she's become a lot more respectful. That's way better than her earlier hostility, but I'd rather just be friends. I hope we'll get there eventually.

After changing into our regular clothes, we leave the *do jang* together.

"So, um, what did you want to ask about?" Kira asks, still slightly nervous.

I make sure no one's within earshot before saying, "When you were on your way to Earth—on the *Horizon*, right?"

She nods.

"Did you notice any groups who sort of kept to themselves or seemed, er, secretive in any way?"

"Former Faxon supporters, you mean? That's who everyone said they were, anyway."

Sounds like my suspicion was right. "Do you know why? Did you actually overhear anything to confirm that?"

"Not personally, but others claimed they did—and it explained why they avoided the rest of us."

We reach Diamond Street and I turn toward Kira's apartment complex instead of heading toward home, so we can keep talking. "How about when you were in Dun Cloch? Did you hear any discussion about groups of Faxon supporters or former supporters there?"

"Again, it was mostly just rumors," she says, "though I remember one guy asking me questions that made me think he was one, trying to find out if I shared their views. Probably because I, um, didn't exactly hide the fact I considered myself a Populist."

My interest sharpens. "Then they had reason to think Populists— some of them, anyway—might join them?"

She frowns uncertainly. "They shouldn't have. The Populist platform is completely nonviolent, nothing like what Faxon and his supporters advocated. But—"

"But every group has its fringe elements. Including the Populists?"

"I, ah, I guess so," she reluctantly admits.

"It only makes sense they would," I say matter-of-factly. "Any movement is made up of individuals, and some of them might not completely agree with the movement's leaders. From what I've read, the official Populist stance makes a lot of sense, but I can see how it might be twisted until it's similar to Faxon's goal of completely eradicating Royals. There's a reason so many people refer to Populists as Anti-Royals."

Now Kira looks even more troubled. "I always hated that term but maybe you're right. Even though they don't advocate violence, the Populists do want to see an end to our hereditary monarchy."

"Which is how Allister and Lennox convinced you to help them?"

She nods, abashed. "I...I'd bought into all the propaganda about you and was convinced—"

"I know," I interrupt gently, not wanting to put her on the defensive. "I'm well aware there are at least three different groups that would like to see me gone—Populists, any Faxon supporters still out there, and a fair number of staunch traditionalists who think my relationship with Rigel proves I'm unfit to be Sovereign."

What I hadn't considered until this week was what could happen if all three groups joined together to oppose me...or worse. It would be an awfully unlikely alliance, but not an impossible one. Maybe if some strong, charismatic leader persuaded them that they all share a common goal...?

"I don't suppose you ever saw Devyn Kane while you were in Dun Cloch?" I ask on that thought.

Kira shakes her head. "He's back on Earth? I didn't even know that. I saw him on the Nuathan feeds, of course, during your Acclamation campaign, but I've never met him in person."

Hm. "Did Allister or Lennox or that woman Enid ever mention *anyone* else in Dun Cloch—or outside of it—who was helping them, supposedly for the Populist cause?"

"Not that I remember. They really didn't tell me much. I...should have realized sooner they weren't really Populists, even though they claimed they were—so I'd help them. But it never occurred to me they could be involved with Faxon supporters. I mean, they're Royals."

"They probably would have been willing to work with anyone who could help them get rid of me. That woman, Enid, isn't Royal, is she?"

"No, I think she's Informatics or something. She's the tech genius who figured a way around their communication blocks and set up that special omni they gave me. She seemed totally devoted to Lennox, though. I got the impression she'd do anything for him."

To include murder, apparently. I store that tidbit away for future reference. We're nearly to the Diamond Terrace apartment complex now, where I see Sean waiting for Kira—which reminds me that Rigel mentioned meeting in the arboretum today. Before reaching out to him mentally to confirm, I ask Kira one more question.

"I don't suppose you know where anyone in Dun Cloch you thought might be a Faxon supporter was planning to settle?"

She frowns thoughtfully. "Seems like I remember the one guy who talked to me saying something about Idaho, but I could be confusing him with someone else. He mostly avoided me after I went on a rant about Faxon that first time he approached me."

Sean told me about the atrocities Faxon's goons committed in Kira's village, so it's no wonder she feels strongly about the subject.

"Okay, thanks. If you remember anything else you think might be important, let me know. Meanwhile, um, have fun." I nod toward Sean, who waves to us.

Kira grins. "Thanks. I, ah, I'm really glad you don't share his mum's opinion of us getting together."

I grin back. "That would be pretty hypocritical of me, considering I'm with Rigel—no matter how many people disapprove. Seriously, you guys seem great together and that makes me really happy."

With a parting wave to Sean, I turn and head for the arboretum...and Rigel.

·⁺·

MOLLY HAS ALREADY LEFT for some sort of cheerleading event when I get to the O'Garas' house that evening for the now-weekly *Echtran* Council meeting. I hope she'll get back before I leave, because I'm dying to ask how her "date" with Alan Dempsey went this afternoon. She texted me after last night's game to thank me for nudging him her way.

The O'Garas' small living room isn't too cramped yet since the only ones here so far are Mrs. O, Mr. Stuart and Nara, who's here holographically from Washington, DC. As always, she greets me enthusiastically, making me smile. My job would be *so* much easier if everyone on the Council shared her attitude.

The next to appear is Kyna, head of the Council, also by hologram from DC. The rest, all Royals and all now living right here in Jewel, are last to arrive. I try not let my irritation show, since I hope to get their support for at least a couple of things I intend to bring up tonight.

"Now that we are all here—" Kyna looks pointedly at Connor, who was five minutes late— "I propose we begin. Tonight's meeting should be shorter than some we've had lately, which I imagine will be a relief to all of us after recent events."

She goes on to introduce the first item on the agenda, involving the progress at NuAgra—both the agricultural research they're doing and the status of the new government center. As soon as Breann finishes with her report on that, Malcolm jumps in.

"Speaking of the new government center, when will Breann and I be assigned our permanent offices at NuAgra? I understand Connor already has one, even though he only moved here this week."

"I bespoke that office when construction first began." Connor lifts his chin arrogantly. "As the Council member who has overseen the entire immigration process so far, it seemed fitting that my office be centrally located for easy accessibility."

"Not to mention the largest," Breann mutters under her breath. She and Malcolm must have been griping to each other about that before they arrived.

The meeting quickly devolves into a bickering session among all four Royals, including Mrs. O'Gara, about their relative ranks and the privileges befitting each. I listen in disbelief as they debate trivial things like furniture, window sizes and Martian tech upgrades.

Kyna, appearing equally disgusted, waves them to silence. "I recommend the four of you settle these small matters among yourselves without wasting any more of the Sovereign's valuable time. I *had* hoped for a short meeting tonight."

The Royals lapse into disgruntled silence so I quickly voice my top concern.

"Is there any update on when Allister and Lennox will be brought to trial? I was expecting to hear something on that at least a week ago."

"No," Kyna replies, frowning at Connor. "I understand formal charges have yet to be filed, despite our near-unanimous vote on the matter."

I frown, too. "What's the holdup?"

"You must realize that these things need to follow proper procedure, Excellency." Connor's expression is condescending. "Given the distinguished lineage of both men, it is important we take even more than the usual care to make certain we do not rush to judgment, particularly considering the potential penalty."

For treason, the crime they're to be charged with, that penalty is the *tabula rasa,* or complete memory erasure—the closest thing Martians have to a death penalty.

"That is precisely what a trial is for," Kyna points out. "Must I remind you that this Council voted, six to one, in favor of bringing charges?"

Connor's was the only "nay" vote, though Mrs. O's vote was grudging. Understandable, since Allister is her brother.

"Nevertheless," Connor insists, "given the *fine*, rank and former positions of the accused, hastiness in this case would be...unseemly, to say the least."

"Unseemly?" Pissed now, I bite out the word. "Lennox and Allister weren't worried about 'unseemly haste' when they filed false charges against Rigel last year. They didn't even bother with a trial before sentencing him. And do you think they followed 'proper procedures' two weeks ago, when they tried to have me killed?"

His superior look still in place, he speaks soothingly. "I understand, of course, why you might take their actions personally, Excellency, but keep in mind that well before the event you refer to, they had already lost their once-powerful positions, and so would not expect to be held to the same standard as—"

"That is nonsense, Connor, and you know it," Kyna interrupts. "What they did violated all standards, position or *fine* notwithstanding. We mustn't convey the impression that we consider Royals above our own laws."

"None of their so-called crimes are public knowledge, so we needn't worry that—" At everyone else's shocked expressions, he breaks off, then inclines his head in acquiescence, though he doesn't look happy. "Very well. I'll see that formal charges are brought this week. After that, a trial can be scheduled as soon as a jury can be reasonably assembled."

"Thank you." Kyna makes the two words a reprimand. "I would also like to know whether the planned memory extraction has been performed on Enid, the woman who assisted them in their attempted atrocity."

Connor shifts in his chair, his sudden discomfort obvious—at least to me, with my emotion-sensing ability. "I, ah, believe that is scheduled to happen next week. However, former Governor Lennox has expressed various privacy concerns that—"

"I don't care what concerns he has," Kyna snaps. "Delay there could be dangerous, as her memories may well reveal other security threats. For example, I would very much like to discover where and how she obtained that bit of antimatter for the explosive she implanted in Kira Morain."

"I'll, ah, speak to the Mind Healers about it as soon as I can."

I don't get the impression he plans to hurry.

Apparently, neither does Kyna. "Never mind, I'll speak to them myself." Then, turning to Mr. Stuart. "Van, I understand you have intercepted communications recently that could be cause for concern. Will you share what you've learned so far with the Council?"

"Of course," he replies, pulling up a screen from his omni. "Last week, while running a routine test of the new Echtran communication network that is nearly ready to deploy, I discovered coded messages that had been cleverly piggy-backed onto our existing MARSTAR system. Since most of our people only access that system when an official bulletin goes out, I thought it worthy of some digging. What I learned alarmed me enough that I brought it to your attention, as well as the Sovereign's."

"Why not the whole Council?" Malcolm asks peevishly, frowning at me. Like the other Royals, he still has issues with my authority over the rest of them.

"Kyna assured me we would do so tonight but asked me to learn all I could in the interim," Mr. Stuart tells him. "Which I've done."

"And what have you learned?" Kyna, at least, looks appropriately concerned.

Mr. Stuart glances again at his screen. "We've known for some weeks that at least two unregistered *Echtran* communities have been established out west." He doesn't point out that the Council Royals didn't consider them worth investigating. "The messages I intercepted were primarily sent between those two communities and…Dun Cloch."

Now everyone is paying attention. "Dun Cloch?" Breann repeats. "Do you know who there received these messages?"

He shakes his head. "The recipient was extremely well-shielded. I rather suspect the woman just mentioned, Enid, arranged that, as she did something very similar for Allister and Lennox. Perhaps when her memories are extracted we will be able to learn more."

"I hope so," Kyna says. "Meanwhile, what about the messages themselves? Were you able to decipher them?"

"Only small sections so far. The encryption they're using is very sophisticated—also pointing to Enid's involvement. I'll keep working on the decryption as more messages come through. I hope to know more soon."

Kyna's brows go up. "Then these messages are still being sent?"

"Yes, though at irregular intervals. Now that I know what to look for, I'm intercepting four or five a day. One recent message consisted primarily of numbers, but whether the figures refer to people or other items is unclear. Another mentioned training of some sort."

I'm surprised the Royals on the Council still don't seem particularly worried. "Shouldn't we put more researchers on this, in case it turns out to be something dangerous? Kira told me there were former Faxon sympathizers on the *Horizon,* traveling to Dun Cloch. What if they're involved?"

"Do you have any evidence of that?" Malcolm asks Mr. Stuart, who shakes his head. "Then all we have to go on is that Ag girl's word. Even if she's telling the truth, there can't possibly be more than a handful of such people left by now. For all we know, these messages could be about establishing new schools for their children, with attendance figures and lesson plans."

That sounds pretty far-fetched to me. "Why bother encrypting it so well if that's all it is?"

He shrugs. "Maybe it's simply the method they used to send private messages back in Nuath—something *fine*-specific that Van wouldn't be familiar with. In any event, until we know more I suggest directing our energies to the new government center. Such as assigning permanent offices to Breann and myself."

"I do have one more item of business to address," I say before the Royals can start bickering again. "I'd like to know why Connor has applied to have his son Tristan certified as eligible to become Royal Consort. I thought that issue had been laid to rest by now."

"What?" Mrs. O'Gara stares at Connor in outrage. "Why was I not informed about this?"

"I'd like to ask the same question, on behalf of the entire Council," Kyna agrees.

Connor, clearly still irritated from the earlier discussion, immediately goes on the offensive. "I am completely within my rights to have my family's bloodline officially certified. I only submitted the necessary data this week, so by rights it should still be considered a private matter. I would like to know who divulged it prematurely?" He glares at Malcolm and Breann, who both shake their heads.

Nara raises a hand. "That would be me. A colleague asked me to review the application, as I have been tasked with overseeing all issues involving underage *Echtrans*. She assumed, of course, that the Council already knew about it. Such applications are public record, so I felt no hesitation in bringing it to the Sovereign's attention, as the matter closely concerns her."

"It concerns my family as well," Mrs. O exclaims. "It is, after all, *my son* you are attempting to supplant with your own, Connor. Perhaps I was mistaken to consider you a friend—or an ally."

Connor still looks stubborn. "You told us yourself that your son has renounced his claim and that you and his father have accepted that decision. What's more, he has now taken up with the Ag girl who was complicit in the plot against the Sovereign's life. According to recent polls, a growing majority of our people still believe a proper pairing is important. Therefore, it is surely our duty to do what we can to ensure a proper succession so that the ruling bloodline remains robust into the future."

He turns to me then with an attempt at a fatherly smile that reminds me unpleasantly of Allister, back when he used to "advise" me.

"Excellency, I understand that you believe yourself bonded for life to the Stuart boy, but you are both still very young, particularly given the average lifespan of our people. It seems only prudent to have other candidates in reserve should something, ah, change in the future. Of course, neither I nor my son have any intention of forcing an issue that may never arise. That is why I thought it best to keep the matter private for now."

"Nothing between Rigel and me is going to change," I assure him, "so you and Tristan have wasted whatever time and resources you've spent on this. But if it makes you feel better about yourselves to have some seal of purity next to your names, I guess that's your choice, no matter how insecure it makes you look."

From across the room I can sense how strongly Connor wants to retort. He hides his frustration well, though, summoning a tight smile and inclining his head to me.

"As I said, it is merely a precaution, Excellency." Keeping his expression and voice carefully pleasant, he turns to Kyna. "Have we any other business tonight? I'm afraid I still have some unpacking to do at home."

She directs a questioning glance my way and I shake my head. "Nothing from me."

"Very well, then, I believe I can declare this meeting adjourned. Should there be any significant developments on any of the matters discussed, you will of course receive reports. Otherwise, we'll talk again next week."

9

Buffered solution

Molly

It LOOKS like the *Echtran* Council meeting is just breaking up when Amber drops me off after the cheer squad barbecue.

Supposedly our get-together was to brainstorm ideas for Spirit Week, ways we could whip up enthusiasm for Jewel's first playoff game on Halloween. After about half an hour, though, it devolved into a gossip session that centered on Trina's campaign to snag Tristan. I had to bite my tongue more than once to keep from making snarky comments about the similarities between his personality and hers.

Rigel's dad and three Council Royals are leaving the house as I reach the front porch. Breann, Malcolm and Mr. Stuart all nod to me as they go past but Connor, who looks pissed, doesn't even spare me a glance. I'm struck again by how much he and Tristan resemble each other. Inside, M is helping Mum collect up coffee cups and saucers.

"How did it go?" I ask.

M shrugs. "Okay, I guess. Longer than Kyna expected, I think."

"Anything, um, interesting happen?"

Mum gives me a stern glance—she's a stickler about keeping Council business private. "Molly can gather up those dishes, Excellency. You'd best go home before it gets any later."

"I did promise Aunt Theresa I'd try to be back by ten-thirty. Thanks again for hosting, Mrs. O'Gara."

That gets a smile from Mum. "My pleasure, Excellency, as always. Shall I have my husband walk you home?"

"I'll do it," I volunteer. "I can take care of the dishes when I get back. C'mon, M."

Cormac, her Bodyguard, is always nearby in case of trouble but Mum still likes one of us to escort M home after dark.

"So what was up with Connor?" I ask once we're on the sidewalk. "He didn't look happy when he left."

"I'll bet he didn't. He wasn't planning to tell anybody about getting Tristan certified as Consort-eligible, so he was pretty ticked when Nara and I outed him."

That gets a snicker from me. "What did Mum say?"

M grins. "She really lit into him. I had a few choice things to say, too. That was right before we adjourned, so I'm sure he was still smarting about it when you saw him."

"Serves him right. Think they'll give up and move back to Denver now?" I ask hopefully.

"I wish. But no. Connor's taking over as Immigrant Liaison at NuAgra and heading up the new *Echtran* Ministry of Terran Obfuscation there."

We're already in front of M's house.

"You need me to come in and explain why you're late?"

She shakes her head. "Thanks, but now that Aunt Theresa knows what I'm really doing at your house on Saturday evenings, she never grills me anymore. In fact, she mostly tries to ignore the whole Martian thing whenever she can."

"Aye, well, finding out the truth about you and the rest of us shook her world pretty badly."

Up until last month, M's aunt thought M was just some orphan left on her mostly-unwilling hands. Since she used to treat her almost like a servant, I figure any change must be for the better.

"Yeah, it really did." M gives me a wry smile. "G'night, Molly. I'll see you at church tomorrow."

✢

Because my mum and M's Aunt Theresa sing in the choir, our families always get to church early. Dad and I join M and her uncle in our usual pew, the third one back, leaving space for Rigel and his family, who usually arrive a bit later. Sean sits further back with Kira, whose mother also joined the choir recently.

"Is that a new dress?" M asks as I sit down. "It's cute."

"Sort of. I made a few alterations to two of my, um, work outfits." Along with some of M's things, I also brought a few pieces from my *Chomseireach* wardrobe back from Mars. M wore two of her dresses Homecoming weekend but this is the first time I've worn one of mine in public since our return to Jewel.

"Wow, you did a really great job with it," she compliments me. "I can't sew worth beans."

Not that she needs to, as Sovereign. As her Handmaid, it's part of my job description, though on Mars I was allowed to use a Nuathan gadget that saved both time and effort. Still, I'm happy with the result of combining a blue and gray cloud-patterned skirt with a paler gray bodice that matches my eyes.

"If you'd like—" I start to say, then break off with a hiss. "I don't believe it! You'll never guess who just walked in."

M follows my gaze to see Connor and Tristan coming up the center aisle. "I guess telling Connor off last night didn't discourage him as much as I hoped it would."

Of course they walk right to our pew. "Do you mind if we sit here?" Connor asks M's uncle, who's sitting closest to the aisle. "We've just moved to Jewel and I'm afraid we don't know anyone yet."

He acts all tentative, but I'm pretty sure he's using Royal "push" on Mr. Truitt because he jumps up immediately.

"Of course!" He gestures at the length of empty bench between him and M—where Rigel and his parents normally sit. "Please, have a seat. And welcome to Jewel. I'm Louie Truitt and that's my niece over there. My wife Theresa will join us for the sermon—she sings in the choir."

The newcomers introduce themselves, Connor not letting on he's ever met any of us before. Tristan, though, greets M like an old friend, sliding down to sit next to her. "Oh, hey, good to see you again. I have a couple of classes with your niece at school," he explains to Mr. Truitt. "M, right?"

"That's what my friends call me."

She's doing a great job of not looking pissed, considering he took Rigel's spot in the pew. A better job than Dad, who's glaring at Connor and Tristan from my other side. I wonder what Mum will do when she sees them here?

When the Stuarts arrive a couple of minutes later, they're forced to sit in the pew behind us. I can tell Rigel isn't any happier about that than M is, but neither of them want to create a scene in church.

Connor asks M's uncle a few innocuous-sounding questions and Mr. Truitt eagerly talks about his job selling cars and how M's aunt teaches third grade and works part-time at the florist shop. In other words, letting him know exactly when M is likely to be home alone.

I'm about to interrupt with a question of my own but the choir files in and I'm distracted by the outraged look on Mum's face when she spots the two interlopers. She manages to pull it together when the choir starts singing, but when she and Mrs. Truitt join us in the pew for the sermon, her glare is ten times more lethal than Dad's was.

The moment the service ends, Connor introduces himself to M's aunt, turning on the charm full blast. Soon he has her practically simpering—something I'd never have expected from starched-up Mrs. Truitt. M looks as boggled as I am.

"You say you moved here to work at NuAgra?" she asks as we all stand up to leave. "Then I assume you know about—" She glances at M. "That is—"

"Yes, Tristan here happens to be in the same grade as your niece." Connor skillfully evades her real question about them being *Echtrans*. "Of course, moving to a new school more than a month into the semester is going to be challenging for him. I hope some of his class-mates might be willing to help him catch up in his courses, perhaps even tutor him a bit."

She positively beams at him. "Why, I'm sure my Marsha would be *delighted* to help. She did the same for the O'Gara children when they moved to Jewel last year and I believe they found it very helpful."

Though it's obvious what Connor is doing, I have no choice but to agree. "Um, yeah, M was great at getting us up to speed."

Connor turns to M. "That would certainly be helpful for Tristan, if you think you have time, Marsha?" He stumbles a tiny bit over her name, probably the first time he's called her anything other than "Excellency."

Trapped, with so many *Duchas* around, M forces a smile. "Uh, sure. No problem. Maybe sometime later this week?"

"Actually, I see no reason you can't start this afternoon," her aunt suggests, sending a syrupy smile Connor's way. "I would be more than willing to excuse you from your usual chores for such a good cause."

"If you're *sure* you don't mind?" Tristan manages to look convincingly unsure of himself when I know he's anything but.

"Of course not," Mrs. Truitt answers for M. "Why don't you come by around three o'clock?" She gives Connor the address.

"That's very kind of you," Connor says, still oozing charm. "Thank you both. We'll see you at three."

As they turn to leave, I catch a hint of a satisfied smirk on Tristan's face that makes my palms positively itch to smack him.

"Well. They seem *very* nice, don't they?" M's aunt says to no one in particular.

"Hm. Yes. Nice." Mum sounds like she's practically gritting her teeth.

Me, I'm already plotting how to put a crimp in Tristan's plan.

I can tell Mum is ready to explode, but she controls herself while we say goodbye to the Stuarts and start walking home with the Truitts, as we often do.

"Suppose I come by, too," I suggest to M and her aunt after a moment. "I'm Tristan's Chemistry partner and we also have Psych class together."

Mrs. Truitt looks uncertain but M immediately jumps on board. "That's a great idea, Molly. Besides, you're better at both Chemistry and Pre-Cal than I am. I'd hate to tell him anything that's not exactly right when he'll have so much to learn in a hurry."

"That's a lovely idea, Molly," Mum agrees, a conspiratorial gleam in her eye. She knows exactly why I'm doing this.

Mrs. Truitt's brow clears and she smiles at me. "Thank you, Molly. I'm sure Tristan will appreciate your help as well."

I seriously doubt that, but it will keep him from being alone with M, which is my only goal.

.∴.

I show up at M's ten minutes before three, in case Tristan decides to come early. Sure enough, I've just rung the bell when a car comes around the corner—a really nice car. M opens the door just before it pulls up to the curb.

"Hey, Molly, thanks," she says as I go in. "That was quick thinking earlier." Then she looks past me. "Ugh. I thought maybe we'd have a few minutes to talk before he got here."

We both wait in the front hall until Tristan rings the bell. He's smiling when M opens the door again, which must mean he didn't see me come in. Sure enough, his smile dims noticeably the second he spots me.

"Hi, M. It's okay if I call you M, right?"

Nodding, she steps back to let him come inside. "Everyone at school does, or nearly everyone. Let's go into the dining room. We can spread out there, and my aunt just made us a fresh batch of cookies."

He glances at me, then away. "So she's staying?"

"Yep." I give him a big smile that I doubt he notices. "M thought I might be more help for the Chemistry stuff and I brought my Psych book, too, since M's not in that class."

"Oh. That's great," he says, his tone implying the exact opposite.

We all go through the archway into the Truitts' dining room. As promised, a big plate of cookies sits in the middle of the table, along with three glasses of milk.

"M's aunt makes really good cookies," I tell Tristan, mostly because I know it will irritate him. "You should try one." I push the cookie plate and a glass of milk toward a chair on the far side of the table and he reluctantly moves that way.

As soon as he commits, M moves to the opposite chair and I sit between them, at the head of the table. Doing my best not to smirk, I reach for a cookie myself.

"What subject should we start with?" I ask brightly. "Pre-Cal, since it's first period?"

Tristan shoots me another quick, irritated glance, then looks across at M. "The class I need the most help in is English Lit." The only class he and M have together that I'm not in. "What books are we supposed to have read by now?"

M raises an eyebrow. "Didn't Ms. Raymond give you the syllabus? The list is online, too. Being *Echtran*, I'm sure you can catch up on the reading fairly quickly. I like Molly's idea of starting with Pre-Cal, especially since she's so good at math."

"Sure. Okay. Fine." Resignedly, he pulls his calculus book out of his backpack.

Over the next two hours, he tries repeatedly to engage M in more personal conversation, and each time either she or I bring the topic back to schoolwork. It's soon obvious he doesn't really need help in any of his subjects, not that I'm surprised. He's probably already learned twice as much as anything taught at Jewel High, just like Sean and I had before coming here.

M's aunt bustles in a few times to make sure we're well supplied with milk and cookies, and to beam upon Tristan, who's apparently charmed her almost as thoroughly as his father did. At five o'clock, M stands up. "What do you say we call it a day? We've at least touched on all your classes now. If you have any more questions, you can ask at school."

"Okay." Tristan stands, too. "Molly, you probably need to get home, right?"

"Soon," I reply off-handedly. No way I'm leaving before he does.

My expression must make that clear, because he gives a tiny snort of disgust before turning back to M.

"I know you must be busy, so I really appreciate you making the time to help me today," he tells her. "Thanks." He holds out a hand like he expects her to shake it—something normal enough between *Duchas*, or even *Echtrans* of equal rank, but presumptuous with the Sovereign. M has never been one to stand on ceremony, though, so after only a slight hesitation, she gives his extended hand one quick shake.

"No problem. It was a good review for us, too, right, Molly?"

"Right." I notice Tristan frowning slightly at M's hand, the one he just shook. Because of what he felt? Or *didn't* feel?

As he opens the front door, Mrs. Truitt emerges from the kitchen again. "Oh, are you leaving, Tristan? You're welcome to stay for dinner, if you'd like. And you, too, Molly."

I almost laugh at the way he perks up for a second, then deflates when she invites me, too.

"Thanks, Mrs. Truitt, but I'd better not," he says. "My parents are expecting me back." Then to M—*just* M— "Do you think maybe you could come over to my house tomorrow night, so we can finish going over the subjects we didn't have time for today?"

M frowns, since we totally got through everything we needed to and Tristan knows it. "I don't—" she begins, but her aunt cuts her off.

"I'm sure she'll be delighted. If you give me the address, I can drop her by after dinner. Say, seven-thirty?"

"Perfect." He gives Mrs. Truitt a smile that actually makes her cheeks go pink. "Guess I'll see you at school tomorrow, M. Thanks again for all your help today."

Fuming, I wait until he's driven away to say, "I really can't stay for dinner either. I told Mum I'd help with the potatoes."

M and I exchange a glance and she turns to her aunt. "I'm going to walk Molly home, if that's okay? I'll be back in a few minutes to help with dinner."

"I've warned Aunt Theresa not to accept invitations on my behalf," she grumbles when we reach the sidewalk. "I guess I need to remind her again."

"Probably a good idea," I agree, though I'm not sure it will do any good if Connor and Tristan keep using Royal "push" on Mrs. Truitt. "Meanwhile, I can tag along tomorrow night too."

"No, you can't. You have a date with Alan, remember? Anyway, I'll be fine."

I'm less complacent. "I don't trust the way he keeps trying get you alone, unchaperoned. And what was the deal with that handshake? He had no right—"

"Sean did the same thing your first day of school, remember? Oh, no, I guess you weren't there at the time. Anyway, he did. And he watched me the *exact* same way."

I do remember Sean telling me later that day about the jolt he felt from M and how he was sure she felt it, too. At the time, we both considered it proof they were destined for each other, just like tradition dictated, since the stronger the *taghal ardus* tingle on first touch, the better suited two people are for each other, genetically. Or so conventional wisdom has always claimed.

"And?"

M chuckles. "This was nothing like that. Sean's touch freaked me out a little because only Rigel had ever given me a stronger jolt. But Tristan's was just like what I get from any other *Echtran*. Like you." She touches my hand to demonstrate.

I barely even notice that sort of resonance, since I've felt it all my life. It wasn't until I started meeting *Duchas* here in Jewel that I realized it's a specifically Martian thing.

"No wonder he looked so disappointed." I chuckle, too. "Wouldn't it be hilarious if his best match turned out to be from Mining, like Jana? Or better, a *Duchas*, like Trina?"

We both go into a fit of giggles at the idea.

"Except I'm pretty sure Trina has already touched him at least a dozen times," M reminds me, still grinning. "Still, wouldn't that be perfect?"

"*So* perfect! Okay, I'd better get in and help Mum," I say as we near my house. "Thanks for indulging my curiosity."

"And thank you again for playing chaperone today. I know Tristan's the last person you wanted to spend your afternoon with."

I shrug. "True, but it's not often I get to play *Chomseireach* in Jewel, so I'm glad I could at least do that much. See you tomorrow."

10

Failed reaction

Tristan

I'M STILL CONFUSED as I drive away from the Sovereign's house. Because I don't get it.

Before I came here today, my father insisted if I could just touch the Sovereign—without being rude—our *taghal ardus* would be so intense she'd *have* to take me seriously. That it might even be strong enough to break whatever bond she has with Stuart, or at least weaken it a lot.

But just now she acted like she didn't feel a thing. Which she probably didn't, because that touch didn't seem like anything special to me, either. I seriously don't get it.

Touch-resonance is supposed to be strongest between people from the same *fine*—it's why cross-fine pairings are so rare. Back in Colorado, I knew a couple of Royal girls, before their families went back to Nuath this last launch window. I definitely got a bigger *taghal ardus* zap when I first met them than I ever did with girls from other *fines*.

Our family is from a really high-ranking Royal line, especially on Mother's side. And the Sovereign is, well, the Sovereign. *This* first touch should have been my strongest ever, according to Father, but it didn't even feel like a *taghal ardus* at all. Which makes zero sense.

"Well?" Father asks the moment I walk into the house.

Setting down my backpack on the ornate side table in the foyer, I join him and Mother in our spacious living room. This house is bigger than the one we had in Denver. Because housing prices are lower in Indiana, Father says. I was amazed to see how tiny the Sovereign's house is until I remembered it belongs to her *Duchas* guardians, not to her.

"Well?" he repeats more sharply, when I don't answer right away. "Did you make any progress with the Sovereign?"

"Not much," I finally admit. "Molly O'Gara was there, too. She's made it pretty clear she considers it her duty as the Sovereign's Handmaid to keep me from being alone with her."

He snorts. "The Council never should have approved that girl's appointment to such a post just because she was raised by Royals. I said as much at the time. Given that she's a mere Ag, I assumed you'd have no trouble outsmarting her. It appears I was wrong."

His tone is so biting my mother winces, though she doesn't say anything. She almost never does.

"I did invite the Sovereign—just the Sovereign—to come here tomorrow night." That should partly appease him. "Her aunt accepted on her behalf and even offered to drop her off, so they probably won't bring Molly along. It was the only thing I could think of without being outright rude to Molly in front of the Sovereign. Since they actually seem to be friends, I didn't think that would be smart."

My father looks pained. "Yet another example of how far the dignity of our leadership has fallen. Our Sovereign, reduced to being friends with an Ag. It's embarrassing."

Mother leans forward with an encouraging smile. "Even with her Handmaid present, spending two hours with the Sovereign must have been of some benefit? She clearly needs more *Echtran* friends, and friendship is generally the first step toward—"

Father flicks a dismissive glance her way and she subsides. "I take it you were unable to find any pretext to touch her over the course of two entire hours spent in her home?"

"Not until I was leaving."

Clearly startled, Father looks at me more approvingly than before. "Then you did make physical contact? Excellent. Why didn't you tell me that at once?"

"Because…it wasn't that big a deal," I admit. "Sorry." I don't know why I'm apologizing for something that wasn't my fault. Habit, I guess.

"Not a big deal?" He looks confused. "Your first touch should have been a very big deal. Do you mean to say you felt no particular resonance with her? Did she?"

I lift a shoulder but stop short of shrugging. "If she did, she didn't let on. And I doubt she did, because I hardly felt anything myself. No more than I'd get from touching someone I've already touched before. It was nothing at all like you told me to expect." I can't keep a trace of accusation out of my voice.

Predictably, that ticks him off. "You must have done something wrong, then. Perhaps you only touched her sleeve, or—"

"Nope. We shook hands as I was leaving, skin to skin. Unless she's got invisible gloves or something, it was a real touch."

Father and Mother exchange puzzled looks, then Father frowns at me again, still angry. "That should not be possible. You're both Royals, and extremely high-ranking Royals at that."

"Look, I can't explain it either. Unless everybody was somehow wrong about her really being Sovereign Leontine's granddaughter?"

He shakes his head. "No. I saw the results of the *foare rioga* myself. Allister himself was present and affirmed to the rest of us that the test was done correctly. That can't be it."

"Perhaps…" Mother says tentatively. We both look at her. "Perhaps it has something to do with that bond she supposedly shares with the Stuart boy? Could it somehow suppress her ability to resonate with anyone else?"

I expect Dad to snap at her, but instead he just lets out a frustrated-sounding breath. "Maybe that's it. I hope so, since the only other explanation would call our son's bloodline into question."

Her eyes widen. "But…you know full well he is my son and one need only see the two of you together to know he is yours. And you have that certification, haven't you?"

"Sorry." He doesn't sound it, though. Sometimes the way he talks to my mother makes me want to punch him. "I haven't received the official documentation yet but yes, his ancestry has been confirmed. It must be…the other thing."

Which makes me realize something that should have occurred to all of us sooner. "Wait a sec. Maybe this isn't so surprising after all. Sean O'Gara touched her all the time in Nuath, remember? We saw it on the feeds. That must not have broken her bond with Stuart, since they got back together the moment his memory returned."

"True," he says grudgingly. "Though she admitted herself that young

O'Gara's touch had a strengthening effect on her when she and Stuart were separated. I assumed yours would also, should another such separation take place."

This is news to me. "What do you mean, 'strengthening effect'? Did she get weak or something when Stuart came back to Earth without her?"

Father looks like he regrets saying so much but after a moment's hesitation he nods. "Yes. I'm told the same thing occurred during a previous separation last year. Though it's likely the Sovereign has exaggerated the effect, it does appear that when she and Stuart are apart for any appreciable length of time, their health is negatively impacted."

"You mean…they actually get sick? Like the *tinneas* from the *graell* stories?" I definitely never heard about *that*—though it makes sense they'd keep it out of the news.

"So our Healers claim." Father seems irked to admit it. "An antidote of sorts was developed last year at the Council's request, then another, more effective one was created in Nuath before Stuart was sent back to Earth. That serum allowed the Sovereign to carry out her necessary work there without him. Even so, she insisted on reuniting with Stuart upon returning here, despite being strongly cautioned against it."

I suddenly remember something Molly O'Gara said in Chemistry Friday. "Wouldn't it have been bad if they hadn't, though? According to that second MARSTAR bulletin last month, the Sovereign and Rigel Stuart somehow used their bond to repel those Grentl aliens when they showed up here."

"Fine. Yes." He glares at me for bringing up the bulletin he'd refused to discuss at the time. "Rigel Stuart did play an important role in that incident. The Council felt compelled to express its gratitude for his contribution. But the Grentl are gone now and unlikely to return within any of our lifetimes. Useful as Stuart was in that particular crisis, it's now time for him to step aside so that the Sovereign can find a more appropriate Consort."

Which is where I'm supposed to come in. But now, hearing all this stuff about their bond, I'm beginning to worry Molly was right that trying to break them up is hopeless.

"Why didn't you tell me any of this before?" I'm pretty ticked myself now. "If their bond is really that strong, what's the point in my continuing to—"

"Of course you must continue," he snaps. "Bond or not, teen

romances on Earth are notoriously short-lived. Theirs will be no differ-ent. She must have alternatives when the inevitable falling-out occurs. Do whatever you can to gain her confidence, to become someone she trusts. Someone she cares about, even if not—yet—in a romantic sense. Her only Royal friends thus far are the O'Garas, whom she has now largely alienated. That puts you in an excellent position to fill the void. See that you do so."

Muttering something about taking on more than his share of Council responsibilities, he heads to his office. I'm frowning after him when Mother gives a little sigh that makes me look at her. Despite a suspicious glint of tears in her eyes—thanks to Father—she smiles at me.

"Please don't let your father's unreasonable demands spoil things for you here in Jewel, Tristan. Keep in mind that the Sovereign is only sixteen. She won't be ready for a true pairing for some years yet."

I nod. "It's not like we can go to Nuath before the next launch window anyway." Another reason I hoped to become Consort—I've always wanted to go there and I know Mother's been longing to return. "That gives me almost two whole years to work with."

"I have full confidence in you, Tristan," she assures me. "Should you be unable to separate the Sovereign from Rigel Stuart, I have no doubt you will find another way to benefit our people long term."

"I will," I promise. "Though I could do the most good as Consort."

It's not like I don't *want* to pair up with the Sovereign. She's pretty. And powerful. And…nice. I also believe as strongly as Father does that I'd be a way better Consort than Stuart, though it's demoralizing to keep trying when my usual tactics seem to have no effect on the Sovereign. Most girls…

But the Sovereign isn't "most girls." Something I—and Father—should have realized from the start.

⁺₊

Now that I have a better idea of what I'm up against, I play it cool when I see the Sovereign in Pre-Cal the next morning. I just smile and thank her again for helping me yesterday without laying on the charm. I'm even prepared to let her out of the follow-up session tonight if she mentions other plans, but she doesn't. Not yet, anyway.

I also start paying attention to everything she says to Stuart or her friends and what her friends say to each other, since my revised strategy involves getting to know them all better. Yeah, even Molly O'Gara, irritating as she is. So when Pre-Cal ends, instead of trying to catch up with the Sovereign, I hang back and leave with Molly.

"I noticed at the game Friday you're one of the Jewel cheerleaders," I comment as we both head to French class. "Is it fun?"

The look she slants up at me holds more than a trace of suspicion. "Most of the time. It's good exercise and it helped me make friends when I got here last year. I especially like cheering for Sean during basketball season."

"Cheerleading must involve a lot of after-school practice, huh?" Maybe if I keep her talking, I'll find some chink in her armor so she'll tell me something about the Sovereign I can use. "Does it ever get in the way of your other, er, duties?" I remember to keep my voice low so no passing *Duchas* will hear.

She quirks an eyebrow at me and I notice irrelevantly that she's as pretty as the Sovereign is. Not that it matters. She's still just an Ag.

"Trying to find out when you can spend time with M without me around to play chaperone?" Molly is also careful not to be overheard. "My duty to her comes before *everything* else. Always."

"No, I didn't mean that," I hastily assure her, realizing too late that my question probably did sound that way. "I'm just trying to get to know you better—get to know all the other *Echtran* students better. You were right that I was kind of a jerk to everybody but M last week. I'd like to make up for that."

"Finally sank in, did it?" She chuckles. I ignore what a pleasant sound it is.

In answer, I just shrug. "It's possible I came here with certain... preconceptions I'm having to adjust."

Another chuckle. "So, he *can* be taught. I wasn't sure it was possible."

I have to bite back a retort. Being the Sovereign's friend and *Chomseireach* doesn't give this Ag any right to talk to *me* that way. Luckily we reach the classroom then, because I'm itching to explain that to her.

Maybe trying to actually make *friends* with Molly is a bad idea. For one thing, I doubt my acting skills are up to that big a challenge. Still, I need to avoid alienating her if I want to get closer to the Sovereign.

After French, the two of them head to Chemistry together. Hoping to figure out what the Sovereign can possibly see in her presumptuous friend, I follow the girls just far enough back to hear most of what they say to each other.

"When are you and Alan getting together tonight?" the Sovereign is asking Molly.

"He said after dinner, but I can make up some excuse to cancel if you want me to come with you tonight instead."

I'm relieved when the Sovereign shakes her head. "Don't you dare! I think it's great Alan wants to spend time with you again."

"Are you sure? I don't like the idea of you going alone." Ugh. Molly definitely takes her so-called duty *way* too seriously.

"I'm positive. Don't forget I have Taekwondo training. If Tristan tries anything, I'm pretty sure I can take him."

They both laugh and I suddenly wish I'd stayed out of earshot.

Because my ego is still feeling a little bruised when I get to Chemistry, I spend the time before the bell chatting with some *Duchas* girls who are falling all over themselves trying to impress me. *This* is the way I'm used to having girls act around me—even *Echtran* ones.

"If you need any help catching up on the stuff we already studied, I have afternoons free," a tall redheaded girl tells me. "We could meet in the media center. I can even bring snacks."

I can't resist projecting just the tiniest bit of charm when I smile at her, like I did with that woman at NuAgra last week. The redhead gives a tiny gasp, her eyes going wide, and she apparently loses her train of thought.

Reassured, I turn off the charm. "Thanks, but—"

"But he can learn *way* more from me." Trina, the head cheerleader, interrupts. "I'm a *great* note-taker. Everyone says so. I have cheerleading practice after school, of course, but you could come watch me practice, then we can go to my house afterward to study. We have way better stuff to eat—and drink—than anything Caitlin can bring to the media center. What do you say?"

She gives me a syrupy smile that probably works well on *Duchas* guys.

The other girls look disappointed but don't argue, reinforcing what I'd already figured out—Trina is more or less the alpha girl at Jewel High. It's also pretty obvious she's not friends with the Sovereign—at all —but she could still be worth cultivating for what she can tell me about her.

I smile back, adding an extra dose of the charm. "That might be fun...one of these days. Thanks."

Her eyes go gratifyingly wide, too. "Really?" She swallows. "I mean, that would be super! Today? Or, um, whichever day you want, really. I mean—"

The bell rings, cutting off her babbling, but she keeps smiling at me over her shoulder as she heads to her table, her eyes still wide and dreamy. She even bumps into a stool along the way but doesn't seem to notice. The other girls stare after her curiously, making me wonder if it's the first time they've ever seen Trina tongue-tied.

Chuckling to myself, I turn toward my own lab table and see Molly watching me with a way-too-knowing look.

"If that were anyone but Trina, I'd think what you just did to her was kind of mean," she whispers as I sit down. "Unless you really do plan to get together with her after school?"

I shrug, trying not to let her sour my mood again. "I didn't promise anything. What's the big deal?"

"No big deal at all. In fact, you and Trina would be perfect together. You should totally go for it."

Right. Like I could ever be remotely interested in a *Duchas*. "Thanks for the sage advice." Now that I'm warmed up, I give Molly another one of my smiles, this time throwing all I have into it.

Her eyes don't widen at all. In fact, they narrow slightly, mockingly, like she's fully aware of what I'm trying to do. No blush, no nothing. I don't get it. Back in Denver, every single girl I used that on responded, *Echtran* as well as *Duchas*. Even the two Royal girls. Does Molly's close association with the Sovereign somehow make her immune, too?

I give it up. "Anything else you'd like to tell me?"

"Lots, but nothing you'd want to hear," she replies with something resembling a smirk.

Again, it takes a monumental effort to refrain from putting her in her place. I content myself with a quick glare before turning away to open my Chemistry book.

————————————————

11

Rare-earth metal

————————————————

Molly

Oʜ, yeah, there's *plenty* I'd like to tell Tristan but this isn't the best time or place. Not with the teacher about to start class.

It's probably just as well there's no real opportunity for conversation before the period ends. But as soon as the bell rings, Tristan turns to me.

"So what is it you think I don't want to hear? The same tired thing as before, how you want me to leave M alone?"

Instead of answering, I ask a question of my own. "Why, exactly, are you so determined to attempt the impossible? Did your dad put you up to it?"

The grimace Tristan tries to hide confirms M's theory. "It's possible he's the one who first suggested it, but I have my own reasons, too."

We both shove our books back into our backpacks and push away from the table.

"What reasons, if you don't mind sharing?" Knowing his motives might help me do my job. Not that I expect him to answer.

"Sure, why not?" he surprises me by saying. "Maybe then you'll stop trying to block me at every turn."

"I doubt it, but…go on."

As we leave the room together, he slants a wary glance down at me out of those too-perfect brown eyes. "My number one reason is safe-guarding our people's future. Until Faxon, our society was peaceful and prosperous for over a dozen centuries. That was mainly due to our Sovereigns and the qualities inherent in that bloodline."

"Things are different these days," I point out—even though I clearly remember telling M the same thing last year, when she was shocked to learn such an advanced society still had a monarchy.

"Are they? Our people are vulnerable right now and you know it. The last thing we should do is abandon traditions that have worked for so long when we need to rebuild confidence and get everyone's coop-eration."

That was exactly my Dad's argument when he insisted M play to the cameras in Nuath by pretending she and Sean were a happy couple. He said it would reassure the people to think she planned to make a "proper" pairing.

"I also don't want to let my family down," Tristan continues when I don't reply. "You were raised by Royals. You must know how most of them feel about pairing—or even dating—outside our own *fine*."

"I don't agree with it, but I'm aware of that particular prejudice, yeah," I'm forced to admit. Mum's continued resistance to Sean and Kira as a couple is a prime example. So is all the pushback M and Rigel keep getting from the Council—and everyone else—about being together.

"Well, I do happen to agree with it, which makes M my only viable choice. According to my father, she's the only Royal girl anywhere near my age on Earth at the moment."

I huff out an exasperated breath. "That's exactly why that prejudice is so stupid. I said the same to my mum when she was so set against Sean going out with Kira—that she'd be dooming him to staying single permanently if he was only allowed to date another Royal. Because M is no longer available. Not to him and not to you. Maybe you *should* take a closer look at some of the *Duchas* girls, like Trina. You have *them* eating out of your hand already."

He scowls at me. "Look, I tried to explain my position, but if you're just going to—"

"No, I understand perfectly. But it makes no difference, because M is bonded with Rigel. Deal with it. If you really can't consider anyone but a Royal girl, you'd best figure a way to get to Nuath. I'm sure there are at least a few there."

"Yeah, at least two lived in Denver before they went back to Mars last summer. But news flash, there won't be another launch window for almost two years. Even then, they'll only let people go *that* direction for a really good reason. A teenage guy looking to hook up with a Royal girl isn't likely to qualify."

That makes me laugh—but Tristan doesn't. He's serious. Apart from his supposedly "patriotic" goal, he really believes M is the only possible girl on Earth for him. Well, that's his problem. My job is to make sure it doesn't become M's.

WHEN I GET to the lunchroom an hour later, M and Rigel are just leaving, carrying drinks and wrapped sandwiches.

"Eating in the courtyard again?" I ask.

M nods. "We didn't get much alone time over the weekend, between the Council meeting and that 'study session.'" She makes air quotes.

"Cool. Have fun." I head to the lunch line, half-wishing I had someone to share a cozy lunch with.

On that thought, I glance over at the table where Alan is sitting. Since I'm not needed to keep Tristan away from M over lunch today, once I get through the line I carry my tray to what I think of as the "NuAgra table."

Nearly all the new *Echtran* students still eat lunch together, even though M and I have both encouraged them to branch out more. The only ones who have so far are Kira, who now sits with Sean at lunch, and Liam, who occasionally sits with the football or basketball players because he's so sports-obsessed.

"Hi, mind if I sit with you guys?"

Alan looks surprised—and pleased. "Sure!" He nods at the empty chair next to him. "Join us."

Smiling around at him and the others, I sit down. "Thanks. I realized I haven't had a chance to talk, um, privately with most of you for a while. How are you liking Jewel now you've been here almost a month?"

Everyone responds positively except the brown-haired freshman, Jana, who just shrugs. While they all take turns expanding on their experiences so far, my attention is caught by Tristan several yards away. He's standing indecisively near our usual table, tray in hand, obviously wondering where M is. As I watch, Trina accosts him. With my Martian hearing, I can pick up her words from here.

"Hey, Tristan, why don't you come sit with the cheerleaders today? You're way too cool for THAT table, anyway. It's mostly losers who sit there."

He turns half away to scan the rest of the cafeteria. "Where—? Um, okay, sure." With a shrug, he lets her lead him to the cheerleader table, where he's enthusiastically greeted by the other girls and less enthusiastically by the jocks who sit with them.

Hiding a smirk, I pull my attention back to the people around me, getting back into the flow of the conversation. I ask them a few questions about the condensed orientation courses they took when they first arrived from Mars. Considering how brief it was, their instruction was impressively thorough. It even included perfecting their accents to correspond with wherever they supposedly lived before.

"Wow, we had nearly two years to work on our Irish accents in Baile-realta before moving here," I tell them. "Now it's second nature—not that it's *that* different from a regular Nuathan accent, according to M. You all sound exactly like you were born right here in the U.S." They seem to appreciate the compliment.

As the lunch period ends, I turn to Alan. "I was wondering, would you mind terribly if we postponed to tomorrow night? There's something I was supposed to do tonight that I totally forgot about."

"Oh, um, sure. Actually, tomorrow might be better anyway. I found out Tuesday is Trivia Night at the Lighthouse Cafe, which sounds fun. I don't think they have anything special going on Mondays."

"Perfect." I give him my best smile.

Now that I have more insight about why Tristan is so determined to move in on M, there's no way I'm letting her go to his house unchaperoned tonight.

⁺⁺

MUM GREETS me with a big smile when I get home from cheerleading practice that afternoon.

"How was school? Are you excited about your date tonight with Alan Dempsey? Have you decided what to wear?"

It's the most overt interest she's shown in me for a while. "Um, actually, we pushed it back till tomorrow night. Tonight I need to play Handmaid and go with M to Tristan's."

"Why ever would she go to that boy's house?" she demands, her happy excitement giving way to a scowl. "Connor's doing, I presume."

"Tristan's, too. When he was leaving M's house yesterday he asked—in front of her aunt—if she could come over to help him some more tonight and of course Mrs. Truitt agreed. I'm almost sure he used that Royal 'push' thing on her, just like Connor did at church."

Mum makes a "tch" noise. "Those two think just because Sean has some passing fancy for that Ag girl, they can—" She breaks off at my wince. "I'm sorry, Molly, no slight meant to *you*, of course. I keep forgetting that you and Kira are from the same *fine*."

If that were true she wouldn't be so excited about me going out with Alan, but I don't correct her.

"Yeah, Tristan's made it quite clear he wants to stake a claim to M, so I figured I'd better go along tonight to keep him from stepping over the line."

"Aye, your duty to the Sovereign must come first. Is that what you told Alan?"

"Er, not exactly, but he seemed happy to switch our date to tomorrow anyway so we can go to Trivia Night at the Lighthouse."

That gets Mum smiling again. "Well, won't that be lovely? I've no doubt the more time you spend with him, the more you'll discover you have in common. Already he's helped you do a better job with your poor plants."

"Um, right." That was all Alan, not me, but if it makes her happy to believe otherwise, I won't burst her bubble. "Guess I'd better go shower and change so I can help you with dinner. I should be at M's around seven—her aunt will be driving us."

Both M and her aunt are surprised when I arrive at their house a couple of hours later. I didn't text M about my change in plans, afraid she'd try to talk me out of tagging along.

"Hey," I greet them when they answer the door. "Tristan asked me during Psych class if I could come over tonight, too, to help him some more in that subject. Do you mind if I ride along?"

Though M looks skeptical, Mrs. Truitt smiles. "Of course we don't mind, Molly. That's very nice of you. We'll be leaving in just a few minutes, as the address he gave me is a few miles away."

"I still need to change my shoes and get my backpack," M says. "Come on up, Molly."

As soon as we're in her room, she turns to me with a frown. "What's going on? I don't believe for a moment Tristan *asked* you to come along tonight. Don't you believe I can fend him off without your help?"

"I'm sure you can, but Mum pointed out it's still my job to be there in case he tries to get you alone—and she's right."

The corners of M's mouth twitch. "Yeah, at the Council meeting she was seriously pissed about Connor getting Tristan certified as Consort-eligible. Maybe even more than I was. I think she sees it as a direct affront to Sean."

"That's exactly how she sees it," I assure her. "Apparently she still hopes you and Sean will eventually end up together—that Kira and Rigel will just, I don't know, vanish or something. Anyway, I know better than to argue when she gets in that kind of mood."

No reason M needs to know coming along was my idea, not Mum's. Especially since Mum fully agreed once I told her what was going on.

"Your mother can be pretty stubborn. Guess you and Sean both get that from her, huh?" The twinkle in her eyes tells me I didn't fool her at all.

"Not directly, in my case," I remind her. "But maybe from growing up around her."

Though her words didn't upset me, M still winces. "Sorry, I didn't mean—"

"No, I know. It's fine. People forget all the time I wasn't actually born into the O'Gara family. Fairly flattering, when you think about it. Do you have everything you need in your backpack?" I pick it up off the chair by her desk.

More than her words, her wince reminded me yet again of how I don't quite fit in anywhere—not a real Royal and not much of an Ag, either. Now's not the time to dwell on it, though. Tonight I have a job to do. I even decided to wear another outfit adapted from my Nuathan *Chomseireach* wardrobe, so I'll be less likely to forget my mission.

That turns out to be a good thing, once we arrive at Tristan's house.

No surprise, Connor bought a place in one of the newer, swankier neighborhoods on the outskirts of Jewel—an exclusive community of mini-mansions with wide, manicured lawns and gardens. When the door opens, it's obvious neither Tristan nor Connor is happy to see me, though they try to hide it in front of Mrs. Truitt.

"I've told Marsha to give me a call when she's ready to come home," she tells Connor with a simpering smile that must weird M out.

"No need," he assures M's aunt warmly. "I'm happy to drive her back. And her…friend as well. Tristan should have offered to have us pick her up in the first place, as she is the one doing him a favor."

Mrs. Truitt's cheeks go even pinker than when Tristan charmed her yesterday. "Oh! Well. If you're sure you don't mind?"

"Not in the least. I'll have her home by nine-thirty. Thank you again, Mrs. Truitt."

"Theresa, please."

His smile broadens. "Theresa, then. Good night."

Blinking dazedly, she bobs her head a couple of times and makes her way back to the car. I hope she isn't so dazzled she'll have trouble driving home.

Shutting the front door, Connor directs his charming smile M's way. "Excellency, I can't tell you how much both Tristan and I appreciate your willingness to take time out of your busy schedule for his benefit. He's very much hoping to befriend some of his fellow *Echtrans* at Jewel High in addition to catching up with the schoolwork. Having our Sovereign as his first, best friend there will ease his transition considerably. Thank you."

M looks like she wants to say something snarky but just raises an eyebrow and nods.

Connor regards her complacently for a moment, then finally turns to me, his smile vanishing as though it never existed. "Tristan didn't mention inviting *you* this evening, Miss O'Gara."

"That's because I didn't." Tristan looks down his nose at me with the exact same expression his father is wearing. "I'm guessing you lied to Mrs. Truitt to convince her to bring you along?"

"That was extremely presumptuous of you, I must say," Connor agrees, his eyes cold.

They obviously expect me to quail in the face of their combined disapproval—and for a second I almost do. But then I glance down at my blue-patterned tunic top and darker blue leggings and recall my Handmaid training from last spring, before we went to Nuath. I also remember the last time I wore this outfit, while accompanying M to a reception near the Palace. When a guy there tried to get a little too familiar, I didn't hesitate to put him in his place.

Drawing my shoulders back, I tilt my chin up to regard them both straight on.

"With all due respect, sir, it was rather presumptuous of Tristan to invite the Sovereign here without her *Chomseireach*," I inform Connor. "As a member of the *Echtran* Council, you are surely aware that doing so was a violation of established protocol. You must also realize that I would have been guilty of a breach of my duty if I had allowed her to come here alone."

Connor glares at me for a long moment but can't very well dispute my words since I'm absolutely right. Rather than acknowledge that, he just gives a terse nod and turns away.

"Very well, then. I suggest the *three* of you get your study session underway before it grows any later. It is a school night, after all."

12

Potential energy

Tristan

I SHOW the two girls into the library on the first floor. Father suggested this room so the Sovereign and I could have some privacy—not that we'll get it now.

"That was pretty rude of you and your dad just now," she remarks, setting down her backpack next to the square table in the middle of the library. "Why would you assume Molly lied to my aunt? Didn't it occur to you I might have invited her along myself?"

Under the Sovereign's stern, green stare, I drop my eyes. "Sorry. I was just...surprised, that's all."

But not nearly as surprised as I was by what Molly just did. Irritated as I am by her interference, I can't help feeling a grudging respect for the way she stood up to my father's hectoring. Better than I usually do.

"It's...fine that she's here. You and I can still talk, right?" I keep my focus exclusively on the Sovereign.

"I thought you wanted to go over more schoolwork." M arches a brow at me. "That's what you told my aunt yesterday."

In other words, *I'm* the liar.

"Well, sure, but I was hoping we could talk about...other stuff, too." I take the chair to her left—the same place her Consort would sit at a formal dinner. Out of the corner of my eye, I see Molly sitting down on my other side, across from the Sovereign.

"What kind of stuff?"

"For one thing, I've been wondering how you felt when you first learned you were the heir to the Martian throne?"

That elicits a grudging smile. "Nearly as freaked out as when I found out there were actual Martians…and that I was one. Rigel and his parents tried to break it to me gently, but it was an awful lot to take in."

"Yeah, I guess it would be. I grew up knowing about Nuath and *Echtrans* so I always just took it for granted. For us, the big shock was finding out you were alive." I give her my intense look again, trying to find a way in.

Instead of reacting she just looks at Molly, who says, "You should have been in Bailerealta when the news broke. There was a week-long holiday."

I also look Molly's way, despite my intention not to. "The *Echtran* community in Denver was a lot smaller then, but we had a big party to celebrate, too."

Her gray eyes crinkle with humor. "You wouldn't believe how hard it was to convince M what a huge deal that was. When we first got to Jewel, she wasn't even a little used to thinking of herself as important. Her aunt treating her practically like a servant all the time didn't help." She frowns across at M. "Even now she knows the truth, I still don't think she treats you with the respect you deserve."

M shrugs. "Old habits are hard to break—for both of us. She's lightened up a lot."

I don't blame Molly for being indignant. The thought of our Sovereign being ordered around by a *Duchas* is pretty offensive.

"How did—?" I start to say when I'm interrupted by a soft throat-clearing from the doorway. My mother.

"Am I interrupting?" she asks when we look her way.

"Not at all." M stands up, smiling. "You're Tristan's mother?"

She nods, then surprises me by giving the traditional salute, bowing with her right fist over her heart. It's the first time I've seen it in real life and not just vids.

"Teara Roark. I'm so happy to have this chance to meet you." Mother's cheeks are slightly flushed and her eyes brighter than usual. "I doubt Connor has mentioned it, but I was quite close to your mother years ago, back in Nuath. We kept in touch after Connor and I moved to

Earth and Galena visited me in Denver when she and your father first arrived here. Before they—" She presses her lips together, like she's holding back tears.

"No, I didn't know that." M sounds a little choked up, too. "I'm glad you told me. I'd very much like it if you could tell me about her sometime. Almost everything I know about my parents is only from reading about them. I haven't met many people who knew them personally."

I realize that's got to be hard for her. Then I notice Molly watching her sympathetically, too, and it occurs to me *she* probably never knew her real parents, either. There wouldn't even be much of anything to read about them, since they were just Ag villagers.

"Of course, Excellency," Mother says, bringing my attention back to the Sovereign. "I would be honored to speak with you about your mother, any time you like."

"Thank you."

Mother smiles at Molly then, too. "And you must be Molly O'Gara, the Sovereign's *Chomseireach*? It is an honor to meet you as well. I am a great admirer of your parents and everything they accomplished with the Resistance."

Molly looks startled, like no one's ever said it was an "honor" to meet her before. Because…why would they?

"Oh, ah, thank you. I'm pretty proud of them myself."

"As you should be. Now, what can I get for you all to snack on while you study?"

"Oh, we don't need anything, thanks," M tells her.

But I say, "Maybe some of those brownies we had after dinner? And some milk?"

"Of course. It's terribly generous of you both to give up an evening to help Tristan with his schoolwork. Thank you."

With another little bow, she goes to get the brownies and the three of us finally get out our books—even though M and Molly know as well as I do the studying thing is mostly for show. Still, we keep at it for over an hour. I do learn a few things that might make my classes easier but I'd rather be learning more about M.

And maybe Molly? Because I'm still not sure I completely understand the dynamic between those two.

At nine o'clock, my father walks in. "I told Mrs. Truitt we would have the Sovereign home by nine-thirty, so it's time to wrap things up." He gives Molly another withering look.

"I can drive them," I offer, hoping to avoid any more unpleasantness there. Doesn't he realize picking on Molly will only make the Sovereign mad?

"No, I implied I would drive her. You know how some *Duchas* are about teenaged drivers. We don't want to give Mrs. Truitt any reason to discourage the Sovereign from spending more time with you in the future."

Wow, way to be obvious! But I don't say anything, just nod.

When we go out to the car a few minutes later, Father opens the front passenger door for M, since it would be weird to make the Sovereign sit in back. Guess he didn't think of *that* when he insisted on driving. Now I'll have to share the back seat with Molly.

Because it seems rude not to—and I don't want M thinking I'm rude again—I open the back door for Molly. She looks almost as startled as when Mother said she was honored to meet her, but gets into the car without a word. I go around to the other side and slide in beside her, feeling strangely awkward. Not a feeling I'm used to.

Nobody says anything for a minute or two as Father backs out of the driveway and heads toward downtown Jewel. Then M turns to him.

"I don't suppose you've heard any more about when formal charges might be brought in Dun Cloch?"

His shoulders twitch slightly. "I, ah, believe that will happen tomorrow or the next day. A trial should be scheduled soon afterward, though I still don't see the urgency of—"

"Yes, you made that clear." I kind of love the way she can cut him off like that—and how he can't say anything about it. "The rest of the Council feels differently."

There's an uncomfortable silence before she speaks again, this time sounding less official. "I, ah, hope your family likes what they've seen of Jewel so far. Are you settling in all right?"

"Yeah, we are, thanks," I reply before Father can say anything sarcastic. Not that he probably would to the Sovereign, but he's obviously in one of his moods. "Everyone's been great at school."

Father adds, "My wife has met two or three of our *Duchas* neighbors. I don't believe any other *Echtrans* live in our immediate neighborhood."

"Has she been out to NuAgra yet?" Molly asks, making me more aware of her next to me in the dark back seat. "My dad's there most days and she sounded like she'd like to meet him."

Again Father's shoulders twitch. "No. She's been busy unpacking our things and organizing the house." He sounds ticked. Because Molly dared to say something to him?

"I'll suggest it to her," I volunteer. I don't think Mother has left the house since we moved in, except for one trip to the grocery store. Getting to know more *Echtrans* here would probably be good for her.

When we pull up in front of the Sovereign's house, I jump out and go around to the other side of the car so Father won't have to. I reach for M's door first, of course, but she's already opening it from inside. Her hand brushes mine as I step back but I barely notice. Again, there's no special tingle or…anything. Not that there usually is on a second touch anyway.

I turn to Molly's door but she's already getting out, too. "Um, do you want us to drop you at your house?" it occurs to me to ask.

"No, it's just around the corner. I'll walk. But, um, thanks." She gives me an odd look, like she wonders if I really meant to offer. "G'night, M. See you at school tomorrow."

"Night, Molly. And thanks. For everything." They exchange a glance that makes me feel like I'm missing something. "Thank you for the ride, Connor," she adds to my father. "Tristan, I'll see you tomorrow, too." Then she hurries up the short walk to her little cracker-box house before I can offer to see her to the door.

Disgruntled, I get back in the car, in the front seat this time.

Father has barely pulled away from the curb before he starts ranting about what an insult it was that the Sovereign insisted on bringing her Handmaid along, as though she doesn't trust our family to treat her properly.

"Are you really that surprised?" I ask when he lets me get a word in. "Here I am, trying to be more subtle around her at school, getting to know her friends and all, and you make it totally obvious you want me to be alone with her. And then you insult her best friend right in front of her."

He looks pained. "Best friends with an Ag. Don't remind me. I hope I've raised *you* to have higher standards than to go making friends with such people."

"Um, in case you've forgotten, the only other Royal at school is Sean O'Gara. Don't you think becoming best buds with him would be a little strange, considering how we plan for me to replace him as Consort?"

Instead of answering, Father just scowls.

M ACTUALLY GOES out of her way to say hi to me in Pre-Cal the next day. I'd consider that an excellent sign if she weren't also holding hands with Rigel Stuart.

Molly shoots me a knowing look as I sit down, like she suspects I'm already doubting I can ever succeed in my mission. Maybe I am, but I'm not about to give up after less than week at Jewel High. Because I have no desire to listen to her gloat, I avoid Molly after class…but on the way to Chemistry an hour later, she somehow ends up next to me in the hallway.

"Did your dad give you a hard time after dropping us off last night?" she asks. "He seemed kind of pissed."

"He was, but not at me."

She sort of smirks up at me. Which I tell myself is obnoxious, not cute. "More at me, I'll bet. I'd say I'm sorry, but I'm really not."

"I don't know what you think would have happened if you hadn't tagged along. It's not like Father was going to shut the two of us into a room together so I could try to seduce her or something. Even if he doesn't like her dating Stuart, he has too much respect for her position to do anything that out of line. So do I."

Her expression tells me she's not buying it. "Just inviting her over without me was out of line. Uncle Allister used to go on and on about the dignity of her position and their *fine* and we all know how well *he* stuck to his supposed high standards. So excuse me if I don't automatically trust you or your dad to observe the proprieties just because you're Royals. I've known too many of you."

And isn't the least bit impressed. She doesn't have to say it.

I wonder if Allister Adair really did plot to have the Sovereign killed recently? If so, I suppose Molly has good reason not to trust Royals implicitly. The Sovereign might, too.

I'm half tempted to ask Molly what it was Allister did way last year that got him removed from the Council. Father would never tell me, but I'll bet Molly knows. I clear my throat, but just then Trina runs up and links her arm through mine.

"Thanks for keeping Tristan safe for me, Molly," she says, fluttering her eyelashes up at me. "Lots of other girls would have tried to snag him for themselves, but I know you're not like that." Despite her words, there's a warning in the look she gives Molly.

Who looks like she's trying not to laugh. "No worries there, Trina, trust me." With another irritating smirk, she walks ahead of us into the Chemistry classroom.

Trina tightens her grip on my arm. "So, Tristan, how does this afternoon look for coming to watch me practice and…everything? My parents won't be home until late tonight…" Her words trail off suggestively.

She's pretty as *Duchas* girls go, in an overly-obvious way, but I'm not the least bit attracted. Though I have to admit, the look on Father's face if I told him I had a date with a *Duchas* might *almost* be worth the firestorm he'd bring down on my head immediately afterward. Almost.

"I've got to go out to NuAgra seventh period for my work-study program," I tell her. "That usually goes till at least five. Sorry. Maybe another time."

Though I'm careful not to sound too regretful, she's not deterred.

"Oh, right, I forgot you have to do that some days. But not *every* day, right?" Again with the eyelash fluttering.

Reluctantly, I shake my head. "I'm supposed to go at least three times a week to get full credit, but I, um, started later than the others, so—"

"So you'll still have at least *one* free afternoon. Plus there's evenings. My parents are hardly ever—" To my relief, the bell rings. "Oops! We'll talk more after, okay?"

With a wink, she finally releases me and I continue on to the table I share with Molly. Who still looks like she's trying not to laugh.

"That's what you get for encouraging her yesterday, you know," she whispers, gray eyes dancing with amusement. "Serves you right. Maybe I should have warned you that she formally laid claim to you at cheerleading practice, your first day here."

I groan. "Yeah, I wish you had." I definitely wouldn't have laid it on so thick yesterday if I'd known, or sat with Trina at lunch. I won't make *that* mistake again.

The teacher starts class then, so we both turn to face him.

"As you should already know if you did the reading, we'll spend most of this six weeks concentrating on chemical bonds and some of the interesting and useful things that happen when they form…and when they break. I thought today we'd start with a simple but fairly dramatic experiment that demonstrates the formation of a bond, in this case between sodium and chlorine to create sodium chloride, or common table salt. Please turn to Unit Four in your books while I hand out the materials you'll be using."

As he walks slowly up and down the room, he gives us an overview of the experiment—one I first did when I was eleven or twelve. At the same time he's handing out beakers of sodium bicarbonate and little vials of hydrochloric acid, one set per table. Once everyone has their materials, he tells us all to measure out five grams of the sodium bicarb.

Molly and I both reach for the scale on our lab table at once and our hands touch briefly. I could swear I've touched her before, but apparently not since I *absolutely* couldn't have missed the zap she gives me now—an almost-electrical current that races up my arm and makes all the hairs stand on end.

Though I can't help sucking in a startled breath, I try hard not to let anything show in my expression as the sensation gradually fades.

Because there's no way I want Molly—or *anyone*—to know I just experienced the strongest *taghal ardus* I've ever felt in my life, way stronger than when I touched those Royal girls in Denver last year. Not only is it embarrassing, it makes no sense at all.

13

Cooling Curve

Molly

THE JOLT I get when Tristan's fingers brush against mine takes me completely off guard. Though it steals my breath, I sternly force myself *not* to react—at least outwardly. Inside, my heart is suddenly racing, while questions rocket around inside my head. Because that was a crazy-strong *taghal ardus*, way stronger than I got from Alan on Saturday...or from any boy, ever.

Which makes absolutely no sense. Tristan and I are about as *non*-compatible as it's possible for two people to be. Not only are we from two widely different *fines*, we don't even *like* each other!

As we follow the teacher's instructions, Tristan is as careful to avoid touching again as I am—which means he also felt that whatever-it-was, though he didn't let on any more than I did. It's like we've mutually agreed to ignore it—which is fine with me.

The experiment we're doing is super simple but I have a hard time concentrating because I'm suddenly way too aware of Tristan sitting right next to me. It feels like his *brath* is suddenly double or triple what it was before that touch, taking on an almost magnetic quality.

I tell myself it's probably just some other manifestation of that charm-thing he does, maybe one that needed a touch before it would operate properly. Whatever it is, I can't let it distract me from my duty to M.

When the bell finally rings, Tristan and I hurry away from each other. I suspect he's as grateful as I am we don't have fourth period together.

Luckily I've already proofread my short story, today's Creative Writing activity. Otherwise, as rattled as I am, I'd probably be adding mistakes instead of catching them. I pretend to work while puzzling over possible explanations for that bizarre incident in Chemistry.

Then I remember an article I read last month, written by Regent Shim, Rigel's grandfather. In it, he made a convincing, genetics-based case for cross-*fine* pairings, hypothesizing that strong inter-*fine* resonances could be common but rarely noticed, simply because of Martians' longstanding taboos against socializing outside their own *fines*.

The theory struck me as logical at the time, since it would explain M and Rigel's *graell* bond—probably the main reason Shim wrote the article. It would also explain the obvious chemistry between Sean and Kira, though neither of them has ever mentioned an actual *bond*, at least to me. Of course Sean was attracted to Kira from the start, before he even got to know her. Not at *all* like Tristan and me.

It's terrifying to think such powerful affinities might randomly form without any rhyme, reason or warning. Surely more of our people would know about it by now, if that were really the case?

But even if some weird genetic anomaly *is* responsible for whatever happened last period, it doesn't mean either of us have to *act* on it. I won't, and I can't imagine Tristan wants to, either. So there's no reason this has to be a big deal at all, not if we both choose to ignore it.

That realization calms me enough that I'm able to give my short story one final pass before class ends.

AT LUNCH, I hang back to see where Tristan heads before deciding where to sit myself. Predictably, Trina tries to convince him to sit at her table again, but he's clearly spotted M and Rigel at our usual table, so he shakes her off.

"Can't today," I overhear him say. "I need to talk to Stuart about the football program, ask if he thinks there's any way they'll let me at least practice with the team for the rest of the season."

"Oooh, I'll bet you're even better than he is," Trina coos. "How awesome would it be to have you both on the team next year? We'd win

State for sure!" She stops trying to persuade him after that, allowing him to find a seat at M's table.

I'm torn. I *should* sit there, in case Rigel and M need my help discouraging Tristan, but I'd much rather keep my distance as long as possible. As I stand there waffling, Alan comes up.

"You okay, Molly? You look like you're zoning out or something. You want to sit with us again?"

"Oh. Um, sure." Rigel and Tristan are talking to each other, with M on Rigel's other side, so they probably don't need me to chaperone anyway.

"Hey," I greet everyone as I set down my tray next to Alan's. "Since we can't seem to get you guys to spread out, I figure I'll have to start infiltrating your table instead. Seriously, the locals aren't *that* scary."

Most of them respond with nervous laughter.

"This just seems…safer, I guess." Erin, a sophomore with bright red hair, gives a little shrug. "It's the only time at school we can talk without worrying we might accidentally say something we shouldn't."

"I think you're worrying too much. I haven't heard even a whiff of suspicion from anyone, though if you keep shutting them all out socially they may start wondering why. You should try getting involved in stuff. I joined the cheer squad even though it's all *Duchas* but me. And it's been fun."

Erin gives a little shudder but freshman Jana leans forward.

"You really enjoy it? I thought about trying out for the JV squad for basketball season…if I can get Adina to do it with me." She glances at Kira's little sister, who looks alarmed.

"I dunno, Jana. Have you seen the outfits they wear? I don't think my mum would like it." The two girls start arguing good-naturedly.

Alan nudges me with his shoulder. "So, we still on for tonight?"

"You bet!" I infuse my reply with extra enthusiasm so he won't guess I temporarily forgot all about our date. Tonight will be an excellent distraction from obsessing over that weird touch thing with Tristan. "They start the trivia contest at seven-thirty, right?"

"I think so. Want to meet at the Lighthouse, or should I swing by and pick you up?"

"There's not much parking on Diamond Street. Why don't you come by and we'll walk from my house? The weather's nice today and it's not far at all."

He agrees and we spend the rest of lunch talking about the kinds of trivia questions we're each best at, planning our strategy for tonight. Afterward, he walks with me to Government.

"Have you tried the things I showed you on any of your other plants yet? How is that going so far?"

"Pretty good," I lie. "I'm still nowhere near as good at it as you are, but I'm sure I'll get better with practice."

I did try again after he left Saturday, but with no more success than before. I worry if Alan finds out just how hopeless I am, he might lose interest completely—and he *is* the only Ag boy close to my age in Jewel. He's also really cute. Maybe not *quite* as insanely good looking as Tristan, but a whole lot nicer. Plus the idea of us dating makes Mum and Dad happy. I don't even want to think what they'd say if I went out with Tristan. Not that he'd ever ask…

"What?" I realize I missed whatever Alan just asked—because I was thinking about Tristan. Again. Dumb, dumb, dumb.

"I asked if you maybe want to go earlier, like six-thirty, so we can get dinner there before the trivia starts?"

Tristan passes us from behind just then, almost making me lose the thread of our conversation again.

"Oh, um, sure, that sounds great," I say a little absently.

Did Tristan feel what I did when we touched? I wish I had the nerve to ask.

✦

I DRESS with extra care that evening, determined to give a potential relationship with Alan my very best shot.

In both of our afternoon classes, Tristan sat as far away from me as possible. I took that as a clear signal he did *not* want to talk about what happened in Chemistry. Of course, being Royal, it probably freaked him out even more than it did me.

Avoiding each other totally works for me, unless my duty to M forces me into his company. I hope it won't anytime soon.

Predictably, Mum is at least as excited about my date with Alan as I am. "That color is lovely on you, Molly." She beams at my flattering teal top and charcoal-gray jeans.

I even put matching teal laces in my gray sneakers, giving my outfit a pulled-together look without being fussy. Alan won't notice—what guy would?—but it gives me a little boost in confidence.

"Thanks. What time do I need to be home?"

"Oh, as it's Alan Dempsey, I'm not terribly concerned. Coming from a nice Hollydoon Agricultural family, he's sure to have you home at a decent hour."

Weird. Mum is usually strict about my curfew on school nights. She must be even happier about this date than I thought.

Alan again shows up a few minutes early. I hurry to answer the door when he rings to prevent Mum gushing to him how grateful she is he asked me out.

"Hey." I step out on the porch with him. "Ready to go?"

"Um, sure."

Though he looks slightly confused when I don't invite him in, I just call out we're leaving and close the front door.

"So, your folks were okay with you going out tonight?" He glances over his shoulder as we head down the street.

"Yeah, they're fine with it." Massive understatement, at least for Mum. "I promised I wouldn't be too late getting back, though, since it's a school night."

Alan smiles down at me. He's almost as tall as Sean, which is saying something—and he has an adorable dimple in his left cheek when he smiles. "No worries there. I told my folks I'd be home by nine-thirty."

We chat a little about school as we walk. I let my arms swing by my sides so if he wants to hold my hand, he can. But either he isn't ready to move to the handholding stage of our fledgling relationship or he doesn't have the guts to make the first move. Neither do I.

"So, you really like living in Jewel?" he asks after a few minutes. "You moved here last year, right?"

"First week of November—almost exactly a year ago, yeah. We lived in Bailerealta in Ireland before that. I liked it there, too, but it's really small. Not that Jewel's exactly a big city." I laugh. "It seemed that way when we first got here, though, after Glenamuir and Bailerealta."

He chuckles, too—a nice-sounding chuckle. "How big is Bailerealta? I've never been there."

"About four hundred people when we lived there. I hear it's a bit bigger now, with all the new arrivals."

When we reach Diamond, Jewel's main street, there are more people around, so we switch to talking about school.

"Have you thought about our next Government project?" I ask. It's the only class we share, since Alan is a senior.

"Not much, yet. I still need to read up on the Constitution stuff you covered before I got here. Maybe you could give me a quick overview sometime?"

Hm, already planning for another date before we've even had this one? Not that working on school stuff is necessarily a *date*. Those study sessions with Tristan certainly weren't...

I yank my thoughts back to Alan. "Sure, I'd be happy to."

The Lighthouse Cafe isn't crowded—not surprising this early on a Tuesday. We snag a table by the windows, well away from the nearest group of *Duchas* so we can talk more freely.

"I've never been to Dun Cloch," I say after the server takes our drink orders. "What's it like?"

"A lot bigger than Bailerealta. When we left, the permanent population was over two thousand, twice what it was before this past launch window. Of course, they have plenty of room to expand, since it's nowhere near anything else. Now that orientations are over, they should have time to build better housing than we had." He grimaces.

"Yeah, M said they had to scramble to accommodate all the new arrivals on such short notice, not just there but in Bailerealta, too."

When we landed there in July on our return from Nuath, it was weird to see the hundred or so temporary flats that had been slapped up since we left. They looked oddly out of place in what was otherwise a quaint Irish village.

"There's not nearly as much space to spread out in Ireland, so I doubt Bailerealta's population will have doubled," I tell him. "Even an extra fifty people would be a lot."

"Wow, I guess so," he agrees. "I know they had a whole complicated system to decide who could settle where. We got to make requests, but not everyone got their first choice—especially if they wanted to come here. We were really lucky to be chosen for Jewel."

The server comes back with our sodas, so we break off to look at the dinner menu.

"I'll have the fish and chips," I tell the server. "They're really good here," I add to Alan.

"Then I'll have the same. Thanks." He hands her the menus with a smile. She looks slightly dazzled when she smiles back, reminding me of how Tristan made Trina go nonverbal before Chemistry class yesterday.

"No problem," the server says with a big smile. "I'll put this right in for you."

As she walks away she glances back at Alan, reminding me how lucky *I* am to be out on a real date with one of the best-looking guys in Jewel—and a senior, at that.

"So, where were we?" he says when she's out of earshot. "Oh, right. Dun Cloch. It took some getting used to, especially the weather. The night we landed, it—" He breaks off with a slight frown, his attention suddenly caught by something behind me.

I turn and see Sean and Kira, who apparently just walked in. I stifle a groan. *Surely* Sean didn't come here to supervise my first date with Alan or, worse, join us?

Even as I think that, Sean spots us. After a startled moment, my glare apparently registers because his surprise gives way to amusement. He winks at me, then leans down and whispers something to Kira. She looks our way and nods, and a second later they leave. Guess they weren't here to put a damper on my evening after all.

I turn back to Alan, relieved. "Well, that could have been awkward." I say it jokingly, though it's true.

Alan swallows a couple of times, still watching the door. "Er, yeah, I guess. Wonder why they left?" His ears are noticeably redder than before.

"I never told Sean where you and I were going tonight, so it was probably just chance they showed up. Glad he decided to leave when he saw us instead of going all big brother on me—though I don't *think* Kira would have let him do that."

"Oh. Right. Yeah." Alan still looks uncomfortable, clearly rattled by the almost-encounter.

I debate with myself for a moment, then decide to tackle the issue head on rather than ignore it. Like M, I've developed a strong aversion to secrets.

"I, um, guess you and Kira knew each other pretty well before coming to Jewel?"

His sky-blue eyes snap to mine. "What? I mean…sure. Sort of. We both lived in Hollydoon, though she was a year behind me in school there. And then we were on the same ship to Dun Cloch, so we went through orientation together. We're, um, both into *caidpel*, so we had that in common, too. The two of us even scraped a little group together to play in Dun Cloch not long after we got there."

None of that answers my *real* question. "So…did you two ever actually date?" I ask straight out. From the way he always acts around her, I assumed they did and she broke it off. But he shakes his head with what looks suspiciously like regret.

"Not date, exactly, but we did hang out a lot in Dun Cloch. *Caidpel*, our classes, plus we went jogging together most evenings. Stuff like that. I did kind of think once we got to Jewel, things might... But then famous Sean O'Gara started paying attention to her and she didn't have time for me anymore, so—" He breaks off. "Sorry."

Though I should probably drop it, I can't. "*Famous* Sean O'Gara?" I repeat incredulously.

"Well...yeah. Your whole family is pretty famous, at least in Nuath. For the Resistance stuff. Plus he was on the feeds constantly with the Sovereign, destined Royal Consort and all that." Maybe he's trying to hide it, but Alan still sounds pretty bitter to me.

"I guess I never thought of them that way, since they're, you know, my family. But you can't really think Kira's just going out with him because he's famous? I mean, she was pretty famous herself back in Nuath, right? Sean said she was one of their biggest *caidpel* stars—he was a fan before he ever met her. But I honestly don't think fame had anything to do with them getting together, on either side. From what I've seen, they really do care about each other."

Alan shrugs. "If you say so. I just worry Kira will get hurt when... if...he decides to go through with the whole Royal Consort thing after all. Guess I still don't completely understand why he's not."

"Um, because M is totally in love with Rigel and not Sean?" I suggest, eyebrows raised. "Not to mention their *graell* bond. Sean had no choice but to back off once he finally understood how things are between them—how important it is for them to be together. I mean, it was that bond that kept the Grentl from blasting us with an EMP last month. I thought everyone knew that?"

"Yeah, I saw that last MARSTAR, though it didn't say exactly *how* they did it. So sure, along with everyone else, I'm grateful for however Rigel helped. But my folks aren't the only ones who think he should step aside now."

I shake my head at his obtuseness, determined to change this *one* mind, at least.

"He can't, even if M was willing to let him—which she's not. They're *bonded.* As far as anyone knows, including our Scientists, that's permanent. So if what you're *really* worried about is Sean dumping Kira to go back to M, you can relax. He won't."

"Okay." If anything, he looks unhappier than before. Which means I probably did convince him.

Our meals come then, a welcome distraction. After a minute or two of eating in silence, Alan clears his throat, his expression contrite.

"I'm sorry, Molly. I should never have said any of that stuff about your brother, or Kira or anything. I wanted tonight to be just about you and me getting to know each other better."

I smile so he won't think I'm mad, but my heart's not really in it. "Yeah, me too."

After that we both try, but we never quite get back to the comfortable companionship we enjoyed before Sean and Kira stopped in. Alan, I suspect, is still brooding, now he knows his case is even more hopeless than he thought. And I'm silently kicking myself for not heeding the warning signs sooner.

When the trivia contest starts half an hour later, I can tell Alan is as relieved as I am to abandon our halting attempts at conversation. Unfortunately, whether because he's still distracted or because he's so new to Earth and American culture, I out-score him by more than two to one in the first round—which doesn't help his mood.

"You want to go?" I ask before the second round starts. "This looks like it could go late." *And this date is obviously a disaster,* I add silently.

"Oh. Sure. Yeah. Let's get out of here."

We go and pay at the register rather than wait for the check. I insist on paying my half even though it's barely ten bucks. I'd rather not be obligated.

Our conversation on the walk back is even more awkward than when we were sitting at the table. Alan tries again to apologize when we approach my house, but I tell him not to worry about it.

"It's fine, really. If we're going to be friends at all, it's better to know where we both stand on things from the start, right?"

"Um, right. Well, I guess I'll see you at school tomorrow. G'night, Molly."

"Good night, Alan."

I wait on the porch until he drives off, then turn and walk into the house, trying to decide what to tell my family. Who are all sitting in the living room, in full view of the front door.

"You're back early," Mum exclaims, since it's not even nine. "Alan didn't have time to come inside?"

"Er, no. He still had homework to do."

Luckily she doesn't try to "read" me or she'd know I'm lying—but the look Sean gives me tells me *he* isn't fooled.

"I consider that commendable, even if it did cut your date short," Dad says bracingly. "It shows that Alan is serious about his schoolwork."

Then Mum joins the gushing. "Such a nice *Echtran* boy. And so handsome! Did you two make plans to go out again anytime soon?"

"Um, not yet. But we'll see each other at school."

"Of course. Oh, I forgot to change the laundry." She hurries off and Dad goes with her. So they can congratulate each other on my date?

But Sean gives me a too-knowing expression. "Let's go out on the porch and talk."

I shrug and follow him back outside. "What did you want to talk about?"

"Tonight. You and Alan. Kira and I didn't ruin things by stopping by the Lighthouse, did we? I could tell you weren't happy to see us. We never would have gone there if—"

"I know. I could tell it wasn't on purpose. And yeah, I guess that was sort of what ruined things, but it was probably just as well." As I say it, I realize it's true. "It got us talking about stuff we wouldn't have otherwise and we found out we're not as...compatible as we thought. Better to know that sooner than later, right?"

He frowns at me in obvious concern. "But I thought—"

"I know," I repeat. "And I still think he's cute and all. But his views are a little too...traditional for my taste. If we kept going out, we'd always be arguing."

I don't add that he's also still hung up on Kira. No point prejudicing Sean against the only other senior *Echtran* boy at Jewel High.

"Well...okay. I was kind of hoping you two would hit it off as well as Kira and I have."

"So was I. Especially since it would make Mum and Dad so happy. And I'm not saying I'll never go out with him again. Maybe if he comes around to a more forward-thinking perspective it'll work out after all. Just...not right now."

Not until he's well and truly over Kira, anyway.

14

Critical point

M

"Dinner was wonderful, Dr. Stuart, thank you. Can I help clear the table?"

Rigel's mom smiles and shakes her head. "Thank you, M, but I believe Van wants to talk to you about some new discoveries he's made since Saturday's Council meeting. Rigel can help me carry everything into the kitchen."

Curious now, I look at Mr. Stuart, who nods. "Yes, I think you'll be interested to hear what I've found so far."

"Don't say anything too interesting before I get there," Rigel says, half-jokingly. Then, just to me, *Don't worry, I'll be quick.*

I follow his dad into his office and involuntarily glance at the enormous vidscreen on one wall—the one where I "met" with half a dozen world leaders last month to tell them about the Grentl.

"I take it you've been able to decipher more of those messages you discovered?"

"A bit, yes," he replies. "It's clear they are *not* about setting up schools, at least not for children. I've come across more than one transmission referring to some sort of 'long term plan.'"

A shiver goes through me. "That sounds...ominous."

"Indeed. I also did some research based on what you learned from Kira and discovered that almost everyone who has disappeared so far once had a reputation as either a Faxon sympathizer or a radical Populist. In other words, people who already didn't get along well with others because of their extreme views. That likely explains why their families didn't search for them right away. It looks like a pattern to me, one I think justifies more attention from the Council."

I blink. "Yeah, I'd say so. Have you shared this with Kyna yet?"

Rigel hurries in just then. "What did I miss?"

His dad fills him in, then turns to me. "I spoke to Kyna shortly before you arrived this evening. I had hoped she'd get back to me before dinner, but— Ah, that must be her now."

He reaches into his pocket and pulls out one of those cellphone-omni combos the whole Council has now. I've requested one for myself but haven't received it yet. Supposedly it's taking a while to add the extra security features Mr. Stuart insisted mine have.

"Kyna," Mr. Stuart says into the phone. "You got my message, then? Yes, she's here right now. Very well."

He sets the device on the edge of his desk and a moment later Kyna's hologram appears in the room with us, her expression somber.

"Good evening, Excellency, Van, Rigel. I thought face to face would be preferable, as I have some rather disturbing news to report."

Uh, oh. "What?" all three of us ask at once.

"Enid, the woman who worked closely with Allister and Lennox in Dun Cloch, was scheduled to have her memories extracted this afternoon. However, I have just been informed that she died before the procedure could be performed."

"Do they know the cause of death?" I ask with a sense of foreboding —and déjà vu.

She nods. "Poison. Apparently self-administered."

Kira did say Enid was devoted to Lennox. Would she commit suicide rather than risk further incriminating him?

"That's twice now that someone who tried to kill me has died before we could get any information from them," I point out. "Somehow, I don't think that's a coincidence."

"Nor do I," Kyna agrees. "We are trying to discover how the poison came to be in her possession."

I huff out a frustrated breath. One less lead to follow—and one more incident pointing to a broader conspiracy than Allister and Lennox holding grudges against me.

"Do you think this might be linked to those unauthorized *Echtran* groups we discussed on Saturday?"

"We don't have enough information yet to determine that, but the possibility certainly warrants further investigation," Kyna replies. "It would be useful to discover whether Enid was in communication with those groups, though the most urgent matter is to find out where she obtained the antimatter that was used in the attempt on your life. We expected today's memory extraction to provide those details, but that is of course impossible now. As she—or someone—no doubt intended."

Mr. Stuart frowns. "So there is some doubt as to whether she died by her own hand?"

"Little is known for certain at this point, including how or when she obtained the toxin. It's possible she already had it secreted on her person before she was incarcerated."

"Wasn't she searched?" Rigel sounds indignant. So am I.

Kyna lifts a holographic shoulder. "Presumably, though as skilled and innovative as Enid was with technology, it's conceivable she devised some method of concealment that our scans were unable to detect."

I exchange a worried glance with Rigel. "Like that bomb she implanted in Kira's neck? Do you think she designed that herself?"

"There is no reason to assume otherwise, unless other evidence comes to light. Kira Morain did mention certain features included in the omni device Enid gave her that were far from standard. Was enough of it salvaged for analysis?"

Regretfully, I shake my head. "No, I'm sorry. Rigel and I, um, kind of incinerated it."

"Pity. Still, it might be helpful if Kira could describe those features for our Scientists, along with anything else of a technical nature she can recall. That information could offer clues as to whether Enid, Allister and Lennox were working with anyone else."

That makes sense. "I'm sure she'd be willing to do that. I'll ask her."

"Won't you get that information out of Allister and Lennox when you probe *their* memories?" Rigel's been even more furious at those two since their attempt to kill me. That, after they tried to kill *him* last year. They'd have succeeded, too, if not for that incredibly awkward deal I made with the Council involving Sean.

Kyna's lips compress into a thin, irritated line. "I certainly hope to do so…eventually. Unfortunately, there are some on the Council—and in Dun Cloch—who are resistant to the idea of performing memory extractions on Royals."

"I know Connor argued against the *tabula rasa*, but now he doesn't even want you to do the extractions?" I'm getting angry myself now. "Last spring, the Royals on the Council approved not just an extraction, but *erasure* of Rigel's memory—even though he hadn't done anything wrong. Allister and Lennox are guilty of attempted murder twice over!"

"And treason. Formal charges *are* finally being brought. However, it will be difficult to achieve convictions without those memory extractions."

Suddenly I understand. "So those fighting it don't want you to get enough evidence to convict. I'm guessing Connor is the one driving this opposition, too?"

Kyna's humorless smile is answer enough. "He was closer to both Allister and Lennox in the past than anyone else on the Council, save Lili O'Gara, as Allister's sister."

"But even she voted to charge them with treason," I remind her.

"True. But while she has not been as outspoken as Connor against a memory extraction, she has cautioned strenuously against undue haste in the matter."

I have to restrain a snort. "Did you point out that the longer we wait, the more opportunity we give someone to silence them permanently, like Enid was silenced?"

"I will. However, I have the distinct impression she would see that as less of a stain on her family than a conviction and the resulting *tabula rasa*."

"You mean she'd rather see her own brother dead than proven guilty?" Much as I've always detested Allister, I find that disturbing.

Mr. Stuart clears his throat. "For most of us, Excellency, a complete memory erasure has always been considered a fate *worse* than death," he tells me gently. "I imagine Lili would prefer to spare him that."

"Understandable," Kyna agrees, "but certainly not helpful to our investigation. Any delay in discovering the source of that illegally obtained antimatter could prove extremely dangerous. If there is a security breach that serious in Dun Cloch, we need to address it immediately."

She's right. Considering the explosion that microscopic bit of antimatter produced after it was removed from Kira, if someone got hold of more, they could create a devastatingly powerful bomb that might be virtually undetectable until it's too late. I shudder.

"I'll call Kira tonight to see when she can talk with the Scientists," I tell her. "Rigel and Sean and I can be there, too, in case there's anything we can remember from that final confrontation that might be useful."

Kyna smiles for the first time since appearing. "Thank you, Excellency. That is precisely what I'd hoped. Meanwhile, I will attempt to convince the holdouts on the Council to move forward on those memory extractions. Van, do let me know if you learn more from those encrypted communications, won't you?"

"Of course," he replies.

With a parting bow to me, she vanishes.

Mr. Stuart picks up his omni and glances at it. "It's after eight-thirty, so perhaps you should take M home?" he suggests to Rigel.

"Probably, yeah, if I want to stay on her aunt's good side. Ready, M?"

Nodding, I get my backpack from the living room. We intended to do some homework together after dinner, but it's probably too late to start now. Plus there's something else I need to do as soon as possible.

Tonight, if I can arrange it.

⁺₊

I MAKE my call to Kira while Rigel drives me home. Next spring I hope to get my own driver's license—for all the good it'll do me without a car.

"Hi, Kira, it's M. I just talked with Kyna from the *Echtran* Council and she was wondering if you'd be willing to talk to some Scientists this week?"

She says sure, but sounds slightly apprehensive about it.

"Don't worry, they just want to ask you about the tech stuff Enid had in Dun Cloch, so they can get an idea of what else she might have been developing and who she might have been working with. She apparently killed herself before they could do a memory extraction—Kyna just told me."

"Yikes," Kira exclaims. "She was obviously one messed up woman. When do the Scientists want to talk to me? And where?"

"I'll let you know, but soon, I think. Thanks, Kira."

I hang up and turn to Rigel. "I think she's still worried the Council might try to charge her with something after all. I've told her I won't allow it, but—"

"Yeah. Considering how completely Allister betrayed her, I can see why she'd have a little trouble trusting Royals now."

So do I, we think to each other at the same time.

The only Royals I *really* trust are my Sovereign ancestors, in the Scepter Archive. I wish I could consult with them about this new development right away, but since Molly's out on her big date with Alan tonight, there's no way she'll be home yet.

Even though it means putting off that session with my Scepter until tomorrow, I hope their date is going well. Molly's such a sweetheart, she totally deserves someone special of her own—preferably someone her mother won't act weird about, the way she does with Sean and Kira.

Since I'm well ahead of my curfew, Rigel stops the car several houses away from mine so Aunt Theresa can't peer out the window and see us parked out front while we say goodnight to each other properly. Cutting the engine, he unbuckles his seatbelt and turns toward me with a smile that makes my toes curl.

"This is always my favorite part of the evening," I confide as he gathers me into his arms.

"Mm. Mine, too." And then we're kissing and nothing else in the world matters.

All too soon, he releases me with a sigh. "It's nearly nine. If we want to convince your aunt to let us spend more evenings together, we'd better not push it."

"Yeah," I reluctantly agree. I never feel more alive than when I'm with Rigel. *I'm glad she doesn't know about this part, at least. It's not as good as actually having you with me at night, but it helps.*

Agreed. He gives me one last, delicious kiss, then drives me the last block home.

Once inside, I send a quick message to Molly.

Text me when you get home. I want to hear how your date went!

To my surprise, she texts me back almost immediately.

I'm home. You want to come over, or is it too late?

I glance at the time. It's just a minute past nine and my school night curfew is nine-thirty. Later, if official Sovereign business is involved—which I may be able to conduct at Molly's house tonight after all.

I poke my head into the living room, where Aunt Theresa is reading while Uncle Louie watches some reality show on TV.

"Hi, I'm home. But would it be okay if I go over to Molly's for a little while? I need to talk to her about schoolwork and to her parents about, er, other stuff." It still makes my aunt nervous when I talk directly about anything Martian-related, so I try to avoid it when possible. Which is sometimes convenient.

Predictably, my last few words make her flinch. "Very well. Don't be any later than you can help, as you have school tomorrow."

"I won't. Thanks." I pull my jacket on again, sling my backpack over my shoulder and head back outside.

Molly answers the door when I ring. After I say hello to her parents she ushers me up to her room, obviously not wanting to talk about her evening in front of them. Once we're safely upstairs, I turn to her.

"So? Dish. How was the date?"

Her face answers my question before she replies and I belatedly realize I should have "read" her feelings before asking. I wouldn't have been nearly so perky if I had.

"Not great. It's why I'm back so early. Sean and Kira stopped by the Lighthouse just a few minutes after we got there, and—"

"You're kidding me! Oh, I am going to give Sean *such* a chewing out the next time I—"

"No, it wasn't his fault. Really. He didn't know we'd be there and as soon as he saw us they left. But Alan saw them and... Didn't I tell you I thought he might still be hung up on Kira? His whole mood changed after that, then we started arguing about politics and stuff. But I could tell it was mostly about Kira."

"I'm sorry," I say, even though Molly seems more resigned than upset. "It was my idea to nudge him your way in the first place. Guess you were right about the rebound thing."

"Yeah." She shrugs. "I'd rather not have been, but better to find out upfront. Anyway, it's not like I had a full-blown crush on him. I just thought he had...potential. The worst part is how disappointed Mum will be. She was *so* happy I was going out with another Ag. But now..."

Irritated as I am by Mrs. O'Gara's narrow-mindedness about inter-*fine* dating, Molly's probably right that arguing with her about it won't help.

"Maybe don't tell her right away?" I suggest. "It's not like you and Alan broke up, since you never had time to become a couple in the first place. It was just a first date."

"Good point. She's sure to ask when we'll go out again, but I can pretend we're both too busy—at least for a while. Maybe she'll eventually leave it alone. So, um, did you want to do homework or anything while you're here?" She clearly doesn't want to talk about Alan anymore.

I hesitate for a moment. "Actually, I could use a little bit more, um, closet time, if you don't mind? I know it's only been a few days, but I found out something this evening and—"

"No, it's fine. I'll just go downstairs and get us some tea—for when you're finished with your 'closet time.'" She makes air quotes, clearly amused by my euphemism, though I again sense some hurt, too.

I swear, sometimes this "gift" of mine feels more like a curse. "Thanks, Molly."

I wait until she's gone to shut myself into her closet. If Molly knew the *whole* truth, I could access the Archive while sitting on her bed instead of scrunched up in a closet no bigger than mine. I could even introduce her to my ancestors.

Maybe it would be okay? I *am* allowed to tell my closest advisors, and a Handmaid is *sort* of an advisor. Besides, Molly is way more than my Handmaid, she's also my best friend—and I *hate* hurting her feelings. With a sigh, I pick up the Scepter.

"*Chartlann rochtana.*"

Like last time, Sovereign Aerleas greets me. "Hello, dear. I take it you need more advice?"

"I do." I quickly tell her everything I learned from Kyna tonight, including the recent news of Enid's suicide.

"And now a couple of Royals on the Council want to delay Allister and Lennox having their memories extracted, which might be the only way to find out where Enid got that antimatter and who else she was working with. They seem more worried about besmirching the honor of the Royal *fine* than keeping everyone safe."

She frowns thoughtfully at me for a moment, probably reviewing my last report in the Archive.

"My prior advice stands, that your best course may be to enlist the help of the more like-minded Council members, particularly Kyna Nuallan and Van Stuart. However, it sounds as though a more robust security strategy may also be necessary. For that, I would recommend you seek input from Sovereign Leontine."

"Thank you. I'll do that."

I say goodbye to Aerleas, then call up Leontine, her son and my grandfather.

"Emileia, my dear. How are you?" he greets me with that grandfatherly smile I love. Maybe because he's the first one of my ancestors I ever "met," he still feels the *most* real—and sympathetic—of any of them.

"Hello, Grandfather. I'm doing well at the moment, but I do need your advice. Have you had a chance to catch up on my latest updates?" I haven't talked with his image since August, right after I got back to Jewel.

He gets that thoughtful look for a moment that means he's accessing the Archive, then nods. "You do lead a busy life, don't you, Emileia?"

I laugh—quietly. "A little *too* busy, lately. I don't have long to talk, since I'm in Molly's closet and it's late, so I'll get right to the point. Considering what happened today, I get the impression security at Dun Cloch isn't nearly as good as it should be. Also, with the NuAgra facility in Jewel becoming our Earth-based government center, we should probably have safeguards there, too. I wondered if it might be possible to set up something similar to the awesome security system the Palace in Nuath has?"

"Do you have reason to believe your personal safety is still at risk? I am extremely pleased that the recent attempt on your life was averted, by the way. Our people cannot afford to lose you."

Even though I know his concern is an artificial projection of how my real grandfather *would* have reacted, I can't help feeling warmed by it.

"I'm not aware of any direct threats at the moment, but if there's more antimatter floating around out there, who knows? All of Jewel could be at risk."

He nods. "A valid concern. Is there someone you can trust to implement a series of security safeguards if I direct you to the technical specifications? This would be highly sensitive information, not to be entrusted to just anyone, however skilled an Engineer they might be."

"Mr. Stuart is Informatics, not an Engineer, but he's really good at what he does. And I'd trust him with my life."

"Ah, yes, the man who designed your MARSTAR communication system, among other things. I agree he would be a good choice. Do you have a chip available for the necessary data?"

"Oops, not at the moment, sorry. I'm sure Mr. Stuart has extras, though."

He smiles approvingly. "Very well. Return with a blank chip and I can transfer the information he will need to begin."

"Thank you. Do you have any other advice based on what you know now? Like, how to get the Council to do what needs to be done?"

"Aerleas's advice on that was good, as usual. Your Council leader Kyna sounds like a valuable ally in this and other matters. I quite agree with her that the top priority should be tracking down the source of the stolen antimatter. For the other issues you brought up, do try not to borrow trouble, won't you? You generally seem to have quite enough without that."

I can't disagree. "I'll try. Thank you, Grandfather. I'll talk to you again as soon as I can. *Chartlann fionragh.*"

As always, I feel a pang when his image disappears. Consoling myself that I'll be seeing him again as soon as I get a data chip from Rigel's dad, I set the Scepter back in its corner and step out of Molly's closet.

15

Dissociation constant

Molly

I TRY to be quiet when I return to my room with two cups of herbal tea and a plate of lemon bars. Partly so I don't disturb M and, okay, partly because I hope I might overhear something.

Setting the tray on my desk, I stare at the closed closet door. Though I can't make out words, I hear M's voice murmuring. Then I'm almost sure I hear a male voice answer her. Less than five minutes later, the door opens.

"Oh, hey, Molly. I didn't hear you come back. Ooh, those look good." She picks up a lemon bar.

"So, um, everything go okay?"

I try to sound casual but as usual M sees right through me.

"I'm sorry, Molly. It doesn't seem fair to shut you out of your own closet and not tell you exactly what I'm doing in there. I really do wish I could." Her green eyes plead with me to understand.

Even though I don't, I nod. "It's fine. Just let me know if there's anything I can ever do to help, okay?"

"I will, I promise. And I *can* tell you what I learned tonight at Rigel's. Kyna called while I was there to tell us that Enid, the woman who put that antimatter bomb in Kira's neck, committed suicide before they could extract her memory. So now the only way to find out for sure if Allister and Lennox were working with anyone else is to extract their memories—which *some* people on the Council don't think we should do."

"Some people. Like Mum?" I guess. She's never seemed to like Uncle Allister much, but he *is* her brother.

M nods. "And Connor. I don't think the other two Royals are all that keen on the idea either. They all seem, I don't know, *offended* by the very idea of extracting memories from someone in their precious *fine*.

I can't help but chuckle. "Don't you mean *'our* precious *fine*'? You're Royal too, remember. Even more than they are."

"Don't remind me. You don't know how lucky you are not to be, Molly, seriously."

She sounds like she means it—and she probably does, at least right this moment. Not that I've ever seen it that way. Especially not lately, with Mum's new obsession about preserving the social hierarchy.

"Do you want me to talk to Mum about it? See if I can convince her how important it is to get those memories?"

M thinks for a second, then shakes her head. "I don't think the rest of the Council has even heard about Enid yet, so she might be upset that I told you about it first. Let's not give her another reason to complain that you and I aren't maintaining a proper professional distance or whatever." She makes a face.

I laugh, even though she's right. Mum reminds me of that way too often and it bothers me more than I let on, even though M doesn't agree with her.

We talk a little about schoolwork while we drink tea and eat lemon bars, then M has to leave. I see her to the front door but Cormac is loitering at the corner so I don't walk her home this time, just go back up to my room.

Where I go into my closet, as if drawn there. I stare at the Scepter for a long time, though I resist the urge to touch it again. Finally, I sigh and start getting ready for bed.

⁺₊

CHATTING with M and Liam about our assignment before Pre-Cal the next morning, I privately wonder if Tristan will have totally forgotten that weird first-touch thing by now. I wish I could.

The answer is obvious as soon as he walks into the classroom. Instead of taking the desk next to mine, like he has every other day, he goes to one in the far back corner—without even glancing our way.

Which is *totally* fine with me. I actually considered sitting somewhere else myself today, then decided that would be cowardly. Not to mention how leaving an empty desk right next to M would be a dereliction of duty. I'm pleased to see Tristan's a bigger coward than I am.

M shoots a curious glance his way but I pretend not to notice, afraid I might give something away. Instead I make a production of getting my textbook out of my backpack and finding the spot where we left off yesterday.

When M and I get to French class next hour, Tristan's already there… in a seat well away from where we usually sit.

"What's the deal with Tristan?" M whispers. "Did you threaten him with bodily injury if he didn't leave me alone? Rigel swears he didn't, though I know he's been tempted."

"Not a threat, exactly, but I *have* told him to back off at least a dozen times." Which is true. "Maybe it finally sank in?"

M looks skeptical but doesn't press the issue, to my relief. It's almost as hard to get a lie past her as it is my mum. I have trouble concentrating on French colloquialisms, I'm so busy dreading Chemistry class next period.

Once there, I delay going to my lab table as long as possible by stopping at M's to talk until the bell rings. Only *that* gets awkward when M asks Rigel if he's *sure* he didn't say anything to Tristan yesterday.

"Not since we talked football at lunch, and you were right there for that," he replies, looking confused. "Why?"

"I just wondered why he's suddenly keeping his distance today. Not that I'm complaining," she adds quickly when Rigel starts to frown.

The bell rings then and I reluctantly head to my seat. Nervous as I am, I find it mildly hilarious that Tristan won't even look at me as I sit down. Is he really *that* afraid of me now?

I imagine we're both equally relieved there's no lab today, just lecture. That means we don't have to interact, or even acknowledge each other. I keep my eyes resolutely forward while Mr. Abbot talks about covalent bonds, illustrating his explanation with diagrams on the whiteboard up front.

But while I'm careful to make it *look* like my whole focus is on the teacher, inside I'm again way too aware of Tristan just a few inches away. The strange pull I feel from his *brath* seems even stronger today than yesterday, though I'm sure that's just my imagination.

When the bell rings at the end of class, Tristan and I both shoot out of our seats, eager to get away from each other. In our haste we bump shoulders, hard, and I nearly lose my balance. He reaches out to steady me, but snatches his hand back before actually making contact. Luckily my Martian reflexes are good enough to save me from an ignominious face plant.

"Sorry," Tristan mumbles, though he looks more angry than contrite. Like that was *my* fault?

"No biggie," I mumble back, though I feel more like yelling at him.

Then, while I'm bending down to pick up my backpack, he scurries out of the room. When I follow him into the hallway, he's just a few paces behind M and Rigel. I wonder if he'll revert to his usual overly-friendly behavior toward M in their shared Lit class, since I won't be there to avoid.

For myself, I'm nearly as grateful today for the hour-long break from Tristan as I was yesterday. Hopefully by tomorrow the weird after-effects of that stupid touch will have worn off and being around him won't bother me so much.

When I get to the cafeteria, Tristan is already sitting at M's table—which presents a dilemma. After last night's awkward date I'd rather not sit with Alan today. But if I go to my usual table, M's likely to realize something weird is going on between Tristan and me. Finally I take the coward's way out and carry my lunch to the cheerleader table—neutral territory.

Unfortunately, that means listening to Trina gush about Tristan.

"You should have heard the nice things he said to me in Lit class when we were talking about Hemingway," she says with a sigh. "Those brown eyes of his are just the dreamiest, aren't they?"

I nearly blurt out, "Whose, Hemingway's?" but the other cheer-leaders are already chorusing their agreement.

"When he sat right across from me here on Monday, I thought I was going to just melt every time he looked at me," Donna coos.

"Uh-uh, girls. That one is all mine!" Trina scolds her. "But now to business—Spirit Week next week. We're going with Halloween as a theme and I've already worked out who'll do what for decorating the school. I've got streamers covered and Amber, I've assigned you locker stickers. Molly, you'll print up signs for classroom doors and Donna, you and Tiffany will make the hall banners, okay? And remember, wear your uniforms and bows every single day next week. If you need to set aside extra time to keep them fresh, plan ahead for that now."

Once she's sure we're all on board with our Spirit Week tasks, Trina turns to me. "I meant to ask, Molly, did you really go on a date with Alan Dempsey last night? Tiffany said she saw you two together at the Lighthouse and I noticed you sat at his table the last two days."

"Um, yeah, sort of," I hedge. "I mean, it wasn't really a date so much as we found out we're both trivia fans, so we agreed to go compete against each other. I won."

"Is that why you're not sitting with him today?" Amber asks, looking over at his table. "Was he a sore loser?"

A laugh escapes me. "Yeah, you could say that."

"You should have let him win," Trina admonishes me. "You always need to let boys win, they have such fragile egos. Remember that if he asks you out again."

"Right. I will. Thanks, Trina."

✦

"Now that everyone's handed in their reports on the electoral process, we'll be turning our attention to significant Supreme Court cases," the teacher says at the start of Government class.

"For this project you can work in groups of two to four because I expect you to really dig into whichever case you choose. You'll identify the key issues, research precedents and analyze the decision, including any dissents. Then I want you to decide as a group whether you believe your chosen case was decided rightly or wrongly and explain why. At the end of the grading period you'll each turn in an individual report as well as a team report that will include how your discussions evolve as you learn more about the case.

"Go ahead and sort yourselves into groups. I'll come around to check they're well balanced so no one's at risk of doing more—or less—than their fair share of the work. Then you'll spend the rest of the period deciding on a court case to tackle. By the end of class I'd like you to submit that case to me for approval."

I glance over at M. She and I were partners for our first project, on the Constitution, but that was only because Rigel didn't have his memory back yet. The two of them paired up for the last one and prob-

122

ably will again. Ditto Sean and Kira. I don't particularly fancy being a third wheel with either couple.

Two rows up, Bri and Deb are already inviting Caitlin, my partner from last time, to join them. I'm about to ask if they can use one more team member when I feel a tap on my shoulder.

I freeze for a second, then turn to see Alan standing there, looking contrite. I experience an unexpected rush of disappointment followed immediately by relief. Because I absolutely did *not* want it to be Tristan standing there. At all.

"Hey, Molly. I really am sorry about last night. Give me a chance to make it up to you by doing this project together?"

"Oh, um, sure," I reply, despite my surprise. Last night, I didn't get the impression he enjoyed himself any more than I did.

Together we head to the back of the room, where he usually sits. On the way we pass Tristan, who's trying to diplomatically discourage two *Duchas* girls vying to be his partner. I suppress a smirk, thinking he's lucky Trina's not in this class. Janie and Rachel are both nice, at least.

"So, what do you think?" Alan says as we reach his desk, yanking my thoughts back. "Should we pick some case that might eventually have a bearing on *our* people's future here?" He grins and I notice his dimple again.

"What, like Korematsu?" I really *should* give Alan another chance.

He frowns uncertainly. "Um, I'm not sure I'm familiar with that one."

I know the newcomers all received overviews to help them fit in but it makes sense they didn't have time to dig very deeply into specifics. I wouldn't know most of this stuff myself if M hadn't helped me so much with U.S. History last year.

Quietly, since most seniors would know this, I brief him on the case that legitimized the internment of Japanese citizens during World War II. Not surprisingly, Alan looks horrified. I'm still explaining the little I know about what led up to the case when there's a throat-clearing at my elbow.

This time it *is* Tristan.

"Um, I really hate to do this, but the teacher suggested that the three of us work together because Alan and I are new to the class and Molly did such a good job on the last two projects. I don't think she'll insist if you'd rather not, though."

His expression makes it obvious he hopes we'll say no. I'm trying to come up with a diplomatic way to do just that when Alan speaks up.

"Sure you can join us, that'll be great!" *His* expression is distinctly admiring and I remembered how reverently Alan spoke about M and my parents. And even Sean, a wee bit. It's clear he's bought into the whole superiority-of-Royals thing.

If I veto Alan's agreement now, I'll sound every bit as rude as Connor was to me Monday night. "If you want, yeah. Fine with me."

"Thanks." Tristan doesn't sound grateful, though. He takes a desk on Alan's other side, well away from me. "Have you started discussing what case to cover?"

"Molly was just telling me about the—what was it? Korematsu? The one about the Japanese internment camps."

Tristan shoots a glance at me, then quickly looks away. "I've heard of it, but don't remember many details. It was pretty controversial, right?"

Because it's apparent I know more about the case than either of them, I reluctantly give them an overview while avoiding Tristan's eye.

Alan seems impressed. "You must have studied that case before, huh?"

"Not in school. But my mum and dad have brought it up when talking about the risks of letting the *Duchas* know too much about us too soon. That made me curious enough to look it up online," I explain in a whisper. Then, more loudly, "Why don't we all do some research on it tonight and compare notes tomorrow? Then we can decide how to split up the work and stuff."

They both agree to that—Tristan still not meeting my gaze.

Then Alan mentions basketball tryouts next week. "I figured I might as well go out for the team. You should, too," he tells Tristan, who shrugs.

"Football's always been my sport. Stuart says I should talk to the coach this week about practicing with them before the season ends."

I'm not the sports nut Bri is, so rather than listen to that discussion, I offer to go tell the teacher what case we want to work on. That also gives me an excuse to get away from Tristan briefly.

Ms. Kowalski readily approves our choice and thanks me for my willingness to help both boys. "Even though this is a new unit, some things we've already covered will be helpful. I was so impressed by the project you and Marsha did on the Constitution, I feel sure you can bring them both up to speed."

I assure her I'll do my best and go back to discover they're no longer talking sports, exactly.

"—O'Gara?" Tristan is saying, his back to me. "I mean, he seems like a nice enough guy but he's definitely made choices I don't agree with."

"Yeah, no kidding," Alan replies quietly. "You should hear my parents on that subject. They can't believe he—" He sees me and breaks off, his ears reddening. "Oh, um, hey. Teacher okay with our topic?"

Tristan turns toward me, too, also looking slightly guilty.

"She's fine with it," I snap. "So, what were you two saying about—?" The bell rings before I can tell them off properly, so I just shoot them both a dirty look, gather up my stuff and storm off to Psych class.

Still pissed that he and Alan were bad-mouthing Sean behind my back, I abruptly decide I've had enough of dancing around the stupid touch issue. When Tristan again aims for a desk well away from me, I walk over to him before he can sit down.

"Don't you think this is getting a little silly?" I hiss. "We're partners in Chemistry and now Government, so it's not like we can completely ignore each other, much as we both might want to. I get why you were freaked yesterday. So was I. Not only are we in completely different *fines*, we don't even like each other. But it was still just a *taghal ardus*. First touch. It shouldn't happen again, so we both just need to get over it."

As I talk, his initial surprise shifts to embarrassment, then irritation.

"Easy for you to say," he growls. "I'll bet *you* were secretly thrilled to get such a strong resonance from someone like me. You can't even imagine how I feel."

My palm itches to smack that condescending look off his face. "I'm every bit as disgusted as you are, believe me," I snarl back. "Why would anyone be thrilled to have *any* kind of resonance with a jerk like you?"

His jaw tightens. "Wow, you don't mince words, do you?"

"Not if I can help it. Being upfront about things generally avoids misunderstandings later. Maybe you should try it sometime." I return to my desk without a backward glance.

✦

WE'RE JUST FINISHING dinner that evening when my phone rings. Since our family has a no-tech-at-the-table rule, I excuse myself to go answer it. It's M.

"Hi, Molly. I don't suppose you have Tristan's cell number?"

"What? No!" I try not to let my voice betray my sudden panic. How did she—? "Why…why would you think I have his number?"

"Since you're partners in Chemistry and now that Government project, I thought he might have given it to you."

Oh. Whew. "No, sorry. Why do you need it?"

Now an edge creeps into her voice. "You won't believe this, but Connor stopped by the florist shop earlier and convinced Aunt Theresa that it would be perfectly wonderful for me to meet Tristan at Dream Cream this evening to study. She *just* this minute told me."

"But…aren't you supposed to go to Rigel's house tonight, to meet with those Scientists? Sean said at dinner that he and Kira planned to join you there soon."

"That's right. They need to ask Kira about the tech stuff Allister and Lennox had in Dun Cloch and Kyna wants every detail of what they said and did while they were projecting their holograms into Jewel. But Aunt Theresa apparently forgot all about that when Connor used his Royal 'push' on her—even though I *told* her not to agree to anything like this without checking with me. So now I need to tell Tristan I'm canceling."

My fury at him from earlier today surges back. "Those two have no business using their charm or whatever to convince your aunt to go along with their little game. They—"

"I know. It's *totally* inappropriate and I plan to say so at this week's Council meeting. Tristan's probably already on his way there, so I guess I'll call Connor instead and he can relay the message to Tristan. While I'm at it, I can tell Connor exactly what I think of their underhanded tactics. Rigel will be here any second to pick me up, but I can call from the car."

"Won't that make Rigel even more likely to pick a fight with Tristan? Besides, I don't see why you should bother calling either one of them. It'll serve Tristan right if he ends up sitting by himself at Dream Cream all evening. Or—" I break off as an idea hits me. "Tell you what, why don't you let *me* handle it, M? This should be your Handmaid's job, anyway."

There's a startled pause at her end. "Are you sure? What if— Oops, Rigel just pulled up."

"Go to your meeting—that's way more important than this. You can trust me to take care of Tristan. I'm not as nice as you. I'll make *sure* he understands how badly he and his dad screwed up. Then tomorrow I'll tell you all about it."

She laughs. "Deal. You're the best, Molly. Thanks." She hangs up.

I get back to the kitchen just as Sean's leaving to pick up Kira. When M mentioned tonight's meeting earlier today, I felt a little left out. Also guilty, because I *should* have been there for the events they'll be talking about. But now I can do something way more useful than tagging along for no good reason.

"Mum, Dad, is it okay if I go to Dream Cream to meet some friends?" I ask as soon as Sean's gone. "My homework is done."

They're both fine with it and, lucky for me, Mum doesn't ask which friends I'm meeting. Though if she did, I could just tell her the truth. I'm sure she'd approve of me going to tell Tristan off.

A few minutes later I'm heading toward Diamond Street for the second time in two nights. As I walk, I plan out what I'll say to Tristan when I get there, a grim smile on my face.

16

Intensive property

Tristan

"I STILL CAN'T BELIEVE you did this behind my back," I tell my father as he turns onto Diamond Street. "The Sovereign probably won't even show up."

He gives me a quelling glance. "Theresa Truitt assured me she would instruct her adopted niece to be there. By all accounts, the Sovereign still obeys her *Duchas* guardians unless doing so would conflict with her duties. As you seem reluctant to press your suit with her, I've no choice but to take steps myself to move matters along."

"I only met her last week," I remind him. "I thought we agreed I could take my time, try to win her trust first? This isn't going to help."

"Of course it will help, unless you botch things again. I've simply arranged for you to spend an hour or two alone with her, something you have failed to accomplish on your own so far. I expect you to put the time to good use."

He pulls up in front of Jewel's little ice cream shop. "Call me when you're ready to be picked up—though you should offer to walk her home first. That will give you extra time together and another opportunity to ingratiate yourself with her *Duchas* guardians. I'll retrieve you from her house."

That was the reason he gave for refusing to let me drive myself—though I suspect he knew I'd be tempted to bail completely if he gave me the chance.

FIFTEEN MINUTES later I'm sitting in a back corner booth at Dream Cream nursing a watery soda, still fuming as I watch the door. The Sovereign was just starting to let down her guard around me at school. Now, even if she shows up, she'll almost certainly be upset about Father's scheming to get her here. I need to convince her I had nothing to do with this plan if I don't want to lose what little trust I've established so far.

Two *Duchas* girls come in to buy ice cream. One glances my way, nudges the other and they both start giggling. I watch them warily until they finish their purchases and leave. At least they didn't ask to sit with me, like the last pair of girls did. I told them I'm waiting for someone so they sat at another table instead. They're still here, which means I'll look like a total schmuck if M never shows.

After another five minutes crawl by, I'm ready to give up and call Father. Then the door opens again. Crap!

I figured the Sovereign would be in a bad mood when she got here, but this is worse. Way worse. The person who just walked in is Molly O'Gara—the very *last* person I want to see—and I can tell at a glance she's a whole lot madder than M would have been.

"Hey there, loverboy," she says sarcastically, sliding into the seat across from me. "Sorry your *date* couldn't make it." Then, leaning forward, she hisses, "What were you and your father thinking, using Mrs. Truitt to set up a private meeting with M? Connor will be lucky if the Council doesn't censure him for this."

I was ready to be honest with M, explain that this whole setup was Father's idea. But there's no way I'll make him look bad—or make myself look like a tool—to this uppity Ag.

"Is it some kind of crime to make friends with her guardians? I thought we were supposed to be trying to fit in with the *Duchas* in Jewel." I whisper too since there are so many interested people—mostly girls—nearby.

Molly's glare could freeze volcanic lava. "Make *friends*? Seriously? You know *dabhal* well he used Royal 'push' to force Mrs. Truitt to go along with your plan and tell M to come here. If that's not illegal, it should be."

I glare back. "Oh, so now none of us are allowed to use our natural abilities around the *Duchas*? What about Stuart playing football...or your step-brother playing basketball? I'm sure *they're* not using any *Echtran* superiority to win all those games."

"That's different. That's sports—and they both hold back a lot so they won't make the locals suspicious. The stuff some of you Royals do is—" She pauses and glances toward the nearest group of girls, who are blatantly trying to listen in. "Never mind. This isn't the best place for this conversation."

I'm not willing to leave it at that, though. Especially after what she said to me earlier today.

"You're right. Let's get out of here so I can tell you what I *really* think about your interference...Ag."

"Fine." With a fluid motion, she surges to her feet and heads for the door. Abandoning my half-finished soda, I clamber out of the booth and follow.

"Hey, Tristan," a girl calls out as I pass—from my Lit class, I think. "Wouldn't you like to—?"

"Not now, sorry." I'm not letting *anything* distract me from finally putting Molly O'Gara in her place.

There are people on the sidewalk outside when I catch up to her, too many for me to speak as freely as I want to. Molly seems irked by that, too. With a withering look that dares me to follow, she heads down Diamond Street toward the end where most of the businesses are already closed.

The moment we're out of earshot from the nearest *Duchas*, I demand, "What did you start to say back there? And where do *you* get off criticizing Royals? Just because you were raised by them doesn't give you the right—"

"Oh, cut the crap." She walks faster, clearly agitated. "If you think Royals are too perfect to criticize, you must not know as much about them as I do."

My legs are longer so I easily keep up with her. "In case you haven't noticed, I happen to *be* Royal. So are my parents."

She snorts, almost but not quite a laugh. "You realize you're only proving my point, right? Though I guess your mum seems nice enough. But other than M and my own family, she's the only nice one I've ever met."

"*Nice*? That's your standard for who's worthy of respect? How about dedication to a better future? My father may not be the *nicest* guy you'll meet but he absolutely wants what's best for our people."

She stops so abruptly I almost run into her when she whirls to face me. We're way down Diamond now, with no one else around.

"What's *best*? I'm sure he does, if you mean what's best for himself and other Royals like you. He's willing to do whatever it takes to ensure that, even if it means ignoring Nuathan laws and endangering every single person on Mars and Earth. In case you don't know it, that's *exactly* what some of the things he's voted for have done."

"You have no idea what you're talking about! The Sovereign is the one who put our people's future at risk when she hooked up with a cross-*fine* nobody instead of her proper Consort. Then your family made things even worse by letting Sean abdicate *his* responsibility, instead of fighting to maintain the Sovereign bloodline and dignity for future generations. I won't even start on what a traitor Stuart is, refusing to step aside even though he has to know most of our people want him to."

She glares at me. "Gah! You are wrong on *so* many counts!"

"Am I? I don't think so."

We're right up in each other's faces now. Her gray eyes catch the light from a distant streetlamp and practically throw off sparks, she's so angry.

"Yes, you are!" she practically shouts. "I swear, you Royals are all alike. Putting bloodlines and *dignity*—whatever *that* is—ahead of people's actual lives! Even my parents and Sean used to spout that garbage, though they mostly know better now. The only Royal I've ever met who has *never* put power and prestige above what's right is M."

I bark out a sarcastic laugh. "M? The Sovereign is the *ultimate* Royal! She has more power and prestige than anyone. And what has she used it for? To ignore the Council and elevate her mongrel boyfriend to a position he can't possibly be prepared for."

"She may be the top Royal genetically, but she has an even lower opinion of Royals in general than I do—and for good reason. If the Council Royals had their way, she and Rigel would probably both be dead, along with half the people on Earth and *everyone* on Mars."

Her cheeks are flushed, her breathing fast as she thrusts her chin forward until only inches separate us.

I want to tell her she's crazy but for some reason the only thing I can force out is, "Yeah?"

"Yeah. Royals have betrayed her at every turn, ever since she found out who she was. So if you think you'll *ever* convince her to leave Rigel for you just because of your stupid *fine*, you're—"

Goaded past endurance, I shut her up in the most efficient way possible. Grabbing her by both shoulders, I yank her toward me and press my mouth against hers.

And my world explodes.

17

Sublimation

Molly

I'M beyond furious at Tristan, so mad I could *strangle* him. Right now he seems to embody every awful thing any Royal has ever done, or tried to do, to M or anyone else. The words tumble out of me, my anger mounting to critical mass until he suddenly silences me in mid-tirade.

With a kiss.

Outraged, I start to shove him away when my fury is suddenly swamped by wonder. Of their own volition, my palms slide from his chest up to his shoulders as a thousand unexpected sensations cascade through me, sensations I've never even imagined. Ecstasy, exultation, energy and a powerful conviction that I could fly if I wanted to. Nothing I've ever experienced has been this glorious.

Or appalling.

After several euphoric seconds we both jolt to our senses, springing apart to stare at each other. Tristan looks as horrified as I am.

"I didn't— I can't—" he starts to stammer.

I shake my head violently, both to stop his words and to clear my thoughts, which are still in chaos. "No! Don't say anything. It…it never happened, okay?"

He frowns, then nods. "Right. You're right. There's no…I mean…can you get home okay from here?"

"What?" I glance around. I barely registered where we were before now, I was so angry. Just a couple of blocks past Opal, near the arboretum. "Oh. Um, sure. I'm most of the way there already. Well, er…bye."

"Bye." He still looks as stunned as I am by what just happened. That thing neither of us is ever going to mention to another soul. Or even think about again.

Feeling a sudden need to put maximum distance between us, I turn and head toward Opal Street, walking faster and faster until I'm jogging. Not until I round the corner do I glance back, almost against my will. Tristan is still standing where I left him, motionless. Maybe in shock.

And no wonder. Because that was— Nope. Not going to think about it. Never happened. After another block I slow to a brisk walk, firmly repeating those words to myself over and over until I get home.

⁺₊

WHEN THE ALARM on my phone goes off the next morning I jerk awake, shoving away the remnants of a vivid dream in which Tristan figured prominently.

"Never happened," I say aloud to my empty room.

Forcefully reminding myself that Tristan is an arrogant jerk I don't even *like*, I grab my toiletry bag and go see if the bathroom is free. With all four of us sharing the one, mornings sometimes get tricky. Luckily, Sean's just leaving it when I step out of my room.

"Morning," he says. "When did you get in last night? I didn't see you when I came home but I didn't want to risk getting you in trouble by asking Mum and Dad."

"Oh, pretty early, actually." I sternly order my color not to rise. "I just met some friends at Dream Cream for a shake after dinner, then came home. I was tired, so I went to bed early."

That's the excuse I gave Mum and Dad last night when I got home, not trusting myself to act normal around them—especially if they asked who I'd been with. Then I went to my room and spent two whole hours reciting an ancient Nuathan meditation, doing everything I could to suppress any memories of my evening.

"I must have been asleep when you got in," I tell Sean now. "How was the thing at Rigel's?"

"Went kind of late. The Scientists kept coming up with more questions to ask Kira, then grilled the rest of us about that final showdown with Uncle Allister and Lennox. Their holograms, I mean. None of us knew enough technical stuff to be much help, but maybe they'll be able to use some of what we remembered. Hope so."

"This is to track down where that antimatter came from?"

He nods. "Kyna's worried there could be more out there and I don't blame her. A bit the size of my pinky fingernail could blow all of Jewel right off the map."

I shudder. "That sounds—"

"Are you both done in there?" Mum interrupts from the other end of the hallway.

"Oops, sorry, Mum. I was just about to go in, but you can go first if you need to."

"No, go on with you. I don't want to make you late for school."

Nodding, I duck into the bathroom and shut the door, hoping my expression didn't betray how my stomach clenched at the word "school."

Where I'll have to face Tristan again and pretend we didn't...I didn't...

"Never happened," I tell my reflection above the sink before splashing my face with cold water.

M IS ALREADY at the bus stop when Sean and I get there. He's recently started taking the bus again instead of riding to school with Pete so he and Kira can spend that extra time together, since neither one has a car. After saying hi to him, M pulls me off to the side.

"So?" she whispers. "How did things go at Dream Cream last night with Tristan? You never answered my text last night."

"Oh, um, yeah, I went to bed early." Might as well keep my story consistent. "I didn't see your text till this morning and figured I'd be seeing you soon anyway. He wasn't too happy when I showed up in your place. Especially when I told him you weren't coming—along with a few other choice things. He, um, didn't hang around after that so I went home, too."

She frowns at me curiously, like she can tell I'm hiding something. Lucky for me, the two *Duchas* sophomores who share our bus stop show up before she can quiz me further. I try not to let my relief show. M may not have Mum's lie-detector gift, but she knows me so well I doubt I can fool her for long.

Once we're on the bus, I whisper question after question about last night's meeting until Bri and Deb join us a few stops later. They're both brimming with gossip about Heather dumping Gary because she caught him flirting with Amber, which keeps M's attention off me for the rest of the ride.

Tristan isn't in Pre-Cal yet when I get there, which briefly delays the inevitable. I go to my usual desk next to M, assuming—hoping—he'll decide to sit in the back corner again.

I'm unprepared for the way my heart speeds up the second he walks in. I have to take several slow, deep breaths to bring it under control. I've nearly managed it when, instead of heading to the back of the room like I expect, he moves to the desk next to me. The same place he's sat every day, until that crazy touch on Tuesday.

Which, I suddenly realize, is exactly what he *would* do if last night—and that touch—never happened. He doesn't say anything to me as he sits down, but he never has before, either. He really is acting like nothing has changed.

Because it hasn't, I remind myself. Definitely not in any way that matters.

Last night was an aberration—some bizarre misfiring of emotions because of how furious we were with each other. An aberration I'm *not* thinking about today. At all. Not today, not ever. Never happened.

To demonstrate how very *un*affected I am by Tristan's proximity, I turn toward M, planning to say something completely inconsequential about class. Except she and Rigel now have their heads together, whispering. Continuing to take slow, deep breaths—*very* quietly—I instead pull out last night's homework and spend the few minutes until class starts checking it over for the fourth time.

When the bell rings at the end of class, Tristan steps past me like I don't exist to talk to M, the same as he did his first day here. Trusting Rigel to run interference if necessary, I cravenly make my escape.

I know it's only a brief respite, since Tristan is in my next two classes, but I need it. Having him next to me for the better part of an hour did really strange things to my heart rate and breathing and I have *got* to find a way to control that before he gets anywhere near me again.

In French he also moves back to his original desk, much closer to mine than where he sat yesterday. Though we persist in ignoring each other, I can't seem to quell the fluttery something still happening in my belly. I chat with M and Kira before class starts but have a hard time concentrating on what either one of them says.

During class, I have an even harder time focusing on the lesson than I did yesterday. Next period will be Chemistry and I'm not at all confident of my ability to keep up the pretense that Tristan doesn't affect me at all. He seems to be doing just fine in that department, which makes my own lack of discipline downright embarrassing.

Tristan again hangs back to chat with M after the bell rings. Because Rigel's not here, I muster enough courage to take my time putting my book in my backpack rather than risk leaving them alone. I still don't look at him, but my other senses are so attuned that I know the moment he leaves for Chemistry.

Which will be our biggest test yet. Mine, anyway.

No matter how many times I tell myself last night never happened and doesn't matter, I still keep obsessing about it. I'm really starting to resent Tristan's superior self-control. Maybe it's yet another Royal ability? Or maybe he really *has* been able to completely put it from his mind.

It occurs to me that a short-term memory wipe, like the one Rigel had, might not be such a terrible thing after all…

Trina is thoroughly monopolizing Tristan when I get to Chemistry, so I go straight to my seat instead of stopping by M's table like I did yesterday. To be honest, I'm a little leery of talking *too* much with M before I can get my emotions under control. Lately I've started wondering if "emotion-sensing" is some new ability she's developing. That would be really useful for her as Sovereign but could definitely get awkward for *me* sometimes. Like now.

When Tristan sits down next to me, we each continue to behave as if the other doesn't exist. Unfortunately, Mr. Abbot's first words threaten our mutual pact of denial.

"Today you'll be working with your partners to observe and record precipitation reactions. Using the reaction plates you'll find on each table, I want you to take turns adding each labeled solution from set A to each solution from set B while your partner writes down the results. This will likely take most of the period, so I recommend you get started."

I steal a glance at Tristan and catch him doing the same thing. We both quickly look away. After a long, awkward pause, I finally clear my throat.

"I'll, um take the first one, okay?"

"Um, sure. Okay."

I use a pipette to add a few drops of potassium carbonate to the silver nitrate in the first little well, then stir the mixture with a toothpick until a solid forms. Without looking at me, Tristan writes down the result. Then he adds ammonium sulfate to the next well containing silver nitrate and I jot down his result.

We make our way down the list, talking only the absolute minimum required by the exercise and being super careful to never brush fingers when we push the sheet with our results back and forth.

Twice my control slips and I peek his way. Both times, I catch him hastily averting his own eyes. Hm. Maybe he *hasn't* been able to totally forget last night? The thought is both reassuring and worrisome.

Well before the bell rings, we finish the exercise, thankfully without any accidental touching. I sense his relief is as strong as my own when he records the very last result.

"Um, good job," he mumbles, rinsing off the reaction plate. Probably because silence would be even more awkward at this point.

"You, too," I mumble back, putting all the used pipettes into the discard beaker.

Then we just sit there, side by side, not saying anything else. If he sneaks any more looks at me, I don't know it—because I actually manage not to do that myself.

Finally the bell rings and we can leave. My fourth period break from Tristan is a blessed relief, a chance to finally get a grip and purge last night's bizarre incident from my memory once and for all.

While pretending to outline my next short story, I remind myself over and over how much I *dis*like Tristan, and why. To that end, I make a list of his worst attributes—like arrogance, prejudice and a sense of entitlement—then tuck the paper into my binder for future reference. Not that I should need it. I hope.

The moment I get to the cafeteria, it's obvious Trina is On A Mission, already talking animatedly to Alan as I get into the lunch line. She finishes by giving him a big smile and a thumbs-up, then hurries over to Tristan, who just left the cashier. By now I'm close enough to listen in.

"—really need tall guys like you to help us hang the banners and stuff. Please say you will?"

He looks skeptical but shrugs and nods. "Sure, I guess so."

"Awesome! Thank you *so* much, Tristan, I knew I could count on you! Meet us in the gym at ten o'clock Saturday morning. The squad should already have everything ready to go by then." Directing a last flirtatious simper his way, she skips over to where Amber and I are nearly through the line.

"Guys! I've lined up some of the cutest guys in school to help us Saturday. Won't that make decorating the school *so* much more fun?"

We both agree, Amber enthusiastically. I'm tempted to ask who else she's talked to. Hopefully a bunch of people, which will make things *marginally* less awkward. I use our upcoming Spirit Week planning as an excuse to sit with the other cheerleaders again today.

"So, Molly," Trina says as I set down my tray, "in Lit class, Jillian said she saw you and Tristan at Dream Cream last night? She said it looked like you were arguing."

"Oh, um, right. I ran into him by chance. He made a snarky crack about Sean and I sort of let him have it." I'm sure my color has risen but Trina doesn't seem to notice.

"Yeah, I've noticed you two don't seem to get along very well. Which is fine, of course. Different tastes and all that."

With a smug little smile, she turns to the other cheerleaders joining us to boast about the boys she's cajoled into helping us decorate on Saturday. They all seem as pleased as Amber was. Then Trina starts discussing her purchases so far.

"Black and gold—okay, orange—crepe paper was on sale because of Halloween, so I bought *tons* of it. We'll have *so* many streamers! And Amber, I found these cute black cat stickers you can use for the lockers. We'll just tell everyone they're Jaguars."

She goes on and on but I mostly tune her out. Obsessing again about that thing that didn't happen.

If Alan notices he's carrying most of the conversation about our Korematsu project in Government class, he doesn't point it out. Neither Tristan nor I say very much, though every now and then one of us weighs in when Alan misses an obvious angle we should cover in our reports. I'm surprised to discover Tristan apparently made more of an effort to study up on the case last night than Alan did. Though to be fair, he'd at least heard of it before yesterday, so he wouldn't have needed as much research.

Still, I wonder if he did that studying before or after going to Dream

Cream? Not that it matters. Except that if he did it afterward, he definitely had a lot more luck distracting himself from what happened than I did.

Gah! I am *so* failing at this whole "didn't happen" thing! Must. Try. Harder.

"We should probably look for old newspaper clips from before the decision went down," I force myself to say, to shift my train of thought. "That would give us a better feel for what public sentiment was like at the time."

Both boys agree that's a good idea and Tristan volunteers to hunt online for some before tomorrow. Alan then starts making a list of who's volunteered to do what, again doing all the talking while Tristan and I take turns shooting furtive glances at each other.

We're all packing up our notes at the end of class when Alan suddenly turns to me, his ears a little pinker than usual.

"Hey, uh, Molly, I was wondering if maybe you'd like me to come by this evening and take another look at your plants? The ones we didn't have time to work with on Saturday, I mean. If, um, you're not busy doing something else, that is?"

It's clearly a peace offering, signaling his willingness to try again. As for me, I'm willing to do just about anything to keep my mind off of Tristan and that crazy kiss. I have *got* to stop obsessing about something that didn't—okay, shouldn't have—happened.

"Sure, that would be grand," I reply without hesitation.

"Great! Say seven-thirtyish, after dinner?"

I nod with only slightly forced enthusiasm. "Perfect!"

From the corner of my eye I catch a hint of a frown on Tristan's brow, but then it's gone. I probably imagined it. Or maybe Alan's comment reminded him even more forcefully that I'm just an Ag, like Alan, and not someone Tristan could ever consider getting serious about? Not that I'd ever *want* him to.

Would I?

18

Physical chemistry

Tristan

ACTING normal around Molly today is even harder than I expect—and I knew it wouldn't be easy. Not after the way my whole world got knocked off its axis last night. And especially not after those dreams I had, reliving that kiss...and more. Now every time I look at her I still feel an echo of that soaring, swooping sensation that swept through me when my lips first touched hers.

Which has me looking at her way more often than I should.

I didn't argue when she declared that kiss never happened...right after it *did*. Because it absolutely *shouldn't* have. Giving into that sudden impulse was hands-down the dumbest thing I've ever done. Something I should *want* to forget. Because that kiss was wrong, wrong, *wrong* on every possible level.

So...why did it feel so right?

After she walked away from me last night I tried, *really* tried, to forget about it, just like she planned to do. I sure as hell didn't mention it when Father picked me up. I just told him the Sovereign never showed —which was true.

I let him assume my silence on the way home was because I was still pissed about his stupid, failed plan. In reality, I was mentally reciting the periodic table of elements in an effort to avoid replaying the life-changing moment I'd just experienced.

No! *Not* life-changing. I can't afford to let one stupid mistake change who I am or what I need to do. Nope, Molly was right. We just have to convince ourselves it never happened. Forget it completely. Except...I can't.

Still, I'm doing my best to *pretend* I have, trying to act exactly like I did last week when I first got here. The difference is, last week Molly got right in my face every time I got too close to the Sovereign. Today, not so much. Instead, she's acting like I don't exist—or like we've never even met.

She's obviously way more determined than I am to forget what happened last night. And doing a better job of it, too, which is humiliating.

Chemistry is the worst. The whole time we're doing the lab together I'm dying to know what Molly's *really* thinking. Is she as crazy-aware of me as I am of her? I doubt it. She's maybe a little quieter than usual, but otherwise normal. Like she really *has* managed to put last night from her mind.

All through lunch and Government I tell myself I'm glad about that. But then Alan Dempsey comes on to her at the end of class and I feel a seriously strong urge to punch him. Not that I let on.

Molly is just ahead of me in the hallway on the way to sixth period. I'm guiltily admiring her walk from behind when it suddenly hits me her whole ignoring-reality plan is the exact opposite of what she said to me yesterday in Psych class. On that thought, I lengthen my stride and catch up with her in two steps.

"Hey, weren't you the one who told me I should try being upfront about things? The one who said it was silly for us to ignore each other?"

She looks up at me, startled, those sparkling gray eyes that haunted my dreams all night going wide. "I, um, yeah. I guess I did. So?"

"So isn't that exactly what we're doing now? I'll admit denying reality sounded like a great idea when you suggested it last night. But maybe it's not the best approach to our...problem."

One dark eyebrow arches skeptically. "Then what is?" If she's finding this as difficult as I am, she doesn't let it show. Probably she's not.

"What you said yesterday. Be upfront about it. Talk things through." Except I already want to do more than talk with her. "You were right that we can't exactly avoid each other, especially in Chemistry and Government."

Unless she drops me from the Korematsu team so she can just be Alan's partner. I don't add that.

"You're right." She manages a crooked grin. "Or rather, *I* was. So I guess I shouldn't ignore my own advice."

"Not when it's *good* advice. Last night, well… I'm not sure either of us were thinking too clearly. So maybe *that* advice wasn't quite so spot on?"

Her cheeks go pink but she nods. "Yeah, maybe not. We probably should talk this through if we really want things to go back to normal." She doesn't say it like a question, but there seems to be one in her eyes.

One I'm not prepared to answer. Not yet, anyway.

"It's settled, then." I try for a matter-of-fact tone. "We'll talk it through. Figure things out. That should make it easier to, um, move forward." I'm just not sure which direction I want that to be.

When we get to class, I take my original desk next to Molly instead of sitting in the corner like I did the past two days. Then spend the next forty-five minutes trying to focus on the lesson instead of the way-too-interesting things her nearness does to me, mentally, physically and emotionally.

It doesn't help that we're studying the sympathetic nervous system and how any sudden stress can automatically increase heart rate and stimulate a fight or flight…or kiss?…response. By the end of class I'm mostly convinced last night was just some anomaly caused by how angry Molly made me. Something that probably won't—and definitely shouldn't—ever happen again.

That conclusion ought to make me feel better. Weird that it doesn't.

"So, when would be a good time to, y'know, talk?" I ask as we put our books in our backpacks after the bell.

She sucks in a quick breath and glances at me, then away. "I, uh, have Chorus next period, then cheerleading practice after that. Trina will kill me if I skip, what with Spirit Week next week. Maybe afterward? Or do you have to go out to NuAgra?"

"I don't have to go every day."

Or at all, really, since Father still hasn't bothered to give me any kind of internship schedule like the others have. He just wants regular reports on my progress with the Sovereign—which I'd rather not give him today anyway.

"This afternoon, then?" She looks like she's trying to read my thoughts.

Supposedly that's something the Sovereign and Stuart can do with each other. It now strikes me as the most embarrassing thing ever. Between that and getting sick when they're apart, it sounds like *graell* bonds are a lot more trouble than they're worth. Not that that's what's going on *here*, of course. At most, it's just a temporary crush. From a one-time sympathetic nervous system reaction.

"Yeah, this afternoon's good," I tell her. "See you then."

With a smile as awkward as I feel right now, I head off to the media center for seventh period. There, away from Molly's disturbing influence, I actually get some homework done.

⁺₊

AFTER THE FINAL bell I head to the football stadium. Even though Molly won't be free for at least an hour and a half, I can use this opportunity to talk to the coach about next season, something I've been meaning to do anyway.

The team's already warming up when I get there but there's no sign of the cheerleaders. Maybe they practice in the gym? Ours in Denver sometimes did, especially if the weather was bad. Though today it's just a little chilly, not—

"Hey, Tristan!"

It's Stuart, motioning me toward the field. Dropping my backpack at the bottom of the bleachers, I trot over to him.

"I told Coach you might be coming by this week, after what you said at lunch the other day. I'll let him know you're here. He's going to get us started on drills in a minute, but then he'll probably want to talk to you. Wait here."

He runs to the middle of the field, where most of the players are already gathered in a loose circle around the head coach. I just stand there, feeling awkward and out of place—something I've never felt on a football field before. As I watch, the coach outlines his plans for today's practice.

Even from thirty yards away I can hear most of what he says with my enhanced *Echtran* senses. It sounds reassuringly familiar: strengths and weaknesses of their next opponent, areas our team needs to focus on, assigning various players their different drills. Listening, I start to relax, back in my element…until the cheerleaders suddenly exit the gym and come jogging out to the track.

With a squeal, Trina runs up to me. "Tristan!" She grabs my arm possessively. "You sounded like you weren't going to come but I just *knew* you couldn't stay away."

"I, uh, actually came to talk to the coach but thought I'd stay to watch practice, too. Football practice, I mean." I need to discourage her enough she won't hang around later, so I can talk to Molly in private.

She doesn't take the hint. "Maybe after practice we can do something together? I've got my car here and my parents are never home before six…"

"Sorry, I can't. I've got a thing. Probably won't even stay for the whole practice." If I have to leave and come back to shake her off, that's what I'll do.

"Are you sure?" She gives me what I'm sure she considers a cute little pout. I mostly find it irritating.

"Yeah, sorry. So…shouldn't you be practicing?"

Now she slants a flirty look up at me. "I thought you only wanted to watch football? I guarantee you'll find *me* way more worth watching."

With a wink, she runs back to the other cheerleaders, already assembled on the track. Molly is showing another girl some complicated dance move, looking disturbingly appealing in a long-sleeved tee and curve-hugging leggings. I drag my gaze away with an effort and see Coach Glazier heading my way.

"Hello there, son," he says, extending a hand. "Stuart tells me you quarterbacked for Rocky Ridge High in Denver?"

I shake his hand. "That's right, sir. I hated to leave mid-season. I figured I'd try out for next year here at Jewel."

He regards me speculatively from under his bushy eyebrows. "You have experience at any other position? As you've probably seen, I've already got a stellar QB."

"I played wide receiver my freshman year," I admit. "I'm, uh, pretty fast."

That earns me a smile and a nod. "We could sure use another decent receiver, especially since our best one's a senior. Think you can come by one day next week to let me see what you've got? Never too soon to look ahead to next season."

We agree I'll attend Monday's practice, then he stalks back across the field to supervise the next drill, leaving me to wait until Molly's finished.

Not until I start climbing the bleachers do I notice the Sovereign is already sitting there—and then I remember Stuart asking her at lunch today if she'd be here. I even made a mental note at the time, thinking it might be a chance to catch her alone...and then totally spaced it. Since I'm here anyway, I may as well take advantage of the opportunity. Something I can report to Father as "progress."

M gives me a wary look when I come up and sit next to her, even though I don't try to sit *too* close.

"Gee, I'd think the Sovereign would have more important things to do than watch a football practice," I comment half-jokingly, to break the ice. Not completely joking, though, since Father often complains she's not focused enough on her duties.

The way she raises an eyebrow reminds me of Molly. "I have to do my homework somewhere." She holds up her Pre-Cal book. "And it helps Rigel if I come to practice occasionally so he can compensate better during the games."

"Compensate?" I have no idea what she's talking about.

"For the way our *graell* bond affects his playing. You know it enhances both of us, right?"

Oh, yeah. "Right. I, um, saw that in the report those Scientists put out."

"There you go, then. I'm sure your father has mentioned how careful we all need to be, since everyone agrees it's too soon to let the *Duchas* know about us. That means Rigel has to scale back how well he can play, especially when I'm nearby."

That does makes sense—though Father mentioned one game a few weeks ago, before we moved here, where Stuart's playing was so over-the-top good the Council worried the *Duchas* would be suspicious. Other than attracting the attention of some college recruiters, though, that apparently didn't happen.

"So, about last night," M says abruptly.

I freeze. Crap! How much did Molly tell her?

"Last night?" I'm amazed my voice doesn't crack. A rush of conflicting feelings flood through me at the reminder.

"I didn't want to say anything earlier, when other people were around," she continues, "but Connor had no business using my aunt to get to me. Even if I'd wanted to meet with you, I couldn't have. I already had something official scheduled."

I swallow and look away, my sudden panic partially subsiding. "Yeah. I, uh, told him going behind your back like that wasn't a good idea."

"No, it wasn't. You mean you didn't help him come up with that plan?"

I shake my head. "I didn't even know about it until Father presented it to me as a done deal, then insisted I play along."

She seems to decide I'm telling the truth—which I am—because she smiles. "Um, Molly sounded like she was kind of looking forward to telling you off when she offered to let you know I couldn't come. Since it was all your dad's idea, I hope she didn't give you too hard a time."

Yikes! What can I possibly say to that? "She...we...argued some, I guess."

She pins me with a speculative look. "Oh? She told me you weren't happy when she showed up but she didn't mention an actual argument. Who won?"

"I, um... I guess it was more or less a draw." I'm desperate to change the subject but I'm coming up blank.

"You shouldn't underestimate Molly, you know," she says, startling me again.

I involuntarily glance down at the track, where two other girls are hoisting Molly into the air like they're displaying her for my own personal benefit. Heart pounding, I turn back to the Sovereign and try to force my voice to sound casual.

"Oh? What do you mean?"

"She's the quickest thinker I know, for one thing. I've never seen her caught flat-footed when she needed a snappy comeback or a plausible excuse for something. I can't count the number of times she bailed me out at home, before my aunt and uncle knew the truth. She can also be incredibly tenacious—some might call it stubborn—when she knows she's right. And she's the most loyal friend anyone could ever ask for. The only person on this planet I trust more is Rigel. If you think you can discount her because she's 'just' an Ag, you're as clueless—and prejudiced—as your father is."

She obviously expects me to argue, but I'm too busy absorbing what she just told me. "I'll, um, try to keep that in mind," I finally manage to say.

"Do. And now, if you don't mind, I need to get some homework done." She pointedly turns away from me and opens her Pre-Cal book.

Which frees me to ogle Molly on the sidelines while pretending to watch football practice. When it looks like both practices are winding down, I say goodbye to the Sovereign and take the precaution of leaving the stands so Trina can't waylay me before I have a chance to talk to Molly.

Circling around behind the bleachers, I find a good vantage point to watch the field without being seen. While I wait, I try to figure out exactly what I want to say to Molly. Though deep down, I know the *safest* course would be to keep my distance from her until this infatuation thing goes away...especially because I'm secretly dying to kiss her again.

19

Resonance

Molly

CHEERLEADING practice is nearly over when I see Tristan say something to M up in the stands, then walk down the bleachers and leave. Did he change his mind about wanting to talk? Maybe because of something M said to him?

I'm so distracted I miss a step and nearly send Amber sprawling when she trips over my foot, which shouldn't have been there.

"Sorry, sorry!" I exclaim, catching her before she can hit the ground. "My fault, totally my fault."

"Seriously, Molly," Trina scolds me from her place at the other end of the line. "You need to get your act together. Don't you realize how visible we'll all be when our team goes to State?"

Belatedly realizing I *again* used super-human reflexes, this time to spare Amber a nasty fall, I nod. "I know. I'm having a hard time focusing today, sorry. Didn't get enough sleep last night I guess."

I'm careful to concentrate on the moves for the last few minutes of practice so Trina won't have any more reason to call me out. At least Tristan didn't see my blunder. Not that I should care.

When practice ends, Trina also notices his absence. "Oh, shoot. I guess Tristan really did have to leave early, like he said," she comments loudly, scanning the stands in vain. "I still need to invite him to tomorrow night's after-party. But remember girls, hands off if he comes!"

With a self-satisfied smirk, she heads back to the gym, the rest of the squad following. I hang back, wondering if I should ask M what Tristan said to her…but worried she'll guess why I want to know. While I'm still dithering, Tristan comes around the end of the bleachers.

"Good. She's gone."

"Who—? Oh, Trina?"

He nods. "She was so determined to get together after practice, I told her I needed to be somewhere. I didn't want to risk her starting up again when you finished so I made myself scarce. Do you, um, still want to talk?"

I glance up to where M is sitting but by now Rigel has joined her from the field for the few minutes they always try to grab before catching their buses. Neither of them is looking our way.

"Sure. Maybe not here, though? Trina will be back out in a minute." I'm actually more worried M will notice us together and ask questions I'm not ready to answer. "How about I go grab my stuff and meet you in the parking lot? Oh, you might want to stay away from the yellow sports car. That's Trina's."

He chuckles and it strikes me I haven't heard him do that before. He has a surprisingly pleasant laugh. "Thanks for the tip."

I run back to the gym to get my backpack and jacket out of the locker room. While I'm there, I tell Amber I won't need a ride today, that I promised M I'd take the late bus with her. That draws a frown from Trina, like any mention of M always does, but I ignore her and hurry back outside before anyone else can tag along.

Tristan is easy to spot in the parking lot, the late afternoon sun glinting off his golden hair and making it practically glow. I quicken my pace, concerned Trina might show up before we have time to talk.

"Hey," he says. "I'm guessing that's Trina's car?" He points at her lemon-yellow roadster a few spaces away. "Um, maybe I should give you a ride, so we can get out of here before she sees us? I wouldn't have parked so close to her if I'd known." He opens the door of his flashy black Porsche.

I carefully scan the parking lot before getting in—I'd rather *no one* sees us together and I'm sure Tristan feels the same. But this will likely be our best chance at privacy for what's bound to be a pretty embarrassing conversation. Besides, my late bus will be leaving any minute and I do need to get home somehow.

Once inside the luxurious interior of the car, safely behind the tinted windows, I relax slightly. Tristan walks around to slide behind the steering wheel and a moment later we've left the parking lot behind, along with any possibility of being waylaid by Trina. For at least a minute, neither of us says anything as we drive past cornfields—about all there is between the school and downtown Jewel.

"So," I finally say to break the awkward silence. "Any thoughts on how we should handle this, um, thing, if we're not going to pretend it never happened?" Not that my mantra was working anyway.

"I, um…not really. I guess having our memories of last night erased isn't a viable option? Anyway, I think the only place they can do that is in Dun Cloch."

Though he's clearly joking, his words still sting a little—even though I had the exact same thought earlier today. I try to force a laugh.

"Yeah, I don't fancy trying to explain to my mum why I'd want to do that. I assume you haven't said anything about it to your dad, either?"

"Are you kidding? He'd—I don't even want to think about what he'd do. But…you really think *your* parents would be upset if they knew?"

He sounds surprised. Which irritates me.

"Why, you think they should be *grateful* or something? That a high-and-mighty Royal might possibly be interested in their adopted Ag daughter?"

Looking a little sheepish, Tristan lifts a shoulder. In other words, yes. It's a timely reminder of exactly how arrogant he is, right when I was starting to soften toward him a little.

"Trust me, my mum feels as strongly about inter-*fine* romances as your father does. You should hear her go on about Sean and Kira—though mostly out of Sean's hearing these days. Not…not that there was anything *romantic* about what happened last night," I add hastily.

"No, of course not," he says just as quickly, looking straight ahead at the road. "It was just a…a momentary lapse in judgment. Or something."

"Right. I mean, we were both really angry. Our emotions were running high and, well, we're both teenagers. It was probably just an adrenaline response, like what the teacher talked about today in Psych class." I speak matter-of-factly, needing to convince myself as well as Tristan.

Though he still doesn't glance at me, he looks relieved. "A sympathetic nervous system thing, yeah. So, um, you agree we shouldn't mention that…whatever-it-was…to anyone else?"

"It's none of their business, is it?" I reply. "It's not like we're planning to go out on dates or anything. I mean, we don't even *like* each other."

"Um, right." He swallows visibly. "You're right. Pursuing any kind of, well, anything, would be crazy under the circumstances. It's not like we have anything in common."

"No, we really don't. Nothing at all, in fact."

We lapse into silence again.

Finally, as we're coming into downtown Jewel, where the county highway becomes Diamond Street, Tristan clears his throat. "We do still have five classes together. So, um, maybe it wouldn't hurt to at least get to know each other a little better? Maybe then we'll stop acting like we're afraid we'll catch the plague or something."

"You're right. I mean, we probably *are* treating this whole resonance thing like a bigger deal than it really is, just like I said yesterday. Okay, yeah, you did a dumb thing last night. And I didn't stop you, which was also dumb. We both know better than to let anything like that happen again, so there really should be nothing to worry about."

He nods several times. "We also don't have to be so paranoid about accidentally touching each other, like in Chemistry. As you pointed out yesterday, the *taghal ardus* is supposed to be a one-time thing." He doesn't sound absolutely positive, though.

To be honest, neither am I. I can feel his *brath* practically tugging at me even now from the other side of the car. Surely that will fade over time, though? I hope so. Otherwise, resisting it day after day will become a real challenge. Not that I have a choice.

He turns without me saying anything when we get to Opal—maybe remembering which way I went last night, when I basically ran away from him.

"Um, that's my house up there," I say as we cross Garnet. "Third one on the right."

He looks surprised when he pulls up. Maybe he assumed my folks, being such high-ranking Royals, would have something bigger and nicer?

"You really do live right around the corner from the Sovereign, don't you?" he comments instead. Then, putting the car in park, he turns to me. "So we're agreed, then? Starting tomorrow, we're just…two regular people who share a bunch of classes, right? You know, talking and stuff. Nothing, um, risky."

Remembering what led up to that kiss last night, I'm not sure talking is exactly risk-free. But *not* talking isn't really an option either, when we have so many classes together.

"Agreed," I say after a moment. "Though maybe we should try to stay away from politics?"

He blinks, his expression half alarmed, half something else I can't decipher. "Oh. Yeah. Uh, probably a good idea."

Again his *brath* seems to surround me, tempting me to sway toward him. I grab my backpack off the floor and quickly get out of the car.

"Good talk, Tristan," I say from a safe distance. "Thanks for suggesting it—and for the ride. See you at school tomorrow."

"Yeah, see you tomorrow, Molly. Bye."

I hear him drive away before I reach the front porch but resist the urge to turn and watch him. At least three-fourths convinced our conversation will let me finally put Tristan and last night's insanity out of my head, I hoist my backpack higher on my shoulder and go inside to give Mum the good news that Alan is coming over again tonight.

⁺₊

MUM IS PREDICTABLY THRILLED by my news about Alan. I don't have the heart to tell her I'm really not that interested in him. And maybe when my stupid infatuation with Tristan wears off, I will be again—if he ever gets over Kira, that is.

When Mum goes off to the kitchen to bake fresh cookies for tonight, I head to my room to start on my homework. I'm only halfway up the stairs when my phone rings. It's M.

"Hey, Molly, are you home yet? Would it be okay if I come over for a few minutes?"

"Yeah, I just got back. And of course."

"Okay, thanks, see you in a few."

Five minutes later the doorbell rings. Mum bustles out of the kitchen to answer it, still all smiles about my so-called "date" with Alan and my plants.

"Oh, hello, Excellency. Molly didn't mention you'd be by. Are you here for a social visit, or is there something official I should know about?"

"Nothing official. I, ah, just wanted to compare notes with Molly about one of our class assignments. Unless you've heard anything more from Dun Cloch or the Council?"

Mum shakes her head, frowning now. "I haven't, no. Should I have?"

"No, I was just wondering. Though Kyna will probably call me if anything important happens before our next meeting. Molly?"

"Yeah, let's go up to my room." I suspect she either wants to talk privately or play with her Scepter again.

Turns out she wants to do both.

"Why is your mother so happy?" she asks once I've shut the door. "Obviously nothing Council-related or she'd have said so."

"Oh, because Alan's coming over to work with my plants again tonight after dinner," I say with a laugh. "Needless to say, she's ecstatic about it."

M looks at me. "And you're not?"

I shrug. "He's awfully cute, and once he's totally over Kira, we'll probably get along fine. I mean, we do have a lot in common—we're both Ags, both grew up in small farming villages in Nuath. And he *is* nice, even if our one real date didn't work out. Before that, when he was here Saturday, he had to notice how badly my Ag skills suck but he didn't make a single crack about it or get impatient with me. He even implied to Mum I was making progress, though I totally wasn't."

"Then what's the problem? You've got a great looking guy interested in you, who you have lots in common with, and who's nice enough to overlook your faults. Except for the Kira thing, which he *will* get over, he sounds perfect. But you don't seem very excited about seeing him again. How come? Just no real…chemistry there?"

The word *chemistry* jolts through me, I associate it so strongly with Tristan. In more ways than one. Fighting to keep my expression neutral, I shrug again. "Not…yet, I guess. But who knows? Maybe if we keep spending time together it'll develop into something."

"Definitely worth pursuing, then. Right?"

M is watching me so intently I wonder what my face gave away. *Can she read my actual emotions?* I'm tempted to ask her outright but worry if the answer is yes she'll demand an explanation for what she senses off me.

Instead, I decide to brazen it through. "Right. Of course!" I force some extra enthusiasm into my voice. "I mean, it's not like there's anyone *else* in Jewel who'd be better boyfriend material than Alan. I'd be crazy not to give him another chance."

"I hope it goes loads better than last time. You'll have to tell me later. Right now I can't stay long. Rigel's picking me up in less than an hour to have dinner there again."

"Wow, that's three nights in a row—though I guess last night wasn't dinner, just official stuff. Still, your aunt must really be loosening up on her rules about that, huh?"

She shrugs. "At least when it's for official business—which this is, though she's starting to look a little skeptical every time I tell her that. I'm hoping to get Rigel's dad to add some extra security out at NuAgra. And maybe Dun Cloch and a few other places."

"Like your house?" I ask. "I know I'd feel better if he could do that. I'll bet Cormac and Rigel would, too."

"Probably not a bad idea," she admits. "Maybe your house, too, since this is where we have all the Council meetings. I'll ask him about it. But first I, um…"

"Need some more closet time?" I guess.

She nods apologetically. "Sorry. But it really should be only a couple of minutes."

"Hey, it's totally fine. That was the whole point of letting me in on the secret about your Scepter, right? So you can use it whenever you want?"

"Right," she agrees. "You really are the best, Molly. Best Handmaid, best friend. And…one of these days I hope I can tell you even more. Seems only fair, as often as I'm inconveniencing you lately."

Even though it still bothers me a little that there are things she's not telling me, her words mean a lot. I smile—and mean it.

"What's a tiny bit of inconvenience between friends? It's not like I needed to use my closet right this minute anyway. Now, if you'd wanted to do this right when I was getting ready for Alan to come over, that might be another matter."

She laughs at that. "Thanks. I promise it won't take that long." Then, with a last grin, she disappears into my closet.

Again.

20

Free radicals

M

ONCE IN MOLLY'S CLOSET, I don't waste any time opening the Archive in my Scepter. All I really need to do is transfer the security system data onto the blank chip Mr. Stuart gave me last night.

Even so, I can't resist talking with my grandfather just a little when he appears. Over the summer, Leontine and Aerleas began to feel like the closest thing to parents I've ever had.

"Emileia, my dear," he greets me. "I hope all has been well with you since we last spoke?"

"Hello, Grandfather. I'm fine, yes. At least, there haven't been any crises in the past two days. I brought an empty data chip this time." I hold it up. "Maybe if Mr. Stuart can put together a few good security systems we can avoid any future disasters, though there *are* still potential threats out there. Especially if it turns out more antimatter has gone missing."

He chuckles. "Didn't I caution you against borrowing trouble, Emileia? While it is wise to prepare for it, there is no need to regard it as inevitable. I suspect your tendency to do so stems from the inordinate number of challenges you have faced over your few short months as Sovereign. Let us hope once we provide Van Stuart with the information to create better safeguards, you will be able to relax your guard some-what. One so young should not live in fear."

Nodding, I insert the blank chip into the little slot between the green stones. While the data downloads, Leontine asks questions about my day-to-day life just like a regular grandpa might.

"School is going pretty well now that I can focus on it again. I'm finally caught up in all my subjects, so Kyna has sent some extra curriculum to my omni—the sorts of things I'd be studying if I lived in Nuath. It's way more advanced than my *Duchas* courses but I'm working my way through it."

"Excellent. I'm very proud of you, Emileia."

Even knowing he's a holographic artifact, his approval warms me. Not for the first time, I desperately wish my *real* parents' images and memories had somehow made it into this Archive. "Thank you, Grand-father. That means a lot to me."

"You won't always feel so cut off from your past, my dear," he says sympathetically, apparently divining the emotion behind my words. "At least, that is my hope. The data has finished transferring, by the way."

"Oh, thanks. I guess I should get going, then. I'll give this to Mr. Stuart this evening, so he can get started right away."

We say goodbye to each other again and I deactivate the Archive.

"Wow, it really was just a couple of minutes this time," Molly says when I step back out of her closet.

Which reminds me that I meant to ask Leontine if it would be okay to tell Molly the whole secret. I'll be sure to do it next time.

"Yeah, I just needed to get some info for Rigel's dad out of the Archive for the security systems I mentioned. But now I should probably head home. I want to change before Rigel gets there and you need time to get ready for your, um, date tonight. What do you plan to wear?"

She laughs. "Probably just jeans and an old sweater, since we'll be mucking about with my plants. It's not like he's taking me to a show or anything."

"Still, I want to hear about it later. Call or text me, okay?"

"Okay."

Molly sees me to the door. I notice her mother is still in excellent spirits when she says goodbye to me.

Walking home, I think about Molly and Alan, hoping they'll hit it off better tonight than they did last time. It's weird, though, how Molly's feelings didn't seem to match her words when she talked about him.

Either she likes Alan a whole lot more than she's willing to admit, or something else is going on between them that she's desperate not to talk about. Neither of which quite seems to fit the blast of emotion she gave off when I asked if they have good chemistry together.

She just shrugged and said, "Not yet," but I sensed an anxiety bordering on fear, along with distaste and something almost like desire, or at least longing. She did such a good job of suppressing whatever that strong mix of emotions was, I couldn't be sure.

Suddenly, I'm reminded of what I felt off of Tristan this afternoon, when he talked with me at football practice. That was also a puzzling mixture of anxiety, rejection and desire, and it didn't seem directed at me. And, like Molly just now, he was working really hard to conceal his emotional turmoil, whatever it was.

Hm.

Molly never did give me any actual details about her confrontation with Tristan at Dream Cream last night. He said they had an argument, but she never mentioned that. Now I wonder why. Whatever happened, they both seem awfully determined to act like it didn't.

⁺₊

When Rigel picks me up half an hour later, I share my interesting new theory with him.

"I think something may be going on between Molly and Tristan, but I'm not sure what. Either they had a huge fight they're both trying to gloss over, or they're really attracted to each other and trying to hide it. Maybe both."

"Attracted?" Rigel sounds both startled and pleased. "After the way he's been coming on to you since he got here, why do you make that sound like a bad thing?"

"Because I don't want Molly to get hurt, of course. Though I don't see how she could possibly be attracted to someone she thinks is a complete jerk and who obviously looks down on her. If she is, though, I can't let him—"

Rigel cuts off my anxious babbling. "M, you know this really isn't any of your business, right? Anyway, it sounds like you're just guessing. Has Molly actually mentioned any of this to you?"

"Well, no, but—"

"Look. If Tristan does anything to hurt Molly, I'll personally break his face if Sean doesn't beat me to it. For now, though, maybe just let them work it out between themselves? Molly's a smart girl. I'm betting she can take care of herself."

Sighing, I nod. Because Rigel is right. But that doesn't stop me from worrying, at least till we get to his house.

There, I have plenty to distract me.

Over an excellent dinner of crab-stuffed shrimp and sweet potato soufflé, the four of us discuss political developments both on Mars and Earth. I marvel at the contrast from my very first dinner here, more than a year ago. Then, I was bewildered by the political conversation involving places, people and events I'd never heard of. It's incredible how much I've learned since then. Maybe *too* much.

"Thus far, the Council Royals have persisted in believing any sort of reactionary movement must be insignificant," Mr. Stuart says. "Earlier, when it was assumed that Crevan Erc's Populists were the primary threat, they insisted that with the launch window closed for the next two years, no further agitation would be likely. But based on what I'm seeing in those messages, it appears these groups may be answering to someone more…local."

"Someone on Earth, you mean, right? Not…someone in Jewel?" Rigel glances at me in concern.

His father shakes his head. "No, there's no reason to think that. None of the communications I've intercepted were sent from or received here." He goes on to update us on the most recent information he's picked up from those encrypted messages he's following.

"Not only do they parrot some of Faxon's old propaganda, I've found at least one indication they may be reaching out to similarly disaffected groups of *Duchas*. Needless to say, that could be extraordinarily dangerous."

"No kidding!" That would be even worse than a coalition between the various *Echtran* groups that already oppose me. "Have you told Kyna about this?"

"Yes, I messaged her as soon as I felt I had enough evidence to do so. She responded that she intends to inform the entire Council about this development, most likely tonight."

Surely they won't be able to brush *this* aside? At least, I hope not.

"I find it hard to believe there are *Echtrans* who would still endorse Faxon's agenda," Dr. Stuart says with a frown. "Our people should be more intelligent than that."

"Even intelligent people can be swayed by clever rhetoric—and prejudice," I point out. "Especially if they're convinced they might have something to gain personally by supporting a particular person or group. We've seen it here on Earth plenty of times. Playing the blame game is a time-tested method to whip up support."

Mr. Stuart nods. "She's right. Faxon did exactly that back in Nuath, convincing many in the lower *fines* that their perceived wrongs were the fault of the Royals—in particular, the Sovereigns. Not until it was too late did his followers discover they'd put their trust in a lying traitor who only cared about increasing his own power and wealth."

"Shouldn't everyone's eyes be opened now, though?" Rigel asks. "Even those Faxon minions who tried to kill M last year seemed pretty shaken when Grandfather reminded them of the ways our people are supposedly superior."

Shim's speech in the cornfield that day nearly *did* turn the tide. It probably would have, if Faxon's henchman Morven hadn't had that nasty Ossian Sphere to control them. Once Rigel and I destroyed it with an electrical blast, his little army quickly deserted him. I'd assumed—hoped—they would return to a right way of thinking after that, but obviously not all of them did.

"I guess we can't know what people's *real* views are without resorting to mind probes," I admit.

"True," Mr. Stuart agrees, "though if someone is attempting to unify these scattered groups and perhaps direct their perceived grievances against you or the Council, that obviously needs to be addressed."

Rigel puts a protective arm around me. "Absolutely. The number one priority should be to keep M safe."

"I agree. But until we know where the threat is coming from and what form it is likely to take—assuming there even is a threat—there's not much we can do."

"Actually, I'm hoping there is," I tell him. "After Kyna told us about Enid the other night, I started thinking we really need some safeguards in place in case these Neo-Faxists or Anti-Royals or whoever they are decide to try something else. I was already planning to talk to you about it tonight."

I go on to describe the sophisticated security system in the Royal Palace back on Mars. That system allowed me to neutralize Devyn Kane and my other so-called advisors when I discovered they were the ones who had erased Rigel's memory and then lied to me about it. Otherwise, they almost certainly would have tried to do something even worse to him—and maybe to me, too.

"I'm hoping you might be able to design something similar for NuAgra and maybe parts of Dun Cloch or any other places that could be targets for malcontents."

"Fascinating," he says. "I agree that putting more protections in place —particularly for you, Excellency—should be a priority. But I would need to know a lot more about how that system operates before I could begin such a project."

I pull the data chip out of my pocket. "That's why I asked you for this last night, so I could download the specs for you to study. Hopefully they'll help you to at least get started."

He takes the chip from me, regarding it curiously. "You downloaded them? From where? I would imagine that would be very closely guarded information."

"It is." I bite my lip. "I, um, can't tell you exactly where I got it, but it was from a *very* reliable and secure source."

Again I wish I didn't have to keep the truth about my Scepter *quite* so secret—though Rigel knows. In fact, he immediately picks up on my thought.

Wow, I didn't realize it had stuff like this in it. Did one of your ancestors—?

Yes, I think back. *I'll tell you about it later, okay?*

His dad, meanwhile, gives a little shrug. "Then I'll ask no more about it, Excellency. Your word is good enough for me. I'll take a look at the data this evening. But that reminds me, I have something for you, as well."

While Rigel and his mother carry the dinner dishes into the kitchen, I follow Mr. Stuart to his office.

"Here." He hands me a small box. "I know you've been eager to get this."

Opening the box, I find what looks like a smartphone…but must be my new omni that can double as one. Now I can keep it with me all the time without making any *Duchas* suspicious.

"Cool!" I exclaim, not caring how undignified I sound. "Can you show me how to set it up?"

He's still doing that when Rigel and Dr. Stuart join us. I excitedly show it to Rigel, who grins at me.

"You don't know how hard it was to not tell you about it earlier.

Especially since, according to Dad, it's even better than the ones the Council have."

"It has some extra features, yes," Mr. Stuart agrees. "For example, that aural dampening field Kira described to us last night."

I didn't even know such an omni app existed until Kira told us about the one Allister and Lennox's henchwoman Enid loaded onto her souped-up phone before she came to Jewel. "Awesome. I can definitely think of times that might be useful."

For one thing, I'll no longer need to whisper when I use my Scepter in Molly's closet…though I'd rather just tell her about Leontine and the others anyway. She lost her parents before she could remember them, too, so I'm sure she'll understand why I want to spend more time talking with my holographic ancestors.

"Thank you so much," I say to Mr. Stuart.

"You can thank Kyna. She arranged for its expedited delivery from Dun Cloch after you left last night. We both agreed it was only appropriate that you have this as soon as possible. Given recent developments, it's more important than ever that you be reachable at all times."

Which reminds me. "Have Allister and Lennox been formally charged yet?" I ask. "Connor said Monday night he expected that to happen in the next day or two and it's already been longer than that. We've *got* to get those memory extractions."

Mr. Stuart nods his agreement. "Kyna tells me the indictment is scheduled for tomorrow morning. She will insist that the extraction occur soon afterward, though we will likely still get some pushback on that from certain Royals."

"Maybe if we tell them their *own* safety is in question they'll be more willing to move forward," I suggest, remembering how cravenly Connor acted when faced with the Grentl threat last month. He was ready to sacrifice all the *Duchas* to spare the *Echtrans* on Earth—particularly himself.

"I'll suggest that to Kyna." Mr. Stuart gives me a wry smile. "I'm sure she will message you once the charges have been formally read tomorrow."

I hold up my new omni-phone. "And now I'll be able to see it right away. Thanks again for this."

My cellphone number has already been transferred to it, making it the only communication device I'll need from now on. Even as a cellphone, it's a lot nicer than the refurbished one I finally talked Aunt

Theresa into. Though even that was a huge improvement over the land-line hardwired to the kitchen wall that was my only phone before that.

"You, ah, may not want to tell your Aunt and Uncle just how much this device differs from your old mobile phone," Dr. Stuart suggests to me. "Particularly your Uncle."

I chuckle. "Good point. I'll just pretend I dropped my other phone and the Council offered to replace it with this one." No way I'll trust Uncle Louie around an omni again.

We talk a little longer, then Rigel drives me home. Back in my room later, I wonder how Molly's "date" with Alan is going—or went. I'm tempted to text her now but realize it'll be safer to wait until she brings it up, in case it turned out to be another fail.

In which case I'll try harder to figure out what's going on between her and Tristan, if anything. Rigel may think it's none of my business, but Molly's my best friend and I'm *not* going to let her get hurt if I can do anything to prevent it.

21

Uncertainty principle

Molly

"Now then, Molly, I can finish up the dishes tonight." Mum takes the stack of dinner plates out of my hand, smiling at my surprise. "Alan will be here soon and you still need to bring your plants downstairs. As it's already dark outside, you can put them in the living room if you'd like, and we'll clear out. Or would here in the kitchen make more sense?"

It would be funny how excited she is about Alan coming over if I weren't worried she'll end up that much more disappointed later.

"The kitchen, I guess? There's water here and the mess won't matter as much if he suggests repotting one...or something."

"Oh, aye, good thinking. See now, you're already getting better at this. I thought for certain working with Alan would be helpful."

While she racks the dishes in the cleaning cabinet, I run up to my room and grab the first two houseplants off my windowsill. It takes three trips to bring all five down to the kitchen, by which time the dishes are all sterilized and my parents are both in the living room. Less than a minute later, the doorbell rings.

To my embarrassment, Mum greets Alan as effusively as she did the first time. Is she really *that* desperate for me to find a boyfriend? An Ag boyfriend, that is. I shove Tristan from my thoughts for about the twentieth time since he dropped me off this afternoon.

"—*so* appreciates your help, don't you Molly?" Mum turns to me with a big smile.

"Oh, um, of course I do. Definitely. So anyway, Alan, I've put my plants in the kitchen this time. We should probably get started, yeah?" I'm already heading that way, eager to get him away from Mum before she can elaborate further.

"There are fresh cookies in the jar," she calls after us. "And don't forget to offer him something to drink—we have lemonade as well as milk, or I can make you a pot of tea."

I walk faster. "We'll be fine, Mum, thanks," I call over my shoulder.

As soon as Alan and I are in the kitchen I nudge the swinging door shut. Not that that will stop Mum from eavesdropping if she has a mind to.

"Sorry," I mutter, sitting down at the kitchen table. "From the way Mum acts, you'd think I never had a boy over before." Which is *almost* true. The only other one was Pete Griffin, and he only came to the house briefly before the Homecoming dance last month.

"Nah, my folks thought it was great I was coming here, too. Parents. What are you gonna do?"

We laugh, breaking the slight tension between us—though his words also remind me how his family idolizes mine for being Resistance heroes...and being Royal. Not that I'll bring *that* up, since I'm as determined to avoid politics with Alan tonight as I will be with Tristan from now on. Politics and boys clearly don't mix well.

"Should I put out some cookies?" I ask, mostly for something to say.

He shakes his head. "I just ate. Maybe later? Let's take a look at your plants first."

"Oh, okay. Sure."

As he surveys the poor things, I can tell he's trying not to frown—and no wonder. They've already drooped noticeably since Saturday, when he so easily perked them up.

"I, uh, guess you've been too busy to really spend time on them this week?"

It's nice of him to provide me with such a convenient excuse. I gladly seize on it. "Yeah, I have, sorry. I really meant to do the stuff you showed me every day, but..." I shrug.

In fact, I *have* spent more time than usual with my plants since Saturday. At least ten minutes every single night before bed, and almost that much most mornings. It just hasn't made any difference—unless it was to make them worse.

"Hey, it can be hard to establish new habits," he says understandingly. "Maybe try setting aside three or four minutes before bed every night, or when you first get up in the morning? That should be enough if you really focus."

For him, maybe.

"I'll, um, try to do that, thanks."

"Meanwhile, let's see if I can give them another boost for you, okay?"

Nodding, I gesture toward the motley collection to indicate he's more than welcome to do whatever he can. While he works with the plants—which again revive noticeably under his skilled touch—we talk about growing up in Nuath. Since we lived in neighboring Ag villages, our experiences were pretty similar.

Mostly to keep him talking about something other than plants, I next ask him about his family's decision to emigrate and then for more details about his orientation in Dun Cloch. That's what we were discussing Tuesday evening before our date turned sour but this time I'm careful to avoid any mention of Kira or *caidpel*.

When he's done as much for my poor plants as he can in one evening, I make a pot of tea and set out a plate of cookies while we chat about the differences between Jewel and our villages back home.

"Wait till we have our first snowfall," I say, grinning. "Even though we all knew to expect it, it was still pretty amazing—and a little freaky." Especially for Sean, who has a thing about stuff falling from the sky, but I don't say that. I don't want to give Alan another excuse to criticize my brother.

"Yeah? I'm really looking forward to that—though maybe not the cold. Already it's a lot cooler at night than it ever got in Nuath. That was happening in Dun Cloch by the time we left, too, since it's a lot further north."

We talk a little about our Government project over tea and cookies and I promise to give him my notes on the Constitution. Again and again, I have to yank my thoughts away from Tristan.

At one point I actually try flirting a little, though I can't claim my heart is in it. I get the impression Alan's trying a little too hard, too— probably as determined to keep his mind off Kira as I am to keep mine off Tristan.

He leaves a little after nine, after a brief delay in the front hall while my parents thank him *again* and Mum asks how things went with the plants. Like before, Alan gives me way more credit than I deserve. Which would be none.

"Feel free to drop by any time," she calls after him as he finally gets out the door.

The moment it's shut, Dad turns to me with a smile. "Alan seems like a fine young man, Molly. I understand he's already begun to make valuable contributions out at NuAgra. I'm pleased you two are becoming such good friends."

"Yeah," I say with more enthusiasm than I feel. "Me, too. I, uh, guess I'd better get all those plants off the kitchen table, huh?"

Mum and Dad both volunteer to help, so we do it in one trip, both of them still going on—and on—about how much they approve of Alan. We're heading back down the stairs when Sean comes through the front door.

"You're a bit later than you said you'd be." Mum's voice has an edge that definitely wasn't there a second ago.

Sean refuses to let her ruffle him. "Not really," he replies calmly. "Molly, Adina said if you want to come over this weekend she'd be happy to have you work with her puppy, to see if you have any special skill with animals like she does."

"Oh, thanks, I'd been meaning to ask her. I have to help put up Spirit Week decorations Saturday but I'll talk to Adina in Chorus tomorrow so we can find a time that works."

To be honest, I've been putting that off. I seriously doubt I'm any better with animals than I am with plants and I'm not in a huge hurry to confirm I'm a failure as an Ag on all fronts.

I go into the kitchen and rinse out the teacups Alan and I used, then pour myself a glass of milk to take up to my room. As I climb the stairs again, I wonder if *fine* skills are like language skills. Maybe there's an optimal age to learn them and if you miss that, you're sunk. Seems likely. Yet another reason to wish I'd had time to know my real parents.

As soon as I'm alone, my thoughts automatically return to Tristan and our conversation this afternoon...and everything else that's happened between us. I can hardly believe that shocking first touch was only two days ago. So much seems to have happened since then...

And starting tomorrow we're supposedly going to get to know each other better, whatever *that* means. I was pretty startled when Tristan suggested it. But I'm sure he just means we'll talk, like normal class-mates, and not be all weird about accidentally touching.

Even though there's no way it'll be anything like the first time, I have to admit, I'm still nervous about that part. Alan touched my hand several times tonight and I didn't get even a fraction of the tingle I felt from *him* on Saturday. That helped reassure me that nothing scary is likely to happen if—when—Tristan and I touch a second time.

I'm just sitting down to finish up my homework when I remember I promised to tell M how tonight went. If I don't, she'll wonder why—and I'm already worried she suspects something odd is going on with me, even if she can't possibly know exactly what.

I send her a quick text. *Alan just left, everything was fine. Are you still at Rigel's?*

Two seconds later my phone rings.

"So? What do you mean by 'fine'?" M demands before even saying hi. "I assume at the very least you didn't fight this time?"

I force a chuckle, irresistibly reminded of the much more intense fight I had with Tristan last night—and how it ended. "No, not at all. He helped with my plants—a lot, actually—and we talked. Also a lot."

"About what? Wait, you mean your mother actually let the two of you spend a whole hour and a half *alone*?"

That really does make me laugh. "In the kitchen, but yeah. Mum's made it pretty obvious she thinks Alan is the best thing that could possibly happen to me. We talked about lots of stuff—our lives in Nuath, his orientation in Dun Cloch, what we both think of Jewel. Like I said, it was fine."

"Then…you think some chemistry might develop between you two after all?"

I swallow. Why does she have to keep using *that* word? "It's defi-nitely not impossible."

"And he's really helping you develop your Ag skills? That's great!"

"Um, I didn't exactly say that. He made my plants look a lot happier, but I can't claim I had anything to do with it. At all. Even if he pretended I did again, to be nice."

She makes an *aww* sound. "That's kind of sweet of him, don't you think? It sounds like there might be more hope there than you thought."

"Maybe so." At least once I purge Tristan from my system—which I need to do ASAP. "I guess time will tell."

We only talk for another couple of minutes, then I settle down to my homework until bedtime, working hard to keep my thoughts on the assignment in front of me instead of ranging back over every second I've spent around Tristan.

As I climb into bed, I wonder if Tristan will find his way into my dreams again, like he did all last night. Though I know I absolutely shouldn't, I almost hope he will. Because those were *awfully* good dreams…

What really matters, I reason, is staying cool, calm and collected whenever I'm actually around him, like at school. As long as I do that, there can't be any real harm in *just* dreaming.

Can there?

22

Reaction mechanism

Tristan

FATHER DOESN'T GET home from NuAgra until late Thursday evening, grumbling about all the clueless newcomers constantly needing advice about the simplest things.

"Apparently shortening our standard Orientation training was not a good idea after all, no matter how necessary it may have seemed to accommodate the numbers."

"Give them time, dear," Mother says soothingly, setting out our dinner. She insisted on waiting the meal for him even though it's past nine o'clock. "Most have only been on Earth for two or three months and it *is* a big adjustment."

He snorts. "Just because it took *you* forever to—"

I interrupt before he can finish his insult. "I'm glad you're back. I wanted to tell you I finally managed some alone time with the Sovereign after school today."

As I hoped, that distracts him from taking out his irritation on my mother.

"Did you?" His pale eyebrows lift from frown to surprise. "How did you accomplish that?"

"She sometimes goes to the football practices to watch Stuart. They claim it helps him pull back during actual games, because their bond supposedly supercharges him. That gave me a chance to catch her alone in the bleachers and talk privately with her for a while."

No point telling him I totally forgot she'd be there until I got out to the field.

"I also talked to Coach Glazier. He wants me to come back Monday for a sort of pre-tryout for next year's team."

"Never mind that." Father waves a careless hand, nearly knocking over the bowl of green beans Mother just set down. "What did you and the Sovereign talk about? I hope you were able to at least imply that a majority of our people would prefer she make a more appropriate choice for Consort?"

I take a big bite of steak before answering. Even with the snack Mother insisted I eat when I got home, I'm starving. "Um, it didn't come up. I'm supposed to be building trust with her, remember? Criticizing Stuart every chance I get would do the exact opposite. I have to at least *pretend* to like her friends."

One in particular...

"Very well. I suppose it's a start, which is honestly more than I expected of you at this point."

"I'm surprised there were still workers at NuAgra this late." Mother says it quickly enough I can tell she's returning the favor by deflecting Father's attention. "Don't most of them go home before dinnertime?"

Father takes a bite, chews, takes another bite, chews, then takes a sip of wine before answering her. Which is just rude.

"Most do, yes, but quite a few singles are still living at the facility while waiting for more apartments to become available in Jewel. I also had other business to attend to after hours, which I'd hoped to conclude earlier. It was unfortunately delayed by the incessant stream of questions all afternoon. Speaking of which, there is a chance Devyn will be coming to Jewel sometime over the next week or two."

Mother frowns slightly. "Devyn Kane? He's been back in touch, then?"

Before this last launch window, Father and Devyn Kane got together fairly often. But then Devyn took the very first ship to Mars, with an eye to challenging the Sovereign for Acclamation. Father's barely mentioned him since that effort failed, at least in my hearing.

"Yes, he's been visiting family out west. He and I had hoped to see each other before we left Colorado but never had the opportunity."

"Oh. I…didn't even realize he'd returned to Earth," Mother says.

Neither did I. Not that I particularly care. Devyn's barely ever even spoken to me, and always seemed a little too…slick for my taste. Like a salesman. Or a politician, which I guess he is. Probably a good one, judging by the poll numbers I saw from Nuath. He came *really* close to getting Acclaimed Sovereign before he threw his support behind M at the last minute.

"What's he doing these days?" I ask, just to be polite.

"That's none of your business," Father snaps, startling me. It was an innocent enough question. "In fact, it would be best if neither of you mention to anyone else that I've spoken with him, given— Never mind."

That seems weird but I don't dare ask any more questions. Neither does Mother. We finish eating in silence, my mind wandering back to this afternoon's conversation with Molly O'Gara…and everything that led up to it.

Though I know it's stupid, I'm already looking forward to seeing her again tomorrow. I try to convince myself that's only so I can prove—to both of us—that I'm perfectly capable of keeping my sudden weird attraction to her under control. That I can be friendly without any hint I want it to be more.

Because I don't. I can't. That would be crazy.

Especially since she made it crystal clear this afternoon that *she* doesn't. She flat out told me she doesn't even like me. Okay, she actually said we don't like *each other*. I didn't bother correcting her, since before yesterday that was absolutely true. Starting the moment I met her, I saw Molly as nothing but an obstacle, someone I needed to outmaneuver so I could get closer to the Sovereign.

Now? I'm not sure.

I definitely don't *dis*like her. Not like I did before that mind-blowing kiss…and those dreams I had afterward. But whether my desire to get to know her better is a result of whatever weird hormonal thing is going on between us or a symptom of something more…genuine, I have no idea. Surely just the former. I hope so, anyway.

Getting to know her better *should* help me figure that out.

And when I do?

I'd rather not think that far ahead.

⁺₊

Partly because I'm so antsy to see Molly again, I take my time getting to Pre-Cal the next morning, psyching myself up for the role I need to play. Cool. Calm. Casual. With one last, deep breath, I walk into the classroom.

There she is, sitting next to the Sovereign—and the mere sight of her momentarily shatters my hard-won calm. Or maybe it's her *brath*, which I swear I can feel all the way from the doorway. Whichever it is, my heart rate and breathing kick into overdrive. I slow down even more, fighting to get a grip. To act like that crazy touch Tuesday and even crazier kiss Wednesday night never happened.

Because it's what I'd do if that were really true, I stop to say hi to M when I reach her. And then to Rigel, since he put in a good word for me with the coach yesterday. Finally, I take my usual desk—not counting Wednesday when I chickened out and sat in the back.

The desk next to Molly.

Cool. Casual.

I turn to her with a smile—but not too big a smile. "Hey, did you finish last night's homework? Question six was a tricky one, wasn't it?"

It wasn't, though some of the *Duchas* might have found it challenging.

"Um, yeah. I thought that was the hardest one too, but I finally figured it out." She's doing better than I am at the casual thing. Unless she's as jumpy inside as I am? I doubt it.

Mostly to prove I can act completely normal around her, I pull out my notebook and show her my answer. "Is that what you got?"

"I think so, let me check." She does the same. Of course we both got it right, but comparing answers makes for safe, impersonal conversation.

Yeah, we can do this. No problem.

In French class, I'm careful to include M and Kira in a four-way discussion about regional accents. Again, totally casual. Neither M or Kira or anyone else could possibly guess anything ever happened between Molly and me.

I start to think we might eventually be able to forget it ourselves. Then we can go back to ignoring each other, or maybe trading occasional insults, like we did last week.

Except…there's a part of me that doesn't really want to. Even as we compare pronunciation differences, I can feel Molly's *brath* sort of surrounding me, like it's trying to reel me in. Just like in the car yesterday. Weird. I don't think I've ever even *heard* of anything like this before.

Even weirder, I kind of like how it feels, almost like a caress. No! That's ridiculous—and all the more reason to resist it. I'm probably just imagining it anyway.

Imaginary or not, in Chemistry, with her right next to me at our lab table, her *brath* feels stronger than ever. In an effort to distract myself from it, I pull out my write up of yesterday's precipitation exercise.

"Hey, can you look this over, tell me if I forgot anything?"

For an instant, I detect a hint of something almost like alarm in her eyes, then she gingerly takes the paper, as careful not to brush my fingers as she was—as we both were—yesterday. But we talked about that in the car, too.

"Remember how we agreed it's probably going to be impossible to avoid touching each other, especially in here?" I whisper. "And how we've probably been worrying about nothing anyway?"

She blinks at me. "Oh, right. The *taghal ardus* is just a one-time thing, so it probably won't matter at all."

"Exactly. Though, um, maybe we should, y'know, test it? Just to be sure? So we're not caught off-guard if we're wrong."

It's a perfectly logical suggestion, one that has absolutely nothing to do with how much I've been dying to touch her again.

"Um, okay. That's…probably a good idea." She hesitates for another second or two, then gingerly puts her hand on the table halfway between us.

I also hesitate for a moment, steeling myself just in case, then reach over and touch her hand.

Crap!

Molly immediately snatches her hand away.

Nope, definitely *not* a one-time effect. If anything, that jolt was even stronger than the first one—and I was even braced for it.

"Oops. So much for *that* theory," she murmurs.

"Yeah. Well. At least now we know. Guess we need to avoid that after all." I try really hard not to sound disappointed, even though I'm already fighting a powerful urge to repeat the experience. Because as startling as that jolt was, it was also pleasant. Exciting. Invigorating.

And something I absolutely can't afford to become addicted to.

"Okay, so maybe this is going to be a little tougher than we thought," she says after a moment. "More inconvenient, anyway."

No kidding! This crush or obsession or whatever I have for Molly O'Gara is more than inconvenient, it's completely inappropriate. I'm

Royal. She's an Ag. And never the twain shall meet…or something like that.

At some point we're *bound* to build up some kind of immunity to each other, right? Meanwhile, I just have to resist touching her again.

She makes that easier than I expect during the rest of the period, apparently even more determined than I am to avoid further physical contact. Not surprising, since she doesn't even like me. *She* probably doesn't feel the least temptation to try another test. Like I do.

In Lit class, away from Molly's unsettling presence, I can think more clearly. Sternly reminding myself of my original goal in coming to Jewel High, I turn to the Sovereign and engage her in conversation. I flirt some, like before, but my heart's not really in it. This dumb infatuation is messing with my focus. It doesn't help that every time I see M and Rigel together, I'm more convinced that Molly was right and I'm wasting my time.

Sure, I still believe I'd be a better, more effective Consort than Rigel can ever be. But unless something dramatically changes between those two, I don't see any way that's going to happen. Not that shifting my pursuit to Molly is exactly a viable plan, either. She may not have a steady boyfriend but there are other, equally insurmountable obstacles to any kind of long-term relationship between us.

When I get to the lunchroom, Molly is just a few people ahead of me in line, chatting with Alan Dempsey, her fellow Ag. With my *Echtran* senses, it's hard to avoid hearing what they say to each other.

"Did you remember to spend a few minutes with your plants before school this morning?" he asks her.

She nods. "And last night before bed, too, even though they were still looking a whole lot better after all the attention you gave them earlier. Um, so far, so good."

"That's great."

His bracing tone sounds condescending to me. Because he's a senior and she's a junior? He's in her same *fine,* so it can't be that—especially considering her adopted family and close association with the Sovereign, which should put her on a higher social level than he is.

Then he says, "Last night you mentioned giving me your notes, but do you maybe want to get together again instead, so you can catch me up on all the Constitution stuff you did in Government class before I got here? You could come over to my house this time, meet my parents."

The idea bothers me way more than it should. So does the enthusiasm in her voice when she replies.

"Sure, that would be great. Maybe Sunday or Monday?" She sounds like she's actually looking forward to it.

Because they're both Ags, I remind myself.

It's funny how I have to keep reminding myself of Molly's *fine*—maybe because she doesn't act at all how I imagined an Ag would. Of course, she *was* raised by Royals and pals around with the Sovereign every day, so I guess it's not that surprising. Doesn't change the fact, though.

And it only makes sense she'd want to get friendly with Alan, the one guy in Jewel near her age who's in her same *fine*. Just like I planned to with M. Still plan to do. Somehow.

The cashier swipes my card and I automatically head for the Sovereign's table, where I've sat every day but one since I got to Jewel High. I'm not terribly surprised when Molly heads toward Alan's table with him, though yesterday and the day before she sat with the cheerleaders.

Just then, the Sovereign catches Molly's eye and motions her over and she changes course. Alan watches her for a second, like he's trying to decide whether to follow her or not, then gives a little shrug and goes to his usual table.

Good.

No, *not* good.

Just because Molly and I have some freaky resonance thing going on doesn't give me any kind of claim on her. She'd surely be better off with a guy from her own *fine* than she could ever be with me, as different as we are. Anyway, Father would flip if he ever found out I was attracted to an Ag.

Even so, I can't help feeling a little more cheerful when she and I end up with our lunch trays right next to each other, across from M and Rigel. Still determined to play it cool around Molly, I just give her a quick smile before turning to the Sovereign.

"Hey, you won't mind if I sit with you again at the game tonight, will you?" I include Rigel in the question because it seems wrong not to.

"That's up to M," he replies, looking at her.

The warm look she gives him in return makes me wonder what it would feel like if Molly looked at me like that.

"Sure," she says. "Bri and Deb will love it." She doesn't say it loudly enough for her *Duchas* friends to hear from several spots down the table, but I know Molly did.

"Cool. Thanks."

All through lunch, Molly and I keep up a light, impersonal conversation that includes other people at the table. Even so, more than once I notice the Sovereign watching us both closely, sometimes more focused on me and sometimes on Molly. Every time I see her doing it, she quickly turns to someone else—usually Rigel.

I wonder uncomfortably if she suspects something is up with Molly and me and is trying to figure out what. She can't read anybody's mind but Rigel's, can she? Geez, I sure hope not. That would make my original goal even more hopeless than it is already.

In Government class, the teacher again has us work with our teams on our Supreme Court projects. I make sure to talk more today than I did yesterday and notice Molly's doing the same. Whether Alan notices the difference, I have no idea. Once or twice he gives me a quick frown when I say something to Molly, even though it's only about some aspect of our case. Maybe he's feeling a little more possessive toward her after spending time with her last night? Jerk.

Before I can stop myself, I blurt out, "Hey, I overheard you two talking in the lunch line about getting together to go over the Constitution unit from the start of the year. Would it be okay if I join you for that? My old school in Denver hadn't covered it yet when I left."

Which is a total lie. It was our first topic of the year in Government, too.

There's no mistaking Alan's frown this time but after a moment's hesitation he grudgingly shrugs. "Um, sure. I guess that would be okay. If it's okay with Molly?"

He sends her a look that clearly signals he wants her to say no. She nods anyway.

"Fine by me. I can catch you both up at once, no problem."

"Thanks." I include them both in my smile. "I really appreciate it."

At the question in Molly's eyes, I quickly look down at my notes, cursing my lack of control and wondering what the hell prompted me to do such a stupid thing. Except I already know.

I'm jealous.

Of an Ag.

23

Reversible process

Molly

I WATCH Tristan as he fiddles with his notes, wondering what *that* was about. Because I'm sure he mentioned during that first "tutoring" session with M and me that he'd already studied the Constitution this year. And now he's just a little too focused on the papers in front of him, like he's deliberately avoiding my eye.

He did such a good job of acting naturally at lunch, I started to think I was the only one who got such a strong zing from that second touch in Chemistry—the one that *should* have been no big deal but was just the opposite. I *was* the one who yanked my hand away…

Just now, though, Tristan almost acted like he was jealous. Of Alan? Surely not.

When we get to Psych class, I briefly consider asking him straight out if that's what's going on, but I don't quite have the nerve. Not when he's treating me like I'm just some acquaintance who happens to sit next to him in class. I'm careful to do the same, since that's what we agreed to.

A few minutes later, something the teacher says suddenly reminds me again of that article of Shim's I read last month, on inter-*fine* pairings. Now I have more questions about that than ever—and it occurs to me that the best person to answer them is M. The trick will be getting all the details about her and Rigel's *graell* resonance without making her suspicious.

Assuming she hasn't already figured out what's going on.

She watched both Tristan and me so closely at lunch, I half suspected that was the main reason she wanted me to sit there. Other than one trivial question about Pre-Cal, there didn't seem to be anything special she wanted to talk about. If she can actually read emotions, I'd *really* like to know what she's been sensing off Tristan today…

I steal a glance at him, wondering if my *brath* feels as strong to him as his does to me. If so, he's not letting on. Maybe Royals are immune? Something else M might know.

At the end of Chorus seventh period, I remember to talk to Kira's sister. "Hey, Adina, Sean said you might have time to, um, let me work with your dog this weekend to see if I can get her to do tricks?"

She nods eagerly. "Sure! You already met Aggie, remember? That time you came over to do homework with Kira? She really liked you. I bet you'll do great with her."

I doubt that, but I figure I owe it to myself to find out.

"Thanks. I've got to help decorate the school tomorrow and I don't know how long it will take. Maybe after that?"

On the way to the bus, we trade phone numbers. I also offer to teach her and Jana a couple of simple cheers when I come over, since they've been talking about trying out for the JV squad before basketball season.

While sitting next to M on the bus, I gather my courage and ask if she has a little time to talk this afternoon. "I, um, read an article recently and it got me thinking about some stuff I never thought to ask you before."

She looks surprised but not overly curious—yet. "Sure. Do you want to come to my house? Aunt Theresa won't be home for an hour or two."

"Yeah, that would be great." I'd just as soon Mum not overhear anything that might make *her* ask questions. With her I wouldn't be able to fudge my answers at all.

Getting off the bus together, I'm suddenly reminded of the first time I went over to M's to talk with her privately—the day I explained all about *fines*, before she knew about the whole Consort tradition or how Sean factored into it. I wonder if she's remembering that too—and if it will make it harder to pretend my interest is purely academic.

Soon we're settled at her kitchen table with glasses of milk and a plate of her aunt's chocolate chip-walnut cookies between us. Definitely *deja vu*.

"So what kind of questions did you have?" M picks up a cookie.

I launch into my story. "Did you read that article Shim published last month in the Nuathan press, on how resonances tend to work between people from the same and different *fines*? It got me wondering what the difference is between the *taghal ardus,* first touch, and the *graell*. And *that* got me wondering exactly how your bond with Rigel formed. When did you—or he—realize it was more than the usual teen resonance?"

The look she gives me is a little too knowing, but all she says is, "You're right, I guess I never did tell you the whole story. When I first told you about our bond, you were resistant to the whole idea, because of Sean. Then later I guess I sort of took it for granted you knew."

"How about you start from the beginning?" I suggest. "You told me it freaked Rigel out the first time he touched you, right?"

She nods. "It freaked me out, too, but only because I'd never felt anything like that before. And because of the way he reacted."

"How long did it take before you realized it was the *graell*?"

"I obviously had no idea at first—I didn't even know Martians existed yet! But Rigel suspected right away, that touch was so intense. He was so worried about it he actually skipped school the next day."

No wonder. *He* already knew M was the one heir to the Martian throne, even if she didn't. He'd have realized right away how our people were likely to react if he accidentally formed a *graell* bond with the Sovereign.

"So that first touch. Other than 'intense,' what did it feel like?"

"Like electricity zinging all through my body, bringing every tiny bit of me alive. And it wasn't long after that before I started changing—my eyesight, my skin, my hearing, et cetera."

When she first told me that part, I chalked it up to how all Martians are enhanced when they're around others. Later I found out it was a lot more than that. "And then what?" I prompt. "Like...what about the second time you touched?"

"It was every bit as strong, maybe stronger—though not quite as startling."

Uh-oh. Like when Tristan touched me again today. "But...it *eventually* faded, right?"

"Nope. If anything it's still getting stronger. We got used to it over time—but we never got tired of it." She smiles dreamily. "I don't think we ever could."

Not what I want to hear! I'm on the verge of panic when I remember something my brother told me last year. "Wait. Don't you and Sean also have some kind of special resonance? I mean, more than you have with most other *Echtrans*?"

"We used to. The *first* time Sean and I shook hands, I got a stronger jolt than I'd felt from anybody but Rigel."

"But not the second time? So more like a regular *taghal ardus*?"

She shrugs. "I guess? Except it took a lot longer to fade than those do, from what I've heard. You probably know more about it than I do, growing up in Nuath and all."

"I was only thirteen when we left, but yeah, that's how it normally works. That also wouldn't explain the way Sean made you feel better when you got sick from being separated from Rigel."

"Shim thinks Sean and I had the sort of extra resonance same-*fine* people tend to have, only stronger because of the whole Consort-Royal bloodline thing."

I take a sip of milk. "Have you ever felt anything like that with anyone else? You had to shake a whole lot of hands back in Nuath."

"No. Some people's *brath* felt a little stronger than others, but nothing close to what I felt off Sean, much less Rigel."

"Do you still get anything special off Sean these days?"

She shakes her head. "Not really. Not since this last time Rigel and I got back together. I don't get the impression he does, either. Unless he's said something? Sean seems really happy with Kira these days..."

"Oh, he is! I was just using him as an example, wondering how many different degrees of resonance there might be."

M looks at me speculatively, like she's practically reading my thoughts—or at least my emotions. "This isn't really about that article, is it? Or Sean, apparently. So what *is* going on? Have you felt something... special from someone recently? One of the new *Echtran* boys?"

I suck in a breath. She knows! I'm almost sure of it now. Even so, I can't bring myself to admit it out loud, not after the way I've badmouthed Tristan since he got here. Which he totally deserved.

"Well, um, Alan and I sort of had to touch when we were working with my plants." Which is true. "And of course we're both Agricultural *fine*, so it made sense we'd have a little stronger resonance because of that." Except we didn't. "Then I remembered that article and wondered about what you felt with Sean compared to Rigel. That's all."

I can tell she knows I'm still hiding something. "That's maybe not the best example, actually, since I was already bonded with Rigel when I first touched Sean. If I hadn't been…who knows?"

A tiny shudder accompanies her words, which isn't very complimentary to Sean, but I guess I get it. Way more than I should, actually.

Which is scary.

"So you're telling me this is actually about Alan?" M asks after a moment. She sounds skeptical.

I don't have it in me to lie to her face. "Not…completely, though I did sort of expect a stronger tingle from him, since he's the first Ag boy my age I've touched since leaving Bailerealta."

She just looks at me, waiting for me to go on.

To buy myself time, I take a big bite of cookie and drink some milk before continuing. I chew slowly but eventually have to swallow. Then, finally, I heave out a sigh. "Okay, fine. Just…don't laugh, okay?"

"I won't. I promise."

"It's…Tristan." There. I said it. "The first time we touched, in Chemistry class, it startled us both, we got such a strong zap. Way stronger than I got from Alan. It didn't seem to make any sense. Especially since Tristan and I don't even *like* each other."

Every time I say that I have to work harder to make myself believe it. M apparently doesn't.

"You don't like him even a little? I mean, I know he was pretty obnoxious when he first got here, but I noticed he's been talking to you more the last couple of days…"

Do I like him? Obsessing over a guy isn't the same as liking, is it?

"Only because I told him how impossible it would be to keep avoiding each other, like he tried to do at first," I tell her. "He's still plenty arrogant about the whole Royal superiority thing—assumed I'd feel honored by that stupid resonance or something."

She grins. "So *that's* why he sat so far away in Pre-Cal and French Wednesday?"

"Yeah. That first touch was Tuesday and he was obviously freaked, like Rigel was with you. Because I'm an Ag. But then we both agreed ignoring each other was silly, so now we're trying to just act…normal. Talk and stuff. It doesn't mean we *like* each other."

"Have you touched each other since that first time?"

I nod. "That's what worries me. Just as a test, we tried it again in Chemistry this morning. It was…even stronger." I am *not* mentioning that kiss! "What do you think I should do?" I ask a little desperately.

M thinks for a second before answering. "You don't *have* to do anything, Molly. Having a strong resonance doesn't force you to act on it, any more than I acted on the one I had with Sean."

"Yeah, but you already had a stronger one with Rigel," I point out.

"True. But you say you don't like Tristan. Do you think he likes you?"

I'm pretty sure M knows. I'm dying to ask her straight out if she really can read other people's emotions but remember in time that she's the Sovereign and I have no business asking questions like that.

Instead, I say, "I doubt it. Unless… Do you think he does?" Not *quite* as direct.

This time she hesitates so long I don't think she's going to reply. Finally she says, "I think maybe you both like each other more than you want to admit. But that still doesn't mean you need to do anything about it if you don't want to."

"I don't see how we could, anyway. Can you imagine what Connor would do if Tristan and I actually went on a date? Or my mum, for that matter?" I force a laugh because that *should* be funny.

M doesn't laugh, though. "Their opinions shouldn't— Oops, sounds like Aunt Theresa's home."

I quickly take our glasses to the sink to rinse, so M's aunt can't make her do it. She still does stuff like that sometimes, even knowing who M really is. I'm already picking up my backpack to leave when Mrs. Truitt comes in.

"Oh, hello, Molly. Marsha, did you remember to put the laundry in the dryer?"

M gets up. "I haven't yet but I will now. Sorry. Bye, Molly."

Struggling to stifle my indignation on M's behalf, I follow her to the laundry room off the kitchen so I can leave by the back door.

"Don't tell anybody about this, okay?" I whisper before I go. "Not even Rigel, if you can avoid it. Please?"

"I won't. But don't worry, Molly. Things will work out one way or another, you'll see. Somehow, they always do."

I hope she's right, even if I don't see any way they possibly can.

⁺⁺

WALKING HOME, it occurs to me to wonder whether Sean and Kira have any kind of special touch-resonance thing going on. Unlike M and Rigel, they're the *exact* same *fines* as Tristan and me, except in reverse.

Sean is the only one home when I get there. Mum and Dad are still out at NuAgra, where they've both been spending more time lately. Realizing this is a perfect chance to question him privately, I join him at the kitchen table, where he's eating a humongous after-school snack.

"Hey. Is Kira busy or something?" Since her close call two weeks ago, the two of them have been as inseparable as Mum will allow.

"She needed to do a few things at home this afternoon but I'm taking her to the game later on. You want some of these before I polish them off?"

He gestures toward a rapidly diminishing stack of sandwiches. Mum must have made them before she left.

"No thanks, I'm good. Do you have a minute?"

"Sure." He stuffs another sandwich in his mouth. "What's up?"

Using the same pretext I did with M, I mention that article I read and how it brought up some questions.

"One bit made me think about how quickly you and Kira fell for each other, even with Mum doing all she could to keep it from happening. Was there anything…*special* about the first time you two touched?"

His eyebrows shoot up and his ears turn red—a dead giveaway he's embarrassed. "Er, yeah, sort of."

"Only sort of?"

He huffs out a breath. "Okay, more than sort of. Not that it's any of your business. It was in the school gym, the day I introduced her to Earth basketball. You've seen enough basketball games to know it's impossible to avoid touching. A few minutes in I was blocking a shot of hers and…yeah. It was pretty intense. We both tried to ignore it, assumed it was just the *taghal ardus* but…it wasn't."

"How did you know?" I ask, though I have a pretty good idea.

"The intensity, for one thing. It was at least as strong as the first time I touched M. That was also stronger than the usual *taghal ardus* and lasted longer, too, but gradually faded over time. With Kira, though, it… keeps getting stronger."

Again, *not* what I want to hear. "Then…it's still doing that? Getting stronger?"

"Not as dramatically as the first two or three times we touched, but…yeah."

"Isn't that kind of scary?" It's sure scaring the crap out of me!

Sean grins, though his ears go redder than ever. "Not anymore. It's actually pretty great."

Huh. "So…do you think you and Kira have a *graell* bond like M and Rigel do?"

"Who knows? It's definitely not *exactly* like theirs. I mean, we can't shoot lightning bolts or read each other's minds."

"Not yet." I force a grin of my own. "M said it took months before she and Rigel could actually hear each other's thoughts. Maybe you'll get there, too? You've only been dating a couple of weeks, after all."

Weirdly, he doesn't seem at all worried. "True. Like I said, who knows? Whatever we have, it's definitely something special."

"Would you want to? Be able to read each other's minds, I mean?" I'm genuinely curious. "What Mum can do is bad enough. Someone actually knowing what I'm *thinking* sounds way worse."

Sean's mouth quirks up. "Depends on who the someone is, y'know? With Kira, I'm not sure I'd mind."

With Tristan, I'm *very* sure I would. Even though I'm not hungry, I pick up a sandwich and start to nibble—just for something to do while I sort through what I've learned this afternoon.

"Is this really just about some article, Mol?" he suddenly asks, exactly like M did. "Or are you wondering how you'll know if Alan is really 'the one'?"

I try to look like he guessed my secret. "Maybe a little."

"And?"

"Um. I guess it's like the article said, there are different degrees of resonance. Maybe the dramatic kind like you and Kira have, and M and Rigel, only happen between different *fines*?"

His laugh is more genuine than mine was. "That would undercut the whole justification for our pairing traditions, wouldn't it? But…maybe. Of course, Mum would be quick to point out that a sample size of two isn't nearly enough to hang a theory on. Um, don't tell her what I just told you, okay?"

"I won't. But I think maybe you should. It might make her back off a little."

"Or make her even worse," he says with a grimace. "I'll think about it."

I manage an encouraging smile. "Good. Thanks for telling me, Sean. This whole resonance-*graell* thing is pretty interesting."

"Yeah, it is. But hey, don't be too bummed if you didn't get anything special off Alan. Just a few days ago, you said you two weren't all that compatible anyway, and as far as we know, these, er, bonds are permanent."

Permanent??

Sean's smiling, and I can guess why. Meanwhile, I'm fighting a rising sense of panic.

"Yeah, that's a, uh, good point. Well, I'd better go freshen up my cheerleading uniform. Amber's picking me up early since tonight's an away game."

24

Transition state

Tristan

MOLLY'S already warming up with the other cheerleaders on the side-lines when I get to the game. Because we're doing the casual friends thing now, I give a little wave when she sees me…and Trina enthusiastically waves back. Molly just smiles and nods and looks amused.

Way more than last Friday, I notice how good she looks in her little black and yellow cheerleader outfit. The super short skirt makes her legs look amazingly long, even though I know she's a good six inches shorter than I am. Not that a "casual friend" has any business noticing her legs…

Turning hastily away, I scan the Blackford High stands, which are even smaller than Jewel's. Yep, there's the Sovereign, again sitting with her *Duchas* friends near midfield, a few rows up. Unlike last week, she actually seems happy to see me, though not as happy as her two girl-friends.

"I see you survived your first full week at Jewel High." The little blonde, Deb, dimples up at me.

Bri, the dark-haired one, adds, "It's really too bad you didn't get here in time to play football this season. I'll bet you're amazing."

Though I play along with their flirting, I'm careful not to turn on the charm. I don't want the Sovereign—or Molly—to think I'm toying with their friends. Molly already got snarky about me using it on Trina, even though it's obvious by now that Trina's one of her least favorite people.

On that thought, I start to glance toward Molly again but catch myself in time. Tonight I need to keep my focus on the Sovereign and do what I can to salvage my campaign to win her over. I give her a big smile but she just looks at me for a second like she's trying to figure me out, then turns to watch the players running onto the field for the kickoff.

"Molly looks like she's having fun, doesn't she?" she comments to her friends.

Of course that instantly diverts my attention to the sidelines again, where Molly and the other cheerleaders are performing an enthusiastic dance routine to greet the team. She does look like she's having fun. She's also easily the best-looking and most talented girl in the group. My heart speeds up a little just watching her. At least I can't feel her *brath* from here…

With an effort, I drag my attention back to the Sovereign. She's watching me with a definite trace of amusement.

"So, have you given any more thought to what I said about Molly during football practice yesterday?" she asks quietly.

Crap.

"What do you mean?" Not that I've been able to think about much of anything *but* Molly for the past two days.

"I noticed you two weren't avoiding each other today. Does that mean you've realized she's worth getting to know better? Because she definitely is. She'd never tell you this herself, but she's been a real hero on more than one occasion, and not just to me, personally."

Because I'm foolishly eager to learn more about Molly, I can't resist saying, "Really? How?"

But then the game starts, so she doesn't answer for several minutes, not till there's a break in the action on the field. I try to follow the game, too, but it's really hard to keep my focus from getting snagged at the sidelines, where Molly's doing stunts and dance moves. When M finally speaks, it's again in a whisper her *Duchas* friends can't hear.

"Without Molly's help, I never would have been Acclaimed last spring. In fact, I'd have looked like a complete idiot when we first got to Mars if she hadn't been there to give me pointers. She always knew exactly what I should wear and how I should act for each occasion, depending on who would be there. Ditto when I was traveling around later, convincing people to emigrate to Earth. And I can't count how many times her upbeat attitude kept me from melting down when that would have been disastrous. No matter how hopeless things seemed— and they did, more than once—Molly always found a silver lining."

A shadow of pain in the Sovereign's green eyes makes me wonder what really happened on Mars. I guessed from Father's mood last spring it was something really serious, but he would never say what. When I asked, he insisted it was classified. I wonder if Molly knows.

"Does that mean she was involved in absolutely everything you did while you were in Nuath?"

"Everything," M confirms. "And she handled it all like a champ, which is a lot more than I can say for certain adults. *Royal* adults."

I flinch at the scorn in her voice. "She, um, told me you're not a big fan of Royals. Even though you are one." Then I swallow, remembering what happened immediately after that...what *I* did. And how it rocked my world.

"She's right—I'm not a fan at all. Royals have caused me more grief and put our people at more risk than anyone, except maybe Faxon. Actually, it wouldn't surprise me a bit to learn Faxon himself has Royal blood. That would explain his megalomania."

She turns away to watch the game for a while. Just as well, because I have no idea what to say to that. I'd assumed Molly exaggerated about the Sovereign despising her own *fine*, but apparently not.

I want to tell her I know plenty of Royals who care about our people's future. But after wracking my brain for several minutes, the only one I can name who doesn't *also* care about power and prestige is my mother.

At halftime I again offer to get M something from the concession stand. At least she's polite this time when she says no thanks. I head down to the sidelines anyway, thinking I'll just say a casual hi to Molly. Unfortunately Trina spots me before I get a chance.

"Oh, hey, Tristan! Awesome game so far, huh? Or have you been too distracted to watch it?" She gives a little shimmy.

I have, actually, though not by her. "Um, yeah, you're all looking great out there," I say absently.

I glance past Trina to where Molly's talking with one of the other cheerleaders ...just in time to see Alan move to her side, wearing a great big smile. Ugh.

Trina frowns—probably because I said "all"—but then pins her own big smile back on. "So, you should totally come to the after party tonight. It's at Matt's—his parents are out of town."

"After party?"

"We have one after every win—which lately is every game, which is awesome! They're always a *lot* of fun. You'll love it."

I wonder if Molly goes to those parties? If so… "I'll, uh, let you know. Maybe."

"Awesome!" She sure uses that word a lot.

I edge away from her. "Well, um, I was going to hit the concession stand." Maybe on my way back I can snag a few minutes with Molly.

"Oooh, will you get me a Coke? I need to talk to a couple girls on the squad who aren't quite on their game tonight. Thanks, Tristan!" Not giving me a chance to refuse, she turns away to lambast some poor girl who apparently dropped her pompom during one of the cheers.

Shaking my head, I go to the concession stand. Then I have to give Trina her drink on my way back, by which time the second half is about to start. I was hoping to find out whether Molly plans to go to that party, but now I'll have to wait until after the game to ask.

I head back up the stands with my own soda and sit down next to the Sovereign again.

"Molly and Alan seem to be getting along well these days." She says it mostly to her friends, but I feel my gut clench.

"They're really cute together, aren't they?" Deb tilts her head and grins.

"Huh. I thought Alan still had a thing for Kira," Bri says. "I guess he finally decided to move on now she's with Sean? He could definitely do worse than Molly, though I might have made a play for him myself if I'd known."

Out of the corner of my eye I can see M watching me again so I'm careful not to let my distaste for the topic show on my face. Instead I do my best to focus on the team lining up for the second-half kickoff…and the cheerleaders starting their first cheer of the half. At least Alan has moved off.

A few minutes later, while the ball changes hands, M speaks to me again in that sub-whisper her non-*Echtran* friends can't hear.

"You should know that over the past year Molly has become my very closest friend. I honestly think she'd do anything for me—and it's mutual. If anybody were ever to hurt her, *especially* on purpose… Well, let's just say I'd take it personally."

For a second I hope she's talking about Alan—because I'd be glad to help her take him down—but the look she gives me is unmistakably a warning. Somehow, I don't know how, she's figured out I'm way more interested in Molly than I should be.

Meeting her eye, I nod to let her know I understand. Because the last thing I want to do is hurt Molly, Sovereign's best friend or not.

As soon as the game ends, I say a polite goodbye to M and her friends and head down to the sidelines. To have any chance of reaching Molly before Alan does, I need to avoid getting waylaid by Trina.

When I spot Alan moving her way from the far side of the stands I quicken my pace, keeping a wary eye on Trina. The moment her back is turned, congratulating the players on Jewel's victory, I hurry to Molly's side.

"You, um, you're really good at this cheerleading thing," I tell her. It sounds even stupider coming out of my mouth than it did in my head.

She looks up at me in surprise. "Thanks. Great game, huh? It should get us first seed in the playoffs."

"Yeah, that's what Bri said. So, um, are you going to that party tonight? Trina mentioned it earlier."

Looking even more surprised now, she shakes her head. Her short ponytail bounces behind her, her brown hair glinting under the stadium's bright lights. "No, I never go to those. There's always drinking, so Mum doesn't like me going to them."

"You *told* her about that?" I would never mention something like that to my parents.

"She asked. Maybe you haven't heard, but my mum is like a human lie-detector. There's no fooling her, not when she asks a direct question."

"Oh, right. My father's mentioned that."

I see Alan closing in from a short distance away, a definite frown on his face—because I'm chatting up Molly, I assume. Like he's the only one allowed to do that?

Even though I know it doesn't work on her, I project a little of my charm thing. "In that case, what do you say to doing something together tomorrow night?" The words are out before I can stop them. Where did *that* come from?

She stares at me with something close to shock. A lot like I'm feeling. "Together? Are...are you actually asking me out? On a date?"

"Um... I guess?" Desperately, I try to force my brain to re-engage. "What do you say? There's this restaurant I heard about, this side of Kokomo..."

Now her gray eyes narrow. "So...someplace no one else will see us together? Thanks, but no."

I feel my face flushing—because that's exactly what I had in mind. Much as I want to spend some time alone with Molly, I'd much rather my father never hear about it. Which he definitely would if we went anywhere in Jewel.

"That's not— Okay, yeah. Sorry." I can't lie to her. Even if I tried, I suspect it wouldn't work any better than it would with her mother. "You're right. If we're not willing to be seen together, we shouldn't go out at all."

From the corner of my eye, I notice Alan has stopped, though he's still watching us, still frowning. Waiting for *his* chance to have a private word with Molly. That's when it hits me that I care more about having her to myself than I care about anything Father might say. He never approves of anything I do anyway, so what difference does it make?

"All right then, how about the Lighthouse Cafe?"

She rocks back on her heels, eyes wide. "Seriously? There'll be a ton of people we know there on a Saturday night. That's when they have a band."

I shrug, suddenly feeling reckless. "So what? We have a bunch of classes together, we're...friends. Why should it matter if anyone sees us? Didn't we agree we'd get to know each other better?" At least, she didn't *dis*agree when I suggested that yesterday...

"I, um, guess we did. Sure. Okay. I'd just as soon be out of the house tomorrow night anyway, since otherwise I'd have to stay in my room the whole time the Council meeting is going on."

"And my mother is having some of the NuAgra women over for coffee or something while Father's at the meeting. Do you want to meet there, or should I come by and pick you up?"

Might as well wave it right in Father's face, since he's bound to find out anyway.

Molly glances over my shoulder. At Alan? I don't look to see.

"Tell you what, let's check out that restaurant near Kokomo instead," she says abruptly. "We should probably make sure we're capable of spending a civil hour or two together before we stir up the gossip mill. I'll be waiting at the corner of Opal and Garnet at seven. Sound good?"

I'm a little insulted that she's even more concerned about us being seen together than I am. But I'm also relieved I can put off having to explain this whatever-it-is to my father.

"Sounds great."

A second later, Alan brushes past me. "You, uh, still want a ride home, Molly?" he asks, flicking a hostile glance my way.

"Sure. Just let me congratulate Rigel and the other guys on the team and we can go. See you later, Tristan." She sounds totally casual, not at all like we just agreed to go out. On a date.

As for me, my mouth is dry and my heart is pounding at the very thought of being alone with her tomorrow night.

"Yeah. Later." Deep in conflicted thought, I head for the parking lot.

⁺₊

When I get home half an hour later, Father surprises me with a big smile the moment I walk into the living room. It's not an expression I'm used to seeing on his face.

"Apparently you made a bit more progress with the Sovereign yesterday than you let on," he says approvingly.

Huh? "What do you mean?"

Still smiling, he comes over and claps me on the shoulder. I can't remember him doing that since the time I beat out another guy for top honors at our all-*Echtran* middle school.

"I stopped by Jewel's game against Blackford tonight on my way home, just for a few minutes, and saw you were sitting with her again. It also looked like you were in *very* close conversation, despite all the *Duchas* around you and the distractions of the game. Well done, son."

Great. The first time he's been proud of me for ages, and it's for something I totally don't deserve. "Um, yeah, I think we're starting to become friends." That's not a *complete* lie.

"That's wonderful, Tristan," Mother says from across the room. She's smiling, too. "I'm sure the Sovereign can use more *Echtran* friends."

"Especially Royal ones," Father agrees. "So tell me, do you think it's too soon for you to ask her on a date? We can afford for you to take her someplace much nicer than Stuart has probably done. Perhaps one of the premier restaurants in Indianapolis. We could even rent you a limousine. I believe there is also a touring Broadway show performing there next weekend."

Mother clears her throat. "Dear, we talked about this and I thought you agreed—"

He waves her to silence without glancing her way. "Never mind. That was before I saw them together tonight. Well, son?"

"Um, yeah, I think it's a little too soon for that. She and Rigel Stuart are definitely still dating, so I seriously doubt she'd accept an invitation like that. Not yet." I don't know why I even added those last two words since I can't imagine she ever would. Assuming I ever ask.

"Yes, well, I suppose it's true there's no great hurry." He gives Mother an impatient look. "Be sure to follow up on this progress at every opportunity, though. Our entire *fine* is counting on you. Our Sovereign needs a Consort who can fill the office properly, not to mention the succession concerns. We mustn't risk having the bloodline diluted."

His obsession with bloodlines suddenly seems a little creepy. Funny how it never struck me that way before, especially considering M is only sixteen. Just like I am.

"Right. Well, um, I didn't get anything to eat at the game, so I'm going to have a snack before bed, if that's okay."

"Of course," Mother says. "I'm glad you had a good time tonight, Tristan."

I did, actually. The evening turned out a whole lot better than I expected—though not for any reason I plan to share with my parents.

Not yet, anyway.

25

Freezing point

Molly

"SO WHAT WAS THAT ABOUT?" Alan demands as I walk with him to the parking lot after the crowd starts to disperse. "With Tristan, I mean."

I've been wondering the exact same thing since Tristan left, but the suspicion in Alan's tone makes me bristle. "We were talking, that's all. Why?"

"Talking about what?" He still sounds suspicious. "It looked a little…intense."

We reach his car then and he opens the passenger door for me. I wait till we're both inside to answer him. "We were arguing a little. We have pretty different political views. Not that it's any of your business."

He huffs out a breath and starts the car. "Sorry. It's just… Nothing."

"What?"

Instead of answering, he backs out of the parking space and navigates his way out of the lot and onto the country road that will take us back to Jewel. Finally, after nearly three minutes of silence, he snorts again.

"I just don't like how these Royal guys are going after the only Ag girls in school, that's all."

For about two seconds I'm stunned speechless. Then I explode.

"What the *hefrin* are you talking about? You think just because you're an Ag, you have some kind of...of *right* to the Ag girls in school? You already implied you think Kira only started going out with Sean because he's Royal, and now you're implying the same thing about me with Tristan. Not that we've ever gone out." *Yet.*

Even in the light from oncoming headlights I can tell his face has gone red. "That's not— I'm not saying I have a *right*, exactly, but it just doesn't seem fair, you know?"

"No. I don't. What I *do* know from what you just said is that you're only acting interested in me because Kira's no longer available. And because I'm also an Ag. Not very flattering, Alan."

He goes even redder. "That's not true. I really do like you, Molly, even if you're a little, uh, challenged when it comes to plants."

For a split second I actually consider jumping out of the car I'm so mad but realize in time how stupid that would be.

"Or maybe you're just a lousy teacher," I shoot back, even though I know that's not the issue. "Well don't worry about wasting your time helping this 'special needs' Ag in future. Kira's little sister is an Ag. Maybe you should make a play for her. Or check out some of the younger Ag women working at NuAgra. Because *this* Ag is officially off the table."

Alan swallows, hard. "Look, Molly, I'm sorry. I never should have said that. It's not your fault—"

"No, I'm glad you did. I'd always rather know how somebody *really* feels."

I fold my arms and stare out my window, thinking how that's especially true when it comes to Tristan. If I hadn't backed down, would he really have taken me to the Lighthouse Cafe to be seen by God and everybody? Guess I'll never know, since I was the one who chickened out.

Alan makes a few more apologetic noises, but otherwise we spend the rest of the half-hour drive to Jewel in silence. Which is fine with me. It gives me time to ponder whether I'm more looking forward to tomorrow night or dreading it.

But by the time Alan drops me off in front of my house, I still don't know.

.⁺⁺.

TRINA IS PRETTY OBVIOUSLY hung over when the cheerleaders gather in the gym the next morning. So are a couple of others. Any regrets I had about riding back with Alan instead of going to the party—with Tristan? —evaporate.

"Okay, girls, let's get all this stuff organized before the guys get here," Trina says. "Amber, c'mon. Off the bleachers. We have work to do."

Amber groans. She's apparently in worse shape than Trina is, though she doesn't take it out on everyone else. "Fine. Where are those cat stickers for the lockers?"

"We're calling them Jaguar stickers, remember? They're right over there." Trina bullies the rest of us into action and soon we have the banners laid out on one side of the gym, with everything else organized by where in the school it's supposed to go. We've just finished when the boys show up to help.

"Hi, Tristan," Trina sings out. Apparently a little too loudly, judging by her wince. "You can help me hang these streamers."

He glances my way before joining her, but I just smile and shrug. There's no stopping Trina when she's on a roll.

A minute later Alan enters the gym, followed by Jimmy Franklin and Pete Griffin. Trina really did line up the cutest guys in the junior and senior classes to help us—though I'd rather avoid at least two out of the four...

Predictably, Pete grins and makes a beeline for me. "Hey, Mol! Looking good today."

I glance down at my oldest jeans and a brown sweater that's fraying at the elbows. "Um, thanks?"

I don't know why Pete keeps flirting with me after all the times I've turned him down. He's a senior, and good looking enough to date most any girl in school...and does. My guess is he sees me as a challenge.

"So, what can I help you do?" he persists.

Since Trina has already co-opted Tristan and I have no desire to work with Alan after last night, I summon a smile. Pete's on the basketball team and Sean's closest *Duchas* friend, even if he is a total player.

"These posters are supposed to go on every second classroom door. It'll go faster if we split them up. Here's an extra roll of tape."

"Cool." He grabs the tape and a stack of "Spook the Spartans! Go Jaguars!" signs and follows me out of the gym.

We work our way down one hall, then another. I try to send him down a separate corridor to hang his posters, but he sticks close. Of course. And keeps trying to flirt.

"You busy this weekend?" he asks hopefully, probably because this is the nicest I've been toward him lately.

"Yeah, I am, sorry. Heather just broke up with Gary, though. You should ask her."

He only looks disappointed for a second. "Maybe I will, you're always so busy these days. Just remember you're my first choice, Mol!"

"Right." I laugh so he won't think I take him seriously.

After taping Spirit Week signs on doors along the whole left-hand side of the school, we run into a traffic jam in the central hallway. Alan and Amber are on opposite sides, sticking peel-off Jaguar-cats on lockers while Donna and Jimmy hang a banner across the center of the corridor. Trina and Tristan are waiting for the ladder so they can hang black and orange streamers from the ceiling.

When I come around the corner, Alan and Tristan both take a step toward me, then stop to glare at each other. The sudden tension in the air is palpable.

"You look like you're about done with those stickers," Tristan says to Alan. "We've got enough people to finish up, if you have other things to do."

Alan thrusts out his chin. "Don't you have someplace *you* need to be? I can help with the crepe paper. I'm taller than you are anyway."

Trina laughs delightedly. "Boys, boys! Be nice. It's sweet how you both want to help me, but we don't want the other girls to feel neglected. Maybe we can switch jobs around a little?"

"Sure," Pete says. "Molly and I can do the streamers. We won't even need a ladder—I can just boost her up."

He reaches for my waist but I sidestep him, remembering all too well how those hands of his like to wander. "Or not."

"How about this?" Trina says. "Tristan and I will finish with the signs and Molly and Alan can put up the rest of the streamers. Pete, you can help Amber with the locker stickers. If we all pitch in, we'll have the school covered in Halloween Jaguar spirit in no time."

Neither Pete nor Tristan look particularly pleased with that solution but Alan immediately moves to my side.

"Is there another stepladder somewhere?" he asks.

"Probably in the janitor's closet," Amber volunteers. "Molly, show him where it is."

I reluctantly head that way with Alan on my heels. As soon as we're away from the others he mutters, "Look, I really am sorry about what I said last night, Molly. I didn't mean it the way you took it, I swear. Will you let me make it up to you?"

"It was pretty obvious what you meant, Alan. How about you make it up to me by getting these stupid streamers up as quickly as possible so we can go home?"

And that's what we do, once we have the second ladder. Since Alan's tall, I send him up the ladder and hand him the black and orange streamers and tape. In less than half an hour we've used up all the crepe paper and take the ladder back to the janitor's closet. The others finish around the same time and we all reconvene in the gym.

"Great job, you guys!" Trina seems a little perkier than she did earlier. "The school looks awesome. Our decorations will really ramp everybody up for Friday's pep rally. How about we all head to Dream Cream for shakes to reward ourselves?" She slants a flirty glance up at Tristan.

My insides tighten at the mention of Dream Cream. Tristan looks self-conscious at the reminder, too.

"Um, I can't," he and I both say at the same time, then laugh nervously.

"I need to get home," I quickly add.

He nods. "Me, too."

Alan doesn't show any interest either, so it's just Jimmy and Pete who go off with the rest of the cheer squad. I quickly accept Amber's offer to drop me home on the way, before any of the boys can volunteer.

After making myself a late lunch, I text Adina to see if she's free and she immediately invites me over. I tell my folks where I'm going and head to Diamond Terrace. If nothing else, working with the puppy should keep me from spending the next few hours obsessing over my looming date with Tristan.

✦

THE MORAINS ARE AS DELIGHTED to see me as they were the last time I came over. Then, it was supposedly to do homework with Kira—but really so she could show me how to open rosebuds. Now, with the excuse that I'm here to teach cheerleading moves to Adina and Jana, I find myself back in the same courtyard where I failed so miserably with the roses.

"She really *does* like you," Adina assures me for the fifth time, when I can't even coax the puppy to do tricks Adina has already taught her. "And she's still really young, so she gets distracted really easily."

"It's fine." I don't want *her* to feel like a failure, too. "Besides, I'm sure if I had your gift with animals I'd know already. I just figured it was worth a try. And she is awfully cute." I cuddle the little white fluff ball and she licks my chin—then nips my finger when I pet her.

"Aggie, no!" Adina admonishes her. Instantly, the puppy droops her head and crawls to her mistress to be forgiven. Which she is, of course, but I'm impressed by how easily Adina can control the little dog.

At least I do a decent job teaching the two girls cheer moves afterward. Jana's clearly a lot more enthusiastic about joining the JV squad than Adina is, but after a couple of hours it's obvious neither will have any trouble making the cut.

"Good luck on Monday," I tell them as I leave. "I'll be rooting for you."

✦

WALKING HOME A LITTLE AFTER FIVE, I realize with a surge of panic that Tristan will be picking me up in less than two hours. I haven't even decided what to wear tonight—or worked out a plausible-sounding excuse for my parents, since I have no intention of telling them the truth. Not yet, anyway.

"I'm glad you're back, Molly," Dad greets me when I walk in. "I know I suggested a movie this evening, but I'd really like to sit in on tonight's Council meeting."

"That's fine, Dad." I totally forgot we'd planned on a movie. "I don't think anything new is playing this week anyway. I half-promised I'd go to a friend's house tonight, so I'll just do that instead."

He accepts my fib without question, but Mum will be the real hurdle. Maybe if I come up with enough details to give her, she won't question me directly about my plans. It's my only hope.

Combing through my closet for the perfect outfit a few minutes later, I think up ways to embroider the story I just told Dad. I've just decided on black denim leggings and a hip-length electric blue sweater—flattering but not *too* sexy—when M taps on my open bedroom door.

"Hey, you busy? Your mother told me you were up here." Her eyes light on the clothes laid out on the bed. "Ooh, what's the occasion?"

Though I'm tempted to tell her the truth, I realize this is a good chance to test my alibi. "Amber's invited a bunch of us over to watch a Jurassic Park marathon in their basement movie room. Her mom's making dinosaur cookies and stuff."

M tilts her head to one side. "So...why are you nervous about it? Is Tristan going to be there?"

Blimey, she's becoming as hard to fool as Mum!

"I saw you two talking after the game last night," she explains then. "I wondered if you were making plans or something."

I give it up. "Okay, yeah. We were. He, um, actually asked me out."

"And you said yes? Where does Amber come into it?"

"She doesn't. That's just the excuse I was going to give my mum if she asks. She probably won't buy it either."

"You don't want your parents to know you're going out with Tristan? Why?"

I stare at her. "Seriously? After the hard time Mum's been giving Sean about Kira? This is the exact same thing in reverse. Plus...I'm pretty sure he's not planning to tell his parents about it, either, and if Mum knows, she might mention it to Connor. Who would go ballistic."

"It *shouldn't* matter to either one of them but yeah, you're probably right. Are you really sure *you* want to do this? I just...I don't want to see you get hurt, Molly."

I'm touched by her concern. "Neither do I," I assure her. "Really, though, I think we're both approaching it as a kind of experiment with no expectations on either side. Maybe after this we won't feel quite so weird around each other at school."

"Okay, then." Though she looks a little skeptical, she doesn't argue.

I glance at my clock. "He's supposed to pick me up at the corner in less than an hour so, um, I really need to jump in the shower, if that's okay? Did you want to talk about anything, or do you just need closet time before the meeting?"

"Both," she says with a grin, "but I won't hold you up. They finally filed formal charges against Allister and Lennox yesterday, in case your parents didn't mention it. So now I'm worried that when they do those memory extractions we'll find out there's a way bigger threat out there than we thought."

"C'mon, M, there's no reason to assume that." I pick up my toiletry kit. "You're always borrowing trouble."

She laughs. "You sound like Sovereign Leontine." Then her expression suddenly changes, like she wants to snatch back her words.

"Huh? What do you mean? How would you know—?"

"I, um, shouldn't have said that." She chews her lip indecisively for several seconds, then suddenly gives a little nod. "But since I did, I might as well tell you the whole truth about my Scepter."

I sit down on the bed, my shower forgotten. "Okay."

"There's not time now to explain it properly but the archive in it, well…it's a lot more than just a data bank. It's the actual stored images, memories and personalities of the last several Sovereigns."

"Whoa. Cool! Can you show me? Or is that not allowed?"

She shrugs. "It's *supposed* to be secret. The only people I've told since I found out about it are Shim and Rigel, and even they've never seen it work. But…maybe? When we have more time. Now, though, you need to get ready for your date and I'd better get in your closet if I'm going to consult the archive before the meeting. Do you need anything out of there first?"

"Just my shoes." I quickly grab them and set them on the floor next to the bed. "There. All yours." We grin at each other and I head for the shower.

To avoid disturbing M—or being too tempted to eavesdrop—I take my time showering. Then I dry my hair and put on a little bit of lip gloss and a swipe of mascara—the only makeup I ever wear. I am *not* putting on extra for Tristan.

My closet door is still closed when I get back to my room, which means M is still in there. Talking with her *ancestors*, as mind-boggling as that is. She must have been totally blown away when she first found out what her Scepter contained. I feel a pang of envy—something I almost never feel toward M, oddly enough—that she can actually talk to her grandfather, Leontine. Like M, I never knew my grandparents, any more than I knew my real parents.

I tiptoe to the closet, tempted to see if I can hear anything…then I glance at my clock and curiosity gives way to a mixture of panic and anticipation. Only ten minutes until I'm supposed to meet Tristan! Assuming he hasn't thought better of this whole crazy idea…

I pull on my outfit and give my hair one last brushing, then head downstairs.

"And where are you off to?" Mum asks as I'm pulling my nice rain jacket off the coat rack.

Shoot. I was hoping to slip out without her seeing me, so Dad could just tell her I'm meeting friends. No such luck.

"Amber's," I tell her breezily. "Dad said he plans to stay for the meeting instead of taking me to a movie, so I thought I'd go to Amber's movie-watching party instead."

"Amber's?" Mum repeats, focusing on me a little more closely. Uh-oh. "Will her parents be there?"

Though I know it's hopeless, I project innocence with all my might, keeping my voice upbeat, casual. "I assume so, since she said her mom was going to make dinosaur-shaped cookies," I say, *willing* her to believe me. "It's supposed to be a Jurassic Park marathon," I add when Mum looks confused.

To my utter amazement, her expression clears. "Well, isn't that nice. How are you getting there?"

"Donna said she'd swing by for me on her way to Amber's. She should be here any minute, so I thought I'd wait for her outside. Isn't the meeting about to start?"

"Yes, in just a few minutes, actually." Mum still shows no trace of suspicion, even though I'm lying my face off. "I was going to ask you to help me bring extra chairs from the dining room, but I can have your father do it. Have fun, dear."

She goes toward the kitchen, presumably to get Dad. I stare after her for a second, nearly as boggled as I was when M told me what her Scepter can do. Then, rather than push my incredible luck, I hurry out the door before she can come back.

Out on the porch, I slip on my jacket and take a deep breath, still marveling over the miracle that just occurred. Never, *ever* can I remember sneaking a falsehood past my mother when she bothered to focus. All I can figure is that she was too distracted to do it properly just now. Whatever the reason, even if it never happens again, I'm beyond grateful it did this time.

Hoping it's a good omen for the evening ahead, I go down the porch steps and call out a cheery greeting to Council member Breann, who's just getting out of her car at the curb. Walking briskly toward the corner where I told Tristan to meet me, I wonder what other surprises this evening might have in store.

26

Dependent variable

M

I WAIT until Molly leaves her bedroom to shut myself into her closet because it seems ruder than ever to close the door in her face now that she knows the big secret. Maybe because she wasn't trying to suppress it, her awe and curiosity about the Scepter came through even more strongly than her nervousness about her date with Tristan.

Which still worries me, despite her insistence that she doesn't expect anything to come of it. Because I got a definite sense that her feelings are already engaged, even if those feelings keep shifting from extreme to extreme. Because Rigel's right that they need to work things out between themselves, I resist the temptation to talk her out of going—but it's hard. If Tristan hurts her, I'm more determined than ever to make him pay for it.

"*Chartlann rochtana,*" I say to the Scepter, again settling myself onto the box of books. Maybe next time I really will do this out in Molly's bedroom.

Sovereign Leontine appears in front of me. "Hello again, Emileia. I notice you are finding more frequent opportunities to access the Archive lately."

I planned to give my update and ask his advice before saying anything about Molly, but with that opening I decide I might as well do that first. "That's partly because I, um, told Molly O'Gara what it is I'm doing in here. It seemed only fair, since I have to lock her out of her own closet every time I need to talk to you."

He raises one grayed eyebrow. "Molly? Your Handmaid?"

"Yes, but she's also my best friend, not counting Rigel. She's been a great sounding board, especially when I haven't been able to consult with you or Sovereign Aerleas or any of the others. And she already knows about everything else that's happened, even the stuff the Council is keeping secret, because she was there for all of it."

"I see. Do you trust her? To guard the secret, I mean."

I nod fervently. "I trust Molly with my life. She's proved her loyalty ten times over—even when it meant putting her own father at possible risk in Nuath, after I discovered his role in erasing Rigel's memory."

"If you trust her, Emileia, that is all that truly matters. *You* are Sovereign now, not I, so the decision to confide in her was yours to make."

"Er, thank you."

I never really thought of it that way. In fact, I half expected him to get mad when I admitted what I did. His reminder that I'm the one ultimately in charge is a relief—but also intimidating. It's been reassuring sometimes to think I still answer to someone else. Having that illusion dispelled is a little disquieting.

"In that case," I say after a moment, "will it be okay if I invite Molly to, um, meet you? And maybe your mother? I know she'd love to."

My grandfather smiles down at me. "Again, Emileia, if you truly wish to do so, you need no permission from me. Though I would still caution you not to allow too many people to learn the true nature of this Archive, no matter how trustworthy they may seem. The more who know, the greater the risk of an incautious word that could be overheard by someone less trustworthy."

"I understand. And I don't plan to tell anyone else anytime soon, I promise." I did think about telling Mr. Stuart, but since he didn't press me on exactly how I got that security data, there's no particular reason he needs any extra details.

"And now, I presume you had some other reason for accessing the Archive than confessing what you apparently considered a non-sanctioned decision?"

"Oh. Yes, I did. I wanted to let you know that Mr. Stuart has already started setting up those security systems. He's contacted an Engineering friend in Dun Cloch who has promised to put together the necessary components. Then they can start setting up better safeguards there, as well as at NuAgra and maybe a few other places here in Jewel."

I go on to explain Mr. Stuart's ideas so far, as well as why he trusts his friend to keep his work confidential until it's ready to implement. It seems like the sort of thing that ought to be in the Archive. Just in case. While I'm still talking, I hear Molly come back into her bedroom. I lower my voice since I didn't think to turn on the sound-dampening feature in my new omni.

Leontine listens in silence until I finish, then nods. "I am pleased to hear that the process seems well in hand already. I take it you have had no further cause for concern in terms of your safety since we last spoke?"

"Not me personally, no, though Mr. Stuart did say he found something troubling that he plans to share at tonight's Council meeting. I'll add whatever it is to the Archive the first chance I get."

"Very well. We must hope that whatever it is can be resolved with these new measures being put in place."

Molly's bedroom door closes again, which must mean she's going to meet Tristan. I'd half hoped to see her again before she left, to give her one last word of caution, but maybe it's just as well I didn't.

"Thank you, Grandfather. We'll talk again soon. Right now I need to get downstairs for the meeting, so they don't have to wait on me—and maybe ask what I was doing up here without Molly."

He bids me goodbye and I deactivate the Archive, already looking forward to introducing Molly to my ancestors.

⁘

WHATEVER MOLLY TOLD her parents must have worked because I get zero sense from either of them that they're upset or worried as the Council meeting begins. When Kyna brings up the status of Allister's and Lennox's trials, however, Mrs. O is noticeably less calm.

"While I voted in favor of the charges," she says, "I do hope that the upcoming proceedings will be kept as much out of the public eye as possible. There is no need for our people at large to know the full extent of what the two men attempted—or are suspected of attempting, I should say. Nothing has been proved yet."

"I agree," Connor states emphatically. "Both Allister and Lennox were highly regarded by our people for more than two decades. Many would doubtless find it highly unsettling to learn that two formerly illustrious Royals have been accused of such an atrocity. As they have not been convicted of anything at this point, I see no need for the charges against them to be publicized."

The three non-Royals on the Council all frown and even Breann looks uncomfortable. Nara is the first to speak up.

"Our custom has always been to allow members of our media to witness court proceedings, no matter how high-profile the accused might be. To bar them in this instance would smack of a cover-up. Surely this Council does not wish to give the impression that we have something to hide?"

When Connor and Mrs. O remain stubbornly silent, Breann says, "I'm afraid I must agree with Nara. Shrouding the proceedings in secrecy may do more to undermine the people's trust in their leaders than publicizing Allister's and Lennox's purported crimes. That is not to say every detail must be released to the media, any more than we broadcast every detail of last month's Grentl threat. But I feel we must allow for reporting on the trial itself."

There's some muttering, particularly among the Royals present, but finally everyone except Connor appears to agree. Even Mr. O, who's only here to observe, nods his approval.

"Can we not at least instruct the judiciary panel to review the evidence in private before presenting its summary for discussion and judgment?" Connor asks, still obviously disgruntled. "The memory extractions, for example. Both of those men had access to a lot of classified information over the years. Information that almost certainly shouldn't be broadcast far and wide."

"The memory extractions that will be submitted as evidence for this trial will be limited to those directly pertaining to the alleged crimes," Kyna points out. "There is no reason to believe those particular memories will contain classified information, as neither of the accused was present for any of our meetings involving the Grentl threat. Your concern is noted, however. I can request that the complete memories be reviewed by the presiding judicial member so that anything classified can be excluded prior to being entered into evidence. Anything she finds of particular concern from a security standpoint can be referred to this

Council for a final ruling on admissibility. Will that satisfy you, Connor?"

He frowns for a long moment, apparently thinking through all the possible ramifications, before nodding grudgingly. "I suppose so."

"Lili?" Kyna turns to Mrs. O.

"Yes," she agrees. "That does seem reasonable."

Kyna's expression becomes sympathetic. "I know this is particularly difficult for you, Lili, and I'm sorry. We will do our best to avoid highlighting your family connection, if that is any comfort."

"It is," Mrs. O'Gara replies with a tight smile. "Thank you."

"And now," Kyna says more briskly, "I believe Van has something he wants to bring to our attention this evening?"

Mr. Stuart clears his throat. "As you all know, I've been working at deciphering the encrypted messages we discussed previously while continuing to monitor those still being sent. At the same time, I've been narrowing my search for the precise sources of the communications by triangulating the bounce points from which they're forwarded. I was only able to make partial progress, however, before the transmissions stopped."

"Stopped?" Kyna repeats, frowning. "Completely?"

"I'm afraid so. At first I assumed it was merely a temporary lull. Prior messages were not sent continuously but in spurts, often with several hours between conversations. But there have now been no communications whatsoever for almost two days—not since late Thursday night."

An immediate suspicion springs to my mind. "Do you think someone tipped them off that you were monitoring them?"

As I ask the question, I try to probe the emotions of everyone in the room to see if anyone "feels" guilty—not that I really think a Council member would do such a thing. Some do seem more worried than others, but I don't pick up anything like a silent admission.

"That was my first worry, once the silence continued longer than it ever had before," Mr. Stuart admits. "I wanted to ask whether anyone beyond this Council is aware that I've been investigating those communications."

Kyna looks thoughtful. "We did speak with a few Scientists Wednesday evening, as you know, though not specifically about this issue. Perhaps one of us mentioned it then?"

"I don't remember doing so, but I suppose it's possible," Mr. Stuart concedes. "Excellency, do you recall the topic coming up?"

I think back, replaying that entire evening in my mind—something I'm much better at now that I've developed near-total recall. "I don't think it did. We definitely didn't say anything in front of Kira or Sean, and they were there almost the entire time."

"That is my recollection as well," says Kyna. "Have you called upon anyone else's expertise in decoding the messages?"

Mr. Stuart shakes his head. "I've done some searching in the Nuathan archives I have available, but those searches should have been completely secure. That is, after all, one of my specialties."

"And I have no doubt you followed every protocol," Kyna assures him. "This sudden cessation could be coincidental, but I am reluctant to assume that. At this point, I suppose all you can do is to continue monitoring, in hopes the communications will resume."

"I'll do that," Mr. Stuart says. "I'll also continue parsing the data I was able to compile before they stopped. I may have enough to create an algorithm that will allow me to pinpoint the locations of origin without further information."

The discussion moves to ongoing topics like the acclimatization of the recent *Echtran* immigrants and how their impact on their various *Duchas* communities is being assessed. Finally, a little after nine, Kyna adjourns the meeting.

"Should it become necessary to reconvene to review any potentially sensitive memories extracted this coming week, I will let you all know," she tells us. "Otherwise, we'll meet again next Saturday, as has become our custom since the Sovereign's return to Jewel. I hope you will all enjoy the rest of your weekend."

With that, her hologram winks out and Nara's soon follows. Of those physically present, Connor is first to leave, though Breann and Malcolm aren't far behind. Mr. Stuart stays long enough to thank Mr. and Mrs. O'Gara for their hospitality—something the Royals never bother to do— and to wish me a good night.

When it's just me and the O'Garas left, I off-handedly say, "I hope Molly's having a good time tonight."

"I'm sure she is," Mrs. O responds. "She sounded quite happy to watch movies at her friend's house instead of going to the cinema with her father as they'd originally planned. But I suppose it's not surprising she would prefer to socialize with friends rather than a parent, at her age."

"No, I guess not," I agree, careful not to give anything away. "Well, I guess I should get back. Cormac will be waiting and Aunt Theresa worries when I'm out too late. Good night."

Walking home, I assume Molly must have only given that fake excuse to her dad, timing it so she could be out of the house before he passed it along to Mrs. O. Pretty clever—and a lot safer than trying to fool her mother's lie-detector ability.

Though I'm glad for Molly's sake it worked, I'm still not sure this date was a great idea. I have a sinking feeling it could turn out even worse than her first date with Alan did.

Whatever happens between her and Tristan tonight, I can hardly wait to hear all about it tomorrow.

27

Combustion

Molly

IT'S JUST STARTING to drizzle when I reach the corner of Opal and Garnet. I pull up the hood of my nice black rain jacket and hope my hair won't frizz before Tristan gets here. Though honestly, that should be the very *least* of my worries. I must have been crazy to agree to this.

A couple of cars pass me. I recognize Mr. Stuart's, then Connor's. Oops. It's twilight but not completely dark yet—but even if Connor noticed me, he surely won't connect the dots? Not if Tristan didn't tell him what he's doing tonight, which he probably didn't. He seemed kind of relieved when I caved and suggested sticking with his original plan, after he called my bluff about the Lighthouse Cafe.

It's five past seven when Tristan pulls up in his sleek black Porsche. The rain is starting to pick up now, so I get in quickly.

"Sorry!" he says as I buckle my seatbelt. "I, um, waited for my father to park and go inside."

As I suspected. "It's okay. I didn't tell my parents, either. Like I said last night, we may as well find out whether we can avoid killing each other for an evening before, um, spreading the word." I don't say about what, exactly—and don't analyze it myself, either.

He grins at me and even though I don't *think* he's using that charm thing he has, it still makes my insides do a little backflip. I swallow and look away. "So, I, um, guess we should get going?"

"Oh. Right." He pulls away from the curb and makes a quick U-turn to head back to Diamond Street—something our minivan could never do on a street this narrow.

I know I should be taking advantage of this opportunity to talk to him, find out more about him, but I'm feeling oddly shy and awkward even though *he* was the one who asked *me* out. Or maybe because of that?

"Have you ever been to this restaurant before?" I ask as we turn onto Diamond, mostly just to say something.

"Um, no. But it has great ratings online. A lot of variety on the menu, which seemed like a good idea since I, er, don't know what you like."

He sounds as nervous as I am, which helps bolster my confidence.

"I like most things." Then, after a pause, I blurt out, "Do you think we're insane to be doing this?"

"Probably," he says with a little laugh. "But…I decided I really don't care. Do you?"

I ponder that for a second, then shrug. "I guess not. If nothing else, doing this might help us get past all the awkwardness at school."

Or not. Depending on how things go tonight, it could get a hundred times worse.

He lifts a shoulder. "That's what I'm hoping. It'll also give us a chance to learn a little more about each other. Even if we decide we'll only ever be friends, that can't be a bad thing, right?"

"Right."

Do I only ever want to be friends with Tristan? Or even friends with him at all? I honestly don't know yet. But maybe I will, after tonight?

"You, um, grew up on Mars, right?" he asks after another slightly-too-long silence.

"In Glenamuir, yes. It's one of the little Ag villages north of Thiaraway. Have you ever visited it?"

He shakes his head. "I've never been to Nuath at all. I was born in Denver."

Huh. I didn't know that. "How long had your parents been on Earth before you were born?"

"Just a couple of years. They left when things on Mars started getting dicey for Royals, I think. Because of Faxon."

My dad used to go off on rants about all the Royals who left instead of staying to fight against Faxon, like he and Mum did. Not that I'll tell Tristan that. It's probably one reason neither of them ever seemed to like Connor much, even before he tried to get Tristan certified as a potential Consort.

"Yeah, a lot of people did that," is all I say.

"I really want to see it someday. Mother and I both hoped we might go during this last launch window. She really wants to go back. But Father decided keeping his position on the Council was more important."

I stop myself just in time from making a crack about power-hungry Royals. I resolved earlier not to argue politics with Tristan tonight, if I can possibly avoid it. Mostly because of what happened last time.

"How long has he been on the Council?" I ask instead. "My mum's only been on it since last year, when Uncle Allister was booted off."

"Yeah, I knew that. Let's see, I guess Father's been on it for a little over ten years now? I was just about to go into first grade when he was appointed. That's when we moved into the bigger house in the Denver suburbs where we lived before we moved here. Before that, we were in a place about half that size in Fiarway, the *Echtran* compound."

That makes me wonder what kind of compensation Mum gets for being on the Council. Funny how I never even thought about it before. I guess I assumed it was a volunteer position without pay. Apparently not. Interesting.

"Do you think the rest of the Council will have to move to Jewel?" I ask him. "The only ones who haven't yet are Kyna and Nara, both non-Royals."

Tristan shrugs. "No clue. Father hasn't said anything about it—at least, not in front of me. Uh-oh."

The rain has been getting harder and harder as we've driven north and now I can see flashing red and blue lights up ahead, along with a lot of brake lights. "There must be an accident."

"Yeah." Slowing the car, he squints through the rain, which is starting to outpace his windshield wipers. "Looks like a semi jack-knifed, or maybe even rolled. I think it may be blocking the whole road."

"So we might be stuck here for a while?"

He frowns and punches up the GPS screen on the dash. "There's a side road just ahead. Maybe we can go around it."

"Worth a try," I agree. "It looks like traffic is about to come to a dead stop."

He surprises me with a grin. "You call this traffic? Seriously? You should see Denver at rush hour."

"You know what I meant."

"Sorry. Okay, looks like this road might let us work our way past the accident."

Tristan has to maneuver the car onto the shoulder for several yards to get past the stopped cars in front of us, then we turn on to a narrow country road with no streetlights or much of anything else. The rain gets even heavier, reflecting off the headlights like an uninterrupted sheet of water.

"Can you see—?" I start to ask when something jumps in front of the car, forcing Tristan to swerve violently to avoid it.

"What was that?" he practically shouts, stopping the car.

"A deer, I think. Good thing you missed it. It would definitely have messed up your pretty car if you'd hit it. Wouldn't have done the deer any good, either."

For a moment he remains silent, clearly shaken by the incident, then he nods. "Were you about to ask how well I can see through this? Obviously not very."

I suddenly think to pull out my cell phone to check the radar. "Looks like this is just the leading edge of a line of pretty nasty storms," I tell him. "Probably a cold front. It's going to get a lot worse before it gets better."

"Think we should find a place to wait it out, then?"

"Might as well. Maybe the accident will clear by then, too, so we can go back to the main road."

Tristan puts the car back in gear and drives forward—slowly, since visibility is so awful. I can't see anything off to the side but cornfields.

"How about here?" he says after three or four minutes, pulling into an empty parking lot in front of a tiny church.

"Sure. At least we're out of the road here."

He parks the car and turns off the engine. It's full dark now, the only illumination coming from a security light above the church door. I'm suddenly hyper-aware of Tristan sitting just a foot or so away from me. Of his *brath*.

The rain continues to drum down on the roof of the car, now and then sounding like it's mixed with hail. I shiver.

"Sean would be so freaked out if he were here," I say without thinking, distracted by Tristan's nearness, then immediately feel disloyal for criticizing my brother to him.

"He would? Why?"

Nothing to do now but explain. "When we first came to Earth from Nuath, he had kind of a hard time getting used to the idea of things—like rain—falling out of the sky on us. It never rains in Nuath, of course. He's mostly over it now, but he still wouldn't like *this*." I gesture toward my window.

"No, I get it. My mother's the same way. She still doesn't like rain—or snow—even after all these years. I think the open sky is the main reason she hardly ever leaves the house. I can see how that would be hard to adjust to for someone who spent their whole life in Nuath."

I'm relieved. I was worried he'd make fun of Sean. "Your mom must really miss Nuath, huh?"

"Yeah. She loved Thiaraway. I really hope we—she and I, anyway—can go there during the next launch window."

He sighs in the darkness and the sound makes me shiver again, though it's a different kind of shiver this time. I'm suddenly glad for the console between our seats.

"You'd go without your dad?"

Tristan gives a mirthless laugh. "In a heartbeat, though I doubt he'd let us. Mother and I would both be happier— Sorry. More than you probably wanted to know."

"No, it's okay. When he drove M and me home from your house I, ah, got the impression you and your dad don't get along all that well."

"I don't think he gets along very well with anyone, but especially me. Nothing I do ever seems to make him happy." He sounds bitter.

I hesitate a moment before saying, "I guess if you told him about asking me out he'd be even less happy, huh?"

"Yeah. But like I said, I've decided I don't care anymore. I'm tired of tiptoeing around him, trying to stay on his good side all the time. I'm sure Mother is, too, though she'd never say so out loud."

"You make it sound like she's afraid of him."

Another sigh. Oddly, it makes me want to comfort him. "I think she probably is. Not *physically*," he adds quickly. "He's never hit her or anything—not that I'd let him. But he can be pretty nasty when he's in a bad mood, so we both try not to do or say anything that will tick him off. It gets old, though."

"I'll bet." I'm suddenly a lot more grateful for my own parents than

I've been in a long time. I may not always agree with them, but they're never intentionally mean. Not even in words.

"Sorry," he says again. "I probably shouldn't be telling you all this. But…I guess I needed to get it out of my system. Or something."

I have to fight an almost overwhelming urge to reach over and put a hand on his arm. "No, it's fine. I'm glad you told me. The whole point of going out tonight was to get to know each other better, right?"

He smiles across at me in the dimness and my heart does a little stutter-step. "Right. Okay, your turn. What's it like for *you* at home, the only non-Royal in your family? Do your parents ever give you a hard time about that?"

"A hard time? No. I mean, they know it's not my fault or anything. Sometimes Mum says something that makes me…more aware of it, but never on purpose. It's mostly when she's complaining about Sean going out with an Ag—how it's beneath him. But I think she only says stuff like that in front of me when she sort of forgets I'm *not* Royal. Definitely not to hurt my feelings, because she always apologizes if I let her see it bothers me."

"I'm glad to hear that." He sounds like he means it. "I didn't like thinking they might hold your *fine* against you. Even if…even if I did at first. I'm sorry about that, by the way. Like you said, it's not your fault. Any more than I can take credit for being born Royal."

I can't believe how much more open-minded he sounds than the last time we touched on this topic…the night he kissed me. I wonder if it was that kiss or the argument preceding it that made him start looking at things differently? Maybe both?

"Thanks, Tristan. That means a lot."

We just look at each other for a long moment. I wonder if his heart is pounding as loudly as mine is. When he finally speaks, his voice is husky.

"I didn't want you to think I still think about you the way I did at first. I mean, I do think about you. A lot. More than I should. But not…" He trails off, embarrassed.

"I've, um, been rethinking some of my prejudices, too," I tell him. "Maybe… Well, maybe M and my family aren't the only Royals worth knowing after all." Against my better judgment, I put a tentative hand on the console between us.

He immediately covers it with his own and an almost-electrical burst of energy sizzles through me from the point of contact. It's even stronger than the first two times we touched, but somehow not so scary. This time I don't snatch my hand away. Neither does he. We just keep staring at each other, like we're trying to read each other's thoughts...the way M and Rigel do.

Then, slowly, he leans toward me and I irresistibly sway forward as well, my heart thumping with slightly terrified anticipation. For a long moment I can taste his breath mingling with mine from less than an inch away. It tastes...good. His dark eyes ask me a question and I answer it by closing the tiny gap between us.

This kiss isn't like that first, angry one. This kiss is mutual—and one hundred percent wonderful. The sensations that sweep through me are even more glorious than I remember. I don't want them to end...ever.

His arms come around my upper back, pulling me closer. My hands slide up his arms to his shoulders so I can do the same. The center console I was grateful for a few minutes ago is now an irritant, keeping me from getting as close to Tristan as I want to be.

Finally, after many, many heartbeats, we pull infinitesimally back to stare into each other's eyes. I grope for words to express what I'm feeling but no such words seem to exist. Not in English or Nuathan.

"I..." Tristan whispers, then stops.

"Yeah."

And then he gathers me into his arms again and I'm more than willing to be gathered.

"Mmm. Rain finally seems to be letting up a little," Tristan murmurs against my lips a long, blissful while later.

Reality intrudes and I reluctantly—so reluctantly!—pull away from him to sit up, only now noticing the crick in my back from leaning awkwardly over the center console. I pull out my cell phone to check the radar again and I'm startled to discover we've been making out for more than twenty minutes. Not long enough, but way longer than I'd have guessed.

"Looks like the worst is over, though it won't be totally past us for a little while yet. I, um, guess we should get back on the road?"

"Yeah, I guess." He sounds as reluctant as I feel. For a moment he gazes at me, a half smile playing about his perfect lips. Then he blurts out, "Hey, you want to go to the Lighthouse Cafe after all? It's getting kind of late to go all the way to Kokomo now."

I blink at him. "Really? Do you think you're—we're—ready for that?"

He shrugs, still smiling. "Why not? I sure don't plan to avoid you in school this week, so what difference does it make if we give the gossip an early start?"

Warmed by his words as well as the look he's giving me, I shrug back. "If you're really sure? You'll probably get even more pushback than I will, once our families hear we were out together."

"Like I said, I'm sick of placating my father by doing things I don't want to do. Or not doing things I do want to do. Maybe I wasn't completely positive about that before tonight, but now I am."

"Positive about what?" I ask, thinking—hoping—maybe I know.

"That I want to be with you. That this whatever-it-is between us is real."

I'm half tempted to say, "What about M?" but I don't. I just smile. "It feels awfully real to me, too—no matter how crazy it seems."

"Yeah, well, maybe crazy is underrated. So, Lighthouse?"

Convinced now that he really means it, my smile widens to a grin. "I'm game if you are." I don't add, "What's the worst that can happen?" That would be tempting fate even more than we're doing already.

28

Boiling point

Tristan

EVEN THOUGH I don't want to, I have to let go of Molly's hand to start the car. What I'd really like to do is stay here with her for the next two or three hours—or more—but we both still need dinner. Otherwise...

"You know, it's weird," I say as I head toward the state road that will take us back to Jewel. "I'm almost looking forward to seeing everyone's jaws drop when they see us together."

It's incredible how liberated I feel, now I've decided not to shape my life to Father's expectations anymore.

Molly chuckles beside me in the darkness and the sound sends a delicious shiver through me, making me want to stop the car and kiss her again. "I'll be interested to see their reactions, too. Especially Trina's."

"And Alan's." Oops. I shouldn't have said that.

"So I was right! You really did ask to join our study session because you were jealous yesterday."

I smile sheepishly and shrug. "Maybe a little."

"You don't need to be, trust me. I'll admit, I thought at first that Alan and I might be a good fit—and my mum is probably still convinced of that—but we're not. At all. There's no, um, chemistry there, you know?"

A quick glance sideways shows her grinning.

"I do know. It's like how I expected to feel some special resonance with the Sovereign but didn't. Don't."

"So much for those same-*fine* extra resonances I've heard about all my life," she says. "I think Alan tried to convince himself there was something between us, too. Because he's unwilling to even consider a girl from a different *fine*. Sound familiar?"

All I can do is laugh at myself. "A little too familiar, yeah. Though I do get where Alan's coming from, since I was raised to think the same way. Obviously everything they told us is wrong—or at least not the whole picture. Thanks for broadening my horizons, Molly."

"Anytime."

We're stopped now, waiting to turn left onto the main road, so I look at her again. She gives me a tremulous smile, obviously touched. Nobody's behind us, so I lean across the console and give her another lingering kiss before turning back to the road ahead.

The accident appears to have cleared, though the backed-up line of cars is still moving slowly. After a couple of minutes a considerate driver flashes headlights to signal they'll let me go, so I make the turn, waving my thanks.

It doesn't take long to get back to Jewel and barely fifteen minutes later I pull into a parking space a couple blocks away from the Lighthouse Cafe, the closest spot I could find.

"Looks like you were right," I remark. "It's going to be crowded tonight. I hope we won't have to wait too long for a table."

When we get out of the car, it's still sprinkling and noticeably colder than it was earlier. Beside me, Molly shivers and pulls her lightweight black raincoat tighter. I instinctively throw an arm around her shoulders to keep her warmer and she smiles up at me in thanks. I can't resist another quick kiss.

I keep her close against me as we walk the two blocks to the restaurant. My omni has a climate control app that would keep us both warm and dry, but I know better than to use it out on Jewel's main street. Besides, this is more fun.

The Lighthouse Cafe is packed. Appetizing food smells assail us when we walk in, along with music from the cover band playing on the tiny stage near the back. Not an empty table in sight. Without much hope, I flag down a passing server.

"Any chance we can get a table?" I ask her, using just a touch of my charm—for Molly's sake.

The woman draws in a quick breath. "I'll, um, see if anyone looks like they're getting ready to leave. Maybe I can, er, nudge them along."

"You don't always play fair, do you?" Molly mutters. I look down to see her watching me with the same expression she wore when I used my ability on Trina.

Embarrassed, I shrug. "I, um, thought it might get us a table quicker. You're hungry, aren't you?"

"I am, but… What *is* that thing you do, exactly? I noticed your dad used it on M's aunt, too."

"Yeah, I think it kind of runs in our family—his side, anyway. Have you heard of the Royal 'push'?"

She nods. "Mum definitely has it. So does M, though it took her a while to figure out how to use it."

"I guess it's sort of a variant of that, since it makes people easier to persuade."

"Especially people of the opposite sex." She still sounds cynical.

I lift a shoulder. "Well…yeah. Though it can work on guys, too, just not as well. With them it's more like the regular kind of 'push.'"

"So do you think—?" she begins, then breaks off as the server returns to us, all smiles.

"I convinced two couples who obviously know each other to share a four-top, so I can give you the other two-top now. This way."

We follow. As we sit down, Molly whispers, "Whatever it is, it obviously works. Thanks. I think."

"It doesn't work on everyone," I remind her. "You and the Sovereign both seem to be immune."

"M is probably immune because she's so tightly bonded to Rigel. And I'm…maybe not quite as immune as you think. I just hide my reactions better than most."

The smile that accompanies her words makes me want to kiss her again but I restrain myself, conscious of dozens of interested eyes all around us. A few tables away, I notice a pair of cheerleaders sitting with a football player and a basketball player, all four staring our way. Yep, the gossip mill will be grinding away by Monday morning.

It's startling how much I don't care.

"You definitely had me fooled," I tell Molly, leaning in close. "I could have sworn you didn't feel a thing."

She shrugs. "I may be more resistant than the average Ag, what with living around Royals my whole life. I'd have been pushed around all the time if I hadn't developed some sort of self-defense."

"That makes sense."

Her reference to spending her life around Royals reminds me of something I've been wanting to ask her. "You were with the Sovereign—M—the whole time you were in Nuath over the summer, right?" I keep my voice low enough that no *Duchas* could possibly hear me over the band and crowd noise.

"Just about. She went to some meetings and stuff that I didn't, but I was with her for all the, um, important stuff."

"Yeah, that's the stuff I'm curious about. Stuff my father would never tell me, even though it's obvious he knows."

She frowns. "Some of it's, um, pretty secret. Things hardly anybody outside the Council and a few people in Nuath know about."

I immediately back off. "Hey, I totally understand if you can't tell me. I definitely don't want to get you in trouble or anything."

For a long moment she looks at me, still frowning, then gives a tiny shrug. "Oh, what the heck. I trust you to keep it secret more than I trust your dad. And way more than somebody like Gordon Nolan. Mostly, it had to do with the Grentl."

She goes on to tell me about how those super-advanced aliens nearly destroyed Nuath—and would have, if the Sovereign hadn't been Acclaimed in time to respond to a message they'd sent. Even more amazing, she tells me our Sovereigns have been communicating with them for centuries, using some special device the Grentl left behind when they abandoned the colony over two thousand years ago.

"M never could have managed all that without Rigel. Without their bond."

She looks at me doubtfully for a moment, like she expects me to argue that point. I don't.

"Even so," she continues, "the Council still voted to have Rigel's memories of M erased and to ship him back to Earth without her. The Royals on the Council, that is. Then they faked a recording to convince her it was all Rigel's idea. She…pretty much lost it. Luckily Sean and I were able to keep her functioning enough to deal with the Grentl before it was too late, but it was a *way* closer call than it should have been."

My admiration for Molly increases. That must be one of the things M was talking about when she claimed Molly was a hero in her own right. Along with Sean, apparently.

The server comes back to take our dinner order then, forcing us to suspend the most interesting conversation I can ever recall having. I have a whole lot better understanding now of why Molly—and the Sovereign—have such a low opinion of Royals. Especially Royals on the Council. Like Father.

"M told me you used to cover for her a lot before her *Duchas* guardians learned the truth?" I ask once we're alone again.

Grinning, she nods. "Yeah, I, uh, guess you could say I'm a pretty good liar. Probably from years of trying to fool my mum. Not that it ever worked. Not till tonight, anyway."

"You mean—?"

"Yeah, when I was leaving the house to meet you, I told her I was going over to Amber's house to watch movies. I thought I'd be grounded for sure but she actually bought it. She was pretty distracted, though, and she does have to focus for her ability to work."

The way I have to focus to use my charm ability, I assume. Still, if Father heard about this, he'd probably claim Kira also fooled Lili O'Gara about her role in that plot against M's life. Not that I plan to tell him anything Molly just told me.

"I guess if it was only going to work once, this was a good time for it to happen," I say after a moment.

"True. Though considering how many people are here tonight, she's bound to find out anyway. Then I probably *will* get grounded," she says with a grimace.

I groan. "I didn't even think about that when I suggested coming here. That you might have made up an excuse to tell your parents, I mean."

"That's okay. Neither did I. But I doubt we could have kept it secret long anyway. Um, assuming we ever plan to go out again." Her gray eyes meet mine and I immediately answer the implicit question.

"I sure plan to, if you're willing. What do you say? Want to do something tomorrow night, too?"

She blinks, then smiles—a smile that does funny things to my insides. "I'd love to." That word also does funny things to my insides. "That is, if I don't get grounded."

Pretty soon people we know from school start coming by our table to say hi, starting with the cheerleaders I noticed earlier.

"I can't *wait* to see Trina's face when she hears you two were here together," one of them gleefully tells Molly. "Though I hope she won't make life too hard for you because of it."

"She probably will, but oh, well," Molly replies with a shrug and a grin. "It won't be the first time. Oh, can you let Amber know my folks think I was at her house tonight? Though they'll probably find out I was here anyway."

The other girl nods. "You can always say a bunch of us decided to come here after. Anyway, I'll make sure Amber knows your cover story." With a conspiratorial grin, she goes back to her table, already pulling out her phone.

"Heather's usually the nicest cheerleader," Molly tells me. "At least when Trina's not around. She tends to be a bad influence on the rest of them."

Two girls from our Chemistry class stop by the table then, followed by a small group from my Lit class, including the Walsh twins. Because of all the *Duchas* around, neither Liam nor Lucas comment on Molly's and my widely different *fines*, though I can tell from their expressions they're even more surprised to see us together than most of our non-*Echtran* classmates.

No question Father will hear about this within days, if not sooner. It'll probably be prime gossip out at NuAgra on Monday, as well as at school.

Amazingly, I still don't care.

⁘

MOLLY AND I stay at the Lighthouse Cafe until ten o'clock, by which time it's not nearly as crowded as when we got here. Even for a Saturday night, it's getting late by sleepy little Jewel, Indiana's standards.

"I should probably take you home soon, huh?" I say reluctantly when I notice the time. I wish this evening could go on forever—though the best part was earlier, in my car, in the rain…

She sounds just as regretful when she replies. "I guess so. I'll likely be in trouble enough as it is without staying out past my curfew."

"Which is…?"

"Ten-thirty on weekends, unless I get permission to stay out later for something special. Tonight has been really, *really* special, but I doubt my folks will see it that way."

That gets a laugh from me. "No, probably not. Okay, let's go."

The rain has stopped completely now but it's colder than ever. I again wrap my arm around Molly as we walk back to my car, already dreading the moment I'll have to let her go.

We indulge in another five minutes or so of kissing once we're in the car, which helps. A little.

"Can I take you all the way home, or do I have to drop you at the corner where I picked you up?" I ask when I finally pull away from the curb.

"It shouldn't matter as long as Mum isn't out on the porch—which she won't be, as chilly as it is. I don't think she knows what Donna's car looks like anyway—that's who I told her was giving me a ride."

When we get there I really want to walk her to the door, too, but that would be pushing it. Instead, partly to keep her with me a few moments longer, I suggest trading phone numbers.

"With any luck you can get around your parents' questions with the help of your cheerleader friends. If not, I want to know."

"Same here, if you get in trouble." She gives me an amazingly sweet good night kiss before getting out of the car.

"G'night, Molly. See you tomorrow, I hope."

"I hope so, too. G'night, Tristan." With a parting smile and wave, she goes up her front walk. I wait until she's inside before I drive away.

.⁺₊

"Where have you been?" Father demands from the living room the moment I walk in the door. "It's past ten-thirty. I asked your mother where you were, but she apparently didn't think to ask and you didn't bother to tell her." He shoots an accusatory glance her way before turning back to me.

I'd concocted an excuse earlier about meeting with Molly and Alan to work on our Government project—but I abruptly decide not to use it. It suddenly hits me more than it ever has before what a bully my father is. Maybe because of telling Molly about him earlier this evening.

Dropping my car keys into the ornate metal bowl by the front door, I walk forward to face him. "I had a date. Guess I should have told Mother before I left."

"A date? What do you mean?" He gets up from the couch and comes toward me. "The Sovereign was at the Council meeting tonight and didn't leave until after I did, near nine o'clock. Are you saying you arranged to meet her afterward and somehow *forgot* to mention that to me?"

"Nope. My date wasn't with her. Sorry." Except I'm not. At all.

Father's brows draw down in an angry, confused frown. "Then with whom? Some *Duchas* girl you decided to take advantage of? Did it not occur to you that if the Sovereign learns of this she may be less inclined to—"

"It wasn't a *Duchas* girl, either," I interrupt him—something I hardly ever do. "I went out with Molly O'Gara. And we had a great time."

"What?" he explodes, just like I knew he would. Weirdly, I don't even flinch. "Why would you go on a *date* with that Ag upstart of a *Chomseireach*? Did you honestly think dallying with her low-born Handmaid might somehow endear you to the Sovereign? I'd say it's likely to do just the opposite."

I shake my head, keeping a smile on my face even though his description of Molly makes me want to punch him. "No, I didn't think any such thing. That's not why I asked Molly out. I happen to like her. A lot."

"Don't be ridiculous," he snaps. "How can you possibly *like* a disgusting little—"

"Watch it, Father." For the second time in two minutes I interrupt him, this time in a voice I've never used to him before. I'm not smiling now. "I just told you I like Molly a lot. I'm not going to let you insult her to my face."

His eyes practically bug out of his head, making him a lot less handsome all of a sudden. "Won't *let* me? The *hefrin* you won't! This is my house and you are my son and I'll say any *dabhal* thing I please. And I'm not about to let you—"

"Dear." Mother gets up and comes toward us, putting out a tentative hand. "Perhaps it would be best if—"

"Don't interrupt me and don't you *dare* defend him!" He wheels around and takes two quick steps toward her, one hand coming up like he just might strike her. She flinches back.

I move so quickly it surprises even me and a split second later I'm standing between them, face to face with my father. "Hey!" I yell at him. "What do you think you're doing?"

"Get out of my way!" He's so angry now his face is red.

"Not a chance."

I force my voice, my expression, to stay calm, hoping to defuse the situation before it escalates further. I've seen him mad plenty of times before, but never quite like this.

"You…you disloyal little…" he sputters.

"Little? I'm taller than you, in case you hadn't noticed. If you really feel like hitting someone, you can try hitting me—not that I plan to let you do that, either."

For a long moment he just glares at me, breathing hard. Finally, he growls, "You will have no further association with that Ag girl, do you hear me? I won't have you besmirching our family honor like that."

I meet his glare straight on. "You're the one doing the 'besmirching' by losing control. As for Molly, I'm not making any promises. Anyway, we have more than half our classes together."

His hand comes up again and for a second I think he really might take a swing at me—something he hasn't done since I was ten or eleven years old. I tense, ready to evade and counter, but then he drops his arm and snorts.

"All right, I'll take it up with Lili O'Gara then. I'll warn her to keep her Ag foundling away from my family if she doesn't want me bringing this before the full Council."

I give a bark of mirthless laughter. "You really think they'll care? The Sovereign and Sean are already dating outside the Royal *fine* and they haven't exactly put a stop to that."

Though his face is nearly back to its normal pale color by now, he looks angrily from me to my mother and back, then makes a disgusted noise before turning away and striding toward his office. He slams the door and a moment later, I hear him making a call—to Molly's mother, no doubt, even though it's nearly eleven by now.

I pull out my own cell to give Molly a heads up, then notice my mother still standing there, utterly quiet, looking almost stunned. My message to Molly momentarily forgotten, I reach out a hand in concern.

"Mother? Are you all right?"

That seems to snap her out of it. "I…yes. Thank you, Tristan. That was a very brave thing you just did."

I hadn't felt brave, just pissed—but it's true that I've never stood up to Father like that before, ever. "I actually thought he was going to hit you." Then, at the shadowed look in her eyes, I blurt out, "Has he ever?"

She swallows visibly, then slowly nods. "Not recently, but…yes. I thought he'd learned to control his temper better by now, but apparently not."

And I never even suspected. Feeling like the worst excuse for a son ever, I lead her to the couch and sit down next to her. "Why didn't you tell me? I wouldn't have let him…" I trail off, wondering if that's true. I want to think so.

"As I said, he hasn't become violent for quite some time—more than two years now. I…hoped you would never need to know."

"But then I made him lose it tonight. I guess you're pretty disappointed in me, too—dating an Ag when I'm supposed to be winning over the Sovereign?"

Putting a hand on my arm, she gives me a pained smile. "No, Tristan, I'm not. I've never been prouder of you in my life. Molly O'Gara seems like a very nice, responsible girl, whatever her *fine*. There are more important things than bloodlines, as I've tried to explain to your father."

"What about my responsibility to our people—our future?"

I always assumed Mother believed it was as vitally important that I hook up with the Sovereign as Father did. Like I thought I did. Not that I remember her ever specifically saying so.

"The fate of our people doesn't rest on your shoulders, Tristan. It never has, despite what your father has said. With so many relocating to Earth over the next few decades, it's clear many, if not most, of our customs will have to change. The only reason I hoped you would become friends with the Sovereign was that I thought it would make you happy. If you feel you can be happier with Molly O'Gara, that's all that really matters to me."

Wow. "Thanks. I…really think I can be. Which reminds me, I'd better let her know what Father is up to."

29

Chain reaction

Molly

I'm just about to get into bed, anticipating a lovely night of the best dreams I've ever had in my life, when my bedroom door slams open. Mum is standing in the doorway, looking angrier than I can ever remember. Uh-oh.

"Did you, or did you not, tell me you spent the evening at your friend Amber's house, watching movies?"

I swallow. No way I'll be able to pull off lying to her again without her knowing, but I try to at least minimize the damage. "Um, none of us were all that into the movie so we, er, decided to go to the Lighthouse Cafe after an hour or so."

"I just received a call from Connor Roark telling me you were out on a *date* with his son, Tristan. Did you arrange to meet him there?"

Her blue eyes bore into mine, totally focused this time, ready to pounce the moment I try to fudge. Crap.

I hang my head, breaking eye contact, and nod. "Sort of. He called after I got to Amber's and asked if I could. I probably should have checked with you first, though. Sorry."

Avoiding her gaze seems to keep her from realizing my confession is only a partial one. Not that it helps much.

"Sorry is not good enough. I just had to listen to that *twilly* Connor berate me for letting my daughter out unsupervised and for not respecting our people's traditions. He even implied that your father and I might have put you up to it in hopes of ensnaring a match for you from a superior *fine*. I let him know how wrong he was and that his son was by no means blameless but that does not let you off the hook, young lady. You—"

"What's all the shouting about?" Sean appears behind her in the hall, yawning. "I was almost asleep."

Mum turns to glare at him. "Your sister went on a *date* without telling us. With Tristan Roark."

Sean's eyebrows disappear into his hairline. "A date? With *Tristan*? You're crazy, Mum. She hates Tristan. She's told me so herself."

I wish now I hadn't been *quite* so outspoken when I complained about Tristan to Sean last week. "Um, we've gotten to know each other a lot better since I said that. We're lab partners in Chemistry and on the same project team in Government. He's…way nicer lately than he was at first."

Mum hmphs. "From what I know of his father, any improvement is likely a charade. They clearly mean him to pair with the Sovereign now her *proper* Consort has withdrawn his suit." She shoots a downright poisonous glance at Sean.

"That's not fair, Mum," I exclaim, grateful for even a temporary diversion from my own scolding. "Sean had no choice after M and Rigel got back together, you know that. You've seen yourself how strong their bond is, what they can do because of it."

Sean just shakes his head. "I've told her that a thousand times, Mol, for all the good it's done. But…you don't *really* mean you just went out on a date with Tristan? On purpose?"

I feel my face heating, remembering how much more than "just" a date tonight turned out to be. "Like I said, we're lab partners. We have more than half our classes together. He suggested getting to know each other a little better and I agreed it wasn't a bad idea."

"Not a bad idea?" Mum repeats incredulously. "It was a *terrible* idea. Which you must have known, or you wouldn't have tried to hide it from us."

"I figured you probably wouldn't approve but I…wanted to see how things went. See if we could spend any time together without arguing."

Again with the laser focus. "And were you able to do that?"

"Um, yeah. We actually got along really well. Better than either of us expected." That's the absolute truth, at least.

But Sean's shaking his head again. "I don't like it, Mol. Tristan's a player. You've seen how he's been hanging after M since he got here. Don't let your emotions get involved when he's probably just using you to get to her. I mean, he's Royal, son of a Council member, and—"

"And I'm just an Ag, is that it?" I'm getting pissed myself now, which feels better than guilty. "Is that what you're doing with Kira? Just biding your time until something better—something *Royal*—comes along? Mum obviously doesn't think so, or she wouldn't be so upset about you dating her."

Sean glowers at me. "You know that's not— Anyway, this is totally different."

"Is it? Tristan's a high-ranking Royal, son of a Council member, just like you. I'm an Ag, just like Kira."

When Sean hesitates, Mum launches back in. "One mismatch in the family is quite enough. You are not to go out with that boy again, Molly. Anyway, I thought you and Alan were beginning to come to an understanding."

"Yeah, I understand Alan just fine. He basically confirmed that he was only interested in me because we're the same *fine*...and because Kira's unavailable at the moment." I hadn't planned to tell Sean that, but I'm pissed at him now, too.

"Be that as it may—" Mum begins when my cellphone dings from my nightstand. "Who would be texting you this late at night?"

"Probably M," I say, going to check. The text is from Tristan.

Heads up! I told my father and he freaked. Maybe called your mother.

I'm about to reply when Mum grabs the phone out of my hand and looks at the screen.

"So! Apparently you both intended to hide this so-called date from your parents until Connor forced his son to admit to it? I'll just keep this so you can't make any more plans behind my back, Missie." She pockets my phone.

"Mum! At least let me tell him you took my phone so he won't think I'm blowing him off."

"Just as well if he does. Whatever you want to tell him can wait until Monday at school. Now to bed with you, to think over what you've done."

Shooing Sean ahead of her, she leaves my room and shuts the door. I half expect to hear her lock it—then realize it doesn't actually lock from the outside. With a frustrated sigh, I thump down on my bed.

Just yesterday, the idea of someone else hearing my thoughts sounded awful. But right now I wish I could send a mental message to Tristan the way M can with Rigel, to let him know what just happened. Maybe I'll get a chance to tell him at church tomorrow?

I crawl into bed, still fuming, then gradually relax as I think back over the whole evening, most of which was wonderful. I fall asleep doing just what Mum told me to—though not at all the way she intended.

*+

ON THE WAY TO church the next morning, Sean hangs back to talk to me while Mum and Dad walk ahead of us.

"I know you think Mum wasn't fair to take your phone last night and all, but she really does have your best interests at heart. She doesn't want to see you get hurt, and neither do I."

"Why are you so sure Tristan plans to hurt me?" I demand. "Are Kira's parents worried you'll hurt her? Is she?"

He slants a frown down at me. "I told you, that's different."

"Is it? Why? Because you and Kira really, really like each other? Maybe even love each other?"

Up ahead, Mum gives an indignant little squeak. She's clearly listening to every word we say, so I slow my pace a little.

"Yes. We do. And that makes all the difference in the world." He doesn't repeat the word "love" but it's obvious that's what he means. Wow.

"Well, I really do like Tristan, and I think he likes me, too. We talked a whole lot last night and I have a much better understanding now of where he's coming from. And he's changed his thinking a lot since he first got here, mainly because of things I've told him. Just because his dad's a jerk doesn't mean he is."

Sean keeps frowning at me and I meet his gaze directly, trying to convince him I'm telling the truth, not just what I want to believe. Finally, he lifts a shoulder and looks away.

"I guess time will tell. I hope you're right, Mol, but don't say we didn't warn you if it turns out you're not."

It's only a slight improvement over total disapproval but I'll take it.

Time *will* tell, and I'm convinced once Sean sees Tristan and me together, sees how Tristan has changed, he'll come around. Whether Mum ever will, I'm less certain.

There's no sign of Tristan or Connor when we get to church, but that's not surprising since it's still early. M and the Truitts arrive just after we do. The moment her aunt and Mum go to the choir room, she scoots over next to me.

"Well?" she whispers excitedly. "How did it go? Tell me all you can before Rigel gets here!"

"Oh, M, it was awesome!" I whisper back. "*So* much better than I expected. I...he...we...well, it was really great. Except now Mum doesn't want me to ever go out with him again."

She tilts her head. "So you told her after all? I didn't think you had from the way she talked after the Council meeting last night."

"Um, not exactly. I guess you haven't heard yet, but we ended up at the Lighthouse Cafe, so it wasn't going to stay a secret long anyway. Then Tristan told his dad and his dad called Mum and...badness ensued. She took my phone so I can't even let him know what happened on my end or find out what happened on his."

"I'm sorry. I guess you were right about that part. But if you two really like each other, I'm sure it'll work out somehow. You'll still see each other a lot at school. Maybe he'll even be here again today."

I turn to look toward the sanctuary door behind us. "Maybe."

But he never shows. Connor must have decided the risk of Tristan and me talking was greater than the benefit of him chatting up M again. Not that I'm worried Tristan would go along with that now.

Not much, anyway.

.˙.

WHEN I GET off the bus the next morning, I scan the parking lot for Tristan's black Porsche, hoping for a chance to talk with him before school starts. It's not there yet, so I follow M and her friends inside to put my coat in my locker and swap out my books.

M got a few more details about my date out of me when we walked back from church together, but I didn't feel comfortable telling her how much kissing happened. I just told her we were delayed by rain and traffic on our way to Kokomo, talked a lot, then decided to go to the Lighthouse instead. And that Tristan kissed me good night.

Now, though, it's all started to feel like a dream, making me doubt everything I felt so sure of when he dropped me off Saturday night.

I watch for him on my way to Pre-Cal, then loiter just down the hall from the classroom, hoping to catch him. When he still doesn't show, I start worrying. Would Connor go so far as to yank him out of school to keep him away from me? Finally, when the bell's about to ring, I go in…and discover Tristan already there, in his usual desk next to mine.

"How did you get here without me seeing you?" I whisper. "I was waiting out in the hallway, hoping we could talk some."

He gives me a lopsided smile that goes straight to my heart. "And I hurried to class the second I got here, hoping the same thing."

"But I didn't even see your car in the lot earlier. I figured you were running late or something."

"Nope. I had to ride the bus because Father took my car keys."

My jaw drops. "He took away your *car*? And here I was mad because Mum took my phone. That's why I couldn't answer your text."

"Yeah, Father took my phone, too, once he thought of it."

"I guess he was pretty upset, then?"

The bell rings before he can answer but he nods. "I'll tell you about it later," he whispers as the teacher starts class.

We walk together to French class and my heart turns over when Tristan takes my hand after a sec.

"You don't mind, do you?" he whispers.

I shake my head, too overwhelmed for the moment by the sensations his touch is sending all through my body to respond aloud. All the uncertainty I felt earlier about the accuracy of my memories of Saturday night, about whether Tristan would still be interested in pursuing a relationship, disappear.

"So anyway," he says after a minute, "even though my father didn't take the news about us particularly well, my mother is totally okay with it. Thought you might like to know that."

I'm surprised, but pleased. "Yeah, that's nice to hear. I also don't think my dad's as upset as my mum is, though he won't say so—especially not in front of her. Sean's not too happy either, but he'll come around. It would be pretty hypocritical of him not to."

He laughs. "Yeah, I guess it would. I'm really sorry I got you in trouble, though. I never expected Father to call your parents when I told him about us."

"You mean you came right out and told him? He didn't find out from someone else?"

"Nope. I had this whole excuse ready, but then decided what the heck. I…don't want to hide this, Molly. But I shouldn't have taken that choice away from you."

I grin up at him. "I think that choice was made when we went to the Lighthouse. Our folks would have found out soon no matter what. It just happened a little sooner than we expected. Than I expected, anyway. But I'm fine with it."

His brown eyes hold mine for a long moment, gauging whether I really mean that, then he smiles. "Good. Because I'm *totally* fine with it. Even if I have to ride the bus for the rest of the year."

Seems like he's giving up a lot more than I am—it's not like I had a car to lose—but if he's okay with it, who am I to argue? I smile back.

We walk hand in hand to Chemistry class, too, which earns me an outraged glare from Trina when she notices. I'm surprised the cheerleaders we saw at the Lighthouse Saturday night didn't say anything to her before now. Maybe they were afraid to? Or maybe they did and she refused to believe them. Not that I particularly care either way.

Sharing a lab table with Tristan is a whole different experience today than it was last week, when things were still so awkward between us. Now, when we have to pass a worksheet on compound names and formulas back and forth, we take every opportunity to brush fingers instead of avoiding each other's touch. And every single time, I get that same delicious tingle that makes me feel like I could fly. Judging by Tristan's expression, so does he.

"I could get used to this," he whispers at one point. "Though it's funny—last week I was hoping I could build up an immunity or something. Now, not so much."

"Ditto," I whisper back.

We hold each other's gazes for a long moment that feels almost as intimate as a kiss…then we go back to the class exercise.

"So, this looks promising," Rigel comments when he and M join us in the lunch line later. "M says you two went out Saturday night?"

"Yep." Tristan grins back and I nod happily.

"That's great!" He's clearly pleased by this development—for obvious reasons.

Not everyone shares his sentiments, though. As I leave the cashier, Trina comes up behind me and hisses something about snakes in the grass before stalking off to the cheerleader table. And from across the cafeteria, I see Alan staring at us in outraged disbelief. We're not holding hands now, since we're both carrying trays, so I assume someone must have told him we went out together.

He confirms that in Government class.

"So, everyone's buzzing about you two and your little date Saturday night," he grumps when the three of us go to the back of the room to work on our project. "I guess neither of you are much on tradition, huh?"

"Shh!" I caution him, glancing around. "Not so loud."

He grimaces but lowers his voice. "Friday night when I asked, you told me you two weren't dating. I should have known better than to believe you."

"We weren't yet, when I told you that. Saturday was our very first date." I still feel a little guilty for misleading him…until he proves again what a jerk he can be.

"You don't have to explain to me. You made your feelings pretty clear—not that it matters. It's not like you're a proper Ag anyway."

I huff out a furious breath, tempted to punch him, right here in class. Why did he have to say that in front of Tristan?

"What do you mean, 'not a proper Ag'?" Tristan immediately asks.

I feel my face getting warm. "He means I'm really bad at growing plants. This is the *second* time he's thrown it in my face. Thanks a lot, Alan."

Now Alan's ears turn red and he looks away, mumbling something unintelligible. Tristan, however, is regarding me curiously.

"Why should you feel embarrassed about that? It's not your fault. Besides, how much good would something like that do here in Jewel? It's probably just because you were raised by Royals. Maybe it's one of those things you have to develop before you're a certain age—a developmental window, isn't that what our Psych book calls it?"

I've wondered the same thing, but somehow having Tristan say it out loud makes me feel a lot better about it. "Maybe. Thanks, Tristan."

Alan just snorts. "So are we going to work on this project or not?"

30

Conjugate base

Tristan

I CAN'T SUPPRESS my intense satisfaction at watching Alan crash and burn in Molly's esteem, though I try—a little—to hide it. We spend the last ten minutes of class talking about nothing but our court case. Alan and Molly are coldly formal whenever they speak to each other. Sort of like she and I were after that first touch last week.

Good.

"Thanks again for sticking up for me about my lack of Ag skills," Molly says as we walk together to Psych class. Holding hands again, which feels amazing.

"I don't see what the big deal is. Pretty obnoxious of Alan to say that, though, if he knows *you* think it is."

She gives a cute little snort. "Yeah. It's not the first time he's proved he can be a real jerk when things don't go his way. Remind me to tell you about the one attempt at a date I had with him."

"Can't you tell me now?" Because I'm suddenly dying of curiosity.

"There's not really time, but let's just say it didn't go well. Not only did it become obvious he's still hung up on Kira, he and I have at least as many political differences as you and I do—did?"

My lips twitch. "I'll admit, my opinions may have shifted a bit. I take it arguing politics with Alan didn't have quite the same, uh, effect, though?"

She laughs. "He definitely did *not* try to shut me up by kissing me, no. He just got sulky. The only reason I went out with him at all was because my parents were so pleased by the idea."

"The *only* reason?" She'd be blind not to realize Alan's one of the best-looking guys in school.

"Okay, the main reason," she concedes with another laugh. "It did make sense to at least try, since on paper it seemed like it should have worked out. I'm awfully glad now it didn't." She slants a look up at me that makes me want to kiss her right here in the hallway.

I resist, but with an effort. "I'm awfully glad, too. It sucks that Father took my car away. I was really hoping you and I could go out again soon."

"I'm grounded anyway. But even if we can't go out on any more real dates for a while, this is nice." She glances down at our linked hands.

"It is," I agree fervently. Until a few days ago, I never dreamed I could feel this way about anyone. Now I can't imagine *not* feeling this way about Molly.

I HEAD to the media center for seventh period since today is when I told Coach Glazier I'd come to football practice so he can put me through my paces. When I see the other junior and senior *Echtrans* heading out to NuAgra, I wonder if I'll ever be joining them again. I don't see much point, unless somebody—other than Father—can find something useful for me to do out there. Of course, if I don't I'll lose my work-study credit —not that that's a big deal.

When the final bell rings I head to the gym to change, already antici-pating seeing Molly again while the cheerleaders practice. It's still chilly so she'll probably be wearing something a lot less revealing than the short-skirted uniform she's had on all day, but I don't care. I just want to be near her again.

"Hey, Tristan," Rigel greets me with a grin when I get to the locker room. "Ready to convince Coach you should replace me at QB next year?"

I laugh. It's a lot easier to be friendly with Rigel now that I've lost all interest in wrecking his relationship with M.

"Doubt that'll happen. I've seen you play. But I'm a decent receiver, too."

"Cool. That could work out great."

He doesn't elaborate with all his teammates around but I'm sure we're both thinking that would give the Jewel Jaguars an unstoppable offense next year—assuming we can avoid being so obvious the Council yanks us both off the team.

I follow the rest of the guys out to the field and a couple minutes later the cheerleaders come out to the sidelines—in sweats, as I expected. It's still hard to focus on what the coach is saying instead of Molly and what her *brath* does to me, even from twenty yards away.

After warmups, the coach has me run a few routes—first throwing, then receiving. I've never felt so on my game in my life and wonder if it has anything to do with Molly. Her touch, her *brath,* does seem to energize me. How bizarre would it be if we developed a *graell* bond like M and Rigel's?

"That's some impressive stuff you've got, son," Coach says afterward. "I'll probably put you in as receiver but it's good to have some depth at quarterback, too, in case of injury. Shoot, I'm wishing I could plug you in for the playoffs, now I've seen you in action."

"From what I've seen, the Jaguars will do fine without me," I tell him and get a thumbs-up in response.

I retire to the sidelines to wait for the late bus…and to watch the last twenty minutes of Molly's cheer practice. She catches my eye and grins at one point and I feel it right in my gut. In a good way. As soon as they finish, she comes over to me.

"Hey, I saw you out there earlier. Looking good!"

"Thanks. Coach seemed pleased. You looked good, too, even though Trina seemed to be giving you a hard time."

She grimaces. "Yeah, she's at least as upset as Alan is about us dating. Remember I told you she staked you out as her own personal property your first day here? Funny thing about Trina—she could probably date ninety percent of the guys in school but she *always* obsesses about the ones she can't have."

"So I'm not the first?"

"Hardly." She laughs. "She spent most of last year and the first few weeks of this year doing her best to snag Rigel away from M. You can see how well that worked. She came on to Sean when he first got here, too, then Alan. Anyway, I'd better go get my stuff. Which late bus are you on, do you know?"

I shake my head. "I didn't think to check. How many are there?"

"Only two, so there's a chance we'll be on the same one. I'll tell Amber I don't need a ride today and we'll check, okay?"

When we get to the buses a few minutes later, it turns out Molly and I *are* on the same one. Grinning at each other, we take a seat together near the back.

"I'm sure my father never considered *this* possibility when he took my car." I lace her fingers through mine. "This helps make up for that—especially since I don't plan to tell him."

"I'm not telling Mum, either. She'd probably forbid me to ride the bus if she knew."

"Yeah, let's not risk that."

Her chuckle ripples through me, doing interesting things to my body. But then she turns serious.

"So, you're really sure you're okay with not having a car or a phone for a while? I mean, I'll totally understand if you decide you want to cool things between us until your dad calms down."

My insides clench. "Do *you* want to cool it?"

"No, but my parents aren't quite as…you know. Plus I never had a car."

I relax again. "No, I don't want to cool it. Not just to get my car back. Sure, my father's a bully, but giving in is never the best way to deal with a bully, right?" I can't bring myself to tell even Molly I found out he actually used to hit my mother. I still feel guilty for not realizing it at the time.

"That's what I've always heard." She relaxes, too. Was she actually worried I might take her up on that offer? Not a chance.

"There you go, then. We still get to be together at school and I'll find more excuses to take the late bus home. Even if we don't manage another *real* date until we're both eighteen, I'll take this—" I squeeze her hand. "—over where I was a week ago."

She smiles up at me so sweetly, I'm really tempted to kiss her. "Me, too," she says.

And then I give into temptation, realizing it's the best opportunity I'm likely to get for a while.

⁖

MY NEIGHBORHOOD IS CLOSER to the school than Molly's, so I have to get off the bus first. I steal another quick kiss before leaving her, hoping it'll last me until I see her again tomorrow.

"I won't be able to call or anything, but you know I'll be thinking about you." I grab my backpack and stand up.

"Ditto. See you tomorrow, Tristan."

I'm leaning down for another kiss when the bus driver honks impatiently. "Oops. Okay, bye."

Mother greets me with a smile when I walk into the house a couple minutes later. "You're in a better mood than I expected," she comments when I grin back. "Because of Molly O'Gara?"

Shrugging, I nod. "Is it that obvious?"

"To someone who cares about you, yes. I didn't want to mention it before, particularly in your father's hearing, but I actually had a feeling about the two of you the night I met her."

That's a surprise. Mother's "feelings" are almost never wrong—at least, the few times she's told me about them ahead of something happening.

"Why didn't you want to mention it?"

"I...didn't think you were ready to hear it. At the time, you still seemed determined to attach the Sovereign if possible—and determined to resent Molly's interference in that goal."

I grin again. "You weren't wrong. Then. So you really do like her? Molly, I mean?"

She nods. "As I said, she seems both responsible and intelligent, as well as very pretty. I thought at the time that she reminded me of someone, though I still haven't been able to place who it might be. I rather doubt I met her biological family before leaving Nuath."

"Probably not. They were Ag farmers in Glenamuir and died when she was a baby. If she had any blood siblings who survived I'm sure she'd have mentioned it."

"Likely just a chance resemblance, then. In any event, I'm glad you didn't take your father's harsh words about her too much to heart."

I give a disgusted snort. "Hardly. In fact, I don't think I'll take much of anything he says to heart from now on. Now that I know—" I break off at her distressed expression. "Sorry."

She shakes her head. "I'm the one who should be sorry. I never should have told you about that, as it's in the past now."

Remembering how close he came to hitting her Saturday night, I'm not so confident. "No, I'm glad you did. I only wish I'd suspected sooner. I could have done more to protect you—or at least tried to."

"I never wanted you in the middle of it, Tristan. When you're a parent, you'll understand."

"I doubt it. I don't even understand why you've stayed with him all this time, considering…" I shake my head, honestly baffled.

Her smile is sad. "Your father can be very charming when he wants to be. You know that. He just…doesn't often make the effort anymore. Not at home, anyway."

"No kidding."

It's hard to believe I used to consider my father practically infallible. Silently, I vow to be a whole lot quicker to stand up to him in the future, on my own behalf as well as Mother's.

CONVERSATION OVER DINNER is as strained as it was the night before, with Father sending glowering looks my way while Mother makes occasional attempts at small talk. I mostly don't say anything at all, not trusting myself to avoid another scene and not wanting to make Mother even more uncomfortable.

"Do you know yet whether Devyn Kane still plans to visit us?" she asks when the meal is nearly over.

His brows draw down in a quick frown. "What? No. We've— I thought I asked you not to mention him again?"

"I simply wanted to know if I should have a guest room ready," she replies with more spirit than she usually shows toward him. Good for her. "It sounds as though I need not bother."

"No," he repeats. "It won't be an issue."

The way he avoids the subject makes me even more curious than I was before. Maybe because I don't trust my father so implicitly now? If he and Devyn are up to something they shouldn't be, M ought to know. I wonder if I should mention it to Molly, so she can pass it along…? Not that I have anything concrete to tell her. Yet.

⁺✦

WHEN I GET off my bus the next morning, Molly meets me at the curb, again wearing the short cheerleading skirt that makes her legs look a mile long.

"Hi. I thought that might be your bus in front of ours. Did you sleep well?" she asks.

I lean down and give her a quick kiss. "I definitely had great dreams," I tell her with a wink.

To my surprise, she blushes. "Um, so did I." The look she slants up at me through her lashes tells me our dreams were similar.

"I guess your dad's not softening yet on the car thing?" She takes the hand I hold out to her. "Or your phone?"

I shake my head. "I haven't even asked. He's been in a bad mood since Saturday night—not that he's ever in a very *good* mood."

"Yeah, I've noticed that—though I've mostly seen him when he comes over for Council meetings. I just figured he just doesn't like attending them."

"Nah, almost anything can set him off." I lower my voice so no one else can possibly overhear. "I...I found out Saturday night that I was wrong when I said he'd never hit my mother. She admitted to me he has, though not recently. I asked her because he came really close that night, when she tried to defend me."

Her gray eyes go wide and concerned. "Because of me? Oh, Tristan, I'm sorry."

"Hey, it's totally *not* your fault my father is such an—" I bite back the word I want to use. "I just feel stupid for not seeing it sooner."

She squeezes my hand. "It's not your fault either, Tristan. Please don't beat yourself up over it. You were a kid. Kids don't usually think that way about their parents. Last summer I learned a few things about my dad I didn't like, too. Though he later admitted he was wrong and has done his best to make up for it."

"Yeah, I somehow don't see Father doing that. Nothing is ever his fault, according to him," I say bitterly, then try to shake it off. I'd rather enjoy my time with Molly than dwell on problems at home. "So, I've been thinking up other excuses to stay after school so we can ride the late bus together again. Tomorrow's basketball tryouts, right?"

"Yes, but wouldn't you rather play football?"

I grin down at her. "Sure, but going to tryouts will get me on that late bus, which is all I really care about. Besides, it might be fun."

Over the next two days, we spend every moment we can together, even though there's no chance to be completely private. By Wednesday we get fewer stares when we walk down the halls holding hands or sit slightly apart from the others at lunch. Bri and Deb seem only mildly disgruntled, but Alan and Trina still shoot glares at us from across the cafeteria. Both M and Rigel are clearly delighted—not hard to guess why. That makes me realize again what a jerk I was my first few days here.

Working with Alan in Government is still uncomfortable, but though he frowns a lot he at least doesn't say anything else outright rude. We agree to do all our collaborating outside of class via email, since Molly and I are still grounded. Not that we tell Alan that. He'd be way too pleased.

After seventh period Wednesday, which I again spend in the media center, I head to the gym for basketball tryouts.

"Oh, hey, Tristan," Liam Walsh greets me. "I didn't know you were planning to try out, too."

"Neither did I." Alan sends me a sour look from a few paces away.

Pete Griffin, a senior who was on last year's team, joins us. "Hey, the more the merrier, right?"

He's the guy Sean sometimes rides to school with—the *Duchas* Molly told me took her to Homecoming this year, and who kept coming on to her when we were decorating the school Saturday morning. I try to control my instinctive aversion.

"That's what I was thinking. Football's really more my thing, but since I've already missed it for this year, I figured I might as well show up."

Already, though, I realize how crazy conspicuous it would be to have four *Echtrans* playing on one team—especially at such a small school. Studying the Korematsu case has given me a good idea of what could happen if the *Duchas* found out about us.

Since I wasn't that into the idea of being on the team anyway, I decide to just watch tryouts instead of participating. Sean and Alan do a pretty good job of holding back but Liam's a little over the top. Needless to say, they all make the team. I congratulate them, then head to the late bus, my heart already speeding up in anticipation of sitting with Molly again.

We don't talk much during the ride but I revel in the sensation of having her right against me, my arm around her shoulders. Judging by her occasional contented sigh, she feels the same. When the bus pulls up to my stop, I give her one last, lingering kiss before getting off.

Only to discover my father at the curb, waiting for me.

"So this is why you've been staying after school instead of coming to NuAgra? I suspected as much."

My lingering euphoria from Molly's kiss effectively spoiled, I glare at him. "I went to basketball tryouts, just like I told Mother. And Monday I'd promised the football coach I'd come to their practice so he could evaluate me."

He snorts. "Evaluate you? To play with a bunch of *Duchas*? Don't make me laugh. In any event, it was all time wasted. Since you've clearly abandoned any effort to supplant Stuart as Consort, I believe you'll be better off back in Denver. What I just saw only confirms that."

"What? Forget it! Besides, I thought you needed to be here to help set up that new government center."

"I do. You and your mother do not. I intended to inform you both of my plans for you this evening but now will do just as well."

He turns on his heel and heads to our house, leaving me to follow—and fume. Somehow, I'll have to make sure this "plan" of his doesn't succeed any better than his last one did.

31

Covalent bond

Molly

THURSDAY MORNING, Tristan's already waiting by the curb when my bus pulls up. I hurry over to him the moment I get off. "Hey."

"Hey," he replies. There's something about the way he says it that dims my smile of greeting. I can almost feel his tension, even before he reaches for my hand.

"What's wrong?" I ask, threading my fingers through his. "I can tell something is."

He sighs. "Yeah, well, I won't be on the late bus today, for one thing. Father found out we ride the same one so he insists I go out to NuAgra seventh period instead."

"That's not all, is it?" I'm not sure how I know for sure, but I do. And I'm not wrong.

"No," he says heavily. "He's also threatening to send my mother and me back to Denver."

I stare at him. "Just to get you away from me? Isn't that kind of an overreaction?"

"I told him I'm not going."

"But—?" I can tell he's still not telling me everything.

"But I doubt I can stop him from pulling me out of school if he really wants to. I'm still a minor. Plus…"

When he hesitates, I realize he's conflicted as well as upset. "It would get your mom away from him, so he can't hurt her again?" I guess.

He nods miserably. "It seems, I don't know, selfish of me to refuse to go just because I don't want to leave you, if that would be the best way to keep her safe. I didn't do a very good job of that a couple years back."

"Because you didn't know!" I remind him, giving his hand a little shake. "Tristan, that was *not* your fault. It was your father's and no one else's."

"That still doesn't let me off the hook for keeping her safe now that I do know."

I stare up at him helplessly. I want to talk him out of leaving but realize it isn't my decision to make. We walk together in silence, stopping at my locker, then his, before heading to Pre-Cal.

Just before we go into the classroom, I say, "Whatever you decide to do, I'll support you. I know you'll make the right decision, for the right reasons."

He turns me to face him, gazing down into my eyes, a sad smile playing about his perfect lips. "I don't deserve you, you know that? And I *so* don't want to leave here now that I've found you."

"We'll just hope for the best then," I say as bracingly as I can, refusing to give into the tears I feel prickling. "He's only threatened so far, right? Maybe he'll change his mind, decide it's too big a hassle. Maybe—"

"You're right. No point borrowing trouble."

His phrasing suddenly reminds me of M and her confession to me Saturday—and that she hasn't been to my house since, to keep her promise about the Scepter. Though that doesn't matter to me nearly as much right now as the possibility of losing Tristan so soon after… No. I won't borrow trouble either.

"C'mon." I'm careful to keep my voice upbeat. "Bell's about to ring."

That whole day we hold hands just a little bit tighter in the hallways, sit just a little bit closer together at lunch. It's like the threat of sudden separation makes us both determined to savor what we have together while we can.

So far we've mostly refrained from overt PDAs inside the school but he kisses me goodbye after Psych class that afternoon.

"Since I won't be able to on the late bus," he explains with a crooked smile. "I'll see you tomorrow, okay?"

I swallow. Surely his dad can't just spirit him away overnight? They still have to make preparations—pack and book travel and stuff—right?

"Okay."

.+.

AMBER DROPS me off after practice since there's no point taking the late bus today. I've been so preoccupied by the specter of Tristan leaving, I completely forgot today is Sean's birthday until Mum comes out of the kitchen with her hands covered in flour.

"Good, you're home! Run up and change so you can help me in the kitchen. It's not every day a young man turns eighteen and I want to be sure to have all Sean's favorites on the table tonight."

He and our folks agreed last week we'd just have a little family dinner party on the actual day, since his basketball buddies are planning to throw a bigger party at Pete's house on Saturday. I was invited to that, too, but Mum already nixed me going because of being grounded.

I dive into dinner preparations with spirit, following every order Mum barks at me. I've been working really hard all week to stay on her good side, hoping she might end my grounding sooner—or at least give me back my phone. I'll need that even more if Tristan leaves… I focus harder on the onions I'm chopping for the shepherd's pie, using them as my excuse when a stray tear escapes.

Sean gets home—from hanging out with Kira, I assume—around the same time Dad gets back from NuAgra.

"Dinner in twenty minutes," Mum sings out cheerily. "Sean, no peeking in the kitchen."

He laughs and goes upstairs and Mum turns to me. "I don't suppose you've changed your mind about inviting Alan to join us?"

"Definitely not. He's been a real jerk this week."

"Oh?" She raises a skeptical eyebrow. "He seemed very nice every time he's been here."

I snort. "Yeah, that was before he threw my brown thumb in my face —and that was after implying I have some kind of obligation to date him just because we're both Ags. No thanks."

"I see." She's frowning now, but whether because she agrees Alan was in the wrong or because she'd still rather I be with him than Tristan,

I can't tell. All she says is, "All right, wash up, then, and hurry right back down to help me set everything out on the table."

I'm bringing in the last of the food while Mum sets the table when the doorbell rings.

"Huh. I wonder if M was able to come after all?" I say in surprise.

She told me earlier today she needed to be at Rigel's tonight to get briefed on some new developments, but to give Sean a birthday hug for her.

"I'll just lay out another setting," Mum says complacently. I set the dish of roasted butternut squash next to the big loaf of soda bread and go to answer the door.

Instead of M, Kira is standing there, looking embarrassed. "Is Sean downstairs yet?" she whispers.

I shake my head, figuring she wants to drop off his present or something, but instead she grins and heads straight for the dining room.

"Ah, just in time," Mum greets her, actually sounding pleased. "Sit here, then, won't you, Kira? He should be down any moment."

Mystified, I look from one to the other but before I can ask what's going on, Dad and Sean come thudding down the stairs.

"Wow, everything smells great," Sean says, striding into the dining room, only to stop cold when he sees Kira. "What—?"

"Happy birthday, Sean." Mum lifts her chin and looks straight at him, a determined smile on her face. "I knew you'd like Kira to be part of tonight's gathering, so I invited her myself. She and I thought we'd make a little surprise of it."

Exactly like I just did, he looks confusedly back and forth between the two of them. Kira's smiling too, though she looks slightly wary.

"Thanks, Mum," Sean finally says. "I didn't—"

"I know. You were worried I'd be rude if you invited her. But I've done a bit of thinking lately and see I've been wrong to act the way I have. The last thing I want is a rift in our family and my churlish attitude was creating just that. I want you both to know that from now on, Kira is welcome in our home and I'll not say another word against her— or the two of you."

Sean and I both stare at her, stunned. Then Sean crosses the room to give Mum a big bear hug. "Thanks, Mum. This is the best present you could possibly have given me."

She's sniffling a little as she hugs him back. "You're welcome, dear."

Now Dad steps forward. "I'm afraid my present may seem a bit anticlimactic after that one, but I hope you'll like it anyway. It should be parked outside by now."

"Parked—? You mean?"

Dad nods, grinning. "I know you've been wanting a car of your own and Louie Truitt was able to give me a great deal. It's used, but still in good condition. He said he'd drop it off just before seven."

Grabbing Kira's hand, Sean practically drags her out front to see it and Mum and I follow. It's a metallic blue two-door sedan that from the front porch looks brand new.

"You can take it for a spin after dinner," Mum says when Sean starts down the porch stairs. "Right now, the food's getting cold."

It's the happiest meal our family has had in a while. I do my best not to spoil Sean's evening by dwelling on my worries about Tristan. Still, it's hard not to imagine how wonderful it would be if Mum could see her way to accepting Tristan like she's finally decided to accept Kira.

⁺₊

ALL THE WAY to school Friday morning I worry Tristan won't be there, that his dad might have shipped him off to Colorado overnight after all.

M notices, of course. "What has you tied in knots today, Molly? Sean wasn't upset I couldn't come to his birthday dinner, was he?"

I shake my head. "I doubt he even noticed." I go on to tell her what Mum did—and said. She's grinning at the end of it.

"That's so awesome! I knew she'd come around eventually. So what *does* have you worried, then?"

With a sigh, I tell her what Connor threatened to do—and why. I also hint about his tendency toward domestic violence, to explain why Tristan might go along with it. That gets her frowning.

"I never liked Connor much, but I never…ugh. Anyway, I doubt he could have made arrangements to move Tristan and his mom this quickly —and after what I heard last night, he's going to have other things to worry about. I predict a *really* interesting Council meeting tomorrow."

The bus pulls up to the school before I can ask why—and then I see Tristan waiting on the sidewalk and relief sweeps every other thought away.

M pats me on the shoulder. "See? Still here."

I flash her a smile, then get off the bus as quickly as I can.

"I was afraid you might already be gone," I tell Tristan when I reach him.

He leans down and gives me a kiss that sends delicious shivers all through my body.

"Not yet. Father did check into housing availability in the *Echtran* compound, but that's all he's done so far. Our house out there already sold, so going back to it isn't an option."

"So we have a little breathing room." And I do feel almost like I'm breathing normally after being half-starved for air since saying goodbye to him yesterday.

"For now, anyway. Like you said yesterday, we'll just hope for the best. Who knows? Maybe a solution we haven't even thought of yet will suddenly appear."

I grin up at him. "Look who's Mr. Optimism now! I like the way you think."

"I guess your attitude has rubbed off on me even more than I thought," he replies with a wink, throwing an arm around my shoulders.

Like yesterday, we take every possible opportunity to be together all day—but it still doesn't seem like enough. I suggest eating lunch in the courtyard so we can be more alone, but then it starts raining halfway through fourth period, spoiling that idea.

"Are you coming to the game tonight?" I ask hopefully at the end of Psych class.

Frowning, he shakes his head. "Father made a point of telling me no before I could even ask. Guess he noticed you're a cheerleader and thought you might be there even though you're grounded."

"Yeah, I will—but Mum and Dad are driving me there and back, so it's not like they'd give us much chance to talk even if you could come. Monday seems like such a long way off..."

Tristan swallows. "It does. Maybe—"

"Email me if you think of anything," I tell him. "I'll do the same."

"Deal. Okay, better run. Bye, Molly. I— Bye."

Leaving me to wonder what he almost said, I watch him hurry off to catch his ride to NuAgra.

The thought of two whole days without seeing Tristan makes it hard for me to summon a convincing amount of spirit for the seventh period Halloween-themed pep rally. A lot of people wore costumes to school today, some of them pretty funny. But even the sight of the Math Club dressed like Legos only cheers me up temporarily.

On the bus ride home afterward, I quietly remind M of her promise to show me how her Scepter works. I need *something* to look forward to over the weekend.

"Yeah, I tried texting you, then remembered your mother took your phone away. Anyway, I thought I could come over an hour or so before the Council meeting tomorrow, since we'll both be at the game tonight. How does that sound?"

"Perfect. It's not like I have any other plans," I grumble.

Her green eyes are sympathetic. "Hey, your mom changed her mind about Sean and Kira. I'm sure it's just a matter of time till she does the same about you and Tristan."

"Assuming he's still in Jewel."

"Weren't you the one who told *me* not to borrow trouble?"

We both laugh, but my heart isn't in it.

THAT EVENING IS our first playoff game and also Jewel's last home game of the season. And, sure enough, Tristan's not there. We win handily, but Mum and Dad whisk me home before I can even congratulate the players. Trina's Halloween after-party is obviously out of the question—not that I feel much like going anyway. Instead, I'm home early enough to hand out candy to the last few trick-or-treaters.

After that, there's nothing else for me to do tonight but hope I'll dream about Tristan again.

⁺⁺

AS PROMISED, M shows up at my house a good hour and a half before the Council meeting Saturday evening.

"Molly and I thought we could work on a couple of school projects in her room, if that's okay?" she says when Mum's surprised to see her here so early.

"All right, Excellency, if it's for school. Keep in mind Molly is still grounded, though, so try not to have too much fun with it, aye?"

I roll my eyes and M laughs. "We'll do our best."

"Can you believe her?" I ask when we get to my room. "You'd think I robbed a bank or something instead of going on a single date with a Royal."

"Um, it's probably more that you didn't *tell* her you were going on a date, don't you think?"

"Okay, maybe. But still."

M just shakes her head, still smiling. "So, are you ready to meet some Sovereigns?"

I catch my breath, indignation at my mother abruptly forgotten. "Ooh, yes! I'm dying to see how this whole thing works."

"It's pretty cool, though it took me a while to figure it out. I mean, it's not like anyone left me a manual or anything."

"I thought you found instructions in some old files at the Palace? The ones that helped you use the Grentl Archive?"

She bites her lip. "Um, yeah, I sort of made that up. It was actually the Grentl Archive that gave me my first clue about the one in the Scepter. Here, I'll show you."

M goes into my closet and comes out with the Scepter and the small, genetically sealed case containing the Grentl Archive stone. "Your door is locked, right?"

I get up and lock it. "It is now."

"Okay." She opens the case and takes out the flat purple crystal I haven't seen since we left Nuath. "Look. See how this stone is the exact shape and size as the pink one at the top of the Scepter? It was noticing how similar they are that made me wonder if the pink stone might also be an Archive. And it is."

"Huh, so it's that big jewel at the top that's the Archive? Cool!" Suddenly a memory niggles at me. "You know, these stones both remind me of one I have. I haven't looked at it or even thought about it in years, but seeing both of these together just made me think of it."

Her eyebrows go up. "Really? You have something you think could be another Archive stone? Where?"

"In my closet of secrets, of course," I say with a grin. "Here, I'll get it." I go in and pull a metal box from a top shelf all the way in the back. Blowing the dust off, I bring it out to show M.

"These are the only things I still have from my birth parents. Mum and Dad kept them for me until I was twelve or so, then said I should have them."

I open the box and take out the few items inside: a bracelet of polished wooden beads that I assume was my Ag mother's, a man's tunic clasp that must have belonged to my real father, a few old letters on real, Earth-style paper, and a translucent pale blue stone.

"Wow, you're right," M says. "It really does look like it could be an Archive. I assumed my Scepter was the only way to access those but maybe they're more common than I thought." She stares at my stone for a second or two, then shrugs. "Do you want to see if my Scepter can open it?"

My eyes widen. "Seriously? Do you think that's a good idea? What if it's not...compatible or something and, I don't know, damages the Scepter?"

"I doubt that's a real risk. Probably the worst that will happen is it just won't work. I'm willing to try if you are, though."

I hesitate for a long moment. If this stone *is* an Archive, will it contain a message from my real parents? Maybe even their images, like M's Archive has of her ancestors? Am I really ready for that? Finally, I nod.

"Okay. But just so you know, if it works I might cry."

She gives me a little hug. "Totally understandable. Shoot, I might, too. All right, let's try it."

Putting her palm over the pink stone at the top of the Scepter, she presses down and twists it to the left and it just...pops out into her hand.

"Whoa!"

"I know. Cool, huh? Now let's put this one in and see what happens."

She picks up my blue stone and pushes it into the spot the pink one just occupied, twisting it to the right.

"There. Okay... *Chartlann rochtana.*"

The Scepter seems to vibrate in her hand, then suddenly two holo-images appear right in the middle of my room, a man and a woman. They look strangely familiar—but nothing like the few pictures I have of my birth parents.

"Hello, Malena," the man says in Nuathan, looking at M, whose mouth has fallen completely open. "We hoped this Archive would never be needed but if you have possession of the Scepter, it appears the precautions we took were necessary after all."

"I... You're..." she stammers, looking wildly back and forth from the man to the woman to me. "Wait, did you call me Malena? My name is Emileia. Sovereign Emileia."

The woman—whose eyes I suddenly notice are the exact same shade of gray as my own—smiles. "Then you did survive?" She switches to

English, probably because M used it. "That is very, very good news, though it appears we did not, if you are now Sovereign. I very much look forward to learning what transpired after we created this Archive. But if you are not Malena, then…" She turns her amazingly lifelike head to look at me. "I assume this must be?"

My own mouth is hanging open, too. I close it and swallow, then somehow find my voice. "Um, no. I'm Molly. Molly O'Gara—though I was born Molly Mulgrew."

"Molly." The woman's smile broadens, making her eyes crinkle at the corners. "Will you put a hand on the Scepter, please?"

Mystified, I take hold of it, right below M's hand.

Looking even more pleased, the holographic woman nods. "I was correct. Eileen Mulgrew did indeed give birth to you, Molly, but she and her husband did not conceive you. Due to the threat our family faced from Faxon, they valiantly agreed to act as your surrogate parents. Your biological parents, however, were Mikal and Galena—us. It is a happy surprise indeed to discover both of our daughters not only alive, but together."

32

Double bond

M

I CAN'T BREATHE. For a long time I just stare at the two images standing in the middle of Molly's room and try to take in what Galena—*my mother!*—just said. "Did you…did you just say *both* of your daughters?"

"Yes," Galena replies, her smile encompassing me as well.

Molly and I share a disbelieving glance.

"I assume from your expressions that you had no suspicion at all before this?"

Together, we shake our heads.

"Doubtless that is the reason you are both still alive," the man— Mikal, my *father!*—tells us. "We took great pains to protect you both, Malena before she was even born. It was on Sovereign Leontine's advice that her embryo was secretly implanted in a non-Royal woman rather than having Galena give birth to the twins she carried."

Molly finds her voice before I do. "Wait, did you say twins? But M— Emileia, I mean—is three months older than I am."

"Yes," Mikal agrees. "Your embryo was put in stasis until an appropriate and willing surrogate could be located to carry you to term."

"We hoped by the time you were born the unrest might have died down," Galena adds. "Then we could have brought you to the Palace in safety to be raised with your sister. Unfortunately, the situation in Nuath continued to deteriorate and—again at Sovereign Leontine's insistence—we were obliged to flee the planet before you were a year old. We created this Archive to be left with the Mulgrews so that you might eventually know your true origins if Faxon's adherents succeeded in carrying out their avowed mission to assassinate us."

Mikal nods. "My father was adamant that such extraordinary measures were necessary to avoid any chance of Nuath being left with no heir at all to the Sovereign line. He claimed that would be far more disastrous than we could imagine."

"Did...did he tell you why?" I ask, finally overcoming my shock enough to speak.

He shakes his head. "He said that I would understand when I became Sovereign—which I assume never occurred?"

"No," I whisper. "I'm sorry. Faxon's assassins did succeed, about a year after you got to Earth. They followed you here." Even though I know they can't *really* feel grief, I hate having to give them the bad news.

"Then Leontine's fears were well founded." Galena appears genuinely sorrowful. If anything, the emotions these holograms display are even more lifelike than the ones in the main Archive. Maybe because these were created more recently?

Mikal regards me curiously. "What I don't understand is how you survived, Emileia, if we were both killed?"

"I...I'm not sure either." This conversation is so surreal I can hardly believe it's happening. "You apparently made it look like I died, too, because that's what everyone believed until just over a year ago. Though Shim, at least, must have suspected otherwise sooner." Why else would he have had Rigel's family searching for me?

"Shim Stuart, do you mean?" Mikal asks. "He and my father were very close, so it would not surprise me if Leontine confided more to him than to me. Perhaps Shim assisted us in the deception that fooled Faxon's assassins. We were to seek him out upon our arrival on Earth, though whether or not we did so is not included in this Archive."

Molly clears her throat. I look at her and see tears running down her cheeks—then realize I'm crying, too. How many times have I wished my father, at least, had been stored in the Scepter Archive? What a treasure we've discovered!

"Did...did you ever check on me after I was born?" she asks the couple in front of us. *Our* parents!

"We could never safely do so before creating this Archive, shortly before leaving Nuath. Whether we tried later would not be stored here," Galena tells her gently. "However, I very much doubt we would have risked contacting the Mulgrews about you, as your only safety lay in concealing your connection to us. Again I must express how grateful we are—or would be, were we still alive—to discover the ruse worked."

"So am I." I give Molly a misty smile. "I can't believe I have a sister… and that she's already my best friend."

Mikal and Galena beam at both of us, looking as delighted as I feel.

"You must add this discovery to the main Archive when you have opportunity," Mikal advises me. "This will be important information for future Sovereigns, particularly as I have no way of knowing whether my father was able to include anything pertaining to it. I presume he died sometime after we left Mars, as you are now Sovereign?"

I nod. "He was assassinated by Faxon just a couple of months after you left, I think. I…don't know all of the details, I'm afraid."

"No matter," Galena says, turning to regard Molly. "The purpose of this Archive is to acquaint Malena with her parents, not to store additional information. Given that, what would you like to know? Or you, Emileia, as you likely have little memory of us, either."

"Everything!" Molly and I exclaim together, then laugh. "Or," I amend, "as much as you can tell us in—" I glance at Molly's clock— "the next forty minutes."

⁺₊

WE ACTUALLY SPEND CLOSER to an hour talking with our parents' holograms, asking all kinds of questions about how they met, what their lives in Nuath were like before Faxon started causing trouble, their main interests… pretty much everything we can think of. Several times during the conversation Molly and I fall silent and just stare at them—or each other—in mutual disbelief.

"I wish we could keep talking to you for hours and hours," I finally say. "And we will, later on! But there's an *Echtran* Council meeting in twenty minutes and I should probably put something about this in the main Archive first…and see if Sovereign Leontine has any advice on how we should break this news to everyone."

"I look forward to speaking with you both again soon," our mother tells us with her beautiful smile.

"I, too," our father agrees. "I'm sure you will think of more questions by then."

I have absolutely no doubt of that. "Okay. Um, bye, then. We…we love you!"

Molly nods vigorously.

Then, regretfully, I say, "*Chartlann fionragh,*" and their images vanish.

For a long moment, Molly and I stare at the spot where they'd been, then turn to each other.

"I…I still can't believe it," she says.

"Me either. Sisters! We're actually sisters!" That fact is even more wonderful than the chance to talk to our parents. I launch myself at Molly and we hug each other tight, crying again.

She's the first to remember we still have things to do. "Um, didn't you want to do something with the other Archive before the meeting?"

"Oh. Right. Thanks." Wiping my eyes, I remove the blue stone from the Scepter and reinsert the pink one. "*Chartlann rochtana.*"

My grandfather—no, *our* grandfather—materializes in front of us. "Hello, my dear." He smiles at me, then glances around in apparent surprise. "I see we are no longer confined to your friend's closet? And this would be that friend you mentioned, your *Chomseireach?*"

"Yes, this is Molly. Except…we just found out that her real name is Malena."

Leontine's eyes widen for a moment, then he blinks. "Malena! Here? I'm afraid I don't understand."

"I know it seems like an incredible coincidence, but after talking with our parents—Molly still had the Archive they left behind, even though she didn't know what it was until tonight—we think we've mostly figured it out."

"Then pray, do explain. I have no doubt this story will be a most valuable addition to this Archive."

I do most of the talking, with Molly chiming in occasionally. I have to talk fast, since it's nearly time for the Council meeting. Even so, I only have time to tell the bare bones of the story—the earliest part of which Grandfather already knew.

"I'll have to fill in the rest later but first, do you have any advice on our best way to let the Council and…and everyone else know the truth about Molly? It doesn't seem right to just blurt it out, somehow."

He smiles at both of us. "At the very least, I would suggest you inform her adoptive parents in advance of any such announcement.

Then, once you have informed the rest of your Council, I recommend you solicit Kyna's input on how best to get the word out to the rest of our people, and on what sort of timetable."

"Thank you, Grandfather. We'll do that. And we'll talk again soon, I promise." I deactivate the Archive and turn back to Molly. "Guess we should get downstairs, huh?"

"Yeah, I guess so." She still looks a little dazed. I'm sure I do, too. "The meeting's supposed to be starting right about now."

We hurry down the stairs side by side and see Mr. O'Gara waiting by the front door.

"We need to hurry, Molly, if we're going to catch the seven-fifteen showing. Excellency, I believe they're ready for you in the living room."

Oops. "People are already here?" I didn't realize we were that late!

He nods. "Breann and Malcolm just arrived and I believe I hear Kyna's voice as well."

"Oh. Um, okay. There's something Molly and I need to tell you first, though."

Mrs. O'Gara comes out of the kitchen just then, carrying her usual large tray of snacks for the local Council members. "Here you are, Excellency! I was about to send Quinn upstairs for you. What on Earth were you two doing up there all this time? Molly and her father will be late for their movie."

"Um, about that. I think Molly and her dad should probably sit in on the meeting tonight."

"Molly? Why ever would Molly need to be there? Quinn can stay if you like, but Molly would do better to wait upstairs or in the kitchen. Oh, there's the doorbell again."

She opens the front door and Mr. Stuart comes in, followed by Connor. So much for telling the O'Garas privately! Still, I make one last effort.

"I was just telling Mr. O'Gara that there's something Molly and I need to talk to you two about."

"I'm afraid it will have to wait until after the meeting, dear. Kyna was quite insistent that we start on time this week as she has some unfinished work to attend to afterward." With that, she bustles into the living room to greet everyone and set out the snacks.

I look at Molly and shrug. "Guess we tell everyone at once, then, huh?"

"I guess so." She looks nervous now.

"It'll be fine," I whisper as her dad goes into the living room, giving us a curious frown over his shoulder. "Come on."

She follows me into the living room and takes a seat in the corner, still looking ill at ease. Molly's never attended a Council meeting before, except for a couple of emergency ones during the Grentl crisis. Kyna raises a brow at her presence but when I give her a little nod to show it's my idea, she doesn't question it.

Connor, however, is another matter.

"Why is the Ag girl here, or Quinn for that matter?" he demands. "I assumed my grievance against her would only be heard by the Council itself. Any response can be made later, through the proper channels."

That distracts me from the announcement I'm planning to make as soon as I figure out the right words. "Grievance? What kind of grievance can you possibly have against Molly?"

"It appears she has insinuated herself into my son's affections, by what means I do not know. I would like the Council's backing to bar her from further contact with him until I can remove him from Jewel and her pernicious influence."

Judging by the expressions on Breann's and Nara's faces, I'm not the only one trying to suppress a laugh—though I have an even better reason.

"The Council will do no such thing," I tell him in no uncertain terms. "Will it, Kyna?" I turn to her.

Her lips are also twitching. "Of course not. You are out of order, Connor. This Council has far more important business tonight than to intervene in a budding teen romance, no matter how it offends your sense of family dignity. As our business concerns you more than anyone else present, I recommend you sit down and pay attention, so that you might consider your response to what I am about to say."

His outrage turns to confusion. "What do you mean? I've done nothing wrong."

"This Council will be the judge of that." She now wears no trace of a smile. "As you should all know if you read my memo, memory extractions were finally performed on Allister Adair and Lach Lennox on Thursday. That evening, I acquainted the Sovereign and Van Stuart with some of the more pertinent facts discovered. We are unfortunately nc closer to tracing the source of the antimatter used in the explosive Enid devised, as she never told either of them where she obtained it. However, we did learn that both men have been in much closer contact with certain individuals in recent months than we had been led to believe. Those individuals are Devyn Kane and...Connor Roark."

Connor's face loses some of its color. "I've done nothing wrong," he repeats. "Allister and Lennox were both friends of mine prior to their, ah, misdeeds and I have occasionally checked on their well-being since their incarceration, but that is all."

"Is it?" Kyna raised a skeptical eyebrow. "According to their memories, you visited them frequently while overseeing the Dun Cloch orientations last summer. You also arranged for Devyn to meet with them, after his return from Mars. The content of some of his conversations with the two traitors would tend to confirm Mr. Stuart's suspicions about undocumented *Echtran* settlements populated by those inimical to our current governmental structure."

"I...I...Devyn asked to see them, yes. All four of us had been friends in years past, so it seemed an innocent enough request. They were allowed visitors, so I broke no regulations in setting up those meetings."

Kyna's gaze bores into him. "No one has accused you of anything criminal, Connor. However, you were aware that the Sovereign and this Council have been curious as to Devyn's whereabouts for some time, yet you volunteered no information on the matter. It now appears likely that he, along with Enid, was a co-conspirator in the recent plot against the Sovereign's life."

"Co-conspirator?" Connor blusters. "That's absurd! Devyn would never— Why, he came close to being Acclaimed Sovereign himself, you all know that. Some of you even suggested he be added to this Council. His exceptional record in the Nuathan legislature prior to Faxon, as well as his Royal lineage, speak for themselves."

"That is not your prerogative to determine," Kyna coldly informs him. "Perhaps you can tell us why you never mentioned his visits to Allister and Lennox?"

The color rushes back to Connor's face. "He...Devyn is a friend. I have always trusted him. He, ah, told me that the Sovereign held a grudge for the part he played in Nuath, in the matter of Rigel Stuart's... memory procedure, so he understandably preferred not to be brought to her notice again."

"I see. Lili, perhaps you would like to ask Connor whether he and Devyn assisted Allister and Lennox in any way as they plotted against the Sovereign's life?"

Mrs. O crosses the room to stand in front of Connor, looking down on him with obvious distaste. "To think you dared to insult my daughter —!" Kyna clears her throat and Mrs. O nods. Focusing closely now, she says, "Connor, did you in any way help Allister and Lennox in what they planned to do to the Sovereign?"

"No! Of course not," he exclaims. "And if Devyn did, which I very much doubt, I was completely unaware of it."

She continues to watch him for several seconds, then turns back to the rest of us. "He appears to be telling the truth. Not that that excuses him for withholding possibly vital information from us before."

"I agree," Kyna says. "This incident casts doubt on your fitness to be a member of this Council, Connor. That matter does not need to be decided tonight, but I believe it should be addressed in the very near future."

There's a murmur of agreement, even from the other two Royals.

"A full report of the results of the memory extractions will be sent to all of you once the transcriptions are complete," Kyna tells everyone then. "Meanwhile, there are a few less urgent matters I thought we might discuss this evening, though briefly, as I would prefer we conclude early if at all possible."

This is my opening, I suddenly realize. Standing up, I clear my throat. "Um, if you don't mind, I have a rather important piece of business to bring up first. It concerns Molly, here. Or, as she should be more properly known, Princess Malena."

If I was hoping for a dramatic reaction, I definitely get it. At least half of those present exclaim, "What?" as every eye turns to Molly—who looks like she wants to disappear into the floor, her face scarlet.

"What do you mean, Excellency?" Kyna frowns at me now. "If this is intended as some sort of joke, I must say—"

"No. It's no joke, I promise. Earlier this evening, Molly and I discovered that her biological parents were not the Ag family she lived with before Mr. and Mrs. O'Gara adopted her, but Mikal, Sovereign Leontine's son and heir, and his wife, Galena. Molly—Malena—is my full-blooded sister."

33

Noble element

Molly

EVEN THOUGH I'M sitting in a corner of the living room, as out of the way as possible, I suddenly feel like I have a spotlight on me. Couldn't M have given me a *little* warning before springing the news on everybody like that?

Hardly anyone looks like they believe it's true—including my parents. Nara is the only one who seems delighted by the news.

"But this is *wonderful!*" she exclaims excitedly, clapping her hands. "We all thought Emileia had lost her entire extended family and now she has a sister! You both must be so happy."

Swallowing, I manage to nod—though right this second I feel more overwhelmed than anything else. Holding my breath, I turn to look at my parents—who are staring at me with expressions almost of horror, as though they suddenly don't recognize me.

"Mum? Dad?" I whisper.

"How...how can this be?" Mum says in a strangled voice, turning to M. "How could you possibly have discovered such a thing since arriving here barely two hours ago?"

M bites her lip. "I, ah, actually can't tell you that, at least not the details, but we, ah discovered some hidden records. Oh, I know! We can have someone do a genetic test on Molly. I'm absolutely positive that will verify what I just said."

"If you'd like, I can ask my wife to come here now," Mr. Stuart offers. "She has the necessary equipment at home to analyze the similarities of the two girls' genomes. However, some may insist on the ancient test Allister used on the Sovereign shortly after she was discovered alive."

"The *foare rioga* is currently in secure storage here in Washington, DC," Kyna says without taking her eyes off me. "I can bring it to Jewel myself, if necessary. For the present, however, I would appreciate it if you would call Ariel, Van. It appears my unfinished work may have to wait until tomorrow."

While he makes the call and we wait for Dr. Stuart to arrive, Kyna quickly reads through the rest of her agenda, tabling most of it until the next meeting.

"Assuming the Sovereign's claim is borne out," she says then, "we will obviously need to discuss what to do with this new information. Meanwhile, I imagine the O'Garas might like a private moment?"

"Yes, please," Dad and I say at the same time. Mum is still speechless.

The three of us get up and go to the kitchen, where I sit down at the kitchen table, across from my parents. "Are…are you guys okay?"

Mum finally finds her voice. "I'm not sure. I feel as though I must be dreaming. How can this possibly be? And how—"

"Like M said, I can't explain *exactly* how, not without giving away a secret that only Sovereigns are supposed to know about. It…had to do with something that was left behind for me when my Ag parents were killed and you adopted me."

Dad frowns. "One of the items in that little box, you mean? Something in there was a clue to your identity and we never realized it?"

That's close enough to the truth that I nod. "Pretty much. It was sort of a matter of…putting the pieces together, once I showed M what was in the box." Which was *literally* the case, though I don't say that.

"How sure are you about this? Really?" Mum asks.

I look her full in the eyes so she'll know I'm telling the truth. "Really, really sure. Believe me, I'm as blown away by this as you are—probably more. I've just had an extra hour or so to get used to the idea."

"I suppose decisions will need to be made, if this is confirmed," Dad says, still frowning thoughtfully. "It's quite something if, in barely over a year, our people have gone from having *no* viable heir to the Sovereign line to having two—though of course Emileia has already been Acclaimed and Installed…"

I suck in a breath. "I don't want to be Sovereign instead of M! That would be crazy. I'm just happy to have her as a sister. I'm not looking to…to share power or anything."

"Perhaps not, at least not yet. But this discovery is bound to have more ramifications than we've yet had time to consider."

"Can't…can't you both just be happy for me for now?" I look from one to the other. "Leave all the political stuff for later? Finding out so much more about my real parents, and especially that I have a sister, is a big enough deal without anything else."

Mum reaches out and takes my hand, then smiles, really smiles, for the first time since hearing the news. "Of course we're happy for you, sweetheart. It's just…a lot to take in, I suppose. As you say, it will take a bit of time to get used to the idea."

"Yeah, it will. Oh! Sean doesn't know yet! Should we—?"

Dad shakes his head. "This isn't the sort of news to give him over the phone. We'll tell him when he gets home tonight. He may as well enjoy his party without distractions while the Council decides what is to be done."

That last bit sounds ominous, especially after what Dad said about two heirs to the Sovereign line. But before I can ask what he thinks might happen, the doorbell rings.

"That must be Ariel. Dearie, dearie me!" Still looking a little dazed, Mum gets up to go answer the door.

Dad and I follow her and soon we're all back in the living room. Once Kyna explains to Dr. Stuart what's going on, she opens her medical bag and pulls out a little silver box.

"This isn't as sophisticated as the equipment they have in Dun Cloch, or even at NuAgra, but it will tell us the degree of overlap between the girls' DNA sequences, from which we can extrapolate the probability of a relationship. If each of you can give me a hair follicle?"

M and I each pluck a strand of hair from our heads and hand them to Dr. Stuart. She first feeds M's longer, lighter brown one into her device, then my shorter, darker one. Then she brings up a small holo-screen, inputs something into it and waits.

Everyone in the room tenses visibly when Dr. Stuart makes a soft, "Ah," sound.

"Well?" Malcolm demands immediately. "What does it say?"

She looks up with a smile. "The results are consistent with the girls' claim of being full sisters, sharing both parents. The odds of such a close match simply by chance are so small as to be negligible."

"Then…it's true?" Kyna sounds surprised. Did she really think M would lie about something like this? Or maybe it's just hard for her to take in. It sure was for me.

"I would say so," Dr. Stuart confirms. "Of course, given the importance of the Sovereign lineage, I imagine a more rigorous test is still in order, but this certainly confirms a close genetic relationship between Molly and Emileia."

"Malena," Mum startles me by saying. "The Sovereign told us Molly's true name is Malena. I, ah, suppose we should get used to calling her that."

I wince. "No, please don't, Mum. Can't I still just be Molly? It's…a pretty good nickname for Malena anyway. Just like M is for Emileia."

"Names aside, it appears this Council has a few decisions to make," Kyna says briskly. "For one, how and when to share this news with the rest of our people. A MARSTAR Bulletin would seem to be in order."

Connor surges to his feet. "Not without more definitive proof! Why, I wouldn't be at all surprised if this turns out to be a scheme cooked up by the Sovereign and her *Chomseireach* to overcome my objections to the girl's interest in my son. Even if there is some relationship, this girl could simply be an illegitimate by-blow, or—"

"Did you not hear what Ariel just told us?" Mum is on her feet, too. "She said that the girls are almost certainly *full* sisters, which would make them both legitimate daughters of the late Prince Mikal and his Consort Galena."

"That proves nothing," Connor insists. "Ariel could be in on the hoax, given the connection between her son and the Sovereign. I'm sure she would prefer Tristan transfer his attentions from the Sovereign to her Handmaid. I demand the *foare rioga* be administered before such explosive news is disseminated to our people."

Mum's so mad now, she's sputtering. "You—! From the start you have been determined to cast aspersions—"

"Enough, please." Kyna holds up a hand. "Connor, given your

tenuous standing on this Council at the moment, you are scarcely in a position to make demands."

Mum gives him a triumphant look and sits back down.

"That said," Kyna continues, "I believe I must agree that given the importance of this discovery, the *foare rioga* should be performed to allay any shadow of doubt before we make a general announcement. I propose that happen tomorrow night, if the rest of you are amenable?"

A quick vote is unanimous. Connor glares at me as he raises his hand.

"In that case, I believe further decisions can wait for the result of that test. I will retrieve the device from its secure location and bring it with me tomorrow." Kyna glances around the room. "If there is no further business for tonight, I'd like to declare this meeting adjourned."

There are no objections and a moment later Kyna's image winks out. Connor leaves immediately too, not even saying goodbye to anyone. Jerk.

Nara lingers for a few minutes to congratulate M and me on finding each other. "I don't know how I never noticed before that you have Galena's eyes," she tells me, on the verge of happy tears. Then she, too, vanishes.

The Stuarts stay to exchange a few words with M while Malcolm and Breann depart, whispering together. Then it's just M, me and my parents in the house.

"So, um, what is this test they want me to take?" I ask M nervously. "Did you have to do it?"

She nods. "Allister insisted. Even though there are now Nuathan genetic tests they can do with hair follicles that are just as precise, they've been using the *foare rioga* for centuries, so the traditionalists still insist on it. It does involve a kind of scary-looking needle for the blood draw, but if Dr. Stuart does it, it shouldn't hurt much at all."

I relax. I've had my share of bumps and bruises and even a bad scrape or two from cheerleading foul-ups, so this should be a piece of cake. "Thanks, M."

Without warning, she practically tackles me with another fierce hug. "I'm so happy we found out, Molly! If I could have picked anyone on Earth—*or* Mars—to be my sister, it would have been you."

"Ditto." I hug her back, hard. "Guess you'd better get home, huh?"

"Yeah. But if you—any of you—" She looks at Mum and Dad—

"want to talk more about all this tomorrow before the meeting, let me know, okay?"

⁺₊

SEAN DOESN'T GET home from the party at Pete's until nearly midnight, but no way I'm going to bed until I've told him the incredible news. Mum and Dad stay up, too, and while we're waiting, all we do is talk about it.

"I still don't understand how this can be," Mum says after making us all a pot of tea to go with the leftover snacks from the meeting. "No one in Glenamuir ever questioned that you were born to the Mulgrews before they were killed."

"That's because I was. Mrs. Mulgrew was my surrogate mother. According to the, uh, record we found, it was all a huge secret to keep me safe. Technically, M and I are twins—though not identical ones, obviously. Faxon's followers were already threatening to eradicate Royals, and especially the Sovereign and his family, when our...mother... Galena, got pregnant. They decided to separate us to make it less likely we could both be killed."

Dad nods. "Given what Sovereign Leontine knew about the Grentl, that made sense I suppose. I presume you were implanted three months later, given the difference in your and Emileia's ages?"

"Um, yeah. I guess embryos can be put in stasis?" That's what Mikal...my father!...said they did.

"Yes, we've had that technology for well over a century," Dad says. "Some *fines* tend to have more trouble conceiving than others, so in vitro fertilization is fairly common in Nuath. Of course, the resulting embryo is usually carried to term by the biological mother."

They keep asking questions and I tell them pretty much everything except about the Scepter and Archive stones. "M thinks we'll be able to find out more, now she knows where to look," I say evasively at one point. "If we do, I'll share it."

"What a mercy we were able to bring that box of mementos along when we evacuated," Mum exclaims.

Wow, no kidding! Getting out in such a hurry after Faxon's people identified my parents as part of the Resistance meant a lot of things got left behind. What if my box—that Archive—had been one of them? I'd have lived my whole life never knowing the truth.

Then another thought suddenly hits me. "No wonder I've never been able to grow plants worth beans!" I exclaim. "I was never an Ag to begin with."

We're all still laughing about that when Sean comes through the kitchen door.

"What's so funny?"

"The reason I suck at growing plants," I tell him, still grinning. "Um, you should probably sit down."

Looking concerned now, he pulls out a chair and joins us at the kitchen table. "What's going on?"

"Do you want to tell him, Dad?"

"Only if you'd rather not. It's your news to share," he replies.

He's right. And I *do* want to be the one to give Sean the news. I can't wait to see the look on his face.

"Okay. You're not going to believe this, but earlier tonight M and I found out I'm not an Ag at all."

"Huh?"

"Turns out I'm Royal—just as Royal as she is and actually *more* Royal than you are. I'm M's sister!"

For several seconds he just blinks at me, then turns to look at Mum and Dad. "What kind of drugs have you given her?"

They're both smiling now. "No drugs," Mum assures him. "What she just said is true. Ariel Stuart confirmed the genetic relationship between the girls and tomorrow night the Council plans to perform the *foare rioga* so they'll have the traditional proof to point to before making the news public. Our Molly is a true heir of the Sovereign line, daughter of Prince Mikal and Consort Galena!"

Sean stares at me, slowly shaking his head back and forth. "I don't... I can't..."

Mum pours him a cup of tea and we spend the next half hour explaining. Again, I only leave out the part about the Scepter and blue stone.

"To think," Mum says when she gets up to rinse out the cups, "all this time we were so concerned to have you meet Emileia so that you could fulfill your role as Consort when we had a completely legitimate potential Sovereign right in our family. Perhaps, had we known—"

Sean and I cut her off by simultaneously saying, "Ewww!"

"That's just gross, Mum," he tells her and I nod. "Molly's my sister. I could never have— Not that it matters now anyway."

"I suppose you're right," she says, though with a touch of regret. "'Twas just a thought."

We all head to bed then, since it's past one and Mum has to be at church early tomorrow for choir. Not till I'm in my room do I finally have a chance to savor the thought that occurred to me right at the start of the Council meeting—how wonderful it will be to tell Tristan my news!

34

Retort

Tristan

It's past nine-thirty when Father slams into the house Saturday night, startling Mother and me as we're watching a movie in the living room.

"Start packing your things," he tells us. "I don't care whether there's a house available in Colorado yet or not, we're leaving. I won't stay here in Jewel to be subjected to any more insults."

"What happened, dear?" Mother asks fearfully.

He glares at her and for a second I don't think he's going to answer. Then he says, "Kyna, the *non*-Royal head of the *Echtran* Council, saw fit to call my honor and loyalty to our people into question. She actually hinted that I might be asked to leave the Council but I don't plan to wait around for that. I'll resign first. Just because—" He breaks off, glowering, then storms off to his office.

"I want you both ready to leave at a moment's notice!" he shouts over his shoulder before banging the door shut.

I look at Mother and she looks back, clearly alarmed. "What do you suppose—?"

"I don't know, but this is crap. *He* can go back to Denver if he wants, but I think you and I should stay put. Whatever he's done, neither of us had anything to do with it."

"Do you really believe your father might have done something deserving of censure by the Council?" she asks doubtfully.

A week ago I might have said no. Not now. "He's awfully ambitious, so who knows? Remember how he didn't want us to tell anyone about him speaking with Devyn Kane last week?"

Even as I say that, I hear him talking angrily in his office—to someone he just called, I assume. Devyn?

"Yes, that did seem odd," Mother agrees. "Still, whatever faults of temper he may have, I always believed he had the best interests of our people at heart."

"As long as it doesn't conflict with his own interests," I add bitterly. "If he *has* done something wrong, I can't imagine him admitting to it. When has he ever?"

I stare at his office door for a moment, thinking, then look at my mother. "Do *you* want to go back to Colorado?"

"Not particularly," she admits. "The sun there is so intense. I never got used to that, nor the harsh winters, despite living there for almost twenty years. After spending time with some of the other *Echtran* women living in Jewel last weekend, I was beginning to feel that we might make a real home here."

"And we will," I promise her. "Like I said, Father can go back to Denver alone if he really wants to leave—and good riddance if he does."

She gasps. "You don't mean that, Tristan?"

"You bet I do. The only reason I considered letting him send just you and me there was to get you away from him. Away from any chance he could ever hurt you again. This would be even better."

Interestingly, Mother doesn't argue with me. She also doesn't agree out loud—but I don't think I imagine the little spark of hope in her eyes at the thought. That solidifies my resolve to stay put. *Especially* if Father insists on leaving.

WHEN FATHER COMES down to breakfast the next morning, he's in a noticeably better mood than he was last night.

"Now that I've had time to think over my options," he says almost cheerfully, "I realize that should circumstances dictate that I leave the *Echtran* Council, I will likely have even greater opportunities available to me elsewhere. In fact, once I've tied up a few loose ends here in Jewel—"

He pauses to regard me speculatively— "I may well be able to secure a position that will guarantee my—and our family's—standing in the social order for generations to come."

Mother and I both stare at him, mystified. "What higher position is there on Earth than the *Echtran* Council?" she asks him.

"Never you mind. I'll share more details when the time comes. Meanwhile, we should begin packing up the house as soon as we finish breakfast."

I wonder what that weird look he gave me was about—and how long those "loose ends" of his will take. How much of a reprieve will they give me to make plans? Given Father's wild mood swings lately, I'd better not count on it being very long. He could still decide to yank me out of school and ship me off without much warning.

With that in mind, instead of packing when I go up to my room, I flip open my laptop and fire off a quick email.

HEY, Molly,

Father came home from the Council meeting last night in a really foul mood and now he wants all of us to move back to Denver, not just Mother and me. Not that I plan to go. Do you have any idea what happened at the meeting to get him so upset?

Love,

I FREEZE, staring at the word I just typed. Because it's true. I'm not sure how or when it happened but I know, with blinding clarity, that it's absolutely true. Crazy as it seems, I'm totally in love with Molly. But because I can't tell her first in an email, I quickly backspace and instead type,

THINKING OF YOU,
—Tristan

SINCE MOLLY'S STILL GROUNDED, she was probably at home during the meeting, though she might not have been able to overhear anything. Still, it can't hurt to ask. The more I know, the better I can plan. Besides,

I'm missing her so much after two whole days apart that even emailing her is better than nothing.

When Father comes to check on my packing progress half an hour later, my laptop is innocently closed. The second I heard his heavy tread on the stairs, I flipped it shut and started flinging random crap out of the nearest drawer.

"You haven't accomplished much yet." He sweeps my room with a critical eye.

"Maybe because I don't want to go." I'd add, *Neither does Mother,* but I don't want him mad at her, too.

He snorts. "Did I ask what you want? You'll do whatever I decide you'll do. Now, get cracking."

The moment he's gone, I open my laptop to see if Molly's replied since the last time I looked. Nope.

I alternate checking my email and pulling more clothes out of my closet and drawers so it looks like I'm at least making an effort to sort through my stuff next time Father stops by. That mostly keeps him off my back, apart from some grumbling about the mess I'm making.

When Molly still hasn't answered me by lunchtime, I start worrying her mother might have taken her computer away, too. The second I get back upstairs, I check my email again with a growing sense of desperation.

Yes!

Hi, Tristan!

Sorry I didn't see your message earlier—it's been kind of a crazy day here. I actually do have a lot to tell you but I don't want to do it in email. Any chance you can escape for a while this afternoon? Maybe we could meet somewhere?

Hoping,

—Molly

My heart starts thudding in slow, painful strokes. What can she have to tell me that she doesn't want to say in an email? What if Father said something to her last night before or after the Council meeting that made her decide to break things off with me after all? That would explain his strangely improved mood.

I'm more anxious than ever to see her, worried Father might not even let me go to school tomorrow. He still has my car keys but my old bike is in the garage…

I look up Molly's address to see how far it is and discover her house is less than three miles away—an easy bike ride. Even if I can't sneak my bike out, it shouldn't take more than half an hour to run there. I email her back.

MOLLY,

If you're sure you can get away, I can meet you near your house. How about the same corner where I picked you up last weekend? I can be there in an hour.
—Tristan

LESS THAN A MINUTE later she responds.

SOUNDS PERFECT. *See you soon!*

I CONSOLE myself that her messages sound upbeat, so whatever she has to tell me can't be *too* bad…except that Molly is almost always upbeat. Will she somehow find a silver lining if Father forces me to leave for good?

Not wanting him to get suspicious, I spend the next fifteen minutes shoving some of my pants and sweaters into boxes. Then I pull on my running shoes and tiptoe downstairs.

Father's not around but I hear clattering in the kitchen—probably Mother boxing up pots and pans. Rather than risk Father blaming her for my absence, I slip out the back door and circle around toward the garage to get my bike. I'm just about to go in when I hear a thump from inside the garage, then Father swearing. Oops. Reversing course, I go around the other side of the house and out to the street.

And start running.

Sure enough, it takes me less than half an hour to reach the corner of Opal and Garnet. It's probably a good ten minutes before I told Molly I'd meet her, so I go to a nearby tree and brace myself against it while I stretch out my calves. It's been a while since I've done much running.

After that, I lean against the tree to wait, since I have a good view of

Molly's house from here. I should be able to spot her whether she comes out the front or sneaks out the back.

The minutes creep by and I start to worry she won't be able to get away without her mother stopping her. I don't have my phone so I can't check the time, but surely the hour is up by now? I push away from the tree, thinking I'll just stroll past her house, then stop before I take a single step.

Because I'm not the only one watching Molly's house.

A scruffy-looking guy I didn't notice before is crouched behind the fence separating the O'Garas' yard from the one next door. He's not pulling weeds or anything, just squatting there and staring at the O'Gara house through the slats in the fence.

Something's definitely off about this. I start moving cautiously in his direction.

I've covered about half the distance when the O'Garas' front door opens and Molly steps out onto her front porch. The man behind the fence instantly tenses, then rises to a crouch. As Molly starts down the porch steps, he begins creeping her way, still hunched low so he's screened from her view by the vine-covered fence.

Seriously alarmed now, I break into a sprint, my rubber-soled shoes making almost no noise on the sidewalk. Molly sees me before stalker-guy does. She smiles and raises a hand to wave at me—which of course alerts the other guy to my presence.

He shoots a quick glance my way, then springs to his feet and lurches toward Molly. That's when I realize he's holding something in his right hand. Something he's pointing at Molly.

Putting on a burst of speed, I lower my shoulder and barrel into the man from the side before he has time to react. He hits the ground hard with a grunt, but immediately scrambles to his feet, now bringing the silver thing in his hand to bear on me, instead.

Molly cries out a warning as an energy beam sizzles past me, less than an inch from my shoulder. I get a whiff of ozone, then hear a crack from behind me from whatever the beam hit. Before he can fire again I duck sideways, but he uses that opportunity to aim at Molly again.

Quickly changing course, I make a dive for the hand holding the weapon, determined to get it away from him before he gets off another shot. My hand closes on his wrist just as he fires and a black, smoking hole appears in one of the fence slats. This guy is playing for keeps!

"Get back inside!" I yell at Molly, keeping an iron hold on the man's wrist. Tightening my grip, I give his arm a fierce twist and the silver weapon goes flying, landing several yards away in a drift of fallen leaves. The attacker gives a strangled cry and tries to wrench himself out of my grasp to go after it, but no way am I letting go.

It's only then I notice the guy's *brath*, though the energy weapon should have already clued me in that he's *Echtran*.

"Go on!" I shout when I realize Molly hasn't moved. "There could be others. I'll hold this one while you get help."

Even as I say that, the guy slips his free hand into a pocket and pulls out another, smaller object that looks like some kind of vial or syringe.

"You think I'm giving up that easily?" he rasps. "Not a chance." He swings the tiny ampule toward my arm.

I have zero doubt it'll be bad if that thing touches me, so I do my best to keep it from happening—without releasing his other hand. Awkwardly, I bat at the glass cylinder with my own free hand while trying to drag the guy toward Molly's house. Any minute, one of her *Duchas* neighbors might look out a window and call the cops. Which would also be bad.

He aims the sinister little object at my arm again but before it connects a foot comes out of nowhere and dashes the ampule from his hand to shatter against the fence.

"No you don't," Molly snarls at him from behind me.

When the guy tries to lunge at her, I finally manage to yank both of his arms behind him and push him onto the ground, face first. Jamming a knee into his back to pin him more securely, I look up at Molly, whose eyes are wide and scared despite what she just did.

"That was quick thinking," I tell her. "Thanks. Now go get your father and Sean, if they're home. We need to get this guy out of sight before the locals get curious."

"Oh. Right. You sure you'll be okay?" She looks worriedly at me as her would-be attacker tries to twist out of my grip.

"Yes—if you hurry."

She nods and hurries back into the house.

I don't have anything to tie the guy's hands with, but I'm bigger and heavier than he is. By now it's obvious I'm stronger, too. He only continues struggling for a few more seconds, then suddenly goes limp— and starts chuckling.

Chuckling?

"Won't do any good, you know." His voice is muffled by the grass beneath him. "You said there might be others? There are. Lots of 'em. I'm only the first. The rest will get here soon enough. Stopping me now, today, only delays the inevitable, and not for long. The ruling *fines* have had their day, lording it over everyone. It's our turn now."

This must be one of those Anti-Royals I've heard Father talk about, who staged protests in Nuath and tried to attack the Sovereign. It wouldn't be hard to find out where the O'Garas live. They probably sent this guy to ambush anyone who came out. He'd have assumed Molly was Royal like the rest of her family.

A minute later Molly and her parents come running outside, Molly in the lead.

"Careful!" I call out. "He says there are more like him—not sure how close by."

Mr. O'Gara strides past Molly to frown down at the man I'm holding. "Molly said he used a, ah, non-standard weapon?"

I nod in its general direction. "It's over there in those leaves. I knocked it out of his hand. Definitely *Echtran*," I add more quietly, so there's no risk of neighbors overhearing.

"I'll alert Cormac, then," Mrs. O'Gara says. "He'll know what to do." She pulls out her phone—probably also an omni, like Father's—and makes a quick call.

"What happened, exactly?" Molly's father asks, looking from the man on the ground to his daughter.

When she hesitates, I answer. "I was, um, out for a jog and decided to swing by, hoping maybe Molly and I could talk. Then I saw this guy crouched by the fence here. That looked really suspicious to me and sure enough, the moment Molly came outside he went to attack her."

"With this, I presume." Mr. O'Gara holds up a small, silver object.

"Yeah. He was starting to aim it at Molly when I, er, tackled him."

"He had something else, too," Molly volunteers, pointing at the fence. "I think it broke when I kicked it out of his hand, though."

Her father goes over and looks at the remains of the vial but is careful not to touch it.

Mrs. O'Gara finishes her call then. "Cormac will be here directly," she tells us.

Sure enough, a moment later the Sovereign's Bodyguard comes trotting around the corner, the Sovereign right behind him. It's the first time I've seen Mr. Cormac outside of school, where he's vice principal.

"What happened?" he asks. "Is everyone okay?"

"Yes, thanks to Tristan here," Mr. O'Gara says. "We're very fortunate he happened by in time to prevent a tragedy. This weapon is set to kill." He gingerly hands the small device to Cormac, who pockets it. "He also had that on him." Mr. O'Gara indicates the shattered vial by the fence.

Cormac leans down and grabs the guy I've kept pinned to the ground all this time and hauls him to his feet.

"I'll take care of this vermin," he growls, "then send someone to clean up and secure the area. Did any non-*Echtrans* witness the disturbance?"

"I don't think so," I tell him. Then, before he marches the would-be assassin off, I repeat what he said after I immobilized him. Understandably, everyone looks even more upset.

"We need to make absolutely sure this time that no one can silence him before we find out what he knows," M says, glaring at the man. Then she blinks in surprise. "Wait, I recognize you! You're the same guy who attacked me last year on Diamond Street."

"A minor setback," the man sneers at her. "We'll prevail in the end, you'll see."

Cormac pulls out something like a zip tie and secures the guy's hands behind his back. "That's enough out of you. Come along." Then, to the rest of us, "I recommend you all get indoors until I can have the whole area scanned for any others."

"An excellent idea," Mrs. O'Gara agrees. "Come along inside, you lot. Now." She ushers us all into the house.

Mr. O'Gara relays everything I told him to the Sovereign as we all take seats in the living room. I snag the spot on the couch next to Molly and to my relief no one objects. I don't quite dare to touch her with her parents in the room, but just being this close feels really good.

"How could that guy have known to attack Molly?" M asks as soon as we're all settled. "Especially so quickly?"

"He was probably just after Royals in general, planning to shoot anyone who came out of the house," I suggest. "Molly just happened to be first. I'm sure a lot of people don't know she's adopted."

Mrs. O'Gara regards me curiously. "Did your father not share any, ah, information from last night's Council meeting when he got home?"

"Um, no. He almost never does. Why?"

Before she can answer, Molly speaks up. "Mum, I…I'd like to tell him myself, if that's okay?"

To my surprise, her parents and the Sovereign all stand up, suddenly smiling.

"Of course," her mother says. Then, to the others, "We'll just go into the kitchen for a few minutes, shall we? I'll make us a spot of tea."

They all leave the room so it's just Molly and me alone. I'm totally baffled, especially since I thought Molly was still grounded from seeing me at all.

"I obviously missed something. What?"

Molly smiles, too, though there's a trace of wariness in her gray eyes. "It's… what I wanted to talk to you about. Something important enough that I thought I should do it face to face."

That bit of wariness along with her phrasing scares me. Is she planning to dump me after all? That would definitely explain why her parents looked so happy.

"Okay." I brace myself for the worst. "Shoot."

"M and I made kind of a huge discovery yesterday, right before the Council meeting. You know how I told you my real parents were Ag farmers in Glenamuir?"

Cautiously relieved, I nod. That doesn't *sound* like the lead-in to a dumping…

"Well, I found out yesterday that's not completely true. The Mulgrews were just my surrogate parents."

"Huh?" Now I'm totally mystified.

"I was born to the Mulgrews, but they didn't conceive me. Because Faxon was threatening to kill off the whole Sovereign line, I was taken from my mother soon after she got pregnant, separated from my twin. The Mulgrews agreed to carry me to term and raise me as their own, as an Ag, to keep me safe. And…it obviously worked."

All I can do for a long moment is stare at her. "Then your real parents…your biological parents, I mean…"

"Were Prince Mikal and his wife Galena," she confirms, her gaze locked on mine. "I was never a real Ag at all. Turns out, I'm actually M's twin sister."

35

Catalyst

Molly

I watch various emotions play across Tristan's face in rapid succession, holding my breath while he absorbs what I just told him. He looks as stunned as I was yesterday, even a little scared, but then, finally, he smiles.

"This...this is really great news for you. Isn't it?" Already, uncertainty is creeping in.

"Yeah, it is. For one thing, I finally know why I've never been any good at growing plants. But the best part is finding out I have a sister. Even better, she's already my best friend!"

Exactly like Sean did last night, Tristan shakes his head slowly back and forth, like he can't quite believe it. I don't blame him. It hasn't completely sunk in for me yet, either. Not even after that attack just now.

"So...wow. I guess our people have another leader now, huh? If you're the Sovereign's twin, you must have as strong a claim to the throne as she does."

I cringe. "My dad said the same thing last night but honestly, I don't care about that. I'm just happy to know where I...I *fit*, you know? Because I was never sure before. Not for my whole life."

Tristan puts his hand over mine and I revel in the lovely sensations that accompany his touch. Now his smile is tender, sympathetic. "I don't know anyone who deserves to be happy more than you do, Molly. I'm really glad for you."

"Don't you mean for us?" I'm only half teasing. "Once everyone knows I'm really Princess Malena, they should stop trying to keep us apart. Especially your dad and my mum. Right?"

To my surprise, he frowns. "You'd think, wouldn't you? Weird that he never said a word about it when he got home last night."

"Probably because he totally refused to believe it, even after Rigel's mom did a genetic test with M's and my hair follicles that proved we're related. He claimed it was some big hoax and Dr. Stuart was in on it. Everyone was pissed at him but when he demanded the official test, the rest agreed it should be done before spreading the word. They're planning to do it tonight."

He's still frowning. "If they agreed, why was he so mad? He came home in a super nasty temper, like I said in my email. He was threatening to resign from the Council, said the leader, Kyna, insulted his honor or something."

"Um, yeah, she did kind of make him squirm last night. That was before M told everyone about me. I got to sit in on the whole meeting, since M wanted me there when she gave the Council our big news," I explain. "They did memory extractions on Uncle Allister and Governor Lennox and found out your dad was in way closer contact with them than he ever let on. That didn't go over very well with the rest of the Council. Kyna seemed especially upset that he never mentioned he'd set up meetings between them and Devyn Kane."

Tristan's eyebrows shoot up. "Devyn Kane? Devyn was working with Allister and Lennox, the ones who tried to kill the Sovereign? Does that mean my father was in on it, too? But…that doesn't make any sense. If he wanted her dead, why was he pushing me to hook up with her?"

"No, my mum asked him that directly. She said he was telling the truth when he claimed he didn't know about their plan. But the Council apparently *has* been trying to track down Devyn for more than a month. Your dad knew that, but never let on to any of them that he knew where Devyn was."

"Huh. It's definitely true he and Devyn have been talking with each other recently. Maybe even last night, though I'm not positive about that. I wonder…"

He lapses into thought and I get the strong sense he's struggling with some terrible inner conflict. I put my free hand over his, where it already rests on mine—partly to reassure him, and partly to intensify the contact between us, hoping it might also increase my understanding of what's going on inside him.

"It's not your fault, Tristan," I assure him after a moment. "You've always said your dad never tells you much of anything that's going on."

"Yeah, but I still could have paid closer attention—to everything. There were clues. Maybe if I'd…" He's silent for another second or two, then suddenly surges to his feet, his expression determined. "Right. Better late than never. I need to talk to the Sovereign, Molly. Now."

Baffled, I accompany Tristan to the kitchen, still clinging to his hand. Mum, Dad and M all look up, startled, when we walk in. Tristan speaks before anyone else can—like he's afraid he'll change his mind if he doesn't say whatever it is quickly.

"You were all wondering how that guy who tried to kill Molly could possibly have learned the truth about her heritage so quickly, right? Well…I think I might know."

Everyone stares at him, including me—though I also tighten my grip on his hand. If he tries to make this somehow his fault, I'm ready to contradict him.

"I… Okay." He takes a deep breath before continuing. "Right after my father got home last night, he made a call to someone. I thought at the time it might be Devyn Kane, because they've been talking a lot recently and Father has been…weird about it. Secretive. After what Molly just told me, I'm guessing he told Devyn about her, and Devyn's the one who sent that assassin after her."

Mum frowns. "But I questioned Connor last night, after we learned he had been in contact with Devyn. He insisted they weren't involved in the recent plot against the Sovereign and I had no sense that he was lying. Why would they want to harm Molly but not Emileia?"

"You just asked if *Connor* helped Allister and Lennox," M points out. "He admitted he didn't know whether Devyn did or not. We have no idea what Devyn's been up to. We didn't even ask whether Connor had spoken with Devyn since setting up those meetings in Dun Cloch. Obviously, he has."

Dad turns to Tristan. "Do you know what they've been discussing?"

He shakes his head. "Father almost never tells me—or my mother—anything. He definitely never mentioned Allister or Lennox. He wouldn't even tell me why Allister was removed from the Council last year when I asked. When Father first mentioned Devyn, it was just to tell Mother and me over dinner that he might be coming to visit us here in Jewel."

"Devyn intends to come here himself?" Mum sounds alarmed.

"I don't think so, not anymore," Tristan says. "Mother asked about it again a few days later and Father said he wasn't coming after all. But both times Devyn's name came up, Father warned us both not to mention it to anyone else. I had no idea then that the Council was looking for the guy, but I still thought that was strange. Maybe if I'd said something sooner to Molly or even to M…"

"You couldn't have known, Tristan," I remind him. "I didn't know they were looking for him either, until last night, so even if you'd told me, I might not have mentioned it to M."

M's frowning now. "Hm. I've wondered if Devyn might be involved with those rogue settlements Mr. Stuart was monitoring. Remember how those transmissions suddenly stopped and we didn't know why? If Connor's been in touch with Devyn all this time, he might have tipped Devyn off about what Mr. Stuart was doing—even if he didn't realize himself what Devyn or those groups were up to."

"When did those transmissions stop?" Tristan asks.

"A week ago Thursday," M tells him. "The day after Kira and the rest of us met at Rigel's to tell those Scientists about the special tech Allister and Lennox had."

"So…the night after I went in your place to meet Tristan at Dream Cream?" I can't help blushing a little at the memory.

Tristan looks at me with an arrested expression and I wonder if he's also remembering our first kiss. But then he says, "It was that same Thursday evening Father first mentioned talking with Devyn—so the timing fits. Also, he said something at breakfast this morning about an opportunity or position he'd been offered. Something bigger than being on the *Echtran* Council."

"What sort of position?" Dad is clearly startled.

"I don't know. Mother asked what he was talking about and he refused to explain, said it was too soon. But maybe it's something to do with Devyn and those groups?"

M stands up. "I need to tell Kyna about all of this before tonight's meeting. The attack, Connor's recent contacts with Devyn, everything. And it sounds like we found that security leak she suspected."

She reaches into her pocket, then grimaces. "Oops. I was in such a rush to follow Cormac here, I didn't think to grab my phone."

"You can use mine, Excellency," Mum offers.

"Thanks. Tristan, I'd like you to come to tonight's meeting, if you're willing. Your mother, too. You'll both be valuable witnesses, and your presence might get Connor to tell us more than he would otherwise."

Tristan looks startled at the request, and not particularly pleased, but then he nods. "Absolutely, if you think it will help. The important thing is to keep Molly safe. Um, to keep both of you safe, I mean."

"I know what you mean." M grins at him. "I'm guessing Molly would also like you here for tonight's official certification of her bloodline."

He turns to me questioningly as M goes into the dining room to make her call to Kyna. I shrug apologetically.

"It *would* make me less nervous to have you there," I admit. "I'm not quite sure what to expect."

"Then count on it," he promises. The warmth in his eyes makes me want to fling myself into his arms but of course I can't do that right here in the kitchen with my parents.

"You were very brave to come forward with this information Tristan," Mum tells him with an understanding smile. "I know it can't have been easy for you to implicate your father, no matter how wrong he may have been."

His expression hardens. "I only wish I'd done it sooner. When I think what would have happened if I'd arrived here just a few minutes later…" He looks at me with anguish in his eyes.

"Mum, Dad, do you mind if Tristan and I go for a walk before he has to go home?" I'm suddenly desperate to be alone with him, if only for a few minutes.

"You and M should both stay indoors until we get the official all-clear from Cormac," Dad reminds me.

Tristan squeezes my hand. "He's right. Anyway, I really ought to get home. I didn't tell my parents I was leaving and they'll have noticed by now that I'm gone. I'd rather not have to tell my father where I was. He might get suspicious and refuse to go to the Council meeting or something."

"I supposed you'd better go, then. But do be careful," Dad cautions him.

"I will," Tristan says. "I want to be sure to attend that meeting myself."

I walk Tristan to the door, grateful when my parents stay put in the kitchen. "I haven't thanked you yet for saving my life," I tell him once we're alone. "You were amazing. If you hadn't been here—"

"Don't. I can't even think about it." The anguish is back. "I...I love you, Molly. Losing you might just have killed me, too."

I catch my breath. My heart suddenly feels like it's about to burst out of my chest, it's so incredibly full. "I love you, too, Tristan. It seems impossible, we've known each other such a short time, but—"

Just like he did once before, he shuts me up with a kiss...but this time there's not a thing wrong with that.

36

Concentration

Tristan

MY FEET barely touch the ground, I'm so buoyed by euphoria as I jog away from Molly's house.

She loves me! That one, incredible fact crowds out all the other revelations from the past hour. Finding out Molly's Royal, the Sovereign's actual twin sister, pales in comparison. She loves me!

Not until the first mile is behind me do other thoughts start to filter in—like how horrifyingly close I came to losing Molly forever because of that Anti-Royal assassin. It twists my gut to think there are people out there who want my Molly dead. Molly, who's always upbeat, who would never willingly hurt anyone... All because she shares the Sovereign's bloodline.

For a block or two, I wish they'd never discovered the truth. Molly would be so much safer as an Ag. But then I have to admit she—we—will have a lot more opportunities open to us now. Exactly what, I'm not sure yet, but I can't forget how incredibly happy she was to discover she and M are sisters. I guess that's worth *some* risk, for both of them. Even though I hate to think of Molly at any risk at all.

Maybe once they do that official test tonight and the Council announces her status to all our people, she'll be a little safer? It seems obvious these Anti-Royals wanted her dead before word got out. Otherwise they'd have taken more time, built in more fail-safes—and I might not have been able to save her.

A shudder runs through me, nearly making me stumble.

The closer I get to our house, the more I start thinking about Father's involvement in all this. It all comes back to Devyn. The guy has always been clever. Persuasive. Power-hungry. He clearly convinced Father to keep his whereabouts a secret when they first talked and has probably been wheedling Council secrets out of him ever since, like the bit about those transmissions.

Since no one outside the Council knew anything about Molly as of last night, Father *had* to be the one who blabbed about her to Devyn. If he didn't believe her claim was true, Father probably just added that "hoax" to his litany of grievances when he called Devyn last night. Not that that lets him off the hook for nearly getting Molly killed.

By the time I turn into our neighborhood, my fury over that betrayal has reached such a pitch that I have to force myself to slow down, calm down. I'm burning to rush home and confront him right now, but I can't.

Not yet.

Because the threat isn't over. From what that assassin said, they plan to keep coming, both for Molly and the Sovereign. Next time we need to be prepared, which means the Council needs to find out more about them—how many there are, what they want, how they're organizing. Father may not know, but I'll bet Devyn does.

If I confront Father, clue him in about the assassination attempt and what I've told the Sovereign, he might cut and run before tonight's meeting. I can't risk that when he's our best path to Devyn—to the truth about the people who sent that murderer after Molly.

With that in mind, when I reach the house I go in by the back door instead of the front. Maybe if I can get a shower before facing my father, I can cool down enough to resist shouting at him...or even punching him.

The living room is empty but Mother pokes her head out of the kitchen as I pass it on my way to the stairs.

"Where have you been?" she whispers. "Your father has been looking for you."

I gesture at my sweats and shoes. "Went for a run. I needed to blow off some steam."

She smiles sympathetically. "Run up and shower. We're eating early again, as your father has another Council meeting this evening. He's in his office on some important call, so if you hurry you needn't face him until his dinner is served. That might help a bit."

"Thanks." I want to tell her what I learned at Molly's but Father could come out any moment so I head upstairs instead.

When I get to the dinner table after my shower, I'm only a little bit calmer than when I got home. It's hard not to glare back when Father regards me through narrowed eyes.

"Your mother says you went out running? Where? I drove around looking for you and didn't see you anywhere in our neighborhood."

"I didn't stay in the neighborhood. Was I supposed to? I don't remember you mentioning that."

Instead of snapping at me like I expect, he gives me a long, assessing look. Then he shifts to an almost pleasant expression that immediately puts me on my guard, given what I learned today.

"No, I suppose I didn't. But now you're here, I want to talk to you."

"About what?" My tone borders on insolent, not that I care. He deserves a whole lot worse than that.

Oddly, he doesn't seem to notice.

"Our family's future. In particular, yours. I'd like to think you've learned your lesson this past week about going behind our backs. I hope so, as it's rather unseemly for someone of your status to ride a bus with common *Duchas*. Tonight I expect to receive news that should benefit us all, one way or another. Given that, I've decided you may have the use of your car again, as well as your phone, starting tomorrow."

In other words, he expects either proof that my girlfriend is the Sovereign's sister…or word from Devyn that she's been eliminated? No matter which it is, he must figure I won't be able to "disgrace" him anymore by being with Molly. No wonder he's suddenly willing to give me my car and phone back.

"Thanks," I grate out. Then, just to confirm my guess, I say, "Does this mean you're okay with me spending time with Molly O'Gara now?"

"Of course. My earlier objections no longer— Well. I imagine you'll find out when you get to school tomorrow," he says complacently, picking up his fork.

It's all I can do not to launch myself across the table at him to wipe that smug look off his face. The only thing that keeps me in my chair is the knowledge that he could be the key to keeping Molly safe in the future, if the Council can get what he knows about Devyn out of him.

His good mood continues through dinner. Mother looks totally mystified by his shift in attitude, but I don't say a word to either of them until Father leaves for the meeting.

Then, the moment he's out of the house, I turn to her. "Guess you're wondering what happened to change Father's mind about Molly and me?"

"Yes." She pauses in the act of stacking the dinner dishes. "Of course I'm pleased that he has, but—"

"It's because of what he found out about her at last night's Council meeting." I go on to tell her about Molly being the Sovereign's twin sister and that no one knew until yesterday.

She gives a little gasp. "Why…of course! Do you recall I mentioned that she reminded me of someone? Molly—or, rather, Princess Malena—has her mother Galena's eyes. The same shape, the same shade of gray, even some of the same expressions. I can't believe I didn't make the connection before."

"Neither did anyone else, obviously," I tell her, smiling. "Why would they?"

"True," she concedes with an answering smile, but then she frowns. "But…if your father learned this last night, why was he so adamant about leaving Jewel when he got home—and so angry? Given your fledgling relationship with Molly, he should have been pleased."

"Because that's not all that happened last night."

I explain how the Council discovered Father's contacts with Allister, Lennox and Devyn—and how they weren't happy he'd kept that from them. Then I tell her about the attempt on Molly's life earlier this afternoon.

Needless to say, she's horrified. "Thank heaven you were there in time to stop him," she exclaims. "Your father should have known better than to reveal her identity to Devyn Kane. Surely he couldn't have wanted something like this to happen?"

"I don't know. Maybe not? Molly said he totally refused to believe she could be the Sovereign's sister, insisted it was some elaborate hoax. Of course, he was already mad because of the other stuff, so it's not surprising he wouldn't admit he'd been all wrong about Molly. He was obviously still furious when got home and made that call, so who knows what he might have said? Anyway, tonight the Council's going to do that official test-thing to confirm Molly's lineage—"

"The *foare rioga*?"

I nod. "Once they do that, Father must know he'll have to accept it. But think about what he said at dinner—that he expects good news tonight 'one way or the other'? I wonder if Devyn's also supposed to let him know whether that assassination attempt was successful or not? Either way—"

"Your father will have no reason to forbid you seeing her," she finishes, looking slightly sick.

"Right. Molly's safe for now, but there are still people out there who want her dead. Along with that official test tonight, it sounds like the Council plans to confront Father about blabbing to Devyn and almost getting her killed. The Sovereign asked if you and I could attend—that we might both be useful as witnesses about his conversations with Devyn, in case he tries to squirm out of it. Are you...okay with that?"

She only hesitates for a second. "Yes. If your father has done what you say, I want him to face the consequences of his actions. When I think what could have happened, if you hadn't gone to see Molly today—" She breaks off with a half-sob. "I have a key to your car. Let's go."

A moment later we're on our way to the O'Garas' house.

"I still find it hard to believe your father would share confidential Council information with Devyn Kane," Mother says as we leave our neighborhood.

"Devyn's an awfully slick talker," I remind her. "Remember those speeches he made when he was campaigning to get Acclaimed?"

She nods. "Even with no genetic claim to the throne, he made a surprisingly compelling case that he would be Nuath's best choice for Sovereign."

"Exactly. He must be super ambitious, too. Maybe now he's back on Earth, he's decided his best way to power is to amass his own army of malcontents—Anti-Royals, Faxon supporters, people like that. He could be promising them who-knows-what to go along with him, just like Faxon did."

"Why, that would be treason! Do you have any reason to believe he's doing such a thing?"

I explain to her about those rogue groups M mentioned—and why I think Father tipped Devyn off that the Council was trying to track their transmissions. "What I don't get is why a Royal like Devyn would be involved with people who want to kill the Sovereign and her sister, maybe wipe out our whole *fine*."

"You said it yourself," Mother points out. "Ambition. Devyn was one of the youngest people ever elected to the legislature in Nuath, on track to become Chancellor before the Faxon upheaval. When we all fled to Earth, he and your father and Lach Lennox all petitioned to be on the *Echtran* Council when a position came open. Lach became Governor of Dun Cloch and your father was given the Council spot, but Devyn had to settle for a minor leadership role in Fiarway. After Faxon was ousted, your father had already agreed we could all return to Nuath when Devyn persuaded him to remain on Earth, on the Council, instead. Then Devyn went to Nuath himself and did all he could to supplant Emileia as Sovereign. He's always lusted after power."

Mother seems so mild most of the time, I sometimes forget how smart she is. But she's right. It does make sense. Devyn probably wanted Father to stay on the Council so he'd have a sure ally there.

As we near the O'Garas' house, another thought occurs to me. Once Molly's claim is proven true, I wouldn't put it past Father to suggest she should put in a good word for him with the Council, because of me. Judging by his smugness at dinner, I'll bet he's already thought of other ways he can make use of my relationship with her.

Molly's way too smart to fall for that, of course, but the idea still bothers me—a lot. If Father starts sucking up to her, will she start to question *my* motives? What if she thinks I only told her I love her so she'll do my family favors? Will I be able to convince her otherwise?

Ugh. Leave it to Father to soil something beautiful.

37

Solution

Molly

NOT FIVE MINUTES after Tristan leaves, Cormac stops by to say he's finished his sweep of the area without finding anyone else suspicious. He escorts M home after that, but of course by now it's way too late for that walk I wanted with Tristan.

I spend the rest of the afternoon trying to do homework but find it almost impossible to concentrate, with that test-thing looming. When I'm not worrying about that, I fret about what might have happened when Tristan got home. What if Connor guesses where he was and what he found out, and spirits them all out of Jewel before tonight's meeting? I might never see him again!

Every time I start to panic, I remind myself that Tristan loves me… and remember that wonderful, parting kiss.

It helps. Some.

"GOODNESS, people will begin arriving any minute," Mum says as she and I are gathering up the dinner dishes shortly before seven. "I'll put together the tea tray if you want to freshen up."

All I have time to do is run a brush through my hair before hurrying back down to the living room. When I walk in, Kyna and Nara are already here—in person this time, not holographically. They both startle me by bowing, just like they would to M.

"Um, hi." What is it M does in response? Not that. Again I feel awkwardly conspicuous and unprepared. That feeling gets worse when the rest of the Council arrives over the next few minutes and every one of *them* bows to me, too. By the time M comes in with the Stuarts, I've remembered to do the little head-incline back.

M winks and gives me a thumbs-up. "I know it feels weird, but you'll get used to it," she whispers to me before sitting down.

Connor is the very last Council member to arrive. *He* doesn't bow to me, though he does incline his head, projecting a tiny bit of that charm thing he does. Hedging his bets?

I also notice he's alone, which I decide is probably just as well. Much as I'd like Tristan's moral support for my test, I know it would be difficult for him to act as a witness. Jerk or not, Connor *is* his father.

Even as I think that, the doorbell rings again and a moment later Mum ushers Tristan and his mother into the room.

"What are you two doing here?" Connor demands, the charm abruptly gone. "You have no business—"

"I requested their presence," M interrupts. "I knew Molly would like Tristan here for her certification as heir to the Sovereign line...among other things."

Though he scowls suspiciously at his wife and son—and me—he doesn't make any other protest, just takes a seat. Mrs. Roark, I notice, doesn't sit next to him, but moves to a chair across the room. Tristan remains by my side, which I appreciate.

"Now that everyone is here, I suppose we'd better get on with the business of officially confirming Molly O'Gara's parentage, hadn't we?" Kyna says briskly, shooting a quick frown Connor's way. She pulls a small, ancient-looking enameled box from a black travel bag by her feet and holds it up. "Ariel, will you do the blood draw?"

"Of course," Dr. Stuart says. "Unless she'd prefer one of the O'Garas —?" She glances at Mum and Dad, who both look a little alarmed at the idea.

"You can do it," I tell Dr. Stuart. "M said it didn't hurt at all when you did it for her last year."

"Very well." Smiling reassuringly at me, she opens the box and takes out a big, antique-looking syringe. "Don't worry, it's quite quick."

Tristan squeezes my shoulder reassuringly and my lingering nervousness vanishes at his touch. Giving him a smile of thanks, I bare my arm to Dr. Stuart. Sure enough, despite how long and scary-looking the needle is, it hardly hurts at all when she draws some of my blood.

Kyna takes the syringe from her and holds it up. "I call you all as witnesses that this is the lifeblood of the girl known as Molly O'Gara. In full view of both Royal and Scientific representatives of the *Echtran* Council, we perform this test to determine whether she is of the true Sovereign lineage, genetically predestined to lead our people in peace, in wisdom and in kindness."

Predestined to lead? They won't really force me into some kind of leadership role, will they? I look wildly at Tristan, then at M. She just gives me a little shrug.

At the same time, everyone else in the room says—no, *chants*—"*Finné muid anois.* We so witness."

Kyna hands the syringe back to Dr. Stuart, who injects it into a device that's apparently part of the little box. It hums for several moments, then a white light flashes on.

"It is confirmed," Kyna announces, now holding the box aloft. "I present to you Princess Malena, full daughter of Mikal, son of Leontine, and his wife Galena."

An excited murmur runs through the room, then everyone rises as one and bows to me, right fists over their hearts—even M, though she's grinning, and Tristan, who looks proud.

Rather to my surprise, Connor's bow is the deepest of all. "Princess, I hope you can find it in your heart to forgive me for anything I might have said while still in ignorance of your status." I can tell he's projecting his charm ability as hard as he can, but my opinion of him is way too low for it to affect me. "Had I the least suspicion, I never would have—"

"Common politeness shouldn't depend on status, Connor," I interrupt, disgusted by the smarminess of his sudden change toward me. "You're only acting nice to me now because you think I might be able to do you favors. I thought Council members were supposed to care more about the good of our people than themselves?"

He flushes but keeps his smile in place. "Of course I care about the good of our people. It is solely for their sake that I hereby withdraw my opposition to your relationship with my son." He gestures toward Tristan, who flinches. "Between his lineage and yours—"

Kyna clears her throat noisily, with a quelling frown at Connor. "Before you make any further plans concerning your or your family's future, I'd like to address a disturbing incident that occurred earlier today. A few hours ago, just outside this house, an attempt was made on Molly O'Gara's life."

Except for Mum, every Council member looks shocked—even Connor.

"Who would do such a thing?" Breann exclaims. "And why?"

"That is what we need to determine," Kyna replies. "Based on certain remarks the would-be assassin made when he was captured, it seems clear he was aware of her blood relationship to the Sovereign. As no one outside this Council knew about that, it appears we do indeed have a security breach among our number." She pins Connor with a stern gaze.

He shifts uncomfortably. "Surely you don't imagine *I* would send someone to hurt the girl. What possible incentive could I have to—"

Again, Kyna cuts him off. "No one has accused you of ordering the attack yourself, Connor. But I would like to know whether you shared the news of her heritage with anyone else after last night's Council meeting?"

"Of course not," he says quickly, just like he did last night. I notice his ears are redder than they were, though.

"Lili?" Kyna says.

Mum steps forward. "Connor, *did* you tell anyone about my Molly's Sovereign lineage? Say, perhaps, Devyn Kane?"

"No." His face is now set in stubborn lines.

"He's lying," Mum tells Kyna. "No question about it."

Connor scowls at her. "All right. Fine. I was justifiably upset after last night's meeting, where I was treated so poorly after all of my years of service. I shared my grievances with Devyn, one of the few people I thought would understand. It's...possible I mentioned the Sovereign's claim about the girl's lineage during that conversation. But I certainly never meant for her to be harmed in any way, especially as she and my son are forming a relationship. A relationship of which I now thoroughly approve, as I said before. Nor did Devyn give me any hint whatsoever that he harbored any sort of ill-will toward her."

"Devyn's involvement will likely be proved or disproved when the assassin's memories are extracted," Kyna tells him. "At the moment, it is your behavior at issue, Connor. Even after learning last night that Devyn might well have been complicit in the plot against the Sovereign, you chose to share this news with him. Nor, I am informed, was last night the first time you'd spoken with Devyn since moving to Jewel—possibly to share other confidential Council business?"

"What? Who—?" He turns his glare on Tristan and his mother. Mrs. Roark looks nervous.

Tristan doesn't.

"Me," he says. "I also told them you asked us to keep quiet about your conversations with Devyn. And what was that bit this morning about him offering you some powerful position if you left the Council?"

"It was...just talk," Connor blusters. "Vague ideas for the future Devyn is considering. Nothing definite."

"Also not true," says Mum, who's still watching him closely.

Kyna's expression becomes even grimmer. "Until such time as we can locate Devyn himself for questioning, I propose Connor be sent to Dun Cloch. Perhaps our security personnel will be able to persuade him to be more forthcoming. I also propose that Connor Roark be removed from this Council, effective immediately. May I have a show of hands in favor of both proposals?"

The vote is unanimous.

"I'll have Cormac escort Connor home to pack his things," M says, tapping a message into her omni-phone.

Kyna nods her approval. "And I will arrange for someone to escort him to Dun Cloch before he can do any more damage, unwitting or not. Tonight, if at all possible."

Cormac arrives a few minutes later with his security team. Angry and humiliated, Connor slouches to his feet, then turns to his wife and son.

"You both still have some packing to do as well. I expect our stay in Dun Cloch will be temporary. After that, we'll return to Colorado. Come along."

"No." It's his wife, not Tristan, who says it. Lifting her chin, she looks him straight in the eye. "I am done taking orders from you, Connor. I've suspected for some time that your frequently-voiced concern for our people's future masked some baser motive. Clearly I was right. Neither Tristan nor I are going anywhere with you."

Tristan stares at her, looking both amazed and proud, then faces his father. "What she said. Mother and I are staying in Jewel."

Connor looks like he wants to argue—or maybe throw something—

but Cormac hustles him out of the house. After the front door closes, there's a long silence. Finally, Kyna turns to me.

"I'm sorry that what should have been a completely happy occasion was marred by such a scene, Princess. Please believe that I am extremely pleased to have the claim you and the Sovereign made last night officially verified. However, in light of today's attack, I'm afraid I must question the wisdom of making any sort of general announcement."

"No, we have to let everyone know," M exclaims. "Don't you remember? Last year we kept my identity secret and Faxon's people did everything they could to get rid of me before word got out. Just like today's attacker tried to do to Molly."

Kyna inclines her head. "You make a valid point, Excellency. Very well. I can prepare a MARSTAR Bulletin to go out tonight, if our newly discovered Princess and the O'Garas are ready for that sort of publicity?"

Yikes! "Publicity?" I squeak. "Does that mean—? You think people will come to gawk at me, the way they did M last year? Like they still do sometimes?"

"I would not be surprised," she replies, "though of course I will again caution our people against doing or saying anything that might draw undue *Duchas* attention."

I look to Mum and Dad, not at *all* sure I'm ready for that.

Mum comes over and puts an arm around me, Dad right beside her. "I know it will be an adjustment, dear. For all of us. But this is your heritage. The sooner you embrace it, the better."

Swallowing, I send a panicked glance at M, who says, "You really will get used to it after a while. Especially since you'll have me here to help."

"And me," Tristan affirms, still close beside me. "We'll all help."

I smile gratefully at them both. "Then...I guess I'm okay with everyone knowing." I hope.

Kyna adjourns the meeting after that and people start heading for the door, each one stopping to congratulate me, even though I didn't do anything but let Dr. Stuart take a little bit of my blood. Tristan and his mother are the last to leave.

"I assume your father wasn't allowed to drive himself to the house," Mrs. Roark says to Tristan. "I can take his car home while you drive yours." Then she turns to me with a misty smile. "When Tristan told me your news this evening, I suddenly realized how very much you look like your mother. I can see that you inherited Galena's courage as well."

"You said that you and she were close friends, back in Nuath?"

She nods. "And now I very much look forward to getting to know *both* of her daughters." Bowing again, she says good night to me and my parents.

Once she's gone, Tristan turns to me with a strange look on his face. "Um, can we talk for a minute before I go?"

"Sure. Mum, Dad, we'll just be out on the front porch, okay?"

Together we go outside and sit next to each other on the porch swing. Now that it's November the nights are getting pretty chilly but almost before I can shiver, Tristan pulls out his omni and switches on the climate control. An instant later I'm toasty warm—or maybe that's just because he's sitting so close.

"By this time tomorrow you're going to be famous," he says after a moment's silence. "If...you want me to back off now my father's been booted off the Council, I'll totally understand. When everyone knows who you really are, a lot of them will think I only want to be with you because of your new status—especially after the way I came on to M when I first got here. Though I swear, it never even occurred to me that—"

I put a finger over his lips to stop his words. "Shh, I know. And no, I don't want you to back off. Why should I care what other people think, especially when I know they're wrong? Back when we both thought I was just an Ag, you took the risk of asking me out on a date and were even willing to face the consequences of being seen with me in public."

"*Just* an Ag?" His brows go up. "You'd better not let Sean hear you say that. Or me either, for that matter. In case you forgot, I fell in love with an Ag—or thought I did. Or have you suddenly decided Royals are superior to Ags after all?"

Both touched and amused, I shake my head. "That would be pretty dumb, wouldn't it? Especially after I told you how stupid *you* were for believing that."

"It would," he agrees. "Besides, look at your surrogate parents—they were Ags, and they were real heroes, risking their own lives to keep you safe from Faxon's people. For all we know, that's what got them killed."

Now I have to swallow a sudden lump in my throat. "You're right. And like you pointed out to me once before, I shouldn't ignore my own advice."

"Not when it's good advice." He's grinning now. "So, if you're positive you're still willing to be seen with me, how about I give you a ride to school tomorrow?"

School! My stomach clenches. "Everyone will have seen the MARSTAR Bulletin by then," I realize as I say it aloud.

"All the *Echtrans*, anyway," Tristan agrees. Then, with a wicked grin, "I have to admit I'm kind of looking forward to seeing how they act toward you. Especially Alan."

A chuckle escapes me. "That's mean. But...so am I," I confess.

"And then tomorrow evening, maybe we can finally go on a second date. How does Dream Cream sound?"

"It sounds perfect." And it does. Looking ahead to tomorrow and all the days to come, I see my whole future suddenly expanding way beyond anything I ever imagined. It's a scary prospect, but also incredibly exciting—especially if I get to share it with Tristan.

When he kisses me, our future looks brighter than ever.

A Martian Glossary

Acclamation: Nuathan electoral process whereby citizens indicate approval or disapproval of a proposed Sovereign.

agoid (AH-gyoyd): organized protest; opposition.

aitlean (ayt-lee-AN): airplane; primitive aircraft used extensively by Duchas; Earth's primary means of intercontinental travel.

Arregaith (ah-ree-GAYTH) (pop. 1,413): town in southeastern Nuath containing spaceport and supporting industries.

ateamh rioga (ah-TEV ree-OH-gah): a persuasive ability shared by some of Royal blood.

athshondis (ath-SHON-dis): resonance.

Bailerealta (BAY-luh-ree-AL-tuh) (pop. 412): village on the western coast of Ireland, est. circa 1575, populated entirely by Echtrans.

Ballytadhg (BAH-lee-teeg) (pop. 1,106): east-central Nuathan village known for Arts fine and industry.

beidan (BID-den): gossip; scandal.

brath: Martian "vibe" detectable by other Martians.

breag fionn (brag fin): discovery of a lie; detection of falsehood.

caidpel (KAYD-pel): predominant sport in Nuath combining elements of the Irish sports of hurling and Gaelic football.

camastall (KAM-uh-stahl): deception; deceit; falsification.

cannarc (KAN-ark): rebellion; mutiny; resistance.

chabhil (KAB-vil): negotiation; debate; (occ.) ultimatum.

chas pell (CHASS-pel): a ball game played by Nuathan children, nearly identical to the Earth sport of basketball.

Cheile Rioga (KEE-luh ree-OH-gah): Royal Consort.

chomhaerle (KOM-ahr-lee): advice; counsel.

Chomseireach (kom-SAY-rik): Handmaid; lady's maid, chaperone and companion to Princess or (female) Sovereign.

Cinnwund Rioga (KIN-wund ree-OH-gah): Royal Destiny.

cloigh (kloy): to overpower or overthrow; defeat; subdue.

comhriteach (KOM-ree-teek): compromise.

cosc damaste (kosk DAHM-uh-stay): damage control.

coslacht (ko-SLACT): appearance; impression; influence.

Costanta (ko-STAHN-tuh): Bodyguard assigned to protect the Sovereign or other members of the Royal family.

dabhal (DOB-uhl) (*slang*): damn, damned.

dhualgis cumann (doo-AHL-gus koo-MAHN): benevolent duty; royal obligation.

dilsacht (DIL-sok): loyalty; allegiance.

doolegar (DOO-luh-gahr): despondency; depression.

Duchas (doo-kas): normal Earth humans.

Dun Cloch (Dun Klok) (pop. 1,247+): largest *Echtran* compound on Earth, founded 1933 in north-central Montana. Main production hub for Martian technology.

ealu (AY-loo): to break free, escape, or elope.

Echtran (ek-tran): person of Martian birth or descent living on Earth; expatriate.

Echtran Council: governing body for expatriate Martians living on Earth.

Echtran Enquirer: unofficial news source for expatriate Martians on Earth. Tends toward the sensationalistic.

edhmiu (FEY-mew): implementation; application.

efrin (EF-rin): Hell; used as a mild curse.

Emileia (em-i-LAY-ah): current *Thiarna* (Sovereign), granddaughter to Sovereign Leontine; sole heir to the Nuathan monarchy.

fasneis (FAHSH-ness): information; intelligence.

fine (feen): genetically related subsets of the Martian population, each with certain attributes.

flach (flok) (*slang*): socially unacceptable swear word.

foare rioga (fair ree-OH-gah): ancient, traditional syringe used for blood draw to verify Sovereign lineage.

gaiscigh (GAH-sheeg): heroism; act of extreme bravery.

giola uresal (gee-OH-la OO-ree-sal): menial servant.

Glenamuir (GLEN-uh-mer) (pop. 898): largely Agricultural village in northwest Nuath; longtime home of O'Gara family during Faxon's reign.

graell (grayl): intense emotional and physical bond believed mythical by most Martians.

grechain (gree-SHAYN): Nuathan information network, both personal and mass-media; news channels within the greater *grechain*.

Grentl (GREN-tuhl): advanced non-human alien race from an unknown part of the galaxy; likely founders of underground human colony on Mars.

hiarmarti (hee-ehr-MAHR-tee): consequences; results; price to be paid.

Hollydoon (HOL-ly doon) (pop. 1,677): largely Agricultural village in northwest Nuath; suffered particularly harsh ravages by Faxon's forces.

Horizon: one of four Nuathan transport ships traveling between Mars and Earth during biennial launch windows.

Insealbau (in-SALL-baw): Installation, as of Nuathan Sovereign.

Installation: Nuathan ceremony signifying a new Sovereign's ascension to power.

Jewel (pop. 5,013): town in north-central Indiana noted for corn, artisan jewelry and annual Jewel Jewelry Festival.

Launch window: period occurring approximately every 26 Earth months and lasting approximately four months, when the distance between Earth and Mars is small enough to allow travel between the two planets.

MARSTAR: official channel for communication from Echtran Council to expatriate Martians living on Earth, generally in the form of MARSTAR Bulletins.

Miochan (mee-OH-kan): healing; curing; a major fine.

moill (mahl): delay; postponement.

naesc geaniteach (nesh gan-it-EEK) genetic affinity.

nimhic (NIV-ik): antidote; cure.

Nuath (NOO-ath): underground human colony on Mars.

omni: a small, multifunctional device developed on Mars.

orinacht (OR-in-ott): propriety; seemliness.

pleanal (plenn-UHL): advance planning; scheming.

Populists: a minority movement among Nuathans advocating equal rights and representation for all fines. (Sometimes referred to as "Anti-Royals.")

probalreith (pro-BAHL-reth): opinion poll; public opinion.

probleid (pruh-BLAYD): privilege; status.

Quintessence (kwin-TESS-ens): one of four passenger vessels used to transport Nuathans between Earth and Mars.

Rigel (RY-jel): a blue supergiant star, approximately 860 light years from Earth, located in the constellation Orion; 7th brightest star visible from Earth, its brightness (or apparent magnitude) making it an important navigational star; Rigel Stuart, son of Ariel and Van Stuart.

rundacht (ROON-dahct): extreme secrecy; classified information.

scar a cheila (scar ah KAY-lah): separated; torn asunder; ripped apart.

Scriosath: memory erasure, the most complete being the tabula rasa or "blank slate," the highest form of official punishment.

Sean O'Gara (shawn oh-GAYR-uh): son of Quinn and Lily O'Gara; destined Cheile Rioga (Royal Consort) to Princess Emileia.

shilcloas (shil-CLO-ahs): hearing another's thoughts; telepathy.

sochar (SO-kar): Nuathan credits, used to purchase anything beyond provided necessities.

spiare (spee-AH-ray): spy; snoop.

stochail (sto-KAYL): preparation, as for a battle or journey.

streach suas (stretch SOO-ahs): resist oppression; underground resistance.

taghal ardus (TAHG-ul ar-DOOS): first touch causing a "tingle" between opposite sex teens, rarely repeated on second touch.

taigde (TAG-duh): research; records.

Teachneaglis (TAK-nee-glish): small minority of Nuathans and Echtrans who prefer to do without most modern advancements, primarily found in the villages of Bailerealta on Earth, and Keary and Eriu on Mars.

teachneoc (TEEK-nee-ok): technology; gadgetry.

teachtok (TEEK-tok) (*slang*): non-omni phone.

threoirach (TRO-rok): instruction; orientation; guidance.

tinneas (TIN-es): physical illness. Rare among Martians except in the very elderly.

toachai (TO-uh-kay): future; destiny.

triail (tree-AYL): test or audition; ordeal by trial.

Tullymayne (TULL-ee-mayn) (pop. 1,993): town in southeastern Nuath containing main transportation hub and supporting industries.

twilly: obnoxious person; jerk.

udaris thusmithoir (oo-DARE-is thoos-MITH-er): parental authority.

unbaen: dictator

About the Author

Brenda Hiatt is the New York Times bestselling author of twenty-three novels (so far), including sweet and spicy historical romance, time travel romance, and young adult science fiction romance. She is as excited about her **Starstruck** series as she's ever been about any of her books. In addition to writing, Brenda is passionate about embracing life to the fullest, to include scuba diving (she has over 60 dives to her credit), Taekwondo (where she is currently pursuing her 4th degree black belt), hiking, traveling, and pursuing new experiences and skills.

For a free Starstruck short story and the earliest news about Brenda Hiatt's books, subscribe to her newsletter at: brendahiatt.com/subscribe

Connect with Brenda:
brendahiatt.com

www.ingramcontent.com/pod-product-compliance
Lightning Source LLC
Chambersburg PA
CBHW032104180726
48284CB00002B/447